HELLFIRE

Hellfire

A Travis Deacon Novel

Rickard B DeMille

 MacDonald, Barclay & Co. ◇ Little Elm, Texas

A MacDonald, Barclay & Co. book

MacDonald, Barclay & Co. (www.macdonaldbarclay.com) is a very new, very small press located in the also very small town of Little Elm, Texas. MacDonald, Barclay specializes in whatever demands our attention. We have a small but talented group of authors covering a broad genre range.

For more information, or permission to use material from this text, contact us by:
Email: info@macdonaldbarclay.com
Mail: MacDonald, Barclay & Co.
        Suite 100-436
        2701 Little Elm Parkway
        Little Elm, TX 75068

DEDICATION

First, a big hug and kiss to my wife for her
patience, putting up with the hours I spent
behind the keyboard writing.
And of course, my heartfelt thanks to the people of
Wales for making me feel at home for the brief time
I was there. A special thanks to the Clan Clarke –
Jeff and Elan, Keri and Chris, Rhiannon and Ben,
Beth and Adam, plus so many others – for decades
of friendship and bonne compagnie. In truth, almost
every day was a day in Wales thanks to them.

Cymru am byth!

Chapter 1

They say that Wales can change a man. I never found out who "they" were, but three grey, eternally overcast days there had certainly changed me.

I was still a hard-charging U.S. Marine, but I'd been Enlightened. I'd come to believe that Welsh dragons were real, while my memories of the sun were simply delusions. And, I'd been converted to the one true religion—Rugby.

This transfiguration had taken place in Swansea, a port city on Britain's jagged southern coast. I'd learned that the Welsh were not English, but a separate and proud people with their own nation, culture and language—a language that seemed to use vowels as a diversion rather than for grammatical consideration. My working theory was that the ancient Romans took the wayward Welsh vowels as tribute and forced them on the Hebrews, who hadn't had any yet.

The previous day I'd almost performed the Heimlich maneuver on a frail old lady in our hotel restaurant. Turns out, she wasn't choking, she was just asking for a glass of water in Welsh.

Anyway, the clock over the bar showed five minutes to

three in the morning. I sat nursing my final beer and waiting for my "mate" and traveling companion, Gareth Jones, contemplating the eternal truths of life. No joke, Rugby enjoyed the righteous fervor of a religion there. At that moment, I still wore my vestments of fandom, the worn-out red jersey that Gareth had taken off and given me when we arrived.

Even at that early hour, the tube showed a replay of the day's gathering of the devout in Ireland. The Irish priesthood were kicking the holy shit out of their brethren from Italy, twenty-five to nine.

I also nursed the culinary remnants of my evening worship, with the High Sacraments of Rugby on the table before me. According to Gareth, this consisted of a pint (OK, four or five pints) of Double Dragon Beer and a local delicacy: cockles. Cockles, for the uninitiated, were like little clams. I found that if you covered them with salt and malt vinegar, they tasted just like little balls of snot, covered with salt and malt vinegar.

Hey, every religion requires some trial of faith.

Irritated, I checked my watch. Gareth was never late, and we had an early day planned with his family. He'd left about noon to "check up on a friend." Like a fool, I forgot to ask if said friend were a woman, and how extensive the checkup was going to be. Maybe I should call it a night.

I took another drink instead.

In addition to observing Rugby, I'd gone back to Gareth's room and retrieved the photo album he'd asked me to critique. Photography was what really brought us together. Gareth was a true genius at capturing people. Not just their images but their souls. All people, any people, anywhere and at any time.

I had skills, don't get me wrong, but he functioned on a different level completely. I could capture precisely what something looked like; his magic could reveal what it truly was. Also, my images were dark, the opposite of his. He celebrated life, I chronicled death.

I had just examined an amazing picture of three men in a café, unaware that they were being turned into art. I could almost hear their whispered conversation. They huddled, secretive and intense. They could have been discussing high matters of international intrigue, or the recipe for barbequed goat. Since the café was in Kabul, Afghanistan, it could have been either.

Gareth and I met in Afghanistan. He commanded a special British unit, while I worked with those sneaky bastards at the CIA. I loved the job. It allowed me to travel the region, meet fascinating people and kill the nasty ones.

It was in Kabul that Gareth once tried to take my picture. I let him live, so he let me be his friend. When he planned two weeks of leave in Wales to watch Rugby, he decided to drag me along.

I preferred to spend my free time in rest and reprobation, but he wanted to cleanse my soul. I told him I liked my soul the way it was, so he promised me the best beer in the universe, as much of it as I could drink. I'd spent the last few years in Islamic nations, so I started packing.

Loud cheering erupted from the Irish devout, so I looked back at the tube. The scene changed, and a news report came on that featured Prince Harry. Apparently, he planned to be here in Wales for the Six Nations Championship this weekend. I'd almost met the Prince in Afghanistan when Gareth pulled an escort assignment. This brought me back to the present; I rubbed my eyes and stretched. The assembly of Dublin appeared to be in halftime, and my body informed me that this would be an excellent time to visit the head. Immediately! Great, I hoped it wasn't the cockles.

Minutes later, bodily demands appeased, I returned to the bar where I found a very large man bending over my table carefully scanning Gareth's pictures. He was muscular, in his early thirties, wearing casual pants and a Rugby jersey for the local club "the Ospreys." He stood a bit over six foot six inches and weighed in at about two hundred fifty-five pounds. That made him a little younger, two inches taller, and ten pounds heavier than me. At least my steel-blue eyes and stylishly shaved head made me better looking.

I then observed another man leaning against the bar. This one was about five feet of anorexic skin and bone. His rumpled blue suit didn't quite conceal the automatic pistol in his belt.

In the mirror over the bar, I saw a third man behind the door. He looked like a gorilla, also in a suit, ready to explode at every seam.

I didn't like this. If things went bad, someone could be seriously hurt, probably me. I turned my attention back to the small man at the bar. He took two steps toward me, buttoned his jacket, and stood erect.

"Gunnery Sergeant Travis Deacon?" His accent revealed he was English, not Welsh.

I smiled sweetly. "No, Margaret Thatcher."

The man standing at my table chuckled. "You've let yourself go, mum."

Good one! I looked back toward my table, at the casually dressed guy with the quick wit, and decided he was not with the others. "Who are you?"

"Call me Brian."

Mr. "Call Me Brian" was definitely Welsh.

He continued, "I'm a friend of Gareth's, and I work for the same people."

That would be the Special Air Service. The Brits

enjoyed a less complicated approach to international problems than we simple colonials. The SAS made the worst of those problems just disappear. Those SAS bastards were tough; I was glad I didn't start anything. We'd all have ended up in the hospital, and Mr. Marriott would have had to remodel the ground floor of his nice hotel.

Brian slid Gareth's album to me across the table and gestured toward the door. The others moved menacingly forward, and Brian turned to face the small one.

"Why don't you and your baby sister get a room, go upstairs, and fuck yourselves. He's coming with me."

The little blond-headed guy did not take this well. His face turned bright red, which made him look even more like a kid. He took a small, defiant step closer. "Or?"

At this point, I'd had enough. Brian seemed OK, but my instincts warned me the other two were trouble. I moved past the SAS man and confronted the little geeky one. "Or, you get to find out how good the health care system here really is."

Blondie looked over at his primate partner, who grinned eagerly and lumbered forward.

Brian stepped between us, "What's he done?"

The man looked uncertain, then glanced over at the small one. Brian bumped the big man with his chest.

"Didn't think so, I suggest you leave."

I was ready to sit, grab my beer, and see how this ended, but the little one pulled King Kong away. Brian laughed and turned back to me, ignoring the two as they stormed out of the bar. Brian finished off my beer, and looked me over as he wiped the foam from his lip.

"They wanted you to start something so they could grab you. What did you do to piss off the coppers?"

I could only shake my head, but I now realized that something was wrong. First Gareth still hadn't shown, then two warring British clans storm the bar where I was waiting.

Brian turned to leave. "My car's outside."

I grabbed his arm. He stopped and looked at me hesitantly; he knew what I was going to ask. "Where's Gareth?"

I studied his face. His expression, rather his lack of expression, told me what I needed to know. I looked numbly down at the photo album. I knew that "act like nothing's wrong" look, I'd worn it too many times myself.

"Shit!"

Chapter 2

I followed Brian through the deserted lobby, then outside onto the drive. To our left, a pair of headlights flared, highlighting us in the middle of the covered pickup area. Unfortunately, the lights weren't bright enough to burn through the fog that blanketed my mind.

I looked up as the large SUV, a black Range Rover, rolled slowly past. I didn't recognize the driver, but I couldn't miss the two dark-suited gentlemen in the back. The assholes from the bar apparently weren't done with me, since they stopped by the exit to wait.

Near the back of the parking area, Brian unlocked a little grey Peugeot and we squeezed in. He started the car, backed carefully out of his spot, then shot past the waiting SUV.

We turned left onto the street, and found ourselves in darkness. A pair of headlights soon appeared in the distance behind us, as the Range Rover sped madly to catch up. They followed, taking up a position just a few meters behind our rear bumper.

Our little procession slowed as it drove past twenty stories of hulking metal skeleton on our right. They were building something big next to my hotel, probably another hotel just off the beach. Unfortunately, that meant everything in the area was under construction, including the roads.

In order to travel north the twenty yards to the main street, we had to navigate a two-hundred-yard labyrinth of orange cones, yellow flashing lights and large wooden barricades. I would normally have made some smartass comment about rats and mazes, but under the circumstances, my heart wasn't in it.

In fact, my heart felt the icy cold blade of grief ripping deep into my chest. I realized that my escort was driving fast like he was in a hurry—not fast like every second mattered.

Gareth was dead. Too many of my friends ended up that way. But Gareth was different. He was like a brother.

We waited at a traffic light, then turned left onto Oystermouth Road. This was a main road running along the coast. There was no traffic and we made good time, the Range Rover following too closely behind. Our convoy moved quickly east, which meant the University of Swansea would soon pass to our right.

Gareth studied languages there. His father was in the Foreign Service, like our State Department, and he'd spent most of his early life in Egypt and the Arabian Peninsula. He spoke perfect Arabic, much better than I.

He once told me that when he got out of the army, he would return to Swansea and become a professor. I was willing to bet that returning there and becoming a corpse was not his second choice.

We turned right and went around one of those damn traffic circles; I was reasonably sure we were now going north. I normally knew exactly where I was and how I got there, but not then. I wasn't technically lost; I just didn't give a shit. I could only stare blankly out the window. The night had turned Swansea's lush greens and vibrant colors into blackness and shadows, which fit my mood perfectly.

I grew up in the flat, brown world of West Texas, but had really started to like it there in Wales. Texas goes on forever, but in Wales everything seemed closer—intimate, not just small. I liked being surrounded by thousands of years of history, but didn't like knowing that Gareth had joined it so soon.

How did a soldier leave the most ferocious battle zone on earth, only to die at home? That just did not compute.

I looked over; my driver was doing an excellent job of ignoring me. This hadn't been a problem, since I needed to sort out my feelings and come to grips with the death of a friend. It only became a problem when I started to wonder what had happened; which was right then. Time to get to work.

"Where are you taking me?"

He ignored me. He appeared to be dealing with his own issues.

"I hope it's not a place with one of your damned Welsh names, that sound like someone's been stabbed in the throat."

He looked over, not smiling but wanting to. It was a start. If I wanted information, this cockle-eating SOB was the only source available.

I felt numb, empty, but at that moment I needed to be charming.

"How did it happen?" I didn't expect a reply, and continued. "Gareth was my friend, too. I worked with him, you probably already know where."

His hands tightened on the wheel, he was thinking

15

about it at least. A little bit of a nudge should be enough.

"We both know I'm not in trouble, or involved. Otherwise, I wouldn't be here with you. I'd be in the back seat of that SUV, sandwiched between Charles and Camilla. The big one's Camilla, right? Too masculine to be Charles."

He snorted.

"Who are they, anyway?"

He glanced at me, and finally spoke, "MI5, probably. They're dressed too shabby for Special Branch."

This didn't mean anything to me, but I had other things on my mind at the moment. I pressed on.

"We don't get many friends in our line of work, but Gareth and I are—were . . ."

Brian glanced over, then stared back at the road.

"I won't leave without knowing what happened. You understand that? You wouldn't either."

He looked over again. "Auto accident, drove off a cliff."

What? How does someone spend years dodging mines and mortar shells in a seven-ton Panther command vehicle, then drive off the paved highway in an MG Midget?

I needed more information. "Where are we going?"

"Morgue."

That meant Gareth was dead when they brought him in. If he'd been alive, or had any chance of resuscitation, they'd have taken him to the hospital.

"How well did you know him?"

He looked at me carefully, then reached a decision.

"We grew up together, joined up together—we were going to retire together."

Brian had to stop for a second to gather himself. It's always tough to lose someone close. "I just got in from Brussels; we were all going to the Six Nations together."

I knew that Gareth and a bunch of his friends had

rented a luxury box; the Six Nations Championship was the Holy Grail of Rugby. I'd have met Brian then; the current timing truly sucked.

We pulled up to a large, ancient, grey brick cube of a building. There were several more black Range Rovers parked out front, as well as an ambulance and one of their stupid little cop cars, lights flashing angrily, taking up two parking spots.

Brian and I exited, then walked up weathered stone steps to the entrance. Brian opened the heavy wooden doors, and we passed from night into death together. We silently crossed the white marble floor of the lobby, worn from decades, if not centuries, of constant use. In times past, this had obviously been a hospital. It had since become a dumping ground for the failures of newer hospitals.

Halfway across the lobby, angry shouts echoed from our right. I spun as I reached for my Beretta, but found nothing. I couldn't carry a weapon in Great Britain.

I saw that there were others in the lobby. Two burly men wearing the familiar dark suits, struggled to restrain a crazed, athletic-looking woman. A short, older man in an expensive grey suit tried futilely to calm her down.

The woman was small, but not tiny. She wore a tan pant suit with a white blouse underneath, and beige running shoes. Her disheveled red hair fell like a veil, completely covering her face.

The small man's soothing words had an effect, and the woman appeared to relax. The older man leaned forward, trying to see her face behind the cascade of ginger. He gestured to the others, who tentatively released their grip on the now docile captive.

"It's Colonel Becket. I should have known." Brian scowled at the well-dressed man. "Charles and Camilla work for him. Why is he bothering Dee?"

I really didn't care about Becket; my attention was on the woman. She sighed heavily, hands rising slowly to brush away her hair. Her freckled face was pale, skin firm and clear. She was pretty and somehow familiar.

Becket seemed like a smooth player as he pretended to smile sympathetically. He leaned closer and whispered, probably hoping to comfort her further; or at least keep her quiet. The woman, Dee, responded with a submissive nod. Becket placed his right hand tenderly on her shoulder.

Dee responded by grabbing his wrist, twisting violently, and throwing him easily toward the man to her left. Becket flew awkwardly forward and both men crumpled to the ground.

Next, her elbow slammed into the gut of the man to her right, who doubled over with a groan. Colonel Becket had jumped nimbly back to his feet, but Dee's left foot executed a beautiful side kick, catching him squarely above the hip. The small man winced, grabbing his side as he flew once more into his dazed companion.

Next, Dee kicked the legs out from under the wheezing man to her right. He fell on his back with a thud, then gasped frantically to catch his breath. She looked around, her emerald eyes flashing angrily as she assessed the situation.

Her face was clearly visible now. She seemed poised and ready to move before the others could even recover. She was nasty, vicious, and had just kicked the crap out of three trained men; I felt myself falling in love. Or maybe those cockles had gone bad.

She bolted for the double doors to our left; the sign above them read "Autopsy Suites." There were two more dark suits there, reaching for weapons inside their jackets.

Brian hurried and got there before the girl, blocking

her path. "Dee, let it go, at least for now."

She looked up defiantly. Letting things go was obviously not in her nature. She glared at the two men blocking her way.

Brian whispered to her. "You can't win this one, you know that."

Her defiance slowly faded. Tears glistened in her pitiful eyes, then began to flow. Sobs followed as she wept dejectedly into Brian's chest.

Her pain became mine. In my entire life, I had never felt a stronger urge to comfort someone, and I wasn't even sure who she was or why I should care. It scared me.

Becket regained his balance, stood on his feet and hobbled angrily across the lobby, followed by his humiliated minions. Their clothes were filthy and disheveled, one of them had a cut on his cheek.

Brian whispered something to the woman, then stepped back. She glared at Becket, who ignored her and gestured at me to follow as he passed. He then limped painfully through the doors toward the autopsy rooms.

I followed, unable to look away from Dee's tear-streaked face. She looked my way, staring at the album tucked under my arm, then up at my face as I passed. She and Brian turned to follow me inside.

The men at the door moved together. The older of the two pointed at Dee and Brian. "Not them."

I didn't know what was going on, and I didn't care. Gareth's body was inside, and these guys were not going to stop me from seeing it. I spoke softly and calmly.

"Your boss won't be happy when I don't show up."

They looked at each other, but didn't move. I was about to force my way past when the woman behind me spoke.

"I'll wait."

Everyone looked at Dee, who nodded to Brian. She then glared at me. I interpreted her stare to mean "Thank you for trying to get me inside," but I could have been wrong. Maybe it was a simple "Fuck you!"

The dark suits parted. This meant that Dee was the problem, not Brian. I would remember that.

Brian and I walked past. As we entered the sterile white tile of the hallway floor, our squeaking shoes announced our approach toward a fallen friend. I looked over my shoulder as I walked. The doors framed Dee's sorrowful face for an instant, then closed and left her alone there.

Seconds later we reached an open door and entered. I had already steeled myself for the harsh smells that assaulted our senses. Long ago I'd gotten used to the odor of cleansers, disinfectants, and other cruel chemicals employed to keep death from escaping a morgue. The door closed, and I looked around at a sterile world of spotless white and gleaming stainless steel.

In the center of the room stood a gurney. On top of the gurney I saw a white sheet, covering what was certainly Gareth's body. I did a quick visual and noticed that the left arm was bent at an impossible angle just above the elbow, which would indicate possible trauma consistent with an automobile accident.

I had known what I would see, but that didn't spare me the impact of seeing it. Less than a day ago, we were eating shepherd's pie and laughing about how drunk we were going to get this weekend. I couldn't help but feel the sting. I smiled weakly at the body.

Don't worry buddy, I'll get drunk enough for the both of us.

Nearby, someone cleared their throat, and I returned to the world of the dead. A rotund woman wearing white surgical garb, probably the medical examiner, took a step toward the gurney. I noticed there were only two others in the room, Becket and a man who may have been his assistant.

Without a word, the medical examiner yanked back the sheet. Gareth Jones' mangled, blood-caked body reposed there in naked death. They had done nothing to clean up the body. The bastards had even left his eyes open. Becket grimaced slightly, but the rest of us maintained a stoic detachment.

Then, for some reason, they all looked at me.

"No one here has seen him in months." Becket was speaking to me. He had a nasal, cultured voice and spoke with irritating precision. I got the impression that if he wasn't a Lord something or other, it was on his to-do list.

They wanted me to ID him? That was bullshit. Gareth worked for the British government; they could have had his dental records there in a second. His face was almost untouched, and Brian had known him for years. Something was very wrong about this whole situation.

Well, I was very good at this; and I did want a closer look. I stepped next to the gurney and looked down at my friend's lifeless shell.

Gareth's remains were in bad shape, but I'd seen worse. The CIA used missile equipped Predator drones to track down and neutralize bad guys from Al Qaeda, the Taliban, and other assorted evil-doers. A Hellfire missile erupting in someone's lap made a real mess. One of my jobs was to dash in when necessary, get a positive ID and DNA sample, then disappear before the locals showed up. These bodies were my photographic specialty, my darkness to Gareth's light.

I took a deep breath, slipped into combat mode, and started my examination. I recognized Gareth at once, but began a walk around anyway. Mentally, I captured every image. First came the old scar from a 7.62 round in his right shoulder, he never mentioned where he got that. Next, I mentally photographed a knife scar above the right hip; he got that freeing a reporter in Basra.

Moving to the opposite side of the table, I recognized the faded dagger tattoo on his left forearm. I also saw the little round scar of a pistol wound next to Gareth's heart, a reminder of how much I owed him. I'd seen more than enough to ID the body, but not enough to satisfy my growing curiosity.

I bent down to examine the left arm, crushed several inches above the elbow. I then noticed there were no corresponding wounds to his side; his arm had been extended when the trauma was inflicted. This also allowed me a closer look at the large avulsion on his hip; avulsions are when chunks of flesh have been torn away, several small chunks in this instance.

I looked to the medical examiner, who indicated some of the more massive wounds on his lower body.

"His MG left the road, then tumbled down a rocky ledge to the beach. It could have been worse."

I looked at his face again, surprised at the lack of trauma there. An open coffin would be possible, though I didn't know why this mattered to me.

But I did know. I remembered why that woman, Dee, looked familiar. Gareth kept a picture of his baby sister, Deirdre, from the day she graduated the police academy. He talked about her often; I could tell she was special to him. Becket made Gareth's sister wait outside, alone.

What an asshole!

I pushed this topic to the back of my mind, I would deal with it later. I went back to my examination, and moved next to the head. I put my left hand over the pistol scar and his heart, then slowly closed his eyes with my right. I stepped back, snapped to attention and saluted a friend and fallen comrade. After a moment of respect, I turned to face Becket.

"It's Gareth."

Becket had been watching me. The arrogant little jerk had known it was Gareth. For some reason, what he really wanted was to gauge my reaction to the death.

Why? How did he even know I was in Wales?

Becket forced what he intended to be a sympathetic smile and nodded, but it looked more like gas pains to me.

"Is there anything you'd like to add?"

I shook my head, grateful he'd put the request that way. I wouldn't lie, but I didn't want to elaborate until I could analyze the situation myself. They could find out on their own that Gareth had been tortured then murdered, but I had no doubt that they suspected something already. I was equally certain they had no idea what that something might be.

The signs on Gareth's body were subtle, but I'd seen this handiwork before, and recently. My commanding officer had some of the same signs after having been captured in Pakistan. I had reached Lieutenant Ibarra too late to save his life, but soon enough to examine his body. If those sadistic bastards were there in Wales, then something very, very bad was about to happen.

I would make sure that it happened to them.

Chapter 3

The medical examiner snapped off her gloves, signaling that the autopsy had ended. The final hour had been tough to watch, but nobody asked to leave. The examiner turned to Becket, but said nothing. Becket turned to face Brian and myself.

"Thank you all for being here. This was clearly an unfortunate accident," he smiled at the doctor, who nodded back seriously.

That was it. Gareth's death was deemed an accident; I had no doubt that Becket decided the ending before we ever arrived. This entire process had been a show, a circus macabre, with that little asshole as ringmaster. The rest of us, captivated, simply watched in amazement from the bleachers.

Did I say captivated? I meant held captive.

Becket was either the world's biggest anal retentive, or he was scared shitless and trying to cover his ass. Either way, one of my new life goals was to never see him again.

Brian and I left the autopsy room, and I went off duty.

Gareth and I had been friends for quite some time, and as I emerged, I found myself struggling to deal with the conflicting emotions. No longer protected by the demand for professional fortitude, I battled to keep my grief under control. In the hallway, I saw Dee by the lobby door, still flanked by the two guards. She watched with intense, but unreadable eyes. I looked at Brian. "Is that his sister?"

Brian nodded. I took a step toward her, but Brian grabbed my arm and whispered.

"Not now mate, give her some time. They were close. Besides, she's not all that social on her best of days."

At that moment, our Colonel from hell stormed out. He paused, hands on hips as he surveyed the hall. He gave us another phony, sympathetic smile and gestured toward an exit down the hall.

I looked back at Dee, but Brian grabbed my elbow and led me off. "I'll call her later. You don't want her wondering if you're with that wanker Becket."

I reluctantly followed, watching over my shoulder as Deirdre moved defiantly up the hall and into the autopsy room.

We reached the door and exited into chilly darkness, then turned left toward the parking lot. I needed to clear my head, but not even the biting cold breeze could cut through the haze of grief clouding my mind.

Brian followed me patiently as I walked to his car, and found myself looking through the window at the steering wheel. Damn backwards cars! Embarrassed, I opened the door for Brian and walked to the other side. I didn't think I would ever be able to drive there.

Both in our proper seats, we left the parking lot. In the silence, I reexamined the mental images of Gareth's lifeless body. It wasn't the first time I'd seen those wounds.

First Lieutenant Ricky Ibarra's body had looked worse,

the injuries more obvious. Ibarra was a goofy kid from Idaho who didn't smoke, swear, or screw. Hell, he'd never had a beer in his entire life, if you can call that a life. Maybe that's why he was such a damn fine combat soldier. Twenty-six years of frustration had to work itself out somehow.

Last fall, a Predator Drone iced up and crashed intact in Pakistan. When one of our drones went down in hostile territory, the CIA would send in another drone to destroy it. If they couldn't neutralize it from the air, a combat team was dropped in to blow it up on the ground.

A group of terrorists knew that, and were waiting. The four Marines with Ibarra were killed in the ambush, Ibarra survived. I took a full squad in to rescue him, but we were five minutes too late. We missed the cowards and the drone, but did recover the bodies intact. We never found out who was responsible, but had to admit they were clever. We'd been close, but close didn't cut it.

I felt I was close again, and wanted the ass of anyone responsible.

Brian didn't need to know this, not yet. But, should I tell Dee? She was a cop, this was her turf, but no—no way in hell could I say, "And if you look really close here, you can see where this chunk of flesh was clearly ripped from your brother's side, and by a pair of pliers, not a rock."

I could always tell her later, or better still—never.

It would have been nice to examine the body in more detail, but I'd seen enough. You don't have to read an entire letter when the signature at the bottom will tell you who wrote it. Some sadistic, SOB terrorist had signed his gruesome work. My job now was to read the signature and decipher the message.

I pictured Gareth's body in my mind, and had to fight back a growing sense of rage. I needed to be a professional once more. I needed information, and I needed it fast. I looked over at Brian.

"Who is Becket?"

"Colonel Becket, may he burn in hell, works with MI5, like your FBI. He's actually in the RAF, Royal Air Force Intelligence, and heads some kind of joint task force. I only met him recently, but I hear he showed up on base a couple of weeks ago, asking questions. He's also been visiting local police stations. No one knows what he's about, and no one's happy about it."

"You don't trust Becket?"

"Not hardly." That was a problem. MI5 was the logical agency to approach with my concerns, but Becket seemed to be a bigger one. I tried a different approach.

"Dee is Gareth's sister, right?"

Brian nodded.

"Isn't she a police officer?"

Brian nodded suspiciously. "Don't get her involved. Besides, the cops will just contact MI5."

I didn't trust the police anyway, not at all. That left me without official options, which would actually keep things from getting complicated. I didn't want anyone looking over my shoulder.

"Who sent you to get me, Dee or Becket?"

This seemed to confuse him; he actually squirmed as he glanced over.

"Gareth."

Not the answer I was expecting! "How?"

"Gareth sent me a text, about dinner time yesterday. Told me if he wasn't back when they kicked me out of the Crossed Swords, a pub by the base, I was to fetch you from the hotel and come find him."

He had to pause for a moment, pretending to concentrate on his driving. I sat quietly and let him gather his emotions.

"So I leave to find you. I call Gareth on the way, but he's not answering. I call Dee to ask where he is, and she tells me about- about what happened."

He stopped talking. We were entering the construction labyrinth outside my hotel, and he really did need to watch his driving here. As we neared the entrance, he looked over and examined my shirt.

"That was Gareth's"

"How did you know?"

"I have one just like it. We got them autographed after the ninety-nine world cup." He pointed at names written on the

shoulder. "Thomas, Charvis - Williams and Jones are still playing."

I examined the Jersey; I'd never taken the time to check out the autographs. "He really wanted me to like Rugby. I do."

The morning's events had clearly taken their toll on Brian as well, and even this professional soldier had to look away to control his feelings. Moments later, we stopped under the deserted canopy of my hotel's front entrance. As I got out, Brian grabbed my arm and said, "If you've got something planned, I want in."

I had barely begun piecing things together, and shook my head.

"No plan, just questions. Why don't you ask around, see if anyone knows what he was doing? I'll call you later."

He nodded, took a pen and paper from his glove box, and wrote his number down for me. I gave him mine, then exited the car. He spoke up before I could close the door.

"Want some advice?" He smiled for the first time.

"Sure," I said looking back in.

"Take a fucking shower, mate, you reek. And wash the

jersey in cold water, gentle cycle; even better, by hand."

The car door slammed on its own as Brian peeled away. I could see why he and Gareth were friends.

I liked Brian. I just wished we'd met for a beer instead of a body.

Chapter 4

The lobby was quiet, only a nervous-looking clerk with a bushy mustache who fussed behind the check-in desk. He glanced at me suspiciously as I crossed to the elevators.

I pressed the "UP" arrow, and the door opened immediately. I entered and hit the three button as a nauseatingly happy voice told me again that the hotel restaurant was world famous for its leg of lamb. I was about to hear about their renowned concierge service when the doors opened and I escaped. The quiet of downstairs did not extend to the hallway of floor number three.

I discovered that the giants had declared war on the munchkins. Two large men, in the now familiar dark suits, were trying to force their way past a beleaguered trio of local cops. Two small, red-faced women and a diminutive male corporal struggled to stop the jacketed primates from entering Gareth's room.

Dee had gotten her people there before Becket's cyborgs could arrive. Good for her. I attempted to make use of this confusion and move quietly past, since my room was on the other side of Gareth's. The smaller of the MI5 agents, wearing a tailored charcoal-grey suit, blocked my way.

"Where do you think you're going?"

"My room." I held up my card key.

Mr. Grey Suit stood straight and crossed his arms. I really didn't need this right now, or maybe I did. Tearing two belligerent assholes into small, bite-sized pieces would be immensely therapeutic.

Unfortunately, pissing off the authorities even more would be counterproductive. I decided to play it cool, and took a step closer. "If you don't move, I'll call the police."

He frowned, confused, and stole a glance at the still defiant officers standing right next to him. I had him going and pressed my advantage.

"Who are you?"

"MI5."

"Not housekeeping? Too bad, I asked for the turndown service. Can I see some ID?"

Irritated, he pulled out his creds and flipped them open. I leaned forward, and reached for his ID case as I spoke.

"Doesn't look like you."

Instead of grasping the case, I "accidentally" knocked it out of his hand. "Sorry."

"Hey!" he complained, and bent forward to catch his ID.

I reached also, but instead of going for the case, I head-butted him in the nose. It's not assault if I can make it look like he started it.

"Shit!" He reeled back slightly.

He reached for his nose as it erupted into a torrent of fresh red blood, raining down on expensive-looking leather shoes.

"Did I do that?" I pressed forward.

He moved back instinctively, and I stepped on his foot as his weight shifted. He lost his balance and tumbled backward into his partner, who tried unsuccessfully to keep him from landing on his ass.

I looked at the other agent in his cheap blue suit. "Is he always that clumsy? Let me go to my room and get a towel for that nose."

Agent "Off the Rack" frowned, still supporting his partner, as the cops giggled. I pushed past and hurried into my room before anyone could object.

Inside my room, I dropped Gareth's album on my bed and moved quickly to the back, opening the sliding glass door to my balcony. It didn't matter which of the two groups outside got into Gareth's room first, I'd be kept out. I really wanted to look at his quarters. Out on my balcony, I hopped up and balanced on the railing.

I leaned forward and leapt the five feet to the balcony of Gareth's room. I landed, regained my balance, and prepared to force open his balcony door.

That wouldn't be necessary; someone with the proper equipment had been there before me. Whoever it was had cut a softball-sized hole through Gareth's glass balcony door and had neglected to close things back up when he left. I stepped through the already open sliding glass door to Gareth's room.

I wasn't surprised to discover that the room had been expertly searched. Every drawer was open, Gareth's hanging clothes were piled in the center of his bed, and his toiletries had been emptied into the sink. The vents in his room had been removed, and the back was off the TV.

I didn't think they'd found what they were searching for. The stupid saying "It's always in the last place you look" seemed to apply here. People tend to stop looking when they find what they're searching for; which, in fact, makes it the last place they looked. The person or persons searching Gareth's room went through everything—no finding, only looking. Apparently, the contents of his mini-bar were significant, though, since its door lay open and the shelves were empty. Maybe MI5 could issue a nationwide alert for anyone carrying a box of Toblerones and an eight-ounce can of Coke.

I picked up an overturned chair by the small desk and sat. I felt as muddled as the room. It had been a long, shitty night, and I felt confident that another load of shit was already on its way.

I heard loud voices outside, and quickly examined the room. I slipped back into combat mode and observed. There had been at least two intruders. The exhaust vent cover from the bathroom fan was on the sink outside the bathroom, meaning the person who removed the cover had probably handed it to someone else, who then set it outside on the sink. A single intruder would have simply set it on the toilet back or tossed it out of the way.

Next to the vent cover on the sink was a small, twisted lump of metal, and I walked over to retrieve it. It was copper colored, attached to a leather cord by a rough metal loop. The copper lump was mine; at least it had been fired at me.

This nine millimeter Makarov pistol round had left the scar next to Gareth's heart. Gareth, like a dumb shit, had jumped in front of the pistol and taken a bullet for me, even though I was wearing a Kevlar vest and he wasn't. I remembered him in my arms, bleeding from a bullet meant for me. He survived that, only to die at home.

Why the hell did you have to go and die? Why hadn't I been there? What was I doing last night? How? Why?

I felt tears and had to blink to clear my eyes. I sat back

down in the chair; death hadn't affected me like this in a long time.

There was a sound at the door. It flung open an inch, but a bar attached to the frame banged loudly and kept the door from opening.

I slipped the necklace over my head, stood, and shouted. "Hold on!"

Again, I would have preferred having a little more time, but doubted it would have made any difference. Besides, I needed to get into the field, which meant I needed to get out of here.

I grabbed a towel from the bed and walked to the door. I closed it briefly and swung the tapered bar away from the hook on the door. I opened the door and moved aside as Dee and Becket struggled to be the first inside. I suspected that they had raced each other here, and had settled their jurisdictional issues by agreeing to enter together.

I walked back to the desk and knocked the chair back onto its side, then gestured around the room.

"This is how I found it."

Becket didn't even glance at the room. His puckered, red-faced, beady-eyed attention was all on me.

"What the bloody hell are you doing in here?"

I held up the towel and smiled innocently, which I hoped would piss him off even more. "I'm getting a towel. Your man out front fell and hurt himself."

Becket's mouth opened and closed; he must have been trying to find something intelligent to say. Failing that, he turned and yelled out the door.

"Tibbs!"

Agent Clearance Rack squeezed in, and Becket was in poor Tibbs' face like this was his fault. Well, in part it was his fault, but why be picky?

"Take this man to the airport. Put him on the next flight out of the country." Tibbs looked more hapless than before. He glared at me briefly, then literally cowered to Becket.

"Sir, they don't really have much of an airport here. I'm sure there are no international flights."

Becket was not someone who let facts get in his way. "Then take him to Cardiff. No, put him on a skiff, run him out to international waters and throw him overboard! We need to get back to London, no more interruptions."

While I enjoyed a good swim as much as the next guy, I had luggage. I also had a plan of my own. I decided to share it with the group: "Sorry, your lordship, you can't do that."

Becket did that mouth thing again, opening and closing. He looked like a little trout out of water.

"What? Why the hell not?" Becket's face contorted. He didn't like being played like this.

I walked up to Dee and held out my arms, hands up and wrists together. To her credit, it only took her a second to catch on. She pulled out her handcuffs and slapped them around my wrists, rather roughly I thought. "Because he's being detained, suspicion of unlawful entry." Before Becket could respond, Dee grabbed the cuffs and dragged me curtly into the hallway. She turned to the smaller of the two female officers stationed outside the door.

"Constable Wells, put this man in the back of my Panda car and keep him there. If he resists, beat him senseless."

Officer, or rather Constable Wells looked up at me, clearly skeptical about her chances if it came to that.

Chapter 5

I scowled out the window, more than a little pissed off. The sun was rising, and I'd been sitting there for over an hour, stuffed in the back of that little white shoe box of a cop car. They must call it a Panda Car because only a little stuffed animal could be comfortable in such a tiny space.

Sheri, Constable Wells, got tired of waiting after half an hour and left to find the DS. DS stands for Detective Sergeant, referring in this instance to Detective Sergeant Deirdre Jones. Sheri and I had been getting along great, despite the fact that she'd been forced to open the windows a crack. I guess I did reek after all.

Constable Sheri Wells was short with dirty blonde hair rolled up under her hat. She had the skin of a teenager, regrettably a teenager with acne. The Constable didn't quite have an hourglass figure, think shot glass. She also had a pale round face with too much eyeliner. Actually, she looked more like a panda than the car did.

She was extremely nice and seemed to be a bit of a flirt. She definitely had a great personality, and yes that was also a commentary on her looks. It's not that she was unattractive; it's just that—well yeah; she was. In fact, she was about two chocolate bars and a bad hair day away from ugly.

I started feeling a little guilty, was I being cruel? Yeah, probably, which made me feel even worse. Sheri Wells seemed to be really a great person. She had an infectious personality, she carried herself like a real professional, and sounded very intelligent. I definitely appreciated the company and enjoyed talking with her a great deal.

Honest!

I told her that if she ever came to West Texas, I would show her around our ranch. I mentioned that she could get close enough to pet some of the steers we breed, and even promised to buy her a ten-gallon cowboy hat.

OK, I may have laid it on a little thick, but I needed her to take off my handcuffs and bring me my morning coffee, or maybe just let me go. What I absolutely had to have was Gareth's photo album. If Becket got his hands on that, I'd never see it again.

I was making progress until she remembered the DS told her to keep me on ice. I got the impression that no one crossed Deirdre Jones without a good reason, or a really good place to hide. Anyway, Sheri eventually left me there, promising to do what she could and hurry back.

Through blurry, caffeine-deprived vision, I glanced at the hotel entrance. Sheri exited the hotel lobby with the corporal; and behind them strolled Detective Sergeant Jones, sipping a mug of steaming hot liquid, arguing with Becket. Sheri glanced over her shoulder to make sure Dee wasn't watching, then scurried over to the car where I sat entombed.

She opened the door and dropped the photo album on the seat next to me. She'd saved it, God bless her, but where did she have it hidden?

Sheri shrugged sympathetically, slammed the door, and hurried to catch up with the corporal at their car. With a last look back and a cute little wink, she was gone, along with my best chance of getting into the field any time soon.

I looked back toward the hotel as Detective Sergeant Jones and Colonel Becket split up, neither of them looking happy. Becket had his cell phone out before he'd taken a second step, but Dee took her time. She looked tired, head down, strolling along the walk. If I felt like complaining about my day, I just had to remember that hers had been worse.

She looked back up at the hotel, threw her shoulders back, then turned and strode toward the car. She opened her door, plopped behind the wheel, and slid the plastic cup into a holder on the dash. I was expecting the deep, rich, satisfying aroma of the hotel's freshly brewed finest.

She was drinking tea, what's the deal with tea around here?

The Detective Sergeant, however, was expecting a different aroma as well, and scowled over her shoulder. She snorted and rolled down the windows. Next, she fastened her seatbelt, after which she took a slow, obviously exaggerated satisfying sip.

Constable Wells must have mentioned I was Starbucks deprived. While the fresh air from the window was nice, I really did want some coffee. I leaned a little toward the center of the car to let her know I was still alive. Dee didn't react, so I leaned further and looked at her image in the rearview mirror.

I saw part of her face reflected there. Dee still had the cup to her lips, but she just stared up at the balcony of Gareth's room. I could only imagine what she was thinking and feeling, so I sat back quietly to let her have a moment.

She was holding things together like a pro, no tears or smears, but there was enough red and puffy around the eyes to hint at what she was dealing with on the inside. I could wait a few minutes more.

But just a few! If I was going to prevent more innocent people from joining her brother in the morgue, I needed to get going- now.

Suddenly, without looking back or any word of warning, she started the car and cranked the fan button on the dash to high. She raised the window and seconds later, she was expertly navigating the parking lot maze, approaching Oystermouth Road.

We turned left again. I had already been down this road a few times today, but now the morning traffic was in full mayhem. At least that's how it felt from the back. This was my first experience with their rush-hour commute, and I found myself leaning, trying to get back on the right side of the road. It had to be a malicious, Red Coat plot; nobody would choose to drive like this.

I again noticed the University of Swansea coming up on the right. The trees that lined both sides of the road were easily visible in the clear morning light. The vegetation edging the north boundary provided a measure of privacy for the campus. The leafy perimeter did, however, have gaps in several places. Right now we were nearing the wide, well-kept entrance leading off to what must have been the main campus. Cars came and went, and a few energetic students walked down paths leading to a new day of enlightenment.

With a slight turn of the head, I watched a moment longer, and then slumped back in my seat. Through the next break in the trees, I saw the Rugby field. Two makeshift teams, sides, were scrimmaging. The field was half in the shadow as they ran and collided with obvious enthusiasm, a nimble young man dove across the goal line for a score as we passed.

I, on the other hand, was completely in the shadow of today's events. I would save my enthusiasm for when I could start ferreting out what had happened. I couldn't wait to score one for the good guys, with all the accompanying body bags. But damn it, I needed to get moving.

"You don't find things to your liking?"

Dee watched me in her rear view mirror. I sat up and leaned forward.

"Excuse me?"

"You don't appear to be enjoying your surroundings. Wales doesn't agree with you?"

"Wales is fine, great actually. It just doesn't seem real. For all these people, life goes on normal and happy. Gareth should be here, so no, things aren't right, normal or happy for me."

I held up my still handcuffed hands and grinned. "And besides, there's really nothing that says 'Welcome to Wales!' like being in restraints, stuffed in the back of a toy police car."

Her reflected face considered me with suspicion; those deep green eyes really were pretty. With a frown, she jerked the wheel to the left. Crossing a lane of angry, honking traffic she pulled over to the tiny shoulder, barely off the road. She spun toward me with remarkable dexterity.

"Maybe you're NOT welcome."

Anymore. I almost corrected her. Her brother's death, murder, changed that. I wondered again at the emotional tsunami that must be roaring through her heart, and realized I'd never told her how I felt about her brother.

I'd seen dozens of my friends dead. Two actually died in my arms. I'd learned to push that into the dark corners of my soul, the mission comes first. Grief needed it's own time and place. Dee only had one brother, and now he was gone.

"I understand. I haven't said how sorry I am about your brother, he was an amazing man. He was my friend. "

Her eyes welled up, then narrowed. "Friends don't break into each other's rooms."

I patted my front pocket.

"Absolutely, that's why he gave me his card key. I couldn't use it with everyone guarding his door. I went to his room earlier that night to get this album." I looked at Gareth's album on the seat next to me. "For some reason, he wanted me to look it over."

She considered this, then looked curiously down at the album. "What time?"

I knew why she was asking. "About one-thirty. Whoever searched his room did it after I was there."

Dee looked me in the eyes, still undecided.

I held up my hands again. "I have questions about what happened."

Like who killed him.

"I know you were his friend, but I don't know if I can trust you."

The honest answer to that was, Of course you can't trust me. I will lie, steal, threaten or kill to find the person who murdered your brother.

One truthful answer did come to mind.

"Gareth did."

I watched as her face transformed from determined and professional to heartbroken. It was amazing, a revelation. Her face didn't really change, and her body remained absolutely still, yet somehow the entire universe seemed to have faded from light to dark in her face.

I felt something different, something strange.

I'd called in airstrikes that vaporized   dozens of al

Qaeda leaders in an instant. I'd run through buildings killing men before they could reach for their weapons. I once beat a man to death with his own artificial leg before he could detonate a roadside bomb. Those were hard things, brutal things, just another day in the Corps.

I again examined the subtle changes on Dee's face, now soft and vulnerable. Soft, subtle—for these things I had no defense.

Dee turned and sat facing forward, fishing in her pants pocket. She retrieved a small round key, and without taking off her seat belt, she spun again in her seat. She reached into the back, grabbed my cuffs and yanked. She struggled briefly to get the key into the tiny hole, but in seconds my hands were free. Immediately after that, she was again endangering dozens of the lives she had sworn to protect by forcing her way back into traffic.

"Thank you."

She said 'you're welcome' by scowling viciously into the mirror and asking sarcastically, "My pleasure entirely, is there anything else I can do?"

How do you pass up such a nice invitation? "As a matter of fact, tell me why this is called a Panda Car?"

Her reflected face went blank, then frowned.

"It's what they're called."

"Why?"

She shook her head. "Who cares?"

At this point, I cared. I rubbed my wrists; the indentations from the cuffs were still deep and red. If I wanted to escape now, there was nothing DS Jones could do to stop me.

I could, but should I? Maybe later. I remembered that Mumbles was on this road, just outside of Swansea, so we were probably headed to the accident scene. This would save me a trip. I rubbed my eyes and realized I hadn't slept in almost twenty-seven hours. This was not really a problem in itself, but I had no way of knowing when I would get a chance to relax again.

I turned sideways and rested my head against the door. I folded my arms across my chest, closed my eyes, and slept.

Chapter 6

I sprang awake to the exhilarating sensation of face on fabric, as my cheek slammed against the back of the passenger seat. Dee brought the car skidding to a halt, coming to rest almost sideways on the side of the road.

I love the smell of nylon in the morning.

I opened my eyes to Deirdre Jones' smiling face. Or, maybe it wasn't smiling, perhaps it was leering; it's hard to tell when you're just waking up. What had become painfully obvious was that she had a bit of a mean streak. I shouldn't have been surprised; I'd already seen that in action.

I smiled back. "Glad I could brighten up your day."

"Gareth could do that."

"What?"

"Sleep anywhere, at any second."

I was about to assure her that it was simply the slumber of innocence, but she had already hopped out of the car. As she walked toward a small group of people near a large police van, I realized she had no intention of letting me out. That would be a problem, since I had no intention of staying put. I needed to get a look at the 'accident' scene, and sitting quietly on my ass in the back of some car was simply unacceptable. So, I knocked politely on the window, forcing her to run back before the glass shattered under my delicate touch. She flung the door open.

"Knock it off!"

Her mean streak again neared critical mass. I asked politely.

"Let me out, please?"

Dee hesitated, then gave me a little half smile. By half smile I mean she only used the left side of her mouth, which to the untrained eye may have looked like a smirk.

I smiled sweetly and continued, "I thought we had this whole trust thing sorted out?"

She looked at her watch. "I don't have any intention of letting you wander about sightseeing."

"And I don't have any intention of staying in this car."

She stared impatiently back up the road for a second. "Five minutes."

I couldn't look into her face right now and lie.

"Ten."

She was still skeptical, so I went on.

"You probably know I won't play by your rules, the best I can do is promise to be honest with you."

I didn't believe for a second that I was the first man with an offer of honesty, but I needed her to trust me.

"I need to see this. I won't be any trouble—at least not right now."

"You've got nine minutes left."

She turned, leaving the door open, and walked away. I exited and watched as she hurried toward the cliff about ten meters to my right, aiming again for the police van, which was uncomfortably close to the drop off.

I followed, analyzing the scene. The accident had

occurred on a curve in the road. Coming out from Mumbles the road curved right, but Gareth had been headed toward Mumbles so it would have been curving left for him. He would have had to cross the oncoming lane of traffic, through the wide dirt shoulder, then smash through the guardrail and over the cliff.

I examined the shoulder area. It measured twenty meters long, and looked wide enough for a small car to pull off safely, but barely. There was definitely not enough room for the eight police cars and a van now crowded around it. I could see that orange cones had been placed up and down the road with officers directing traffic safely past.

At the far end, where the accident had occurred, a large wrecker had backed up to the edge of the cliff, cable trailing into the void below. I could see where the guardrail had been breached, leaving a finger of twisted metal pointing off into the cloudy sky. Men, and a few women, stood in groups, each with their jobs to do. They talked, smoked, and some even joked around—it was just another accident scene to them.

That changed when DS Jones arrived. As we reached the van, a constable holding a clipboard noticed us and waved urgently to the group. They turned toward Dee, standing straighter and looking sadder. I slowed down and let them perform the meet and greet ritual in private. Everyone looked genuinely sympathetic, and Dee looked truly appreciative.

I felt sorry for Dee too, but my goal was making sure the people responsible experienced the next round of suffering. I wouldn't have a nice day until I looked into the eyes of the person who killed Gareth, and watch with satisfaction as those eyes turned vacant and lifeless.

I'm a firm believer in the power of positive thinking. Dee, at that instant, seemed occupied with Officer

Clipboard and his magic papers, so I wandered over to the wrecker to get a better look. I needed to examine the guardrail, then see what I could learn from the wrecker operator.

The guardrail itself was a long ribbon of metal anchored to heavy wooden posts. There were three posts, one at each end and another in the middle. The rail had been torn from the post at the far side, but was still anchored to the post in the middle. I examined the twisted guardrail metal, then looked at my watch.

I had eight minutes left. Dee noticed my wanderings and sent a skinny little baby-faced officer to keep an eye on me. Geez, he looked about twelve.

I turned away before he reached me and started questioning Trevor, the tow-truck driver whose name was printed in marker over his left breast pocket. Trevor carefully watched the tension on his tow cable as it reeled slowly in. He glanced over and smiled when I said hello.

"Trevor, how long have you been on site?"

"'Bout four hours. Fuckin' Bobbies had me standing with my thumb up my arse forever. Then them bloody twats in black suits made me park back on the roadway while they took measurements and made pictures of everything."

I nodded sympathetically. "Assholes, all of 'em."

"Every fucking one, and their mothers, brothers and sisters as well!" Trevor plucked the tow cable like he was playing a harp. With a common enemy and our bonding complete, I began to pump my newest best friend for information.

"How far did the car fly down the hill?"

"Not far, bloody amazing it went down at all with them posts being so stout and such. They're not far apart, and if he'd caught one of them, his little toy car would still

48

be wrapped 'round it."

Interesting. I nodded my head in agreement and examined the scene closely. Things still didn't make sense. I walked over to the edge and peered down. The car was almost to the top. I could clearly see that the trunk had been damaged, but that was all I could make out. I turned back to the wrecker.

"Skid marks."

Trevor and the baby-faced Bobby looked at each other and scowled.

"How long are the skid marks, the car?"

Down to seven minutes.

"Oh, right. See for yourself." He checked the cable again, then we walked around his truck to the edge of the pavement. He pointed to a pair of curving black rubber lines starting up the road a few meters and curving nicely toward the dirt shoulder where we were standing.

Things were still not coming together for me, so I closed my eyes and turned back time. In my mind, I could hear the screech of skidding tires, I could now smell the burning rubber in the night as Gareth's little green MG left the road.

I turned and walked to the thick post where the nearest end of the guardrail was anchored. I examined it briefly then closed my eyes again. Now I could hear the crunch of tires on gravel as the car slid over the dirt shoulder. This was followed immediately by the crash of metal on metal and a squeal from the twisting guardrail. Finally the rattling, bouncing rumble of Gareth's car as it careened down the cliff.

My visualization ended, and a final curtain came down on the incident. Now that I knew what had happened, I needed to get away from my babysitters. It was time to get on the trail to retribution.

I clapped Trevor on the arm and smiled. "Don't let the bastards get you down."

He grinned back. "Not a chance!"

I looked back at the cliff. If I'd had more time, I would have liked to get a better look at the car itself, but that really wasn't necessary. What was necessary was that I got moving. As I looked around for suitable transport, meaning anything with wheels and the keys still in it, I saw a caravan of black Land Rovers pushing their way impatiently onto the crime scene.

Shit, I thought I still had five minutes left.

They stopped. Becket bounded from the lead vehicle, still the happy-go-lucky leprechaun of MI5. Maybe he heard me and Trevor complaining about bastards and assholes and he thought we were calling him.

This pompous little prick was going to continue making things difficult, I could tell that already. So, should I stay or should I go? I spun to the kid Constable and held out my wrists.

"Cuff me."

Baby-face just stared and blinked. I held my wrists a little higher.

"You have handcuffs, right?"

He nodded. Good, he spoke English. I unzipped my fly, then actually stuck my wrists in his face.

"Then put your handcuffs on me, and drag me over to Detective Jones."

He stared blankly. God, I didn't need this right now.

"Just do it! Now!" I couldn't yell, so I made my normal voice as angry and threatening as possible.

Junior finally woke up from his nap. He blinked three times and pulled out his cuffs. After a moment of fumbling, he finally got them on me. I hustled toward where Dee and Becket were arguing, my escort running to keep up.

Becket saw me approach and growled. "You let this man wander around the accident scene?"

Dee fumbled for an answer when I stopped in front of her and raised my cuffed hands. Then, as if embarrassed, I reached down and zipped my pants.

"Thank you. The back of your car will now stay dry and fresh."

She played along without missing a beat. "Fine, then maybe you'll stop being such a bloody pain in my ass."

She turned to my breathless chaperone in blue. "Covington, put this man back in my car and drive him to Central Station. Don't do anything else, just wait until I call. I'll handle things when I get there. And no one talks to him, understood?"

Covington saluted and we turned to leave. Becket began to sputter like an old boat motor.

"I think not! I need him."

Dee straightened herself to an imposing five feet, six inches of red-haired fury.

"This man is officially in my custody; what do you have that officially transfers him to yours?"

Becket was at a loss. Bullying and intimidation weren't working for him this time, mainly because Dee had been doing the bullying and intimidating. He hesitated but didn't give up.

"You'll be giving him to me in an hour, probably less."

"I don't have to give you shit, though you certainly deserve a ration or two." She spun to glare at me. Constable Kiddie and I had been standing there enjoying the show.

She growled. "Covington!"

Constable Covington jumped, grabbed my cuffs, and dragged me to the car.

I heard Becket bark behind me. "Tibbs!"

We got in Dee's car, and I extended my hands into the front.

"You can have these back."

As Constable Kiddie fumbled for his keys again I saw Tibbs and his partner hop into one of the Range Rovers. We had a tail, and from Tibbs' expression as he glared at me before mounting his vehicle, I knew there would be a rematch.

Chapter 7

I paced around Dee's police car and surveyed the parking lot. Again! Dee had radioed Covington with instructions to leave me there with the car while she attended to "another fucking crisis the bastard brought me." I assumed that I was the bastard, but didn't know what the crisis could be. But then again, I was new to the country.

I never enjoyed waiting, and considered calling Brian. I really didn't like just standing around when I had a mission to run, but I really didn't want to drag him into this yet. My CIA friends could make sure I got out of the country safely, but Brian was stuck here. Crossing the wrong people could cost him his job, or freedom.

Besides, my preferred approach to problem solving involved the liberal application of high explosives. From the small bangs that propelled searing hot chunks of metal out of the barrel of a gun and through the tender flesh of a human body, to the ultra-cool mega-booms that made mountains into molehills. I once called in an air strike on a

Taliban cave in the mountains near Pakistan. I received confirmation the strike was in progress, then instructions to light up the cave entrance with a laser designator—a little point of light to show the flyboys what to hit.

I was holding the laser on target when the mountain erupted, and the earth convulsed from the violence of the bomb's impact.

It must have been a GBU-28 Bunker Buster. There's nothing like four thousand pounds of high explosives detonating nearby to give one's colon a thorough cleansing. Who needed Six Flags Amusement Park when you could watch an instrument of chemical annihilation, twice the size of your average import car, reduce a granite mountain to driveway gravel?

That Bunker Buster had probably been three times the size of the little Meter Maid cart then peddling through the parking lot. I looked closer and realized it was a car, not a meter cart. I hated those tiny 'eco' cars. Like mosquitoes, they buzzed around and annoyed people. Apparently, this one intended to annoy just me.

It shuddered to a stop beside Dee's police vehicle. The tiny car now rested perfectly centered over the white line of a parking spot. I couldn't see past the tinted windows, but I remembered the car taking up two parking spots at the morgue; Dee had returned.

Sure enough, Dee exploded out of her car and marched to her police cruiser. She unlocked it, opened the door, and rummaged around inside. She stood back up, holding a small bag of woman stuff and Gareth's album.

After closing and locking the door, she noticed me admiring her parking job and inquired politely.

"You got a problem?"

I shrugged. "No problem, I just need to get used to the way people drive around here. In the states we park between the lines, in Wales, I guess you straddle them."

Dee walked over, slammed the album into my stomach, and returned to her eco-car. She opened her door, then raised her right hand, finger extended in the universal symbol for "Straddle this, asshole." She plopped herself inside and slammed her door.

I must have hesitated a moment too long, because she let out, "Get in already!"

I walked to the tiny transport, curious as to how I was to accomplish this 'getting-in' miracle. The shiny round top reached just above my navel, at any moment I expected an avalanche of clowns to pour out.

The horn honked, the passenger door flung open, and Dee's dulcet voice floated out. "You friggin' deaf? Get in!"

Deaf? No, but I'd had to be blind to think I could fit in a roller skate with radials. Still, I bent over and examined the interior. It actually might have been OK, if my name were Frodo and I lived in the Shire.

I inquired courteously. "You can't be serious?"

The pissed-off stare said she was. I examined the seat, exhaled and folded my arms. I managed to sit on the edge of the seat and swing my right leg in. My knee rested about three microns from the flimsy dash, a good sneeze and I might make a softball-sized dent. The left leg followed, and I closed the door.

This was ridiculous! This was also her personal car. I knew that because I saw two bottles of makeup in the tiny tray between the seats. I then examined a pile of tissues on the floor under my feet. A huge mirror covered the entire sun visor, smudged with fingerprints of assorted color and texture.

Her car labored out of the lot, and we soon headed into a residential section of Swansea. I hadn't been to this part of town yet, but it had been on today's schedule with

Gareth. I didn't think I should mention that to Dee. In fact, Dee hadn't glanced my way since we left the lot.

I realized that my safest option was to just wait her out. Unfortunately, I almost always chose action over inaction, so I looked over at her and smiled.

"You seem to have a problem with me today?"

This worked better than I expected. She spun, eyes open almost as wide as her mouth. Her face turned so red her freckles nearly disappeared. She breathed in and out in short gasps, like she was in labor. It was all I could do to keep from laughing, but I didn't want to let success get to my head.

"Problem with you? You are the bloody problem, you dozy prat. First off, Sheri, Constable Wells, tells me I best not be scrumping her new squeeze. So I ask what she's on about. So she says you chatted her up, that a bird like her doesn't get many chances with any real talent. I think she plans on having it off with you, and if you're just winding her up, I'll have your bollocks in a blender!"

All I could do was stare. I didn't think she'd taken a breath since practicing her Lamaze breathing a few moments before.

Our car drifted into the lane to our left, and some guy in a yellow Mercedes hit his horn. She swerved back without looking at the road, and still without taking a breath. Miraculously, there was more air in there somehow, and she ripped into me again.

"Just like a fucking bloke, wants to shag anything with a slit twixt the gams."

Something really had her in a lather, but I had no idea what it was—or what she was saying.

And, she still hadn't taken a breath! I was actually getting worried at this point. Come on, don't pass out on me. She finally started breathing, but it was that weird panting thing again. It was a little annoying, actually.

She used that fresh influx of oxygen to renew her assault.

"Well, what do you have to say?"

What could I say? Only one thing came to mind at the moment.

"I speak five languages, and I just found out that English isn't one of them."

She furrowed her brow, confused.

"Dee, I have no idea what you just said!"

She was finally breathing normally again, and I no longer had the urge to yell "Push." However, she still glared at me, suspicious.

"No idea, really? Did you or did you not flirt with Constable Sheri Wells?"

I suddenly got the feeling I had entered an active mine field. "We had a nice conversation, but I wasn't flirting."

"She thinks you were coming on to her!"

I shook my head to imply 'no',' and 'I'm confused.'

"You didn't tell her she'd 'enjoy petting your Texas Longhorn?'"

I responded hesitantly. "Yeah. Well, something like that."

She sat straight, head high, a triumphant look on her face.

I asked. "What's wrong with that?"

"So! You want me to believe it's the whole cow you have stuffed in your shorts, and not just the sausage?"

That sounded quite clever, but what did it mean?

Oh! My Texas Longhorn, she thought. Sheri thought . . . I was in trouble. I started to explain.

"Constable Wells and I were talking about Texas, where I'm from. That's it! She said she'd like to visit. I said if she did, I'd show her around . . . if I were there at the time. I, we, my cousins and I, have Longhorns on our ranch. It's a starter herd, but they're nice animals."

"Oh, right! And didn't you say she could ride your wild stallion?"

"Napalm."

"What's a napalm?"

"My stallion."

"Fuck off!"

How had things gotten so screwed up? I kept trying to make her understand.

"I bought a ranch with my cousins, several years ago now. I have a small herd of Texas Longhorns. I also have a cream Palomino named Napalm."

Now she looked confused. "What about the exotic day together?"

I shrugged, with only a vague idea of what she was asking about now.

"I said we can take a day and see my exotics. We've introduced blesboc, urials, and even some bongos and watusis."

She turned red again. "What the FUCK are you on about?"

"Animals . . . African . . . we have them . . ."

It was time for me to shut up. I folded my arms, slumped down in my seat to see out the windshield and stared straight ahead. I could've sworn that I was speaking English, but I guess I was wrong.

A little while later, we were deep into the residential district. Several apartment buildings came up on our left. Dee looked over suspiciously, out of the corner of her eye.

"You have a ranch?"

I nodded. I felt safer keeping my mouth shut at this point.

"What's it called?"

I wasn't sure my answer was going to help, but she was obviously going to wait until I replied.

"The Eagle, Globe and Angus."

She laughed, but she didn't actually look all that amused. I tried to explain.

"My cousins and I were all Marines. Two of us still are. The Marine Corps symbol is the Eagle, Globe and Anchor."

"And you thought that 'Eagle, Globe and Angus' sounded like a good name for a ranch?"

"It took a lot of beer, but eventually, yeah."

Dee pulled up in front of a tall, brick apartment building. It had a nice gated patio area with a lawn, gardens and wrought-iron benches out front. Dee grabbed a bag that had been stuffed between the seats, and tossed it into my lap.

"I got you some clothes."

I couldn't wait to see them! I took the bag, and Gareth's album, and we both got out of the car.

I could see the complex had an expansive tiled entryway, which was now visible through double glass doors.

"Looks nice." It did appear much nicer than I'd expected.

She followed my gaze, smirked, then turned to cross the street.

"I'm a cop, remember?"

Across the street stood an old, two story beige apartment building. It looked like it might have been pre-war, meaning the War of 1812. I didn't want to say it was a dump, but nothing worse came to mind at the moment.

She saw my concern and smiled, enjoying the apparent discomfort. "The city tried to condemn it a few years back, but it wasn't worth tearing down. Can't top the rent, though, and it really pisses off the rich gits across the street."

Her logic seemed unimpeachable and her courage unquestionable, so we walked up to the ground-floor apartment on the far left. Truthfully, as I walked across the property, I noticed that it was well cared for. The walkways were all in good shape, no cracks or holes, and the landscaping was almost adequate. Everything seemed to stay green in Wales, so it must have been easy to take care of this tiny strip of grass that protected Dee's building from the encroaching concrete. As we neared the door, I heard barking from inside. I liked dogs, so this wasn't a problem.

Dee glanced over. "Wait here until I call. Come in and just stand in the living room, all quiet like, while Blackjack gets used to you. You should know he does bite at times, but only draws blood if he's threatened."

Whatever, I just wanted to get a shower, put on some clean clothes, and set out on the trail for Gareth's killer. I was only good for another forty-eight, maybe sixty hours without sleep, and I definitely wanted the ass of whoever had killed her brother. I wanted it really bad.

Dee gave me the "are you up for this?" nod, which I returned with an "I think I can handle this" roll of the eyes. She turned and slipped through the door.

Inside, I heard soft growls and panting. There was some jumping and running around, and finally a couple of excited yelps. I had no idea what the dog was doing, but Dee certainly seemed happy to be home. The door opened a crack, and she softly ordered me inside.

I took two steps into the living room area and stopped. In front of me was what looked like a shrunken Doberman. It crouched low, front legs forward and lips snapped back in a snarl. The little guy stood ready to protect his turf and turf-mate, which I respected.

Blackjack was black, no surprise, with brown paws and little brown patches on his snout. He was a really nice-looking beast, except for the a sissy pink collar around his neck. His ears lay back, but I could tell they were cropped like triangles. His tail had been lopped off at about one inch.

Blackjack stood slowly, warily, still checking me out. I looked at Dee. "He'd be in a better mood if he didn't have to wear that ridiculous collar."

She smiled sarcastically and raised her right hand like before, but I couldn't see what she wanted me to straddle this time. Meanwhile, Blackjack circled me slowly, sniffing the air with interest. I wondered if making him smell two days worth of my sweat, dirt and beer constituted cruelty to animals.

Carefully, Blackjack approached. He stood on his back legs and sniffed obsessively at the hem of my shirt, of Gareth's old shirt—Gareth's favorite old shirt. Blackjack whined softly. He looked up at me with eager eyes, then at Dee. He turned and jumped onto the back of the couch. He moved the curtain aside with his snout and eagerly scanned the front of the building.

He barked sharply. I'm pretty sure he was saying, "Gareth, where are you buddy? I'm right here!"

I looked over at Dee, wondering what to do next, and saw her disappear down a dark hallway to my left. Moments later I heard muffled sobs coming from somewhere down the hall. I definitely couldn't blame her. She had earned it. It had been a horrible day, and she'd soldiered through like a real professional. I even found it necessary to wipe a drop of wetness from my eyes.

I turned back to the window. This sucked for everybody, but people could understand. Poor Blackjack would spend every day of his life waiting for Gareth to come home.

I set my bag and the album on the couch. I didn't know how he'd react, but I knelt on the couch facing the window. I opened the curtains with one hand and reached for him with the other.

"It's OK big guy, we'll stand watch together for a while."

I lifted Blackjack higher. He looked at me suspiciously, then turned back to the window. Together we scoured the world outside for a friend who was never coming home.

Chapter 8

Deirdre Catherine Jones, youngest Detective Sergeant in the South Wales Police Service, sterling example of professionalism and poise to all around her, was a mess. She found herself on the verge of losing it; totally and completely. She fought to keep the tears from surging into a river of despair.

The very core of her being had been shattered. Her life lay in useless bits around her. The best of her past had become the worst of her future, a cold dead memory that would surely fester into shadow and regret. The most important person remaining in her life was gone. Mum and Dad had died years ago, and now Gareth joined them.

Worse still, she could not allow herself to grieve.

Her brother's death would be investigated, and she wanted to be on the case. She had to have it, she demanded it. She'd even started investigating on her own, without telling her boss. He'd understood, but hadn't agreed. Gareth's death would be the most important case of her life, and she could not allow the pain and sorrow to show.

If she weren't at her best, someone else would be given the case. It had been ruled an accident, but she didn't care—she would get to the bottom of this.

Getting on the case didn't keep a cruel shroud of misery from descending over her soul. There seemed to be a chill fog roiling from her broken heart, threatening to numb her mind as well. In fact, everything was going bad; even her dog betrayed her. As if she needed more, her best friend Sheri now wanted to scratch her eyes out. Topping everything off, the directors of MI5 were certainly thinking up new and creative ways of making her life a living hell. It had been a ghastly day, and it wasn't even suppertime yet.

To keep her mind from toppling over the edge of sanity and into a chasm of emotional void, Dee resorted to one of the oldest and least understood cures in the history of human evolution.

The Detective Sergeant would take a bubble bath, if she could remember how.

No doubt, there were exotic scents guaranteed to transform a world of pain and sadness into a liquid universe of exquisite harmony. Unfortunately, Dee Jones didn't know about such things. She was a detective, so she investigated her options and made do with what she had.

Dee grabbed a box from under the sink and liberally sprinkled bubble bath under the running water, something pink called "Doctor Bubbly," which had been left there years ago by her little cousin. Scented candles also seemed appropriate, and Dee had been forced to raid her Christmas decorations. The scent of cinnamon soon filled the room.

Dear God, am I really this pathetic?

She glanced at the mirror; puffy red eyes peered back.

Absolutely.

She thought about opening the door and giving the Yank a chance to use the head before she barricaded herself inside, but instead, she marched over and locked the door. Let him piss in the bushes if he needs to. Let the two of them water the shrubs if it came to that. She was taking a bath.

She removed her robe and draped it over the little chair at her makeup table. She turned and gazed down at islands of tiny white bubbles, floating in a bubble-gum sea. She hesitated, then stepped over the edge and dipped her right foot into the water. It was bloody hot, but felt better than she'd expected—inviting actually.

She slowly dipped her left foot in. When it was comfortably submerged, she lowered the rest of her body carefully down into the water. It felt more like the water rose up to her, welcoming her.

Not too damn inviting, it was really hot!

She forced herself to stay in the water, and her body quickly adjusted.

She sat there a moment, letting her consciousness align itself with her unfamiliar new surroundings. Dee splashed a little and smiled. She scooped up a handful of pinkish-white bubbles and blew them at the showerhead, which peered quizzically down at her from the white-tiled wall.

She grinned, the warm embrace of the water and the festive scent in the air had begun to push the day's ordeal from her mind. She slid deeper into the warmth and laid her head back, resting it on the hard porcelain edge of the tub.

That was uncomfortable.

She sat up and looked around the bathroom. Her bag lay within reach, so she stretched and pulled it close. She rummaged through it and retrieved a clear plastic evidence bag with a zip close top. She inflated the bag, quickly zipped it closed, and slid it behind her neck like a pillow.

Much better.

She took two deep breaths, and the warm water began to draw a brutal day's worth of tension from her muscles. Exhaustion numbed her, and not just her body. Almost instantly her mind slipped into a universe that was not quite sleep, but definitely not awake; a grey, quiet, limbo of the mind. It stopped being a place for thoughts, and instead, became a sanctuary for the vague images playing hide-and-go-seek in her subconscious.

If only for a moment, she was at peace.

It was an all too brief a moment of peace as Dee's phone rang treasonously nearby. She dove for her purse, and a tidal wave of soapy, now bubble-free water washed over the side of the tub.

"Shit!"

She hoped the pink tsunami hadn't flooded her shoulder bag, but the ringing continued so she figured her purse was probably OK. She hung over the side of the tub, fishing for the ringing sound that meant her boss was calling. She fumbled with her phone, then finally managed to mutter.

"Jones."

"Detective Jones, so nice of you to finally answer your phone."

Why had Inspector Hill called me at home? What's he talking about?

Dee looked at the display of her phone, which showed two missed calls. How could that be, was her phone on the outs? Then she noticed the time. She'd been in the tub for over an hour. She shook her head and realized her boss was still talking.

"Detective Sergeant Jones, I asked where you are."

Dee sat straighter in the tub. When the Inspector used her full Title, what followed was seldom pleasant.

"Are you alone?"

"Yes, I mean I'm alone in this room. Travis, Sergeant Deacon, is still in my custody. He's in the next room."

Inspector Hill remained silent; Dee wondered if something really had gone wrong with her phone.

"Sir, are you still there?"

He replied quite peevishly. "Aren't you going to ask if I'm alone?"

"Right, if you say so."

This had to be his way of paying her back, which he didn't often do. That meant he was either worried or pissed. Dee was certain that pissed would be the better for her.

"Are you alone, sir?"

"Yes, Sergeant, I mean I'm alone in this room. MI5, who wants to crawl up my ass with a cattle prod, is in the next room. Would you care to exchange places?"

Dee looked down at her naked, now chilly body.

"Not at the moment, no sir."

"I didn't think so. Either way, you've put me in a bit of a dilemma, and I can't decide whether to fire you or give you a commendation."

Dee was tempted to express a preference, but thought better of it. She waited for her boss to go on.

"What did you do to that twat Becket?"

"Colonel Becket? Nothing really, just a disagreement over who should deal with the American."

Actually, Dee remembered that Deacon had gone out of his way to offend Becket. Maybe the annoying American wasn't so bad.

"It's gratifying to hear you're standing firm in defense of our local authority, but MI5 is not amused in the least. One of their senior agents from Cardiff drove here to personally ruin my day. I'm sure the plan was for me to make yours even worse, but I refused. They still want a meeting as soon as their little Colonel shows up, kind of a 'roast Detective Jones over an open fire' sort of affair. I should be able to postpone this until after your brother's funeral, but no longer."

Dee struggled to take everything in.

"Thank you, sir. I appreciate you looking out for me."

"Don't make me regret it, Jones. I'm about to inform MI5 that you've been placed on bereavement leave for two weeks. You will be off duty, and unavailable. Since you are now under MI5's microscope, I would prefer if you didn't call in while you're on holiday, at least not from your cell phone."

Hill seemed to be telling her that her phone would soon be tapped, and in such a way that he couldn't assume that it hadn't happened already. He went on.

"Are you planning any travel?"

This was an odd question. "Why do you ask, sir?"

The Inspector chuckled. "I'm sure our human hemorrhoid, Becket, will be here soon. At that time he'll be looking for blood.

Since they can't have yours, your Marine will probably be moved to the top of his list."

She hadn't thought of that.

"He's still in your custody. My suggestion would be to take him along," he began to speak slowly and with emphasis, "since I'm sure you feel the need to get out and visit with family before the funeral. If you don't want him with you, I can arrange for suitable accommodations downtown. It may be in your best interest to spend a few days on your own in mourning. Don't feel the need to check in."

Was Inspector Hill telling her to hide?

"Now, I have to go and deal with things here. I'm truly sorry about your brother. Take what time you need, and please accept our condolences. Let us know about the funeral details, many of us will want to be there with you."

"Thank you sir, I appreciate your consideration."

She closed her phone and sat there, chin on the side of the tub. The idea of attending Gareth's funeral seemed unreal, like something from a bad movie.

Dee sat up, in shock at her oversight. She had been so caught up in trying to understand what had happened, that she'd completely lost sight of what needed to be done.

She flipped open her phone and found Brian's name in the directory. She dialed, and Brian picked up on the first ring. She found his voice familiar, comforting.

"How you holding up?"

Dee tried to sound normal. "Hanging in. Brian, I have a huge favor to ask."

"Anything."

"Someone, me I guess, has to see to the funeral," she fought back tears. "But I'm not sure I'm up to it. I know it's a lot to . . ."

"Dee, it's being handled. I talked to the base chaplain. He's seeing to all the details. Gareth mentioned, I mean dying is something we've talked about, that he wanted to be buried near your Mum and Dad. Is that OK?"

Dee choked, and this time the tears would not be contained. She nodded, and warm tears splashed into the tepid water below. She managed to chirp out a pitiful "Yes."

She tried not to sniffle, and was embarrassed when she had to reach over and unroll a wad of toilet paper to blow her nose.

"I have to ask, Dee, when do you want to have it? I thought a viewing next week at our base chapel, then the graveside. If that's all right with you?"

"Fine. Anytime, soonest possible I guess. Thanks," she

muttered. "Thank you Brian."

"Call if you need anything, promise?"

"Sure, bye."

Brian stopped her. "One more thing. Is that American with you?"

"Yes." She answered cautiously.

"Let him know that I've asked around, and—"

Dee exploded into the mouthpiece. "Brian Godric Warren! If you get involved in anything about my brother's death, I'll see you de-nutted and singing with the boy's choir."

Brian hesitated just a moment too long before replying, "Nothing like that, we just want him to share a pint, talk about Gareth and all. We will truly miss your brother, we really will."

Dee shook her head, "Bullshit! Do not get involved."

"No really Dee, everyone knew him, he had a lot of friends here."

She hung up and struggled to contain her grief. Had she been too hard on Brian? Thank God he was on top of things; but then again, this was all part of a soldier's world.

It was also part of her world now, just like Gareth was not—and never would be again. Their last time together seemed like a memory from the ancient past.

They'd met, yesterday, for a quick bite. He had been happy, but nervous about introducing her to his friend Travis. Gareth had been dropping subtle hints for months about his big American mate.

Dee had to admit, she'd been looking forward to meeting Travis Deacon as well. Gareth had never set her up with anyone before, ever. He said he didn't want to have to kill a friend if things didn't work out.

The fact that he was even considering the possibility of her and the American was amazing, and somehow enticing.

No one knew Deirdre better than Gareth. He'd told her a thousand times that he wanted her to be happy, and now he wanted her to meet Deacon.

Wanted, but things hadn't worked out so well. She thought again about that last meeting. After they'd eaten, he headed out to meet someone. It didn't seem important at the time, but Gareth acted nervous, anxious to get on the road.

Dee looked down at her phone, and considered the voicemail he'd left last night. She'd gone to bed about seven, since she was on early shift the next day. He mentioned Travis again on the phone, but his voice sounded different, almost like Inspector Hill's at morning briefings. It was information, not chit chat.

And what was she going to do with the big lump of imported American meat in her living room? The Inspector had let her know that she could dump Travis off at the lock up if she wanted, and that she should consider doing so. Travis clearly had his own agenda, one he was not sharing with her.

However, he had kept his word, finding him at her patrol car earlier had been a bit of a shocker. She was glad too, since she had been able to set him straight about Sheri. But he had an explanation for that, as well. Either way, her plan to set Sheri Wells up with Brian had gone up in flames.

Before she decided how to deal with Deacon, she needed to find out if he had been honest with her. She also needed to find out if he knew what Gareth's voicemail meant. She then had to discover where her brother had gone after their lunch. There were a lot of questions she needed answers to.

One issue had been resolved, however. Doctor Bubbly managed a miracle cure, at least a temporary one. She could do this. She could work this case. She felt strong again and wouldn't stop until she found out what happened to her brother.

She cupped her hand and scooped up a bit of bathwater, which she used to wash away the crusty tracks of her earlier tears. Something tugged at the back of her mind. What had Brian said? That everyone knew Gareth and that he had a lot of friends?

Dee wasn't sure that all of them were friends. Detective Sergeant Jones was back and on the case.

Chapter 9

I woke up feeling violated.

As my mind cleared, I lowered my eyes and looked down at the little black head resting comfortably in my crotch. Blackjack's eyes opened slightly, but with a blink and a groan, he closed them and went back to sleep. While my canine companion obviously felt at ease with our moment of intimacy, I did not.

I sat. Reluctantly Blackjack hopped down from the couch and shook his head, ears flopping over softly. He then executed an impossibly wide yawn, and completed his morning ritual with a stretch, back legs pointing almost straight back and head arched to the sky.

Now that Blackjack was ready, he stared at me with a *Get your ass moving!* look. Does everyone think they can order me around over here?

I stood and enjoyed my own yawn and stretch. My mouth felt as dry as the Iraqi desert, so I looked around for the kitchen. I spotted a sink to my right, and stumbled drunkenly toward the linoleum oasis. In the field, I usually wake up instantly. It's nice to ease into the day once in a while.

I jumped as Blackjack sped past me, disappearing through the kitchen doorway. I heard the sound of jumping as I entered, and found Blackjack leaping enthusiastically, trying to retrieve something from the counter next to the fridge. As I entered, he sat glancing back and forth between me and the counter.

I walked over and found a black, retractable leash coiled neatly next to a box of dog treats. I looked down at the beast, trying to decide which he was after. He now sat on his behind, front paws high, begging. I'd seen the commercials, he wanted a treat.

I opened the box, pulled out a heart-shaped biscuit, and held it out to Blackjack. He stood on his rear legs, carefully took the treat from my hands, and sprinted to a mat in front of the sink. In a microsecond of crunching frenzy, he devoured the liver-flavored delicacy and was back in front of me, paws up and head cocked expectantly. I needed an interpreter.

I marched into the living room to ask Dee for clarification, but the delicate sounds of snoring, fluctuating between a chainsaw and a jet taking off, hinted that Dee may have fallen asleep.

I looked back at Blackjack, who glanced at the counter then imploringly back at me.

Fine!

I snatched up the leash, and Blackjack sat expectantly as I snapped it onto his collar. I grabbed a bottle of water from the fridge and moved toward the front door. I stopped to listen for the dulcet, jackhammer serenade that told me Dee still didn't want to be bothered.

I opened the door, and with a bark and a tug we were on our way. The first portion of our journey lasted about two seconds, and Blackjack went leg up, watering the withered bush next to Dee's porch. It hit me then, I had the same need but couldn't see a big enough bush. Maybe the water bottle could be refilled.

We walked around a short, irregular shaped block, then crossed the street and walked around that block as well. As we got ready to cross the street back to Dee's apartment, a new problem arose. Blackjack had been trying to mark his territory, but had been dry-firing for the last half hour.

The next time was different. He squatted right in the middle of the sidewalk and began a little spinning dance. As the spinning stopped the pooping began. What was I supposed to do now?

We were right in front of the fancy brick apartments. I looked around and saw other dog logs of varying size and degree of decomposition, but they were on the narrow grass strip by the fence.

I couldn't leave a dirty mutt-mine on the walk, so I looked around, exploring my alternatives. I saw a small empty bag nearby that had once held some kind of dry, crumbly shortbread cookies. Putting a pile of dog crap inside would actually be a step up. I then located a dried-out branch next to the metal fence, and used it to roll the tiny brown dog droppings into the bag.

This left me, quite literally, holding the bag—and the stick. I looked around for a trashcan, but was interrupted by a voice, a voice from the past, a really angry voice from the past. Agents Nosebleed and Tibbs from the hotel were several meters down the street. As they approached, Blackjack began to growl.

"I thought we'd find you here with your little cop girlfriend."

Tibbs, the big one, smiled maliciously and continued. "We're here to kick you out of England, now! And there's not a damn thing you can do about it."

I was not in the mood for this, and I really had to pee. Maybe I could solve two problems at once, and asked, "Do you kids have a car?"

They looked at each other. Tibbs looked over his shoulder, and the bleeder nodded. I bent down, picked up Blackjack, and gestured for them to lead on.

"Then, let's go!"

They exchanged a surprised glance, shrugged, and turned. The little agent, sans jacket now and with only a trace of blood on his shirt, led off. Tibbs waited and brought up the rear. Blackjack kept a wary eye on both as we marched down the street.

Around the corner, parked facing the wrong way on a small side street, was a black sedan. We approached, and the lead asshole pulled a set of keys from his pocket. He pressed a button on the remote, and unlocked the doors. He then stopped in front of the rear passenger's door and opened it for me.

I ignored him, set Blackjack down, and we walked around to the driver's door. I opened it and pretended to look shocked. "Wrong side, I keep doing that."

They were on the other side, looking at me like I was an idiot. I tossed the bag in the back seat, and while I spoke, I unzipped my pants. "And there are two problems with your plan. First, I'm already out of England."

I moved tight against the open doorframe and began to relieve myself on the seats. They looked confused, then irritated. Mr. Purple-Beak spoke up.

"Fine, out of Britain. What's the second problem?"

"Dee is not my girlfriend. She's my wife." I tilted my head back, smiled and sighed as yellow liquid pooled on the fabric. "I'm feeling much better."

They looked totally astonished, confused couldn't quite

describe it. Tibbs looked tentatively into the car, trying to see what I was doing without letting me out of his sight. The other answered, skeptical.

"What do you mean, your wife?"

"You know the court building's right across from the police station, right?"

They nodded.

"Well, she went to see Justice of the Peace Harris, and got a marriage license. I now have a spousal exemption and can't be deported!"

The look on Agent Nose Bleed's face was priceless. He didn't know whether to believe me or not. The look on Tibbs face was even better, because he had discovered what I was doing in his car.

"You bastard!"

Tibbs rushed around the back of the car as I zipped up. As he reached our side, Blackjack was at him in a fury of fangs. I tossed Tibbs the pooh stick I still carried, business end first, and suggested, "Here, use this."

He grabbed the stick out of the air and was about to swing it, when his nose wrinkled and his jaw dropped. He threw the stick aside and stared at the brown mess in his hand.

Things got very busy, very fast. Blackjack was still jumping, trying to get to Tibbs. Tibbs was shouting obscenities and trying to find something to wipe his hand on. Agent Bleeder was running around the front of the car, hoping to take me from behind.

I had to admit, I was having fun. That was until Tibbs tried to kick Blackjack and missed. I saw he was about to try again, which pissed me off just a little. I took up the slack on the leash and reached for the door handle in front of me. As Tibbs went to kick, I pulled Blackjack to me and yanked the door open. Tibbs caught the bottom of the door with his shin and howled in pain. He was hopping around in agony as the backup agent reached my back.

Just before the second agent got close enough to grab me, I launched a back kick and caught him in the knee. His leg buckled, and he went down with a whimper. I grabbed Blackjack, tossed him in the backseat, and closed the rear door as Tibbs recovered and came at me.

He threw a right cross. I stepped back quickly and closed the front door on Blackjack, who had hopped into the front seat and had almost made it back into the fight.

Tibbs saw my advance to the rear as retreat, and attempted to press his supposed advantage. He executed a pretty good front kick with his right foot, which I blocked with my left arm. I stepped inside and swept his left leg out from under him with my right foot. He flew into the air, arms and legs doing little windmill motions as he tried to control his fall. Instead, he landed with a thud on his back. I saw his head snap back and crack against the concrete. I hoped he wasn't hurt.

I glanced back at the agent with the bright purple nose. He hadn't tried to get up, but had retrieved his weapon instead, which was the right move. I rushed over and kicked the gun out of his hand, then spun him onto his stomach and wrapped my left arm around his neck. I made sure his windpipe was in the bend of my elbow, and with my right hand I pushed his head forward. This compressed the carotid arteries in his neck, restricting blood flow to the brain. I was gentle, and just put him to sleep for a while, instead of forever.

I looked at the unconscious MI5 guys, and realized this was the second time in the last few minutes I would have to pick up lumps of shit off the ground.

I opened the door and untangled Blackjack's leash as he hopped out. I returned the gun, and lifted the dynamic duo and stuffed them back in their car, reclining the seats. I estimated I had at most an hour of slumber time to convince Dee to go with me. Otherwise, I would have to leave on my own.

Chapter 10

Sharing a deep sense of accomplishment, Blackjack and I knocked on Dee's apartment door. I had been unable to get Brian on the phone, but that didn't diminish my joy in seeing a little action. Those MI5 guys were actually pretty good, but training to stay ready is just not the same as training to stay alive. They really didn't stand a chance.

Dee answered from just inside, "It's open!"

I'd barely opened the door before Blackjack pushed his way inside. He bounded into Dee's lap, licking her face as she removed the leash. Having just seen the other things Blackjack liked to lick; I felt an even greater need to shower.

They were genuinely happy to see each other. She was scratching him behind the ears and he was loving it, tongue hanging out the side of his happy face.

I hated to break the magic of the moment, but we had a problem. I told her, "We have a problem."

Dee reached back and lowered the screen of the notebook computer she had been using, then turned over a notepad sitting next to it. She picked up her cell phone, which showed a call in progress, and spoke into the mouthpiece. "It's him, give me a moment."

Without looking at me, she pointed at my bag, sitting next to the bathroom door. "Get cleaned up. The shower works, just make sure the plastic part of the curtain stays inside the tub."

Besides clothes, I assumed she'd bought the essential toiletries so I wouldn't be tempted to use hers. I snatched up the bag and hurried into the bathroom. Before I closed the door I looked back.

"We need to be out of here in half an hour, forty-five minutes tops. If not, we won't be going anywhere."

She stared a moment, trying to decide if I was at all serious.

"We'll see. Make sure you rinse out the tub when you're done. I wash Blackjack in there and don't want him to catch anything."

It occurred to me then that I could actually get to like Deirdre Jones.

* * *

It took just over fifteen minutes, and I exited the bathroom; maybe not a new man, but at least a much better smelling old one. I wore dark sweat pants, a navy blue t-shirt, and had a dark blue hooded sweatshirt over my arm. I had my dirty clothes rolled into a tight bundle, and I set them and the bag next to the couch.

Dee was still at the computer, and she swiveled in her chair to regard me critically. She raised her eyebrows and cocked her head. "You look like a hooligan. Maybe you can spray graffiti on Becket's car or something?"

I smiled, "What a great idea! I just happen to have a

car nearby."

She frowned, shook her head in exasperation, then looked back at her computer screen. "Eagle, Globe and Angus? You must have been totally shit faced."

"Not by Welsh standards, as I've discovered, but obviously drunk enough."

Dee moved aside. I saw that she had been examining our ranch's Website.

"And people pay to kill animals on your land?"

"Some do."

I was expecting a lecture about how all life is sacred, and that animals have feelings too, and how brutal it was, but Dee just turned and looked back at her screen.

"You actually have all of those animals you named."

"And more."

I could tell that something about me still bothered her. "I said I'd never lie to you. I mean that."

Dee spun back toward me, eyes moist. "Then tell me, do you think my brother's death was an accident?"

"No, I don't."

"Why?"

The whole honesty thing had now become a problem. "Several reasons, most too complicated to explain."

Dee's eyes flashed and she leaned forward, face getting red. "You don't think I'm smart enough?"

The honesty thing had already become a BIG problem.

"Not at all!" Was that the right answer? I should clarify, "I mean, that's not the reason at all, I can tell you're very smart."

Dee sat on the edge of her chair, almost bouncing now. Poor Blackjack looked confused, probably trying to decide whether to comfort her or attack me.

I had to decide what I could tell her without making her feel worse about Gareth's death. Murder. I went on.

"I've seen a lot of injuries; accidental, combat related, even self-inflicted. When I saw Gareth's body, it didn't look like an accident. When I saw his car, I knew it wasn't."

She looked skeptical, "Why is that?"

Now I had something to bargain with. "If I tell you, will you let me go?"

"Not bloody likely!"

"Then no information."

She smiled and looked at her dining table. Gareth's album was there, open. She hesitated a moment then looked me directly in the eye. "How about we share information?"

What information could she have that would help me? She was a cop and this was her city–country, whatever. She was also his sister; maybe she could help me get started.

"OK, I believe his car was pushed off that cliff."

Dee scowled, skeptical. "Because?"

"All of the damage to the rear of his car was above the rear bumper. If the impact to the rear was from hitting the ground as it bounced down the cliff, the damage would have come from below, not above. And I don't think Gareth was going very fast when he went over the cliff."

"That's it?"

Negotiation time. "No, but it's your turn."

"You haven't given me all that much."

"And you haven't given me anything. Besides, I think you suspected something from the start."

She hesitated, but only a moment. She picked up her cell phone and speed dialed. I could hear the faint sound of ringing, followed by a mechanical voice. She pressed another button, then activated the speaker phone.

The digital voice droned out. "First saved message."

Gareth's voice suddenly filled the room. Blackjack jumped up, putting his front paws on Dee's leg. "Hey Sis, it's me. Something's come up, I may not be back in Swansea until morning. If you can't get in touch with me, find my friend Travis. He has what you'll need to find me. I really hope you like him, I think you two . . ."

Dee fumbled with the phone and ended the call, a little embarrassed. We sat in silence, except Blackjack who whined and went to the window.

I looked at Dee. "Gareth called Brian last night and told him to find me, to take me to you."

Dee nodded. "That can't be a coincidence. Gareth was into something and didn't want us to know just yet."

I said sharply, "Or wasn't sure yet. "

I stopped talking and let the frustration go. Why hadn't she mentioned this earlier? As if she could read my mind, she went on.

"I wasn't sure I could trust you, or if you could help me figure out what's going on. I need to know everything you know, or even suspect."

One thing I'd learned from the CIA was that if not enough information was bad, too much information could be worse. I needed to convince her that she needed my help, without giving her time to wonder why.

"I believe your brother was murdered. I saw injuries that make me believe . . ." How did I put it without using the word torture? "I don't think all of the injuries were a result of the accident."

Her eyes narrowed just a bit.

I continued, "You're a police officer, is there any way you can check the cell towers, find out where he made that call from?"

"He didn't use his cell phone. He made the call from a land line."

"So you have the number on your caller ID?"

Dee shakes her head. "The number was blocked."

Damn, that would make things harder. But Dee was a detective, and one step ahead on this one.

"However, someone is checking on that for me. All I know right now is that it came from Tenby."

I went through my limited knowledge of Welsh geography, and came up empty. If I were right about Gareth, though, then the accident was staged to make it look like it happened while Gareth was on his way back. Tenby was probably west of Mumbles, so we had a place to start.

I stood up, "I need to get to Tenby."

"We will go to Tenby, first thing in the morning."

I shook my head. "If we don't go now, we don't go at all."

Now she stood to face me. "Maybe you don't understand how this works, but you are in my custody. You will go where I go, when I go there. Or, you can go to jail. I'm still not sure which I prefer."

One of us didn't understand how things were going to work, and I was pretty sure it wasn't me. I tried to explain.

"There's a car across the street with . . ."

She interrupted. "I called Sheri, Constable Wells. She's going to contact Dyfed-Powys Police and find out what we need. Tenby isn't in South Wales, I have no jurisdiction there."

Tomorrow was not an option. "I just beat the shit out of Tibbs and his MI5 partner," I pointed toward the door, "right there across the street. When they wake up, they will call some friends and come after us. We have about ten minutes."

She looked at the window, then hurried toward the door. She stopped suddenly and looked back at her computer.

I asked before she decided to take it with her. "I'd like

to check my e-mail."

She eyed me suspiciously.

"Just your e-mail?"

I nodded. "You should check fast, they may be awake already."

She scowled at me suspiciously, then hurried out the door.

I had only lied a little bit, and logged into a CIA external site and downloaded a keyboard encryption program. This would allow the rest of my activities to be completed securely. I needed to contact a friend at Langley, Hamilton Dupree.

I could trust Ham. He owed me his life; at least two-thirds of it. That's how much of his body I pulled from a burning Humvee before it exploded. They encourage field agents to have legs, so they gave him a desk job at CIA Headquarters. We'd kept in touch, he'd even gone hunting on the ranch once.

I felt a creeping worry that time was not something I had enough of, and was willing to put my butt on the line to speed things along. Ham didn't really have a butt any more, so it was no big deal for him.

Dee stormed back into the apartment and marched into her bedroom. She refused to look at me. She came back minutes later wearing casual clothes and a really nasty frown. She set down an overnight bag and snatched up her computer. She pressed the power button until the screen went blank, then she slipped the notebook into her bag. Still without speaking, or even glancing my way, she snapped the leash on Blackjack's collar and stood stiffly.

"Are they alive?"

"As much as they were in the hotel this morning."

She spun, grabbed her bag, and led Blackjack toward the door.

"Wait!" I need a security blanket, just in case my worst fears prove correct.

She turned, hands on hips, and glared.

"I need a gun. Your backup weapon should be good enough."

Dee's face went slack. He jaw dropped and her eyes grew to the size of dinner plates, at least that's how it seemed. She shook her head slowly and finally managed to speak.

"Are you out of your bloody mind? I don't have a gun. I've never fired a gun. I hope to live my entire life without ever touching a fucking gun. Any other questions?"

Yes, but she wasn't going to like it. "Where can I get one? We may not be safe if we aren't armed."

After a long, agonizing wait, the daggers in Dee's eyes faded. She dropped the leash and marched slowly past me and down the hall. She returned a few second later with a large flat piece of wood, which she jammed into my stomach as she returned to the dog. I grabbed the stick by what was obviously a handle, laughed, and swatted the air. I smiled at her in disbelief. "So, if we find the people that may have killed your brother, you want me to paddle them."

"It's not a paddle, you idiot, it's a cricket bat; and it's all the weapon you're going to get."

I swung the thing again. I knew a paddle when I saw one, I'd become intimately acquainted with them as a teenager. I tucked it under my arm, hurried across the room, snatched my bag, and followed her out. If I had things figured out correctly, I would have a gun before long anyway.

I saw Dee lead Blackjack toward her car. "Shouldn't we leave the dog here?"

Chapter 11

The sun had set, which I found a little disappointing. I really enjoyed the Welsh countryside, when not planning painful ways to deal with Gareth's killers, that is. The history there in Wales was incredible; you just never knew when you could see a church, castle, maybe even an Old World outhouse that was older than the entire New World itself.

Pretty neat, actually.

I wondered briefly if my sightseeing was a little disrespectful under the tragic circumstances, but I didn't think so. Gareth wanted me to love Wales, so instead of disrespecting his memory, I tried to honor his wishes.

Dee was navigating her tricked-out roller skate down the highway. There must have been a tailwind because she managed to keep up with traffic. We were currently on a two-lane road with the designation of A478; it had a name, but I would have had to actually care what it was in order to find out. We had just passed a little village called New Hedges. After driving past places called Llanllwch and

Pibwrlwyd, it was nice to find a town whose name I could actually pronounce.

I wasn't kidding about the whole vowel thing.

We passed under a place where the trees grew over the highway, almost like an arch welcoming us as conquering heroes. As I thought about it, I bet the whole conquering thing had happened a bunch of times over the last few thousand years.

Like I said, pretty neat.

And I didn't care about the hero part, only the conquering. I couldn't let myself lose sight of why we were there. On the left, I looked and could see a brick retaining wall, unfortunately Dee's car was so low I couldn't see what was on the other side. In fact, I could barely see over the small bump of a curb that bordered the road. On the right, we passed a bunch of two-story houses, buildings that seemed to be assembled from the same kit. Actually, they were duplexes. The small front yards were separated by fences, each side with a different entrance.

We drove through what was mainly a residential area, but soon found ourselves on narrow streets surrounded by stores. The lighting wasn't great, but everything seemed colorful and very nicely kept. The street was clean, even though it was active with people, and I thought back to the arching trees. I was ready to do some conquering. Merrick, a dangerous name from the past, lived there. I knew that any slapping backs and shaking of hands in greeting would soon be followed by the shedding of blood.

Still neat, and getting neater.

Dee had received a text message as we left Swansea, probably from Constable Wells. She then managed to drive a large truck off the road as she entered information into her GPS. She adjusted the device on her windshield. Death cheated, she returned her attention to hogging the road.

The drive had taken almost an hour, and on two occasions I attempted conversation. Each time she asked me politely to wait. Her exact gesture was 'fuck you,' but I'm sure she meant it in the nicest way. She finally looked over, and after glaring at me a moment she asked. "You've met this Naismith fellow?"

"He tried to kill me, if that qualifies as meeting."

She smiled, "I like him already."

"Not so fast, first he threatened to kill your brother. That's what inspired me to kick the shit out of him, which resulted in a small knife wound for me and an extended period of hospitalization for him. You know, guy stuff."

She glanced impatiently over, "Why did he want to kill my brother?"

"Your brother got him court-martialed and kicked out of the SAS."

She glanced at me quickly. That had her attention, so I continued. "Kind of a sad circumstance, but Gareth had no choice. A member of Merrick's team disappeared in a little town near the Pakistani border. Merrick was team leader, and they started looking for their teammate. It started getting darker, so Merrick started looking harder. At dusk, things turned dark, in a moral kind of way as well. Merrick did a little field surgery on two of the town elders, removing their capacity to reproduce. Merrick did save their buddy before the Taliban fighters could get him over the border, but word got out. Like I said, Gareth didn't have any choice. Your brother actually went to bat for the guy. He only got a year's confinement and was kicked out. It could have been worse."

Dee's face took on a look of horror. "He sounds like a monster."

"He sounds like a guy who went too far in trying to save a buddy."

She eyed me suspiciously, then asked, "You two fought?"

"I never liked Merrick, but he always hated me. Gareth wanted to talk to him alone. Your brother didn't realize that alone meant with me following him. Merrick got mad, got physical, then got hospitalized. Shit happens, but I wasn't going to let it happen to Gareth."

Dee stared at me a moment longer, then turned her attention back to the road. After two lefts and a right, we pulled to the curb on a street full of what looked like rundown apartments. She looked across the street.

"That's the address."

I bent down and followed her line of sight. A plaque over the door identified it as the "The Downs of Tenby," but the rest of the building identified it as "The Run-Downs of Tenby." It looked like shit. A faded white banner flapped lazily under the second-story windows. It offered discount rates by the day, week, or month. If I did find out that Merrick was involved, they may need to add 'rest of your life' to the discounts.

The Merrick's building was clearly visible from a hundred windows and doorways on the street, and I didn't like that. I frowned at Dee and asked, "Shouldn't we have parked somewhere else and checked this place out first?"

She just turned and glared at me, but I didn't care. Until I knew the situation and all of the players, I wanted to be careful. Besides, I had started to doubt the whole Merrick connection. The bastard was definitely capable of engaging in a little torture, but I didn't think he would've carved up Gareth. Something else was going on, but this was all we had, for the moment.

Dee reached for the door handle, I grabbed her arm and asked, "What are we going to do?"

"I'll go in and talk to him."

"I don't think that's safe. Why don't I go first, then you can talk to him while we wait for the ambulance?" I gave her my sweetest smile. "I couldn't live with myself if anything happened to you."

She shook her head. "You're a prick, you know that?"

I nodded. "He may not want to talk to us."

"There's only so much we can legally do."

"Then let's go straight to illegal. How do we get in without letting him know it's us? You've investigated a bunch of break-ins and burglaries, what would a slick crook do?"

She looked at me, and I was suddenly glad that cops there didn't carry guns. She reached a decision, and burst out of the car like she had been shot from a cannon. I set Blackjack, who had slept through most of the trip, over on her now vacant seat and hopped out to follow. Dee ran across the street and bent over to talk to a kid of about twelve. The boy nodded a couple of times, and Dee handed him a couple of bills. The boy ran inside, and about a minute later he burst out and ran back to Dee. She handed him another bill, and the kid ran off.

Dee looked back, shouted "Wait here!" and then entered the building.

I ignored her and rushed inside as well. The first door on the left sported a battered wooden 'OFFICE' sign. Dee stopped in front of it, folded her arms, and waited. I stood safely behind her, and looked around. A trash bin overflowed by the front door. A vending machine offered snacks, but the ones on the top row looked half eaten by rats. Next to that stood a rack of faded brochures from when the "Downs" may have actually been a hotel.

I strolled over and grabbed one titled "Tenby, A Jewel By the Sea." It had the picture of a young couple running onto the beach from the ocean. The woman looked like the

Welsh hottie Catherine Zeta Jones, which is why I noticed it in the first place.

I turned back to find Dee glaring at me over her shoulder. I was saved when the office door banged open, and a fat, greasy looking man with Mediterranean features stumbled into the lobby. He struggled to button his shirt and almost ran into Dee, who barely stepped aside in time.

"What the . . ." He stopped short and looked her over.

Dee raised her ID case and asked, "Something wrong?"

The man stared, nodded stupidly, started to speak, then hesitated again. He finally managed to mumble, "Yeah, right, somebody in 3-D is calling out the window for help."

I stuffed the brochure into my pocket and asked, "Who lives there?"

"Some bloke named Naismith."

Dee glanced at me, then suggested, "Maybe we should come along."

He nodded stupidly and ambled toward the stairs. He started up, but by the first landing he was winded. He struggled on, but had to stop at the first floor. Dee seemed willing to wait for our host, but I sure as hell was not.

I looked up to the next floor and cocked my head, "Was that a scream?" The others looked at each other, then craned to see up the stairwell. I took a couple of steps toward the second floor, and held out my hand to the man. "Give me the keys, before it's too late!"

Dee glared at me as our rotund escort fished in his pocket for a large ring of keys. He assiduously examined each key until he found the one he wanted, and I snatched the entire bunch from his hands. Dee's cell phone chimed with an incoming text message, and when she looked down I bounded up the stairs.

"Wait, you bastard!" she shouted and leapt to follow.

94

As I reached the third floor, I was surprised to find Dee right behind me. She was fast.

And she was pissed. As we reached the third landing, she snatched the keys from my hand, shoved rudely past, and rushed to Merrick's apartment. She unlocked the door, opened it, and turned to face me.

"I want you to wait here, understand?"

I nodded in agreement, then rushed past her.

The one-room apartment was small, but spotless. The bed had been made and stood ready for inspection. Next to the bed waited a small dresser that looked like it also functioned as a nightstand. The large digital clock there flashed 6:47 p.m. I looked at my watch, the clock was three minutes fast.

Rounding out the décor we had a faded wardrobe of some dark, indistinguishable hardwood. The door on the left hung by a single, heroic hinge. The right door, sporting an impromptu mosaic that began life as a mirror, leaned up against the wall. The clothes looked almost out of place, perfectly laundered and impeccably organized—dress shirt, then T-shirts (by color), then pants. I had to fight the urge to find a pair of white inspection gloves.

This guy was squared away! My preference was to organize my off-duty clothes by the color of their stains – reds, greens, blues, and the rest. If you're wondering about where I put the clean clothes, don't. The base laundry sucks, so the stains don't come out. No really clean clothes, problem solved.

We continued to look around. To our left was a tiny kitchen area, whose sink appeared to do double duty since the open door next to the stove revealed a toilet. Everything was neat, clean, and orderly – except for the area next to the sink itself. Resting there were wads of cloth, rolls of white tape, and a large knife. We walked, side by side, to the kitchen and looked around. We looked into the sink, then stared at each other in shock. The sink was splattered with dried and drying blood. The bottom was littered with more bandages, some red, others brown with dried blood.

Maybe I should reconsider giving Mr. Merrick a pass on Gareth's murder.

Dee staggered forward, steadying herself with both hands on the counter. She stared into the sink a moment longer, then looked back at the loud wheezing sound announcing the approach of the red-faced manager. She turned to him and asked, "Where is he?"

The fat man shrugged, "Hell if I know. We ain't engaged or nothin'." He looked around the room and nodded approvingly.

"Not bad, probably the neatest flat in the building." Dee moved menacingly forward. "He filled out an application to move in, right?"

The manager nodded three times, then shook his head twice. "Not exactly. He ain't turned it in yet, but he pays rent in cash, with a full month up front, so there's no big hurry."

I hurried over and turned the man's bulk back toward the door.

"I want you to go back to your office and look for anything you have on Merrick Naismith. We'll be down in a minute."

Our greasy host shook his head, "Ain't got nothing, promise."

I pushed him toward the door. "We still want you to go to your office and look. I'll lock up and bring the keys down in a minute."

The manager looked around blankly, then nodded in understanding. "Right, I'll just leave you two to lock up."

He left the room, and I closed the door behind him. I turned to Dee, who was still standing over the sink, head down and eyes closed. I moved to her side and tried to sound as comforting as possible.

"This doesn't mean anything, there are a thousand explanations for this."

She asked without looking up. "Such as?"

"Maybe he cut himself shaving." I regretted saying that before the words had even left my lips. "I don't know, but let's not get ahead of ourselves."

Dee stood erect, but she looked exhausted, beaten. She moved to the tiny Formica table and sat in the solitary, brown metal folding chair. She barely glanced up as I went to the dresser and started going through the drawers, looking for anything that might help us find him. Dee looked over and shook her head.

"You can't do that."

I nodded, "I know."

I finished with the bottom drawer and closed it. Dee reached for her cell phone as I stood and looked at the wardrobe.

She started dialing. "I'm going to call the local police, I have no jurisdiction here."

She stopped when her phone chimed again, another text message. I moved to the wardrobe, opened it, and started looking through the clothes. She stopped dialing and checked the message.

"It's Sheri. They traced Gareth's call last night to here in Tenby. He called from a phone number belonging to. . ."

I interrupted, "Tenby Harbor Services."

Dee looked over, surprised, then nodded. I held up a bright blue T-shirt, with the picture of a forklift in the center and "Tenby Harbor Services" in block white letters around it. The color returned to her face. Her eyes focused, and she stood up. She had the next lead, and was ready to go. As she reached the door, I called out.

"Wait, we forgot something important!"

She stopped and pivoted. I rushed over to the tiny fridge next to the table, opened it, and examined its contents. I reached inside, liberated two cans of Brains beer, then hurried out behind her.

Chapter 12

We left Merrick's place and headed toward the dock. On a narrow street bordered by shops, Dee's phone rang. She answered, looked at me, then pulled over. I noticed she had the courtesy to leave room for the pedestrians to squeeze by on the little bit of sidewalk she didn't block. There were a lot of people squeezing by my window, and Blackjack hopped up in my lap to take in the sights, nose leaving smudges on the window.

Dee got out so that I couldn't hear the conversation, which seemed a little rude to me. I watched her pace back and forth behind the car, pushing pedestrians out of her way as she moved. It was nice to see her tormenting someone else, maybe she would get it out of her system. Before the call, she mentioned that this was a favorite spot for the trendy and chic of the area, and that people from all over England came here on vacation to see the sights and enjoy the local restaurants.

A restaurant sounded good, since the cockles weren't sticking with me that well. I was thinking steak and fries, but the brochure from Merrick's place was touting mutton and leeks. No wonder the first colonist got the hell out of this place. You're supposed to take leaks not eat leeks, right?

Anyway, according to the brochure, Tenby had been there for a while, like at least twelve hundred years, probably longer. I read that there had once been a Tenby Castle here. The Normans, and here the pamphlet was very specific, were actually Vikings and not French. They visited here and grew to like the locale. In medieval times, liking a place usually meant it offered good defenses and an easy resupply through the harbor. I could appreciate that on a professional level.

I looked around. We had pulled over in front of a bright blue building, with fluorescent white trim around two huge display windows. I couldn't tell if it was a neighborhood market, a gift shop, or a card shop, since a sign over the front awning promised "Food – Cards – Gifts" in large block letters. Colorful shelves offered food and souvenirs in the windows.

The streets there were narrow, and the sidewalk almost nonexistent. Even with a car small enough to hide in a clover patch, Dee managed to block most of the sidewalk, plus an entire lane of traffic. I saw that Dee had finished her call, and was looking through the window of the gift shop. As she headed toward the door, I called out, "Get some food, peanuts or something. And some bottled water."

She scowled back, something she did a lot, and without a word she went inside. I really wanted out, my back hurt and my legs were starting to cramp. Instead, I waited with Blackjack, who now had his front paws up on the window. Three amazingly beautiful girls with long, jet-black hair walked by and stopped when they saw Blackjack. They bent down and tapped on the window, so to be polite I rolled it down. They immediately began to fuss over the little Min Pin in Spanish, the Andalucian dialect, by the way they pronounced the letter "s."

One of them asked Blackjack, *"Como te llamas?"* or "What's your name?" in the familiar form of Spanish. They were definitely from Andalusia.

I answered in only slightly accented Colombian Spanish, explaining that his name was Blackjack. They were excited to find someone they could communicate with, and asked if I would show them around. They were with a cruise ship that was spending the night in port, and wanted to have some fun.

I tried to explain that we had work to do, and they were quite explicit in their explanation of why Blackjack and I would have more fun with them. Dee came out, stopped and stared as the three gorgeous women tried to pull me out of the car. She marched around to the driver's side, got in, and put the car in gear. She glared into the rearview mirror as we forced our way through the thickening foot traffic.

"What was that all about?"

Several clever answers came to mind, but I decided to go with the truth.

"Don't know. It's a curse, but I barely notice it any more."

Dee reacted by throwing a brown paper bag in my lap, then hitting her horn and forcing a group of teenagers to press themselves against a wall for safety.

I opened the bag and took out the nuts; Blackjack knew what they were and tried to sit. I opened the bag and was about to give him one when Dee glanced over and snapped irritably.

"Water first."

"What?"

She grabbed a water bottle from the bag, a sports type that squirted liquid out of the top. She pulled the top open and squirted water at Blackjack. It was like a Las Vegas animal act. Dee squirted an arch of water across my lap, and the little MinPin managed to get his mouth in the stream, tongue lapping like crazy. They had obviously done this before, but they didn't have it down perfectly. My lap was soaked, and Dee seemed pleased.

It was nice to see her smile again, even if it was at my expense.

I divided up the peanuts, and we feasted as Dee checked the GPS. She nodded to herself, then hit the accelerator. It was dark now, and she reached for the light switch, almost killing a young bicyclist as she swerved back onto the street. In less than ten minutes, we reached the shore. I spotted a boat in the distance, moving slowly through the deepening darkness ahead.

I swallowed a helping of nuts and looked at Dee. "Who was that on the phone?"

"Sheri." She didn't go on, and I could tell something was bothering her.

"What did she say?"

After a second, Dee tensed and explained, "Sheri found out the exact address of where Gareth called from." She glanced over. "He called from the Harbor Services office on the dock." Both trails were leading toward that office, and I didn't think that could be a coincidence. Dee didn't think so either, and her hands tightened on the wheel. She squeezed and twisted, first her hands then her face. I could see her getting upset.

I needed to get her mind off Gareth. I had noticed that the buildings on my left had been replaced by a partially lit old wall – no, an ancient wall. We forced our way forward, and came to a large, high, curved section of the structure. I squinted and saw several arches in it, and higher up in the wall were shadowy arrow slits for the defenders. The wall appeared to have battlements on top, and I turned my head to watch small crowds of people move in and out. "That looked like a keep, is this a castle?"

I looked over at Dee and pointed at the ancient wall that was still next to us. She shook her head and grimaced. "Does that look like a castle to you?"

Actually, it did or I wouldn't have asked. Her attention was back on me, though, so I continued.

"Then what is it?"

"It's the old city wall, built around thirteen hundred I think."

Wow, that was old. In fact, these walls probably dated back to the time of the Crusades. I had studied the Crusades, understanding them actually helped me understand the geopolitical situation I was dealing with professionally. Europe had moved on. For them the Crusades were a part of history, a distant past that students did their best to forget. For many Muslims, it happened yesterday, and they were still battling the infidel invaders from the west.

Actually, their brand of Islam was very inclusive. They didn't just hate us Crusaders. They would kill pretty much anyone.

We reached the end of the wall and turned left. I saw the bay, harbor, whatever, on our right. Several boats moved across the water, running lights glistening like jewels in the dark. We quickly turned right, and descended a steep road toward a small pier reaching out into the harbor. I looked left out my window and saw cliffs, the city was now above us. The low cliffs above the beach were crowned with sparkling lights coming from the buildings there. Most of the structures lining the bluff were bright and colorful, a dazzling parade of lights separated by brief sections of black or simple white.

It was very picturesque; I wish I had my camera or camcorder. Then I wondered if Gareth had ever photographed the city. I imagined him there, early in the morning, trying to capture the vibrant colors of the buildings with the gold and red backdrop of the rising sun. Maybe when we finished this, I'd take that picture in his memory, my feeble tribute to his special talent.

The view reminded me of a beautiful little village I once visited, located on an island off the coast of Greece. A companion and I stopped there one lovely night, much like tonight. We boated ashore to meet a Yemeni gentleman who we killed, along with his five bodyguards. He'd helped finance the bombing of a destroyer, the USS Cole. The CIA gladly made interest payments on those kinds of investments. We go out of our way to make sure that kind of debt gets paid back in full.

Dee drove quickly past an "Official Vehicles Only" sign, and parked under a sign that said "No Parking," on the side of a small white block office building.

She turned off the car and announced: "This is Harbor Services office."

What the hell was I thinking? What was she thinking? Didn't she listen to me outside Merrick's place? But this wasn't really her fault. I quickly scanned the area. It was a security nightmare. There were only a couple of small buildings on the pier, but there were literally dozens of places on the cliffs above where observers could be positioned.

I had obviously not learned my lesson from earlier, and placed us in danger as a result. I really need my professional paranoia to step it up a notch. We hopped out and closed the car doors before Blackjack could follow, and I hustled Dee inside the office.

I closed and locked the door behind us, then examined the room. There were only a few small windows, which was good. I hurried around the office drawing the shades on all except one large window facing the water.

This drew the attention of a short, fat, little bald man with a scraggly brown beard. He jumped up and protested loudly, "Hang on, what are you doing?"

I ignored him and took Dee aside, gently explaining my concerns. "When we're going someplace, we don't just pull up and go inside. Remember? What if this place is being watched? We don't want Merrick, or MI5, or anyone else to know where we are or what we're doing."

She just stared back, clearly not getting my point.

"We don't know what Gareth did, or with who. We both suspect that someone grabbed him, and we have to assume that they may be waiting to see if anyone comes to investigate."

Dee was not convinced, so I continued. "Someone kidnapped him, whether anyone believes me or not. Humor me, allow me my paranoid moments. In the future, let me check out the places we visit before we expose ourselves. Please?"

She continued to stare, more annoyed than upset. After a moment, she shook her head. "You're more than just a little mad, you know that?"

In fact, I did know that, but it had no bearing on our current situation. Before I could bring that to her attention, the fat guy behind the desk finally leaned forward and asked loudly, "May I help you?"

He didn't sound sincere, I think he just wanted us gone. However, I decided to take his word, and spread my hands as I looked down at my still soaked crotch. "My panty shield failed, have you got any paper towels?"

He blinked, looked at my soggy pants in astonishment, and stammered, "Uh, over there."

He pointed to a little coffee bar area, then slid his chair back and stood up. The round mound of a man struggled to get around his desk, but before he even reached the side, he found Dee in his face. He started to speak, but Dee held up her ID and tried to quiet the situation down just a bit.

"I'm sorry to barge in on you like this, but we're conducting an investigation and time is limited. I need to ask you a few questions."

He relaxed a little and plodded back the two feet he'd just traversed, plopping down into a worn leather desk chair.

He stared at me as I rubbed on the front of my pants. I got the impression he was about to comment on my predicament, but instead politely asked, "What the fuck do you think you're doing? This is my office."

Dee attempted to calm him down. I prefer a more proactive method for securing a person's cooperation and so I started around the desk, ready to stuff the wet paper towels down his throat.

"Travis, give us a moment, won't you?" I could have gotten everything this little worm knew in about thirty seconds, but hey, this was her turf. I decided to look around the office while we tried things her way.

She leaned across the desk and offered him her hand.

"I'm Detective Sergeant Deirdre Jones," not bothering to introduce me. He took her hand, "And you are?"

She refused to let go until he introduced himself. "Alun Pendergrass."

She stood, looked around the office, and gave a frown when she saw me going through papers on a bulletin board next to the coffee bar. She looked around the office a moment longer and turned back. She gave Alun her most disarming smile.

"Nice office," she pointed to a large, green, bush looking thing against the wall. "What kind of plant is that?"

Alun barely glanced over. "A plastic one."

Dee smiled. "It's very nice. May I sit? I just have a few simple questions, and then we'll be off."

Alun Pendergrass, if that was a real name, simply glared at her. He then set his jaw and slid his chair back from the desk.

"No, you may not!"

He opened the middle drawer of his desk. I turned immediately from the duty schedule that I'd been studying and got ready to jump over the desk and strangle Mr. Fatass. Instead of pulling out a weapon, he mumbled while he searched for something inside.

"They told me someone might be coming here asking questions, and that I was not to say a word, to just send you off. Then I was to call MI5 and tell them you were here."

In triumph, he pulled a card out of the drawer and waved it at us.

"If you don't get out, immediately, I'll call!"

This was very interesting, but I decided it was time for me to get involved. I sat on the side of his desk, leaned toward him and winked. "You're going to call anyway when we leave, aren't you?"

His jaw dropped just a bit as he thought about it, so I pressed on, "And what's the word?"

He furrowed his brow, confused, as I hoped he'd be. I stood and took a step toward him. "They told you not to say 'a word.' What word did they tell you not to say?"

"I . . . what?"

Now I was around the desk, next to Alun.

"Who are you supposed to call?" I reached and

snatched the card from his hand, "Thanks."

I examined the expensive looking paper and scrolled lettering, then showed it to Dee. On the front, in large script letters it said simply: "Colonel M. Becket."

On the back was a handwritten phone number. Dee pulled out a pen and paper and jotted the number down. I asked, "What exactly does Harbor Services do?"

"Lots of stuff."

I pointed to the bulletin board. "You have the names of ships with dates and numbers. Why?"

Alun looked even more suspicious, but finally answered, "We provision ships, food, water, supplies, anything they need. They fax us their orders, we have the supplies ready when they get here. Sometimes they pick them up, sometimes we boat them out."

I found this interesting, but I didn't really know why. "Any ships from Spain in port now?" I remembered the three girls from town.

Alun nodded. "The Iberian Gold."

Dee was not as interested in this as I was, and interrupted, "Is that all you do?"

Alun shrugged.

"Every so often a small cargo pulls in, we help load and unload, that's about it."

Dee pressed on, "A call was made from this office yesterday. I'm trying to find out about the man who made it."

Alun scowled, then squinted.

"I wasn't here yesterday. I have no idea who called, nor why."

That stopped Dee temporarily, but I had a few questions and pressed on.

"You've had that card for a while." Thinking about how long it took him to search around in his desk drawer to find it. "How long have you had it?"

He frowned, thinking.

"About a month. These scary looking blokes in suits came in and talked to us."

"Who is 'us?'"

"Everyone what works in the office here."

"Does that include Merrick Naismith? He works here, doesn't he? But I don't see his name on the schedule."

Jabba the Hut scowled out of the window facing the pier. "That's for office people. Naismith works on the dock."

Dee stepped in. "Doing what? Did he work yesterday?"

Alun didn't like being questioned, and whined, "I said I wasn't here yesterday, so I don't know. Naismith loads supplies onto our supply tugs, nothing to do with office material at all."

My turn to be the bad cop. I pressed on, "When does he work? Where is his schedule?"

Alun fell back in his chair and rolled as far away from me as possible. I was afraid his panty shield was about to give out. He literally cowered as he spoke, "His schedule is at the warehouse, I'm pretty sure he's there now. Don't hurt me."

I smiled. Alun was going to be of no help, but I now knew where to find Merrick. I handed the card back and patted him on the shoulder.

"Thanks, mate, you've been very helpful. If you decide to call these assholes, please give us an hour or two to get back to Detective Jones' office first." I turned to Dee, "We should get back. You can get a court order to look through the files here, then bring Merrick in for questioning."

Dee looked as confused as Alun. I hurried around the desk, helped her to her feet, then ushered her toward the door. I could see she was mad; I shook my head vigorously. She gave me the evil eye, but came along quietly. We left the building, and I saw our friend Pendergrass had picked up the phone before we were all the way out of the door.

We hurried to the car and got in, Blackjack leaping into Dee's lap and making sure his tongue was clean by working energetically on her cheeks. She pushed the dog gently away and faced me, royally pissed.

"What the hell was that all about?"

"He's calling Becket right now."

Dee started the car, "I know that."

"I want Becket to think we're going back to Swansea, and I didn't want the little fat man to warn Merrick before we find him."

I saw her glance in the same direction Pendegrass did when he talked about Merrick. There was a single, large, well-lit metal building at the end of the dock. She looked back at me, nodded thoughtfully, and suggested, "Our next step is to find Merrick."

I nodded in agreement, and she reached behind her seat and handed me Blackjack's leash.

"Give him a good walk," she pointed at the entrance road to the cliffs above. "Maybe up the hill and back. I need to make some calls. It may take me a while to find our Mr. Naismith."

Liar! I smiled, "Good idea."

I snapped the leash on the beast's collar and looked over. "Honk if you need me."

She smiled and nodded. I lifted the dog out, and without looking back, Blackjack and I strolled back up the hill.

Chapter 13

We stood in the darkness, out of view, about a hundred meters from the car. Blackjack and I had stopped at the first curve in the road and waited. We both smiled as we watched Dee down below, sitting in her car pretending to talk on the phone. I was amused that she thought she could fool me. Blackjack was just glad to be out of that damn shoebox on wheels.

Dee had only glanced back at us once, which was good. Better would have been to adjust her mirror to watch us without glancing at all. I'd mention that to her when we got back.

Dee soon got out of the car and began pacing. With each turn, she looked in our direction, and after three casual turns, she abandoned all pretense and stared in our direction. Satisfied, she turned and marched toward the end of the dock. She covered the distance in minutes, while we simply watched from the shadows. She reached what appeared to be an office door, stopped, and turned back. She examined the dock, then did a final scan of the road back to town.

"Mommy thinks she's sneaky," I whispered to Blackjack.

Blackjack looked up, then did a little spinning dance at the end of his leash. He was ready to go, and so was I. I looked down and watched Dee step inside. The door to the warehouse closed behind her.

"Showtime!"

I started out at a jog, then stepped it up just a little. Blackjack had no problem staying with me. As we reached the dock, the slope leveled out, and I picked up my pace. I looked down at the blur of legs and flapping tongue beside me and smiled—he enjoyed this as much as I did. In less time than it took Dee to walk across the dock, we covered four times the distance and neither of us was out of breath.

I grabbed the doorknob, turned and yanked on the door. It didn't move. I checked the deadbolt, she'd locked it behind her.

Excellent!

Dee had thought ahead—good for her but bad for me, and possibly worse for her if Merrick weren't a gracious host. I turned left and ran toward the nearest corner of the building, there would certainly be doors on the opposite side, facing the dock. We hurried to the back of the warehouse, and slowed to a walk as we approached a cluster of men, milling about and smoking.

We walked casually up and I asked, "Merrick?"

A small man gestured inside with his cigarette, ashes flying into the face of the large man behind him. "In there with some bird, a cop. She kicked us out."

I walked toward a raised garage door, expecting protests from the muscular exiles outside, but none of the men even glanced over. We went inside and looked around a large, open warehouse space. It looked like the discount grocer I used back in Texas. Grey metal shelves held bulk quantities of food and supplies. I saw one bundle of toilet paper that stood as tall as Dee's clown car. We walked toward the back of the space, past huge boxes of corn flakes and something called "Porage Oats," until we heard raised voices rumbling from an open door to our left.

We hurried over and slipped inside.

This room was smaller, cooler. It had the same grey shelves around the walls, but with large bins full of fruits and vegetables occupying the center. At the far end, a large man had Dee backed against a huge tub of potatoes. He waved his finger in her face and shouted angrily as we approached, "I don't give a fuck who you are. I ain't talking to the cops. I suggest you get out."

Blackjack saw what was going on and barked, pulling at his leash. The man turned, and I saw that we had indeed located Merrick Naismith. I also saw that his face was cut and bruised, someone had done a number on him. Merrick looked down at the dog, and I pulled Blackjack back until he was beside me. This didn't make him happy, since getting his teeth into the man threatening Dee had become his entire world.

Merrick scowled down at Blackjack then glared up at me. After barely a second, his face went slack in surprise. Two heartbeats later, his eyes narrowed and his lips curled up in a smile. He raised his arms slightly, stepped forward, and led with his left.

No, not dancing, though a foxtrot may have been appropriate since Blackjack was going for his ankle. I pulled the little guy back in case Merrick tried to kick him, and the knuckles of his left hand caught me on the side of the jaw.

I staggered back, still more worried about Blackjack than myself. I handled this bozo a year ago, and didn't anticipate any problems this time either. I locked

Blackjack's leash and tossed it into a bin of pineapples, hoping that would hold him, then rocked back to avoid another left jab.

I remembered Merrick as being more of an uppercut and front-kick kind of guy, and barely missed the right cross that followed the jab. I shuffled away from Blackjack and raised my hands slowly, palms forward. "I don't want to fight you."

"Then don't." He launched himself forward and threw a roundhouse kick toward my head.

I stepped back again and took up a defensive stance. "I'm not here to . . ." I had started to say 'cause trouble,' but changed it to 'bleed' as I blocked a combination of punches designed to make blood spill from my face.

Dee had recovered and was rushing toward us. I yelled to her, "Don't let Blackjack get loose."

She hesitated, then rushed to the four-legged set of jaws that had almost freed himself from his restraints. She grabbed the leash as it slid over the side of the bin, and Blackjack jerked to a halt.

Meanwhile, Merrick had become a man on a mission. That mission was to inflict as much pain and damage to my person as possible, and he was doing pretty well. I had hoped to keep him away until we could reason with him, but he didn't seem to be in a reasonable frame of mind. And, it seemed like he'd changed his fighting style. He now used a tighter boxing stance, instead of the wide-open combat posture from before.

He surprised me with a spinning back kick. I stepped away, but he still caught me in the hip. Those heavy work boots would leave a bruise. Time to get serious. I threw a sequence of front kicks, planning to launch a scissor kick when he blocked them, but he shuffled back instead.

Maybe he did want to dance. He'd at least exercised a

114

little patience, and I wondered when he'd change his fighting style. In the brig? Probably not, he was almost as big as I was, though not as bulky. Not many would survive a fight with him.

My attention returned to the present moment, as my head snapped back. He'd tagged me with a lunging jab, another addition to his repertoire of pain. It was time to end this, so I took up a stance similar to his.

He again jabbed twice with his left, like before, so I was ready for the right cross. I blocked with my right, and followed through by grabbing the sleeve of his shirt and yanking, using his momentum to pull him off balance. I pounded my left fist into his kidney, and he staggered forward into a rack of soup cans. He covered his head as the cans clattered down around him.

As he stood to face me again, I heard shouts from my rear. I glanced over my shoulder. Two men rushed in; they must have heard the barking and brawling inside. The lead man, the one I'd talked with, pointed and yelled.

"Leave 'im alone, there."

They rushed forward, and I spun to meet them. The small man reached for me, so I grabbed his wrist and twisted, forcing him to his knees. The other was close now, and I gave him a side kick that launched him into a bin of carrots. I gave the small man kneeling next to me a back-knuckle blow to the nose, and he collapsed forward as the blood began to flow.

I heard more noise, and more men rushed in. Dee looped Blackjack's leash over a hook holding large plastic bags and hurried to meet them, while the dog struggled to get to Merrick. Badge held high, Dee intercepted the newcomers and shouted, "Police, get back!"

I spun to face Merrick, who had started to move toward me again.

I held up my hands. "Stop! Someone's going to get hurt."

He took one more step, but hesitated as his bleeding coworker staggered up with bloody hands. The second man rolled out of the bin and hurried over to support the first. Merrick looked at them, then glared at me. He finally looked back at his friends and said calmly, "It's OK."

They looked skeptical, but Dee arrived and stuck her credentials in their faces. Reluctantly, they left as she shoved them rudely out the door. Alone now, Merrick and I faced off.

He pointed at me menacingly, "I promised to kill you."

Dee appeared, and put a hand in his chest to keep him from advancing toward me and said, "I understand your feelings, believe me."

She spun to face me. I'm sure she wanted to express her gratitude, but since we were in public, she decided to wait. She smiled, well maybe it was a grimace, and said, "I'll deal with you later. Get the dog."

She turned back toward Merrick as I hurried to free Blackjack. I heard Dee bark, in her best command voice, "I asked you a question."

"I don't remember."

Dee pressed on, "You don't remember why there are bloody bandages in the sink of your apartment?"

I picked up the beast, and we hurried back. I saw Merrick furrow his brow and shake his head. "No, I don't remember the question."

Now Dee shook her head. "There's blood in your sink, whose is it?"

Merrick looked genuinely confused. "Mine, whose else would it be?"

Dee didn't give him time to think. "Why were you bleeding?"

He gestured to his face. "Cuts," he glared at me, "from before you and this cock sucker showed up."

"How did you get cut?"

He looked down at her, "Fighting."

Dee crossed her arms suspiciously, "You seem to do that a lot."

He shook his head and looked down nervously, "Not like that, boxing. Bare knuckles. You know, fight club. It's illegal, but nobody gets hurt. Mostly. I need the extra money."

That would explain the change in fighting style. It also explained the blood in his sink, and the cuts and bruises on his face. It fit, if it was true.

Dee changed tactics. "You called me a while back, about Gareth, said you had a message for him. What message?"

Merrick crossed his arms. "Ask your brother."

"I'm asking you."

He hesitated, then shook his head. "Sorry, I promised."

I put my hand on Dee's shoulder before she could reply. This guy may be a royal asshole, but he didn't kill Gareth. I said softly, "Gareth won't mind. He's dead."

It took a second, but Merrick's eyes went wide, then his jaw dropped just slightly. He blinked twice then looked back and forth between our faces, hoping that he'd heard me wrong.

"When?"

Dee started to speak, but had to stop when she began to choke up. I replied, "Late last night, outside Tenby," I let him think about that. "What did you two talk about?"

Merrick looked even more confused, he shrugged and frowned, "What do you mean? I didn't talk to Gareth yesterday."

Dee recovered, and took up the questioning. She seemed to be good at this. "Were you working yesterday?"

He shook his head, "Day off."

"Where were you last night?"

He looked at us tentatively, then continued, "I had a fight, a private gym near Saundersfoot. My fight ended about three. What happened to Gareth?" He asked insistently.

Dee hesitated, her voice caught as she replied, "Auto accident."

Merrick thought a moment, then looked at us suspiciously. "If it was an accident, why are you here bustin' my balls about where I was?"

I was about to start busting more than his balls, but Dee kept on the pressure. "I asked you before, what was your message to my brother."

His face softened just a bit, and he shrugged, "Thanks, just thanks."

I had a hard time with that answer and took a small step forward. "I don't think so. Gareth got you court-martialed, you wanted to kill him too, as I recall."

Merrick looked away, then nodded slowly, "That I did, but I had a lot of time to think while I was in the Glasshouse." He looked down at Dee. "I would have had a lot more time there if it weren't for your brother. He went out on a limb for me, got my sentence reduced. He got me this job when I got out."

That sounded like Gareth, doing enough was never enough for him. He would always go above and beyond when he felt it was needed. I started to slip away into grief. There weren't many people like Gareth Jones, and now there was one less. I would miss him. Blackjack squirmed in my arms. I held him closer, and forced myself back from the darkness.

Merrick looked at Dee, then directly at me. "Again, why come to me if Gareth was killed in an accident?" His face turned red, and his voice grew louder. "I'm trying to move on, and you come here to rub my face in it? I'm not proud of what I did back there in Sandland, but I did what I had to for a mate." Now he stepped closer, "You sayin' you wouldn't do the same?"

I had to think about that, I had already thought about that. What would I have done in his place, how far would I go to save a friend? How far am I willing to go now to find out what happened to Gareth? There were no easy answers to those questions. I shrugged, then calmly looked him in the eyes and said, "I don't have a problem with what you were trying to do. Yes, I would have tried to rescue a teammate, same as you. But when you start acting like one of them to do it, you need to be stopped."

He didn't react, and we just stood there, staring at each other until a voice came from the open door behind me.

"Do I need to call the police?"

Merrick called out, "Not a problem. They're just leaving."

Dee didn't agree, "I'm not sure I'm done."

Merrick pointed to the back, "Look, I got to get back to work. I can't afford to lose this job. Dee, I'm sorry about your brother. Truly sorry." Dee nodded and looked down. "But I didn't know a damn thing about that 'till you just told me."

He looked at me. "I want to know, was Gareth killed in an accident or not?"

I looked at Dee. She nodded, so I answered. "Gareth was in an accident, but I don't think that's what killed him. I think he had been . . . worked on."

Merrick nodded, but didn't say anything else. We turned and walked to the back. As we reached the door, he

119

called out, "Deacon, you're still a royal prick!"

I smiled and shouted back. "Why does everyone assume I don't already know that?"

We walked out of the room, then through the larger storage area and out to the dock. I set Blackjack down, then had to pull him along when he stopped to growl at the building behind us. I looked at Dee as we wandered toward the car, she looked exhausted.

"Maybe we should get some rest," I suggested.

She looked out at the harbor, unable to hide the pain in her voice. "We need to get another bloody lead. Damn, I thought we were on to something."

We reached the car. I opened the door and set Blackjack inside, then stared at Dee over the roof.

"We do have a lead," I pictured the bulletin board I'd seen on the Harbor Services office wall, reading a name from there in my mind. I didn't even try to pronounce it correctly, "Someone named Newyddlyn Reese."

Dee stared back, confused.

"What does this have to do with Dylan?"

Chapter 14

I looked down amazed. The pint-sized carton in my hand held a chaotic, frozen mess. I had never realized that Chunky Monkey was a real flavor of ice cream, and I took another bite to make sure. Then, to be thorough, I dug my spoon in again, capturing chocolate, nuts and banana in a glob of goodness. I then closed my eyes, and slid the magical lump from its plastic cradle and onto the warm embrace of my waiting tongue. Wow, that tasted good.

I opened my eyes and returned to walking my post. Besides expanding my gastronomical universe, I currently manned the forward observation post in our quest for justice. Disguised as a simple shopper, I had stationed myself strategically between the diapers on my left and the plastic dinnerware on my right. From there I could see out the front window, watching both the parking lot and the street beyond.

A few feet away, guarding the canned vegetables, stood Dee. She occupied the next aisle, a little closer to the door. I could hear her cursing under her breath, probably at me, but that was just too bad.

We were waiting for Dee's cousin Dylan in the "West Tenby Supermart" near his home. I'd insisted on reasonable precautions, and Dee insisted on being unreasonable about everything. We compromised and did it my way. Dee was not happy at the moment but hey, I'd gotten used to that.

While Dee attempted to beguile, then befuddle Alun at Harbor Services with her skills and charms as a detective and a woman, I poked around the office. On a bulletin board by the coffee machine, I found the work schedule for the month. Simple math determined that Alun had not been on duty when the call was made from that office, Dylan Reese had been.

Locating Dylan was much easier than anticipated, since Dee already had his number in her phone. Turns out, Dee's mom and Dylan's mom have the same mom, and dad. Dylan was a musician who apparently lived a secret, double life as a dock supervisor. Dee wanted to simply drop in, chat with the family, and find out what he knew. I vetoed that idea.

I could not get Dee to recognize the danger of our situation. She wanted to conduct an investigation; I had concluded that we were engaged in a combat field operation. Anyone who would torture Gareth, would not give a damn about her rules. In fact, they wouldn't believe in rules at all.

Her rules would get us killed, guaranteed. My rules were better; they at least had odds. Long ones, but still a chance.

I understood her problem better than she understood mine. The police in Britain were very professional, and in most cases well respected. The uncooperative suspect she normally dealt with might cut and run, trying to stay ahead of the law. Our current suspects, if they got the chance, would cut off our heads before they ran, which was part of their law.

This was a subtle, but important difference that I hoped Dee would come to understand, quickly.

We had parked at the bookstore next door, walked to the Supermart, and called Dylan from a payphone inside. Dee pretended to be a different cousin, Mary something or other, and told Dylan he needed to hurry over and help her carry her grocery bags home.

Dee was sure Dylan knew it was a bogus call, but seemed curious enough to come anyway. All we had to do was wait inside, out of sight and out of our minds. This was not secure enough, but I gave in. I couldn't shake the feeling that we were running out of time, and this was the quickest way to our next clue.

A blue ford Cortina pulled up out front and a man fitting Dylan's description got out. He looked off to his right, squinted, then marched to the double glass doors at the entrance.

He pushed his way inside, stood on his toes and looked around, then frowned.

"Dee, what the bloody hell is going on?"

Dee's voice rasped in what she intended as a whisper, but carried through the store.

"Over here, and be quiet."

Why do people think they can shout and whisper at the same time?

I heard Dylan walk toward us, then turn down Dee's aisle. They greeted each other, hugged, and Dylan asked, "Are you mad? Why are we meeting like this?"

"I needed to ask you some questions, privately. I wasn't sure you'd recognize my voice."

"I didn't recognize your voice on the phone, but I saw

your stupid little car parked up the road."

I couldn't stop myself and spoke between two rows of plastic cups.

"I told you we should have parked behind the building."

I couldn't see him, but he didn't sound surprised when he responded, "Is that Gareth's Yank?"

Dee spoke before I could answer, "Yes. We need to ask you some questions."

"Fine, but why didn't you just . . ."

I walked down the aisle, and missed what they were saying. I hung a left at the toilet paper, then turned again and walked up their aisle. When I reached them, Dylan looked confused, and just a little angry.

Dylan was short but very muscular, and with red hair and green eyes, he looked more like Dee's brother than cousin. He was asking Dee a question, but she put her hand to her mouth, choking back tears. She looked up at me for help, and Dylan turned to me for information. "What the fuck is going on? Yes, I talked with Gareth yesterday, two days ago, whatever. But if you want to know what we talked about, you need to ask him. And what's the matter with her?"

"We can't ask Gareth."

I could have just said "he's dead," but this seemed like a softer way of breaking the news. Dylan processed that statement and his eyes grew wide, anxious.

"The official finding was that he died in an auto accident. I believe he was murdered."

"We believe," Dee added, though she was on the verge of losing control. Dylan looked at her, she nodded then looked away.

"When? How?"

"Yesterday, very early morning. Just this side of

124

Mumbles."

Dylan spun to face Dee, confused, his expression asking her if this was real, since he couldn't seem to find the words. She nodded, and Dylan turned slowly back to me.

"I can't believe it, and murdered you say?"

I nodded. Dylan looked down, stunned. His face clouded and it appeared he might also start to cry. After a few seconds, he shook his head and spoke, "It's my fault."

We didn't say anything, letting Dylan clear his mind, and heart. After a moment, he went on, "I called him, told him about a Beeb poking about the dock, asking questions. Gareth came by the day before yesterday. We talked, then he went on to Pembroke."

I asked, "Why did you call Gareth? Why not the police?"

"I called the police, they took the report. Understand, this happened over a month ago."

Dee was starting to think like a detective again and asked, "Start from the beginning, why did you call, who was the Beeb, etc."

I had to interrupt, "What's a Beeb?"

Dylan spoke up first, getting angry again, "A rag head, diaper dome, camel jockey, sheep shagger – an Arab. Seems they're all named Habeeb, right? So they're called Beebs. We have names for everybody here."

I smiled. "A bit insensitive, don't you think?"

"Hey you kill 'em, don't get more insensitive than that."

Good point. Dee didn't seem to mind the reference, and pulled out her notepad. She looked up at Dylan and began her questioning.

"Did you get his name?"

Dylan grinned, the initial shock beginning to pass. I

pegged Dylan for a happy drunk, friendly guy with a good-natured heart.

"Goat humper said his name was Habeeb, no shit! So I knew he was lying."

There was an obvious inconsistency there, but I let it pass.

"Beeb shows up at the dock, asking about work. Says he works in Cardiff, but he's askin' questions about tonnage and . . ."

Dee interrupted, "Short version, Dylan, no need for his life story."

"Right, whatever. He was askin' questions on the dock, and some of the hands got suspicious and called me. I talk with him a bit, and realize he isn't from Cardiff. I ask more questions, and he mentions the ferry and a couple of other details about his dock."

Dylan had a satisfied look on his face.

"He's from Pembroke, maybe Milford Haven, but I'd bet my life he works those docks."

Dee looked away, but poor Dylan had no idea what he'd said. He'd bet Gareth's life, and lost. I had more questions and got the narrative moving again before he could think about what he'd said.

"Great thinking Dylan, but why did you call Gareth."

"When Beeb leaves, I call the police, tell them there was a Muslim gentleman here asking about the docks and acting suspicious. That afternoon two detectives come to the office, and I told them what happened."

Dee understood the process and commented, "That was a good response time. Police take that sort of information very seriously."

Dylan had his own opinions.

"Too seriously. Three days later, a couple of blokes from MI5 from London drop by my house after hours.

126

They tell me they've investigated and determined there were no security issues. Everything's fine, they say. Then they go on and tell me that if I talk about it, I would be guilty of disseminating false information, and maybe causing public panic. Can you believe that?"

Actually, knowing what I know now, I would expect that. I asked Dylan, "Was one of them a big guy, named Tibbs?"

"Yeah, Tibbs, the big one."

Dee and I look at each other. Becket. Dee followed up.

"But you didn't forget it."

"No. After sleeping on it, I realize that everything may not be all fine and dandy, maybe that's just what they want me to think. Pissed me off, actually, so I sent an e-mail to Gareth asking him what to do."

A little bell went off in my head, "When was that?"

Dylan thought about it, then looked down at his watch.

"A month tomorrow. Gareth calls me the next day and asks me about it."

I made some quick mental calculations. The very next day, Gareth asked me to join his Welsh Rugby excursion. Interesting, especially since he never mentioned coming to Wales before Dylan's call.

This may all be a coincidence. Sure, and Osama bin Laden was killed by a stray bullet. What the hell had Gareth learned from Dylan? I started to ask, but Dee beat me to it.

"What did you tell him?"

"Just what I told you."

That couldn't be everything, but again Dee beat me to the question.

"That can't be everything."

"Yeah, that's about it. We talked a little more about Rugby, he tells me that the Yank here is a major bad ass and will make a decent fly half when he learns the game."

He laughed, sad but still amused at the thought. He looked at me and smiled.

"Gareth told me what you said about that."

It took a second, but I remembered, and couldn't help but smile as well. Dylan continued his explanation.

"So when Gareth gets home, he calls, and says he'll stop by. He shows up yesterday and I tell him the same thing, so he calls you from my office and . . ." Dee interrupted, "What did Travis say? About being a fly half?"

Dylan smirked, "Our Rugby virgin Yank hears 'fly half' and checks his zipper. Says fly half sounded like Gareth was telling him is zipper was open."

Dee laughed out loud, then looked over at me, "Not really?"

I could only shrug hoping it would keep me from crying. I couldn't let myself think about Gareth, not the way he was back then—not yet.

And I couldn't help but be moved by the strength Dee and Dylan were exercising. Getting to know Gareth, and a couple other Welshmen over there in Sandland, had convinced me they were my kindred souls. No situation was so desperate that they lost their love for life or sense of humor about it. We were only hours away from the death of her brother, and she was laughing about something that simple.

And it happened again. Seeing Dee laugh made me feel a little lightheaded. I couldn't let myself worry about that right now. I focused back on Dylan, who'd started speaking again.

"And after he leaves you a message, he asks me to print out a picture of the Beeb for when he comes back. Then he leaves."

Dee asked the obvious questions again. "He thought

this big meat head could play fly half?"

Well, maybe not the obvious one.

Dylan shrugged, and I asked my question, "What picture?"

"Gareth wanted me to print out a picture of our Sand Monkey for when he came back, he didn't have time to wait."

"You took his picture?"

"On the docks we video everything, hell in the UK you can't take a piss without some blighter watching you on closed circuit. MI5 took the originals. I had to go through the backup disks, but I found it and printed out a picture."

Dee got excited and asked, "Do you still have the picture?"

"In the car, I'll get it."

Dylan left, and I asked Dee, "How far is Pembook?

"Pembroke, and it's not far."

Damn, I can't even pronounce the easy ones. I rushed to the front of the store, there were things I needed before we parted ways with Dylan.

I got back after Dylan did, and he and Dee were examining a fuzzy black-and-white picture of a bearded face. It wasn't great, but it was good enough. With this we may be able to find our 'Beeb.' Then we could find out if Gareth had found him, and what he discovered.

I handed them both a cell phone, the prepaid minute kind that couldn't be tied to us. If MI5 was still interested, I was pretty sure our phones were being tracked.

"Here, use these phones if we need to talk to each other, I've programmed in the numbers."

I handed him a small grocery bag. He looked inside and frowned. I felt I should explain, "Dog food, and a couple of sports bottles of water. We need you to keep Blackjack while we follow Gareth's trail."

A look of horror contorted his face, and he actually took a step back.

"No fucking way! You keep that devil dog away from me."

Dee was instantly in his face. "If you didn't try to kick him, he would . . ."

I interrupted gently, "Quiet! It will only be for a day or so."

They both looked at me and barked in unison, "No!"

"Just for a . . ."

"FUCK NO!"

That didn't work out as I'd hoped. Maybe the second part of my plan would work out better. I smiled at Dylan.

"And we'll need to borrow your car. Hers is too easy to spot."

Dylan now took a step forward, "I'm not driving that little poofter car."

Dee was right behind him, "And I'm not driving that piece of shit Cortina."

They resumed arguing, but I interrupted and stepped close to Dylan. "I am going to find the person who killed Gareth, does anyone have a problem with that?" They both shook their heads. "Dylan, it appears that Blackjack will be leaving in your car, which one will you be in?"

Dylan reluctantly pulled the keys from his pocket and handed them to Dee, who already had hers out. They exchanged keys, and Dylan shoved the bag of dog items into my chest and growled, "For Gareth, but I'm parking your little priss-mobile in the back here, and calling a mate to pick me up."

That was actually better, and I couldn't blame Dylan at all.

Two other details popped into my head. The first was a question for him, "Do you know Merrick Naismith?"

Reluctantly, he nodded, "Yes."

Dee asked, "How?"

"Gareth asked me to get him on with Harbor. It's entry level, but he's doing OK. I make sure we're on different shifts."

We looked at each other. Merrick's story checked out.

I continued with the last detail. "If you don't hear from us in two days, report your car stolen. It will give you cover if there are. . . complications."

Dee spoke up, "Don't tell anyone we were here, or where we're going. Say I called you from Swansea, that I need to be alone and can't be reached."

Dylan looked at Dee and nodded anxiously, almost fearful. It finally struck him that we would be following Gareth, maybe all the way to the grave.

Chapter 15

Abdul al Maliki looked at the man in front of him, Naseem Hassan, and marveled again at his father's wisdom.

Maliki thought back to the occasion of his twelfth birthday. His father had invited the young Abdul to accompany him to work, at the large building in the mountains that he used as an office. The boy grew excited. Even though he was the eldest son, he had seldom been exposed to his father's business. The boy knew only that his father was wealthy, a political leader in their rural region of Pakistan, and controlled the loyalty of many men. Men respected his father, maybe even feared him, which made Maliki revere his father all the more.

They sat on the porch while servants brought them hot tea. As they chatted and sipped the tea, a large man approached them hesitantly. The man stopped at the railing just a few meters from his father, removed the flat, round pakol he wore from his head, and dropped his eyes.

His father took another sip of tea then set down his cup, bidding his son to do the same. He looked at the young man seriously and explained, "You are of age now Abdul, and must learn to be a man. This training begins today with two simple truths, ones that you must never forget." He pointed at the terrified man still standing at the rail. "Truth number one is that stupid people do stupid things. This is simply the way things are."

His father nodded toward the man at the rail. "This man just returned from Afghanistan. He had been instructed many times that while there he was to avoid towns and valleys. He was vigorously reminded that he must have no contact with the agents of Kabul or their Russian masters." His father glared at the man, whose head dropped so low that his face could not be seen at all.

His father went on, "This man was not wise. He did not follow instructions. As a result, he lost his entire shipment, and almost his life."

His father finished his tea, then raised the glass above his head. A servant scurried over and took it from him to be refilled. His father slid his chair back, resting his hands in his lap. His posture had relaxed, but his face became serious. He stared at the boy intently.

"This brings me to the second truth you must learn today, my son. Since you can't stop stupid people from being stupid, it's best to just kill them before they make things worse."

His father's hand rose from below the tabletop, holding a small automatic pistol. The gun swung quickly toward the man and fired. The single shot startled the boy, but he didn't flinch. The weapon had been fired into the top of the man's head, and he dropped like a puppet whose strings had been cut. Abdul then stood to look over the rail, marveling at how peaceful the dead man looked.

The adult Abdul looked again at Naseem, blinked twice, and returned to the present. Maliki smiled casually at this person who had jeopardized his intricate plan. He must determine if this man was so stupid that Truth Number One had been satisfied.

Maliki pointed to a nearby wall, "Please, look there."

Together they stared at a large, ultra-high-definition TV displaying maddeningly low resolution security footage of two men standing on a dock. Maliki wanted Naseem to validate or disprove the first truth before they moved on to Truth Number Two.

Maliki pointed at one of the men on the screen, "Who is that man?"

Naseem looked at Maliki confused, then back at the TV. "How did you get this?"

"Please answer my question."

"Me, that is me. Many days ago."

"Good, who is the other man?"

Naseem thought briefly, then shook his head, "I don't remember his name, but he's just a dock worker from Tenby."

"No, he's not just a dock worker, and why are you talking to him?"

Naseem smiled excitedly, squirming like a puppy wanting attention. "I was trying to find a different port for this second cargo. I remembered that you lamented having to bring both shipments into the same port. I visited other ports in the area hoping to find an alternative."

Maliki smiled indulgently. "I did say that, but the reason we didn't use a new port is that you are a supervisor at the old one. You can make cargo and any other inconvenient paperwork disappear."

Maliki's men had prepared this second shipment in a nearby building, weeks before. It had been loaded on a cargo ship, sailed around the world, and unloaded at a major Welsh seaport without a scrap of documentation.

Unlike the first cargo, however, it had not gone undetected.

Maliki shook his head remorsefully. "The man you are talking to became suspicious. He called the police, who then called MI5."

Naseem's face grew concerned, but then he relaxed. "That should not be a problem. I did not give him my real name, nor tell him where I was from. I told him I was looking for a new job and asked him about what types of cargo they handled." He shrugged, "There will be no problems."

"Naseem, there have already been problems. I have been able to distract MI5, but there was a man, an SAS man watching you unload the final cargo."

Naseem looked around, startled, as if that man may still be watching them. This was a stupid man.

"I took care of him as well, but I've just learned that still others have been asking questions. Unfortunately, you can't go back to your job. People may come looking for you."

Naseem sounded small and weak as he whined, "What should I do?"

"I think you should disappear, do you agree?"

Naseem nodded. Maliki stood, lifted the other man from the seat, then called to someone outside the room.

"Come!"

A powerful looking man strode in calmly. Maliki put his hand on Naseem's shoulder.

"This is Ahmed. He will make sure you are not found by the authorities."

Naseem looked at Maliki and nodded gratefully, "Thank you."

Maliki turned to look out a window and said, "I am always happy to help a brother."

Suddenly, Naseem went stiff as something small slid

136

over his head. He attempted to turn and look at Ahmed, but the garrote bit cruelly into his neck. Naseem's frantic hands first tried to pull the piano wire from around his neck, but it was too tight. He then tried to reach Ahmed, but that also proved impossible. Soon Naseem's struggles became weaker, slower, then stopped entirely.

Truth Number Two had been invoked.

Ahmed maintained the pressure for a minute longer, then let Naseem slump limply to the floor. Maliki spoke without looking at the body.

"There is a furnace in the main house."

Ahmed nodded, heaved Naseem's dead body over his shoulder, and left.

Maliki touched the window. It faced east toward Mecca. East toward where his aged father lived with his wives. His father's body was failing him, though his mind was still able; able enough to appreciate what his son would soon achieve. Very soon, his father would be beside himself with joy and pride.

Maliki glanced outside at a perfectly manicured garden, bordered by a stand of evergreen trees. This manor, with almost a hundred acres of surrounding property, belonged to one of his unwitting British partners. It was a 'fly in' estate with its own landing strip. This made perfect sense since the owner was an Air Force pilot, now a Brigadier General, who regularly flew to London, Cardiff, and several resort islands off the coast of Europe and Africa.

Not only was it logical, it was practical, since no one ever considered searching his plane. Maliki implemented this brilliant enterprise years ago. The esteemed General knew he had been importing Persian rugs illegally, but not that each had been wrapped around several kilos of heroin. The old fool actually believed he received a million pounds a year by cheating the crown of its duty on rugs, not drugs.

Maliki spun and walked confidently back to his desk. He remained certain that nothing could disrupt his plan. Not only was God on his side, but so was the clock. The time of his success could be better measured in hours than in days. In fact, it would be less than two days until the world, starting right here in once Great Britain, would be forever changed.

Still, any good battle plan provided for rearguard security.

Maliki picked up a cheap, disposable cell phone and pressed a speed dial number. The phone buzzed, and someone answered on the second ring. Maliki didn't wait for a greeting.

"Gamal, there have been others in Tenby."

Gamal answered in perfect, if somewhat vulgar, English, "Who?"

"I don't know for sure who they are, or where. Nor do I care as long as they don't interfere with our operations. There is little possibility that anyone has the time or resources to pursue us, but we must be certain. Wait at the port. If anyone shows up, kill them."

"Sir, what if the others return?"

Maliki considered this. The British police were barely competent at times, but perhaps they could be of some help.

"I will make sure they return. They will probably occupy the same location as before. Watch them as well. If someone shows up asking questions, make it look like they killed each other. That will keep everyone occupied until it is too late."

"God willing," Gamal hung up.

Maliki felt better. Gamal Thahim had been born in Khyber, but grew up in a very rough section of Liverpool. There, from an early age, he had been forced to defend his faith against the bullies and ruffians who lived around him. His faith, strength, and hatred for the British all flourished in that harsh environment. He was not well educated, but he was ruthless, intelligent and cunning. Gamal had become a valued employee, and a lethal tool.

Gamal would ensure that their trail would not be followed, and this comforting realization would allow Maliki to return to more immediate issues. He picked up a house phone and dialed Nadja, the Russian whore he kept there. She had been given to him as the sweetener on a large arms purchase; anti-tank missiles were worth much more than women in the former Soviet Union. She had also been placed in charge of maintaining that house, which she did with skill and enthusiasm. Nadja was both talented and beautiful, and on Maliki's instruction, she had offered to help at the manor house. It had not been long before she enjoyed a room very near the master suite, and her maintenance duties were now of a much more intimate nature.

Nadja finally picked up her phone. Maliki smiled as she promised to be there soon.

Maliki hung up, walked to the wet bar and poured a glass of scotch. Two problems had been solved. He had progressed two steps closer to his victory.

Chapter 16

I watched from the shadows as Dee walked back to the parking lot where we'd left Dylan's car. She didn't like having to sneak around and keep in the shadows, but it didn't take much to convince her to go along. After all that had happened in the last two days, I think she wanted an excuse to be paranoid.

We were at the docks; it took only twenty minutes to get to Pembroke. Then we spent half an hour locating the exact dock where Dylan thought we should start. We had watched and waited from various spots around the area, and Dee was getting impatient. She wanted to start asking questions. I wanted to live long enough to use any information we discovered. However, I had seen enough, it was time to be off on my own. Dee was ready to sit, and I convinced her that Blackjack needed a potty break and a little water.

The truth was, I needed a break from her. For some reason, she didn't trust me to follow proper procedures. Maybe I shouldn't have told her I didn't give a damn about proper procedures.

She disappeared around the office building next door, and I turned to face away from the docks. I already knew what was happening out there. I began to examine the places where I would be if I had to set up surveillance of the docks.

Across about a hundred meters of water, on a small outcrop of land, stood a two-story building in what appeared to be an industrial area. I looked again for a weak flicker of orange light in a second-story window, and finally I saw it for the third time. I felt sure it meant that somebody just lit a cigarette in an otherwise dark room. Assuming that someone had been instructed to maintain covert surveillance on a person or place, smoking was a lazy mistake. It would be like putting up a neon sign that said: "Here we are!"

They say smoking can kill you, and if those were the people that nabbed Gareth, I just might get the opportunity to make that a fact. Before I visited the building, however, I needed information from people on the dock. I needed to know who our Beeb really was, and if possible, a list of his friends and acquaintances.

Moreover, this is where Gareth probably came when he left Tenby. I needed to follow Gareth's movements. That meant I needed to know if he'd been there, and where he went after. If there had been men watching the dock, they may even have grabbed him here. Gareth was always alert, but he was only looking for a longshoreman. He didn't know how dangerous things were, or he would probably still be alive.

When people in our line of work understand a situation, we know what precautions to take. I was taking them. My counter surveillance indicated this dock may well be under the eye of someone in that nearby building, or maybe they were just kids in there doing drugs. I would find out. If we were being watched, the watchers had lost the element of surprise, and would soon be losing more.

I tossed the hood from my sweatshirt over my head and walked carefully around the building, staying in the darkness. A cool breeze off the water hit me as the dock came into view. The smell of salt water and diesel fuel were stronger now, and I moved toward the voices of laboring men.

Against the building, I found boxes waiting to be moved. I lifted one to my shoulder, keeping it between the suspect building and my face, and walked into the harsh halogen glare of work lights. I looked around and started toward the man who seemed to be in charge.

Keeping my back to any watchful eyes, I set down the box and pulled Dylan's picture of the unknown Beeb from my pocket. I tried to look casual as I showed it to him, as if I had brought him a piece of routine paperwork.

I asked, "Do you know this guy?"

The supervisor craned his neck a little and nodded, "Yeah, but why'd they give you a picture."

He looked around, then pointed to a group that was hoisting a large crate from the deck of a small freighter, "You're over there."

No, I'm pretty sure I'm here. I held the picture a little closer.

"I'm trying to find this guy."

The supervisor looked at me confused. He looked back at the picture then at me, "You're not the temporary replacement?"

"I don't even know who he is."

"Naseem, Naseem Hassan the regular dock supervisor, he's missed his last few shifts and I have to fill in for him, so I asked for a replacement to work my job. That's not you?"

I shook my head and considered congratulating him. I felt certain the promotion would soon be permanent. I extended my hand, "Travis Deacon. You don't know where he is?"

The supervisor took my hand. "Rys, Rys Miller. Why is everyone looking for Naseem?"

Had Gareth been here?

"How many people have been looking for him?"

"A couple, one guy two nights ago. Then some coppers last night. Is he in trouble?"

"Was the guy two nights ago about your height, very fit with a haircut like mine?"

Rys smiled as I lifted the hood from my bald head, then nodded, "That's the one, SAS bloke."

"Exactly, what did he do?"

"He came askin' if I had any Muslim hands, which I do, and if any of them had been acting odd over the last few months, which there was: Naseem."

"Odd how?"

"Normally, the little blighter don't give a shit what we're unloading. He's too good to associate with us, and he's always looking for an excuse to slough his work off on me, like if it's booze or cigarettes. He don't want to unload anything that's unclean—like he didn't need a bath most of the time himself."

Rhys motions to the ship being unloaded.

"A few weeks, maybe months ago we get a ship in from Egypt, and old Naseem's about to cream his knickers. You'd think we was unloading his great grandma's ashes or something the way he fussed and paced about."

This corresponded with the time frame Dylan mentioned. I had to assume the two events were related.

"What was in those crates?"

"The bill said appliances and electronics for some import company in Liverpool. 'Bout the right size and weight, could have been."

"What else?"

"Then two nights ago we get another ship. This one from Indonesia, but Naseem starts acting funny again. It looked exactly like the same cargo, for the same company. It makes you wonder, you know."

I shook my head. No, I didn't know, so Rys explained.

"Why are we unloading cargo for a Liverpool company here? It happens from time to time, but twice? I wonder if he's nicking stuff, or smuggling something, so I ask what it is. The little prat tells me it's dead people and laughs. Couple nights later is when that Gareth bloke shows up."

I can feel things start to come together, but not enough. I ask Rys, "Tell me about Gareth."

"He's in this beautiful little MG, parks at the end of the dock." He smiles and points to a parking area about a hundred meters away. "Sweet little car. He wants to talk to Naseem, but I tell him that Naseem's not here, and may not show up at all. He just goes back to his car and waits awhile, but he must've got tired. He was gone by the time shift ended."

Gareth didn't get tired. He abducted.

"Tell me about the police."

Rys thinks a second and shakes his head before going on, "MI5, don't know why they were here, really. I guess they don't have anything better to do than stop by and tell me everything's normal and not to worry, which in itself ain't normal and caused me a bit of worry."

Naseem is a dead end, but now I need to find out about that ship.

"Do you know who picked up that shipment?"

"No, but they were important. Customs must have

cleared it immediately, since my instructions said to have it loaded directly onto trucks."

"Was there any other cargo?"

The supervisor shook his head, then the sound of crashing wood and swearing came from down the dock. He glared over at a shattered crate, resting on its side. "Damn, I gotta go."

"Where can I find out more about that cargo?"

He looked over his shoulder as he hurried toward the chaos and said, "Harbor Master's office, opens to the public about seven."

Rys was gone, but I knew what my next few steps were going to be. I hoisted my box again and walked toward the parking lot where I assumed Dee and Blackjack would be waiting patiently.

I knew Blackjack, at least, would be up for our next adventure.

Chapter 17

We were back in Dylan's faded blue Ford leaving the docks. We turned left, following the first important looking road we found. It curved to our left, then right. We were now on a decent little road, what the sign called Western Way. I hate to be culturally insensitive, but I really prefer the Western Way. I took our path as a good omen.

I finished telling Dee about our Beeb, now named Naseem. I also explained about the ships and cargos. I finally worked up enough courage to talk about Gareth.

"Gareth was here, looking for Naseem."

She stared at me, wanting to know, but not wanting to hear what I might have to say.

"I think they took him back on the dock. Gareth was waiting to see if Naseem showed up, when he disappeared. Rys, the new dock supervisor, thought Gareth just got tired of waiting and left, but that's not what happened."

We reached a large, poorly lit traffic circle and started around.

I had been looking out my window, to the left toward

the water, and estimated we had reached the finger of land where the suspect building stood. There was a road heading in that direction, Pier Road, and I told Dee to turn.

She pulled onto a narrow two-lane road and stopped. She turned to face me. "Are you sure?" she asked.

"There's no way I can be sure. I believe that someone's watching the dock from a building in this area. Let's find out who and why, then go from there."

She looked tired, and I could understand why. Blackjack was asleep in my lap, and Dee looked down at him enviously. After a second of doubt, she pulled back onto the road and continued on.

The little road was well paved. On our right, we passed what looked like a new supermarket, but the buildings further on looked much older. They were well maintained, but built of block or older wood construction. Most of the buildings looked like offices or shops supporting the activities of the port.

Ahead down the road, I could see a three story white building, but that was not the one I was looking for. The one I needed would probably be to the left of it.

As we continued, I noticed that all the windows had metal bars, and there was a high metal fence that ran almost the entire length of the road. As the fence ended, the warehouses and workshops began. On our right, the buildings eventually gave way to bushes, then a dirt and stone rise of three to four meters. It looked to be an undeveloped green area, with trees and brush growing on top.

We reached the three-story building (the Pier House), and stopped. It looked like a hotel of some sort, maybe an office building. We drove past it. To the left, behind the Pier House, stood a large metal warehouse, a few meters off the water at the end of the peninsula.

There was enough of a moon to see the building, though not clearly. Large double doors at the near end were closed, but at the far end, the one closest to the water, we could see windows high up in the corrugated steel wall. The windows were dark, but I guessed the building had a second story built above the work area inside. The offices would sit above the floor of the warehouse allowing a manager or supervisor to monitor the work being done on the floor below.

Now it appeared the offices were allowing Muslim scumbags to monitor the work being done on the dock. But maybe not, we needed more information.

"Stop."

Dee came to an abrupt halt, and I looked across the road and through a drive leading from Pier Road to the warehouse. I could barely make out the rear end of a vehicle, parked almost entirely out of view from the road. Before she could protest, I put Blackjack in her lap and hopped out.

I leaned back in and said, "Turn around, wait for me up the road a few hundred meters."

I stood, shut the door, and hurried toward the drive. I vaulted a gate meant to keep out only vehicles and disappeared into the weeds and brush inside the wire fence.

I moved silently toward the warehouse, weaving my way through the brush. It was only about twenty meters before I reached the parking area of the building. Sitting in the corner, as out of sight as possible, was a black Range Rover.

I slipped silently through the bushes until I was in front of the Range Rover, then crept to the driver's window in a crouch. I peeked inside, the vehicle was very clean and neat. There was a radio mounted under the dash, with a handset hanging near the steering wheel. On the console, I could see a black notebook with an official logo on the front.

I slid back into the bushes, moved carefully to the road, and hurried toward where Dee was waiting. As I jogged on, I analyzed the situation. I suspected that the terrorists would want to be watching the dock. The planning and execution so far had been meticulous, which would also make the mastermind behind this plan difficult to locate and neutralize.

MI5, however, had taken the only good observation point in the area. If the terrorists couldn't watch the dock, what would they do? By the time I passed the place where the Cortina should have been, I had a pretty good idea what those assholes would be doing.

About two hundred meters past that point where she should have been waiting, I found the petty and peevish Dee, parked and pissed off. At that point, I had also decided what our next course of action should be. I got in and explained, "MI5 has the dock under surveillance."

"You sure it's them?"

"There's a black Range Rover with a sign that says 'Official

MI5 Business' on the dash."

It was only a small exaggeration, but it kept her from asking more questions. I knew who it was. I also knew we were running out of time.

"Becket's people have the only good observation point occupied, which means the bad guys will find an alternative location. If that's impossible, they will be watching the watchers. After checking things out at the pier, I think they'll have chosen the latter."

Dee's face went blank. She shook her head and barked, "What the bloody hell are you talking about? Why would anyone watch the dock, and how in god's name did you come up with that nonsense?" She squinted suspiciously and continued, "What are you trying to pull?"

I needed to speed things along, and decided an object lesson was appropriate.

"We can spend an hour discussing it, or I can take ten minutes and show you."

She hesitated, so I did not. I snapped the leash on Blackjack's collar, and we hopped out. I leaned back inside, retrieved the paddle, I mean Cricket bat, from behind my seat where I'd stowed it. I then informed Dee of her part in my little demonstration.

"When I text you, drive forward and stop at exactly the same place you dropped me off before, in front of the warehouse. Roll down the window and call Blackjack, keep calling him until he comes."

She did not like this at all.

"Why would I do that?"

I kept talking, not giving her time to ask questions.

"Get out of the car and be ready to catch Blackjack."

"What do you mean catch Blackjack, where will . . ."

I interrupted forcefully, "Just listen. It's important. He may jump from the rise to your right, in fact, pull over on the right side of the road. Once you catch him, get back inside and close and lock the doors. If anyone but me comes out of the trees, drive away as fast as you can and call the police. Understand?"

"Not a word!"

But I knew she had. She wouldn't miss something like that, so I went on.

"Good, don't be late! You need to be there to catch him."

She hopped out of the car, mad as I'd ever seen her, and yelled. "Stop!"

I closed the door and started jogging up the road

before she could respond.

She got louder. "If you hurt my dog, I swear I'll cut off your balls and shove them down your throat!"

I hated using Blackjack like this, but I would make sure he stayed safe. Probably. Anyway, I knew he wanted to get Gareth's killers as much as I did.

As I passed the last building on my right, the dirt and bushes began. I grabbed Blackjack and carried him. I couldn't have him barking and chasing little forest creatures.

The incline was gentle here, but a few meters further on it became a sheer drop to the road. I stopped as I disappeared completely into the brush and typed a text message to Dee. All I had to do was press send.

I didn't know exactly where the stakeout would be. I didn't know for sure if they were there at all. I just had to assume they would make sure no one followed their trail. So, if these were the guys who killed Gareth, they would be here.

I moved deeper into the woods, then circled left. The wind was coming off the water, from the west, so I had to circle about forty meters before I turned back toward the road. The wind not only carried smells, but sounds as well, so I made sure to approach from downwind.

We slipped silently toward the road for a minute or so, when Blackjack's head jerked up. His ears swiveled forward to catch any sound. He lifted his nose and sniffed, then began to tense. I put my hand over his snout and whispered for him to be quiet, which he did.

I liked this little guy more and more all the time.

We moved warily forward, stopping every few meters to listen and test the air. Blackjack seemed to understand what was going on; hunting was built into his genetic code. I took another step, when Blackjack's head bobbed up again. I froze. I waited for a couple of minutes, but my senses couldn't detect a thing.

I started to move forward when I heard a sniffle from in front, and about ten degrees to the left. The sniffle earned a muted rebuke in Arabic.

Bingo!

I slowly reached into my pocket and pressed send on my phone. I then slid silently to my left, about fifteen meters, which I estimated would put the sniffling snoopers directly between us, and the place where Dee would stop.

I knelt and set Blackjack on the ground beside me. I slowly unsnapped the leash from his collar, my other hand on his chest to keep him from bolting. I estimated Dee should be there now, and tensed for action.

I heard whispers from ahead; they may have spotted the car. Then I made out the sound of the engine and tires on pavement, and the whispers became more animated. Finally, there was silence.

"Blackjack!" Dee's voice carried through the trees. "Come here boy."

She had parked exactly where I'd indicated, and her voice came from directly ahead. Blackjack barked once, answering excitedly. Dee must have heard him. She called out again, "Where are you? Get over here now."

Blackjack was ready to go, so I let him loose. He sprinted forward, with me close behind. I held the Cricket bat behind my back as I moved after the Min Pin. It was my turn to yell, "Blackjack! Where are you? Go to mommy."

My placement was perfect. As I ran forward, I saw Blackjack bound between two prone men and scamper down the hill.

I yelled again, "Blackjack, go to mommy."

The two men looked back toward my voice.

I heard Dee scream and hoped she had caught the little daredevil. The two men looked forward again toward the scream.

I was almost there. The man to my right had a rifle with a large night-vision scope. The other had night-vision binoculars. They were both kneeling now, trying to see over the edge of the rise just a short distance in front of them. The one with the rifle heard me coming and turned onto his side.

I yelled in Arabic, "Stop. It's me!"

The look of confusion on his face was replaced by a spray of blood as the edge of my paddle smashed into the bridge of his nose. A sickening crunch indicated cartilage had become pulp. He whimpered and collapsed on top if his rifle, hands over his nose.

The man to my left was rolling onto his left side, reaching with his right hand to where a pistol probably waited. I swung the bat in an arch, from near the face of victim number one, and propelled it down toward the face of the other man, who became victim number two.

The second victim barely managed to get his arm up to protect his face. The violent crack of bat on bone told me he now had a second elbow, and the wooden bludgeon still kept going and smashed into his forehead.

Victim number one was struggling to his feet; he had been partially covered by weeds when I first saw him and was larger than I anticipated. He wiped his eyes with his left hand and blinked rapidly, trying to clear away the tears and blood. With his right hand, he reached for the pistol in a holster on his belt.

I swung the bat in a horizontal arch and smashed it into the side of his head, just above the ear. It was lights out for Number One, who became instantly limp and slumped to the dirt.

I was really getting into it. Every Cricket game should be played like this.

I spun back around, but Number Two was staggering into the woods, reaching frantically with his still functional left hand for something in his right pants pocket, probably a gun.

I started toward the unconscious terrorist Number One. I wanted his gun. It's not a good idea to bring a stick to a gunfight, and I was sure that Number Two was armed. Unfortunately, he was also moving faster than I'd anticipated, and I was forced to hurry immediately after him.

After a chase of several seconds, I caught him. He hadn't been able to retrieve his pistol, but he reached behind his back and pulled out a knife. I recognized it immediately. It was the long, thick, angled blade of a Kukri, the knife of the Gurkhas.

These are wicked knives when used as a weapon. They're not as effective for stabbing, but for slashing or cutting they were unequalled. My adversary dropped into a fighting stance, and even using his off hand. I could see he was dangerous.

I circled to my left, his right, toward the side of his body where his forearm dangled limply, broken clean through. He had to be in considerable pain, but rage and fear were pumping adrenaline through his blood, masking the agony.

As I looked for something to use as a weapon, he sensed his only chance was to attack before I could arm myself. Since he could not stab me with any effect, he screamed and cursed in Arabic as he raised the knife to slash at my right side.

I spun to my left and launched a side kick into his mangled right forearm, and his wrist swung like a pendulum

155

from the impact. No one produces enough adrenaline to mask the pain that kick had caused. He cried out and dropped to his knees, cradling his right arm. He grimaced in pain, but still struggled to raise his knife in a defensive posture.

I'd had enough and reached down, picked up a large stone, and hurled it into his face. He slumped backward and lay on his back, moaning. He was still conscious, which is what I wanted.

I kicked the knife away, then moved behind him and flipped him over onto his stomach. This may have been a little uncomfortable, since he screamed in pain. I frisked him quickly, retrieving a Makarov pistol, probably of Chinese manufacture. At this point, my phone rang. It was Dee.

"Aren't you done yet?"

Wow, she was tough to please.

"I'm fine, thank you for asking. As it is, I just subdued two heavily armed terrorists with a stick, retrieved several weapons, and have been offering timely advice on pain management."

"If you insist, but you still need to get down here, you and your playmates have been making a bloody racket. We need to get out of here before someone shows up to investigate."

"No, what we need to do is to make sure the terrorists are properly restrained, secure their weapons and equipment, and then interrogate them."

If they're conscious, or alive, I didn't actually say that, but I did want to reinforce my point. "Unless you're comfortable leaving a sniper rifle and various automatic pistols here for the local kids to deal with?"

She remained silent for far too long, as if she were actually considering that. She finally replied, "We need to call the local police."

"We have MI5 across the street. When everything's secure and we have all the information these two can provide, we will wake up Becket's thugs and let them have the prisoners."

I heard silence on the phone again, and finally.

"Fine."

She hung up, and I dragged Number Two back toward Number One. I had to make sure they were both safely restrained before I began to collect their equipment. Then we could load everything up in the car and head out. We weren't going to the MI5 agents, not just yet. I had other plans. In fact, I had only just begun to drive Dee crazy for the night.

Chapter 18

I lay next to the small cliff, upper-body hanging over so I could see the road below. I lowered one of the terrorists' backpacks down to Dee by its strap. She hurried to put it in the trunk of their car as she had with the other items she'd retrieved. I, meanwhile, stood on the rise above her and looked at the three remaining items.

Dee and I had been working rapidly, but it had still been almost twenty minutes since the operation went lethal. I had used most of that time interrogating Number Two, who had been lowered just before the backpack. I hadn't learned much, except that the surviving terrorist had a very low tolerance for pain.

I looked up and down the road. Even on an out-of-the-way stretch of road like this, someone would drive by eventually. We needed to hurry.

I lifted the Russian manufactured Dragunov sniper rifle to my shoulder and stared through the matching Russian night-vision scope, into the building across the road. I had seen two flashes of orange light during the last half hour, and suspected there were at least three men, all smokers, pulling stakeout duty.

From the vantage point the terrorists had selected, they could actually see into the building where the MI5 stakeout team was hiding. In fact, they could see all the way through and out another window to the harbor on the opposite side of the building. Also clearly visible was the head of an MI5 agent, probably watching Rys and his crew on the dock.

If the terrorists were patient and waited for the right moment, they could easily kill two MI5 agents before they even caught wind of what was happening. They would shoot the one looking out the far window first, then the second when he rushed over to see what had happened.

That's why this wasn't fair, that's why I was the one who needed to track these bastards down. Local authorities enforce the law. They have rules, and the terrorists know that. They are fighting a different war. Different rules, different tactics, and an entirely different mentality. Law enforcement eventually realizes what's happening and adapts—too late for the ones who've already died.

The attack on 9/11 happened that way. The London subway bombing happened that way. I had no doubt that this attack, whatever they unloaded from those ships, would happen that way. I had to run this like a combat mission, because that's what our enemy was doing.

To make a point, I removed the magazine and put it in my pocket. I ejected the chambered round, caught it before it fell to the earth, and put it with the magazine. The weapon safe, I then looped the rifle's sling over a forked branch, about six feet off the ground. The barrel swayed a little but finally stopped, pointing at the back of the MI5 agent's head in the window across the road.

They would understand what a rifle pointing at the window meant. They were smart, professional, but were handicapped by their own rules. Maybe this would finally get someone's attention. The rifle secured, all that remained to be lowered was the Cricket bat and the body. There was enough ambient light to see the fluids and tissue that the terrorists' head had left on the bat. I wasn't sure how Dee would react if she saw it, so I wiped it off on the dead guy's shirt.

I moved to the edge and lowered the bat, handle first, to Dee. She reached up to take it carefully, and then lowered it to her side.

"Is that it?"

No, but I didn't know if she could support the weight of Number One. Besides, his head was still oozing gooey green stuff, and I didn't want it dripping on Dee's clothes. We didn't have time for a shower and change of wardrobe.

Out away from the trees, there was enough light to examine the body. I rolled up the sleeves, examining the arms for marks or tattoos. I opened the mouth and looked inside as I spoke to Dee.

"Dee, how many cell phones were in the backpack I just lowered?"

There were none in the backpack, I had them both, but this would require Dee to bury her nose in the bag and search. Meanwhile, I lifted the dead terrorist by his belt. I walked to the ledge, dangled the body with its legs down, and simply tossed the lump of inert flesh over the edge.

It landed on the pavement with a disgusting thud. Dee leapt out from behind the Cortina, startled. Disgusted, she stared at the body, then she looked up at me even more disgusted.

I spread my hands helplessly and whispered, "He jumped, what could I do?"

She glared back, and didn't bother mentioning the phones. She was starting to understand me, which scared me more than any terrorist.

I hopped down, stuffed the lifeless jumper into the trunk and managed to slam the door closed. I looked at Number Two in the backseat, still unconscious and tied up with Number One's bootlaces. Both had been carrying ID, and the names on all their documents matched. Those documents asserted that Number One was Gamal and Number Two was Youssef, but I wasn't sure. I didn't want to get locked into a name, unless I was certain it was correct. Besides, One and Two were easier to say.

I got in the passenger side and looked over to Dee, who didn't look back, and did not look happy. She just sat there, staring ahead, and it took a second for me to realize I hadn't told her where we were going.

I reached into my shirt pocket, pulled out a motel card key, and smiled. "Let's find the MotorLodge."

Dee stared at me a moment longer, then without a word she started driving. She pulled out her prepaid cell phone, pressed a couple of buttons with her free hand, and put the phone to her ear. Seconds later she said, "MotorLodge Suites, Pembroke. Thank you, that would be wonderful."

I could hear the phone ring several times. A female voice finally answered, but I couldn't make out what she was saying.

Dee asked, "Where are you located? Where is that from the Pier House? Thank you."

She looked over, made a u-turn, and hurried back up the road as fast as the car would go. We reached the traffic circle, took the first left again, and one minute later we pulled into the parking lot of a nice, new motel.

Dee glared over at me with a 'now what?' look on her face. I motioned around the parking lot. "Just drive around," I said.

She reluctantly put the car in gear as I retrieved a set of car keys from my pocket. As we drove, I periodically pressed the unlock button on the remote attached to the key chain. In a far corner of the last row tail lights flashed on a dark, older looking minivan with tinted windows.

Dee pulled up behind it and I got out. I looked around, but there was no one else in the parking lot. Only a half-mile away, the dock was a constant vortex of action, loading and unloading all day and all night. Here it seemed like the world enjoyed its rest. I don't think I'd been to a place in Wales quite this quiet.

I mentioned my observation to Dee as she got out. She simply looked around, then stared at me like I was an idiot. "No pubs," she said.

I still had a lot to learn about Wales.

Chastened, I opened the back of the minivan. "We need to transfer our stuff."

Instead of opening the trunk she leaned on it, folding her arms defiantly.

"Now we're stealing a car? When is this going to stop?"

I guess I needed to go easy on her. She was probably exhausted, on top of the stress from what she'd been through over the past two days. I doubted that she fully understood what was at stake; one doesn't encounter hardcore terrorists in civilized company. The people at MI5 probably knew what they were capable of, but for some bizarre reason they thought I was the problem.

I probably was a problem for them, but that was because they didn't have all the facts. Or, maybe they had the wrong facts. Maybe they had lies instead of facts. I began to think about the possibility of disinformation when Dee interrupted, "No comment?"

"About what?"

"How long are we going to go on like this?" She stood and moved half a step forward, gesturing to the car. "I have a dead man in my trunk and another one that's almost dead in my back seat. How is all this helping us learn what happened to my brother?"

"Dee, I know what happened to your brother. We're trying to get the people that did it before they do it to someone else."

She rubbed her eyes as she spoke. "How could you know? You only saw him for a moment."

"I knew what to look for."

She crossed her arms, not satisfied, but I wasn't ready to tell her the truth about what Gareth had suffered.

"Ask the M.E. to examine the wounds on his right side and his left arm again, carefully. When you have her conclusions, I'll be able to explain. Otherwise it's just too complicated."

I hated putting her off, and I hated that she knew I was putting her off.

Dee was a huge benefit to me right now, but I was beginning to wish she were gone; her presence complicated things. I wanted her safe. I knew that was becoming important to me. When it became as important as finishing the mission, there would be problems. But, I couldn't deny that my chances of success were significantly better with her help.

But if anything happened to her . . . I couldn't think about that now.

"We have to hurry. These two are neutralized, but there are probably others staying in this motel."

That got her attention, she looked over her shoulder at the motel entrance then at the semiconscious man in the Cortina. She looked down, thinking a moment, finally crossing her arms defiantly.

Getting a different car was important, but getting moving was more important. We had to get to the Harbor Master's office and find out about that cargo before morning.

I nodded.

"Fine, but think about how long before MI5 figures out what we're driving. They have cameras all over the docks, remember? Either way, we have to go to the Harbor Master."

She weakened, but kept her body in front of the rear hatch. She finally nodded, which was all I really needed right now. I implemented plan B, and hurried over to the driver's side of the van, and opened the door. I then popped the hood and opened the engine compartment. It had a six-cylinder engine with a standard ignition system, which was good. I reached in, popped open the distributor, and pulled out the rotor. I slipped the rotor into my pocket, replaced the distributor cap, and closed the hood.

With the rotor removed, the car would try to start normally.

Everything would sound fine, but no electricity could reach the spark plugs. No spark, no ignition, and the van would be sitting there when we got back, just in case Dee changed her mind.

I walked back to the Cortina and got in. Blackjack hopped into my lap and we both stared at Dee. I hit the remote, locked the doors, and started rubbing Blackjack's belly.

I looked at her again. She hadn't moved at all, so I urged her gently, "We really need to know about the shipment Gareth was watching."

Chapter 19

I never imagined Dee could get so mad, livid, apoplectic. I wasn't even sure those grim modifiers adequately described her red-faced, gasping state of agitation. She stood on her tiptoes until we were nose to nose, and literally spat the words in my face. "Not a fucking chance! Never. No way in hell! Never!"

She had already said never a dozen times, and I had started to believe she was serious. I decided to give it one last try. I was supporting terrorist Number Two with my left arm, and the body of Number One rested peacefully in our car down a set of office stairs. In my right hand, I held the little Makarov 9mm pistol. I grasped it by the base of the grip so that she could see it clearly.

"Dee, you may need this, and it's small and easy to shoot. This guy is a terrorist, and if we meet any of his friends, they'll be terrorists. They'll have guns too. Probably bigger ones."

"Never!" Her face was getting redder, and her freckles were doing the disappearing thing again. "Ne-ver, e-ver," she pronounced syllabically to dramatize her conviction.

Dee spun and knocked mercilessly on the door. After a minute, she knocked again, but still no one came. We stood in front of a second-floor entrance, accessible only by a rickety wood staircase. It had a heavy wooden door worn by years of exposure to salt air and saltier dockworkers. We looked around, there were windows spaced about every three meters apart.

Dee leaned over the rotten wooden railing and tried again to look inside through the window to her left. Finally, she shook her head and looked up at me, "Maybe they're out making rounds. We can wait downstairs."

I held up the pistol again, but this time by the barrel. I pretended to knock on the door with the base of the grip. "Makes a great knocker!"

What she did with her eyes was amazing. She managed to open her eyes wide and squint at the same time. They were like glowering, demon eyes.

I gave up on the gun, but waiting didn't work for me. I cocked my head and asked, "Do you hear something? Someone coming, have your ID ready."

She shifted Blackjack to her other arm and pulled out her ID case. She had insisted we bring him along, that he needed to get out. I didn't object. I got to bring my terrorist, so there was no reason she shouldn't bring her dog.

I cocked my ear pretending to listen and asked, "Is someone coming?"

Case in hand, she leaned left, giving me just enough room. I shifted Number Two in my arms, leaned back and kicked in the door.

Blackjack barked in surprise as wood splintered and the door flung open. It banged on something metal behind it, then rebounded back at us. I moved through the doorway and used the head of my Muslim friend to stop the door from hitting me in the face. He was still unconscious, and didn't mind a bit.

Dee, however, did mind. She set Blackjack down and wheeled to face me. "What the hell are you doing? This is breaking and entering!"

"No, it's a rescue mission. The door was locked, blinds closed, and I heard someone moaning from inside. I was afraid they were in danger. It was our duty to make sure everyone's safe, just like you did in Tenby."

Right on cue, a short, fat, walrus of a man ambled down a hallway and into the room. He really did look like a walrus. His bald head glistened under a thin coat of oil or grease, and he sported a stupid Wilford Brimley mustache. The most disturbing feature, however, was the strange, orange-brown color of his skin.

Dee and I stared as he struggled to fasten his belt, he hadn't even bothered to zip up his pants or button his shirt. It was a disgusting sight. Thinking of Pendergrass in Tenby, I wondered if there was a weight requirement for desk jockeys here on the docks.

And what was that smell?

Dee just stared, not sure how to react. It was our host who got things moving. "What the hell are you doing in here?" he asked.

I thought he looked like Jabba the Hut! No, not fat enough, but only by a cheeseburger or two. Dee shook her head, trying to block out the nightmare in front of her.

He spoke again, "Who are you?"

Dee raised her ID case and let it drop open, "Police."

He looked confused, then startled as I dropped Number Two into a secretary chair behind to an impossibly neat desk. Number Two moaned weakly. I located a roll of tape on the desk. As I taped him to the chair, I addressed our oily host, "We found two men, heavily armed, sneaking up your stairs."

I stopped the tape job and lifted my sweatshirt revealing three semi-automatic pistols. He stepped back, startled. "They were about to break in."

Walrus man blinked, eyes wandering from me to Dee, and eventually to Number Two.

"Where's the other one?"

"In hell, wondering what happened to all those virgins. They may have accomplices. We need to check your video cameras."

He blinked, wide-eyed, trying to catch up with the disturbing events. I needed to hurry him along.

"Now, before they come back!"

He started to turn, but recovered faster than I'd anticipated. He frowned at us and picked up a phone. I rushed over replaced the phone and spun him to face the hallway.

"She's an officer, and we've called for backup. MI5 will be here shortly. Now where are the cameras?"

I looked down at my hand where I'd touched him. It was covered in oil, or grease, or something else. And he did reek, like a fruit stand that had been left in the Texas sun too long.

At that moment, we heard a crashing sound behind us. We spun as Blackjack pulled his head out of the trashcan he'd just overturned, half a sandwich held delicately between his jaws.

Dee rushed over and pulled it from his mouth. She righted the trash can and threw the sandwich back in. Too bad, I was going to ask Blackjack if he'd share.

"No! Come here," Dee said, waving her finger at the dog.

She moved toward the hall, and Blackjack followed. I

spun also, and noticed that Jabba was staring at Blackjack. I needed him to focus on getting me the information I required.

"A drug-sniffing dog, and it looks like he's found something. Are you going to make me take you to jail and then tear this place apart?"

His eyes grew wide, frightened, and he glanced over his shoulder, then back at us. He obviously didn't want us to see down the hall, but being arrested was worse.

"This way!"

He spun quickly and hurried down the hall, eyes on the floor. We followed. Dee led Blackjack, and I pushed the chair with terrorist Number Two taped safely on board.

I looked into the room that Jabba had tried to ignore, disappointed. I'd expected a dancing girl on a chain, a blowup doll, or at least a computer screen with porn. Instead, there was a couch, with a sun lamp on a stand next to it. Colorful bottles of oils and creams lay strewn on the floor around it.

He was working on his tan, and his sickly color probably meant he was using that tan in a bottle crap. I think I'd have preferred porn.

We quickly reached a large room at the end of the hall. The light was off but ghostly shadows from half a dozen video monitors flickered across the wall. He half-turned and gestured around the room. "Here it is."

I was only interested in one video camera's perspective, and not the current one at that. I looked around the room and saw a radio base station, and several walkie-talkies in cradles along one wall. I remembered that Rys had a radio on his belt.

"Jab . . . I mean, what's your name?"

"Matthew Braden, what's yours?"

"Matthew, you know Rys, the new dock supervisor?"

He nodded. "Which camera is his?"

Matthew pointed an oily red flipper at the second screen from the left. I turned to the radios.

"Good. Can you get Rys on the radio? I need him to come up here."

Matthew picked up a cell phone from the tabletop in front of the monitors, and speed dialed his number. We heard the faint sound of ringing, then the call was answered. He spoke to Rys in a whisper, "It's Braden. Come to my office, now."

We couldn't quite make out Rys' angry reply, but Matthew ignored it. "I don't care, come to my office straight away!"

Braden hung up and set the phone down, then looked at Rys' monitor. The foreman was clearly visible on the black-and-white screen, barking orders to another one of the dockworkers.

Matthew began to examine the other screens.

"There may be more terrorists, you said?"

I ignored him and quickly scanned the other monitors. There was nothing significant there, so I turned to Matthew and asked,

"You record these, correct?" He nodded, and I tapped the screen displaying Rys' dock.

"I need you to pull the tapes, disks, whatever else you have from this camera from the last two months."

He shook his head. "We send them to our head office every week; insurance and liability, all that. I only have since Monday."

"I need the recording of two nights ago, then."

He went to a bookshelf across the room and retrieved a large media case. While he searched methodically through pages of DVDs, Dee moved close and whispered angrily, "Thank you so very much for taking over and acting like a fool. I really do enjoy being ignored. What are we looking for?"

I didn't have time for a complete explanation, so I gave her a short one. "Clues."

"What clues would those be?"

"First, Naseem's cargo. Maybe we can get some idea about what it was by examining the video of it being unloaded. If we can estimate the size and weight, it may help. We may find out about the vehicles they used."

Matthew had been eavesdropping, and interrupted, "If I know what ship and which item you're interested in, I can look up exact sizes and weights from the manifest."

Dee smiled at him pleasantly. "That's a wonderful idea, you're so clever."

He grinned stupidly back, and held up a DVD.

"This is the one from two nights ago," he nodded eagerly. "Shall I queue it up?"

Dee smiled again, even sweeter. I had no doubt that the manipulation gene is not in the Y chromosome. Matthew didn't care. He seemed more than eager to help Dee. Before long, he would want a collar to match Blackjack's.

The Harbor Master fumbled the disk into a player on the table and pressed play. A tiny screen came to life, showing a barely adequate view of the dock. He looked up at Dee, smiling. "Here it is, what time to you want to see?"

Dee looked at me. I shrugged and looked at the door, which had just opened. I called out, "Rys?"

"What do you need?" Rys did not sound happy.

"Back here!" I called back.

Rys strode down the hall. Blackjack growled, but Dee had him sit. As Rys reached the security office, he saw me and smirked.

"Not surprised to see you again."

He looked around the room, smiling when he saw Dee. He suddenly recoiled as Matthew, who had maintained his greasy, half-naked splendor, stood up from the screen and waved.

Finally, Rys saw Number Two and whistled in surprise. He took a step closer, "What have we got here?"

I gave him the story about stopping the terrorists, and Rys was duly impressed. I then asked him if he would help us find the video showing Naseem's cargo. Rys nodded and went to the monitor.

He took the remote from Matthew, wiping it gingerly on his shirt. He hit fast forward, and in less than a minute the screen displayed a small freighter at the dock. It looked old but well maintained. In fact, it looked like it had just been painted. I wondered what it looked like before. I noticed the ship's name, probably as new as the paint, written in bold white Arabic characters. I pointed to it on the screen. Dee leaned closer and read it before I could: "Atqaa Allah."

I looked at her, surprised. She frowned.

"I grew up in the Middle East, just like Gareth. In fact, my Arabic is better than his."

She turned back to the screen and translated, "It means 'Fear Allah.' It's usually said as a warning to sinners and infidels. Odd name for a ship."

I agreed. Rys spoke up, bending over to examine the video screen.

"The orders said it was 'The Fear of God.' Sounded a bit off to me."

Matthew ambled at maximum speed to the other side of the room and buried himself in a file cabinet. I looked over Rys' shoulder.

"I bet everything about that ship was a bit off. That probably wasn't its name a month ago."

Rys stood and interrupted.

"There's the first crate."

He pointed at the screen, where a crane lowered a large box to the dock. I stared a moment longer, then commented to no one in particular, "I wish we knew what was inside that crate."

Rys spoke first. "That one seemed to spook Naseem. He was muttering something about dead people."

"Electronics!"

We turned to look at Matthew, who had thankfully buttoned his shirt. I hoped his zipper would be next. He triumphantly waved a handful of papers and explained, "This is the manifest for The Fear. Two crates, different sizes and weights, both containing electronics."

Rys frowned, "There were half a dozen crates."

Then Matthew frowned, "Only two on the manifest."

Four crates were missing, and presumed deadly.

Dee smiled at the Harbor Master again. "That's excellent, Matthew, can we have copies of the ones on file?"

He smiled back dumbly, but shook his head.

"I can't let you copy them."

Dee frowned sadly, almost pouting. Matthew looked like a little boy who just had his birthday cancelled. He took a tentative step forward. "I can let you look at them."

Dee nodded, reached into her bag and pulled out a notepad, and took the papers from Matthew; careful to avoid the grease stains. She sat at a desk and began copying.

I smiled at Braden. "Can you make screen captures to get still pictures from the video?"

He nodded and confirmed, "Digital and paper."

"Please print out pictures of each of the crates. Do you have Email?"

He nodded again.

"Send copies to this e-mail address."

I wrote down an e-mail address and turned to Rys. There were more details left to dispose of, one living and the other dead. And I didn't want to forget about the sniper rifle still hanging in a tree. I asked Rys for his help, he agreed. I explained what I needed. It took a minute, but eventually he nodded, pulled the radio from his belt and began barking out orders.

I moved to look over Dee's shoulder as she wrote. She was copying down way more information than I wanted. I was in a hurry, but took a deep breath and let her finish.

When she was done, I suggested. "Ask Rys to estimate the dimensions and weights of the other crates."

She went to Rys, and soon had a good estimate of the dimensions and weight for the remaining four crates, which is what I really needed. If we needed to, we could now estimate the size of the vehicle or vehicles required to move them, and could adequately describe what we were looking for as we searched. We had a chance. I was pretty sure all of the other details on the manifest were false.

Dee closed her notepad and dropped it into her bag. She smiled and handed the papers back to Braden. "Thank you, Matthew."

I helped her to her feet and pointed her toward the door. "Yeah, thanks, but we have to go."

Braden's smile became confusion as he looked at Number Two, who looked more alert and moaned softly through his gag.

"What about this bugger?"

Dee looked at me earnestly as she said, "We have to get him medical attention. And he must be turned over to proper authorities. We can't just leave him here."

I smiled, "It's being handled."

I walked over to Rys, who carefully watched the view

of his dock. He looked up, grinned, then stepped aside and nodded.

"Almost done."

We crowded around the screen and stared. A large crate dangled in front of the ship being unloaded. Behind it, hidden from view, someone in a lift bucket was working on the side of the ship.

I looked at Rys.

"I need you to wait downstairs with the Beeb. I'll help you roll him down."

Rys frowned. "Why can't I just wait in here?"

"He's got a friend down there, a dead one who doesn't smell too good. I'd rather not bring him up here."

Matthew looked stricken, shaking his head emphatically.

I went on, "I have to keep them together; they're a matched set. I really don't think Matthew is up to it by himself."

Rys frowned, and Matthew looked like he was about to have a calf—I think that's what walrus babies are called. Pup, maybe?

Matthew looked at Rys imploringly, and Rys relented. "This one's not going to keel over on me, right?"

I shook my head. "It's nothing fatal, if he wakes up just try twisting his broken arm around a couple of times, he will probably pass right out. Now, can you have someone fetch the MI5 agents watching your dock, I told you where they were. Have them come to the Harbor Master's office immediately."

Rys smiled slyly and said, "I can do better than that."

He spoke into his radio, and seconds later a crane swung the massive crate away from the side of the ship. It revealed a man with a large brush, painting a message on the side of the ship in large white block letters. It read, 'MI5

Agents. Terrorists in the Harbor Master's office. Hurry."

I smiled and patted Rys on the shoulder, "Very nicely done!" I then urged Dee toward the front door. We had to get moving.

Chapter 20

I gently guided Dee toward the front of the office, then grabbed Number Two and rolled him toward the door. "Blackjack come."

Dee was not happy. "We need to ask him questions, find out what he knows. Where are we supposed to go next?"

I pushed faster, not wanting to answer. I also needed to make sure that Rys or Jabba didn't hear anything they shouldn't.

We reached the front door, and I pushed it over the threshold and onto the top landing. The wind was gentle, bringing the fresh salt air into my lungs. It was fantastic compared to the reek of the Walrus den. I hoped the toxic air inside hadn't caused any permanent lung damage, though I was sure they were at least three shades darker from all the tanning potions in the air.

Rys and I grabbed the chair and muscled it awkwardly down the stairs. The weak overhead light above the stairway made it hard to see, and Rys missed a step and almost dropped the chair.

Number Two didn't like this and began to moan, his head moving back and forth slowly. We set the chair on a landing next to the stairway. Rys looked at the prisoner nervously, then skeptically at me.

"What if he wakes up?" he asked.

I looked around. I noticed the bushes along the wall had a border of large stones set around them to keep the grass out.

"If he wakes up, just rock him to sleep." I grabbed a stone about the size of a grapefruit and tossed it to Rys. "That rock should work."

Dee and Blackjack reached the bottom of the stairs. She scowled at me but didn't comment. I think Blackjack liked my idea, since he hopped up and put his front paws on my leg. At the top of the stairs, I saw Jabba peering over the rickety railing. When he saw me look at him, he hurried back inside.

I had no doubt he intended to call the police, so again we needed to hurry. I popped the trunk of the Cortina, retrieved Number One's body, and dumped it unceremoniously in front of Number Two.

Rys looked aghast, but I didn't have time to explain. Once it got light out, everything became more difficult. As I got in the car, I shouted back, "When MI5 gets here, tell them these two were hiding on the hill behind the warehouse where they're watching the docks. These guys were going to kill them. There's a sniper rifle hanging in a tree behind the building they were in with a clear shot of their window. They need to get it before anyone else does. Can you remember all that?"

Rys thought about it, then nodded. He obviously didn't like having to babysit terrorists, especially since one of them was dead. He spread his hands and said, "You're seriously not going to leave me like this."

"Sorry, I think these guys came from Liverpool. We need to get there as soon as possible and follow up."

We got in the car. I turned to Dee and whispered, "We need to get back to the motel!"

She sped off as Blackjack assumed the position, curled up in my lap. Dee scowled, glared actually, clearly not enjoying our success as much as Blackjack and I.

"What made you say they're from Liverpool?"

I reached into my sweatshirt pocket and pulled out a stack of cards, documents and bills. I showed her the top one, a driver's license.

"The live one, Gamal, was from Liverpool. Besides, I'd rather have them looking for us in Liverpool than where we're going."

Only minutes later, we saw the motel ahead. Dee was tired of my paranoia, but she still stopped outside the parking lot and let me out as I requested. I moved to a position where I could observe the van, and most of the motel at the same time.

Per my instructions, Dee stopped behind the van, counted to ten slowly, then drove around the lot. If anyone was watching, they would have begun to move toward Dee. I would make sure they never reached her if they tried.

I decided we were safe. If there were others inside, they would probably be in the middle of the Fajr, their morning prayer. I felt confident that we had enough time to get away without being discovered.

Dee pulled into a parking spot two down from the van. Before she could get out, I bent and looked in the window. "Open the trunk, then get ready to leave. Follow me, I'll drive the van."

I strode to the passenger side and retrieved Blackjack, the papers I'd gotten from Matthew, and Gareth's album. I then put them in the back of the van, noticed a small can of Sprite under the seat, and tossed it into the front.

Dee watched impatiently as I rushed back to the open trunk of our car, grabbed our remaining baggage, and carried it to the van. Everything stowed quickly inside. I noticed that Blackjack had scampered forward, taking up a position on the console between the front seats. He looked back asking, 'What's taking you so long?'

Blackjack barked encouragement as I popped open the hood, replaced the rotor, and closed the hood back up. We both stared out the rear window as we backed out. With some trepidation, and even more concentration, I began my British driving adventure.

The vehicle fought against my natural instincts as it inched out of the motel parking lot and down the street. A few meters down the road, we turned right and followed the road to the round Criterion Corner where several roads met.

It was exciting, and just a little scary, to drive around the large green traffic hazard. Even more so because it was light, and there were now cars on the road. I probably drove like I had just been thrown out of a pub, because I weaved, slowed and sped up at random. I managed to circumnavigate the traffic circle and turn onto Pier Road. Seconds later, I reached the parking lot of what indeed turned out to be a grocery store.

There were now a few cars at the far end of the lot, probably employees. We pulled into an open spot and waited, engine running. Dee picked a spot between two other vehicles and turned off her engine. The Cortina wouldn't be discovered for days. By then it wouldn't matter if everyone knew we'd been there.

I crawled over Blackjack and the console, into the passenger seat of the van. Dee hurried into the driver's seat and backed out as I congratulated myself.

"Miracles happen. I can drive here."

"Miracles indeed!"

She looked around the lot, put the van in drive, and headed toward the exit. She smiled over at me. The smile made her look so nice that what she said almost escaped me.

"Watching you struggle to make the circle, I said a prayer for us all, my first prayer in over a dozen years. That certainly qualifies as a miracle."

We smiled at each other, enjoying the moment. But it was only for a moment, and as we moved down the street, my mind went back to our dilemma. There was so little time, and so many decisions to be made.

I looked over at Dee, who rubbed her eyes wearily.

"We're making progress! I think we should head back toward Swansea while I make a few calls."

She shook her head slowly and glanced at me through the corner of her eye.

"I think you need to sit back, maybe sleep a bit, because I decide what happens next. I haven't slept in forever, and poor Blackjack is getting stressed."

Blackjack looked up at the mention of his name. He glanced at Dee, then turned to stare at me with his big, brown eyes. Two against one, no fair.

We didn't really have time to rest, but she was almost out of it. It was time to make a point though. We were getting closer. I just wished I knew to what. I nodded at the black trash bin sitting between the seats. It was stuffed with papers, wrappers, and other disgusting refuse from a life of terror.

"I bet these guys like Toblerone chocolates."

Dee looked at me like I was an idiot, but I simply smiled back. "Go ahead, check."

She stared at me a moment longer, then shook her head in disgust and resumed driving. I bent down and began to fish through the refuse. At the bottom of the bin, I retrieved the yellow wrapper of the suspect confection.

Dee looked over, unimpressed, as my hand displayed its trophy. "So what? They like chocolate."

Reaching behind my seat for the eight-ounce Sprite can that soon joined the candy wrapper on the console, she inspected my evidence, but failed to make the connection.

"These were the people that searched your brother's hotel room." Her eyes went just a little wider, and she understood what the trash on the dash meant. She turned back to her driving, but she looked a little more energetic, and significantly more focused on our mission. We were getting closer. And I was, in fact, getting a little tired.

My left hand searched the side of my seat, but didn't find a lever to recline the seat back. Denied again.

The need to keep driving toward Swansea kept prodding me. I looked over at Dee, but she looked exhausted. A new problem began to occupy my mind, how would I find out who killed Gareth, and keep Dee safe at the same time? Maybe I could convince her to go back to her police friends. Brian might be able to help me from here. It would be life or death from now on, and Brian was used to it.

"Dee, the people chasing us are very dangerous."

"I know what I'm doing."

Her eyes stared at the road ahead, ignoring me. Her thoughts were clearly somewhere else. If she were with Gareth in her mind, I hoped it was at a happier time and place.

I climbed into the back of the van, and managed to find a lever that reclined the bench seat there. I took off my sweatshirt and rolled it up to use as a pillow, then curled up and tried to get comfortable.

My eyes faced the rear, away from the light coming in through the front windshield. It only took me a few seconds to drop off, but before I did, I felt Blackjack hop onto the seat and curl up in the space behind my bent knees. He squirmed and twisted to get comfortable, then dropped his head to my leg to sleep.

I'd had dogs since I was a baby, on a ranch they're a necessity. We had dogs on the Eagle, Globe and Angus, working dogs that I really loved. Mutt and Jeff were my cattle dogs, and Slick Willey was my retriever. They were colleagues. We all worked together.

I'd never had a dog that was just a friend, a buddy. Blackjack's only job was to be there. He'd been there for Gareth. He would be there for Dee, and I got the impression he would be there any time I needed him as well. As my mind slipped into the comfort of sleep, I realized that I could get used to having a buddy.

Chapter 21

I woke up, instantly alert. Something was wrong.

It took only a second to realize that the van's engine was still running, but the vehicle was stationary. My internal clock said that over half an hour passed since we pulled over. Dee had grabbed Blackjack, she said they needed to get out and do doggie things. Half an hour wasn't long enough to become alarmed, but definitely long enough to become alert.

I heard the latch of the rear hatch door click. Someone started to open the rear door. I rolled off the bench, retrieving Number One's Sig 40 caliber from my waistband as I fell.

The rough carpet of the van floor scraped my arm as I aimed under the seat at a space between Dee's computer case and my bag. It was only a few inches, but enough for a clean shot. The problem would be getting a positive ID, though if they started shooting first it would simplify things considerably. The door flew up, and Blackjack bounded over the bags and onto my makeshift bed. He looked down at me and barked sharply, a kind of 'get your ass in gear' kind of yelp. So, I got my ass in gear.

I sat, slid open the side door and looked around. The van was parked in front of a very well kept, two-story house, surrounded by a large green yard. The yard was surrounded by fields, with a barn and several outbuildings off to the left.

I looked back at the house, at a sign hanging off the front porch, but couldn't make out what it said. Nothing in my field of vision posed a threat, except maybe the old lady tending to her rose bushes across the street, who was glaring at Blackjack. She appeared decidedly unhappy to have a four-legged visitor in the neighborhood.

I would have liked to recon the area first, but if Blackjack said it was OK, then I could relax a little. We hopped out and walked to the rear of the vehicle where Dee was unloading our bags. From here I could read the sign over the porch. The lettering was in Old English and read "The Good Knight Bed and Breakfast." It appeared that Dee planned on staying here a while, my plan involved moving, finding and kicking ass. I looked at Dee, who looked almost dead on her feet, and decided to give her plan a try. Before she could pick up her computer, I put my hand on her arm and asked, "How did you pay for this?"

"Cash."

Right answer. If she'd used a credit card, MI5 could trace us. However, paying with cash had its own problems. I needed more info. "That didn't seem suspicious?"

"Not when I explained why I didn't want to use a credit card."

She smiled at my look of concern, then with a smug expression she picked up her computer and overnight bags and walked toward the steps to the front porch. I grabbed my duffle, adjusted my shirt to conceal the guns in my waistband, and hurried to follow.

"What did you tell them?"

She looked over her shoulder with a wicked little smile.

"That we're on vacation, touring Wales. That you're married, and you don't want your wife to know about me. We pay cash, so there won't be any records. Apparently, it happens all the time."

Great idea. I wondered if this trick had worked for her before.

We walked up a small path toward the old two-story block building. It was light blue with the porch and trim a slightly darker shade of blue. One of the upstairs windows stood open, and white sheer curtains waved to us from inside.

We climbed three concrete steps to a polished concrete porch. Dee opened the door without knocking and we entered, walking down a long, narrow entry. On the left was a small sitting area, where a small woman sat watching TV. She had grey hair and wore an orange-flowered dress. She waved without looking, not wanting to miss a moment of the obnoxious game show on the screen.

On the right was a beautiful dining room that literally grabbed my attention. On the back wall stood an enormous fireplace with an intricately carved mantle around it, figurines of knights and medieval soldiers battling across the top. However, the most amazing feature was the large table and chairs in the center of the room.

The antique looking chairs were a dark, heavily lacquered wood with high backs. A delicately carved dragon perched on the top of each chair back with red flames blazing from gaping jaws. The center of the equally ancient table held the beautifully inlaid figure of a Welsh dragon. It was strikingly vivid, from the black of its raised talon claw to the curved, crimson, arrow-point tail behind.

I'm not into antiques at all, but I still found the room to be amazing.

"Get a move on!"

I looked ahead. Dee beckoned to me from the second step of the staircase leading up. I pulled myself away and followed.

We went up the stairs to a landing, and the bathroom welcomed us with open doors. I saw a large iron tub with a white plastic curtain hanging like a halo above it. To our right ran a landing with four white-wooden doors along its length. Dee entered the landing and turned right, then walked to the last door. This room would face the front of the building, which meant we could watch the narrow street in front of our lodgings.

The door was unlocked, and we entered. Our room measured about ten square meters, with a large metal-framed bed against the far wall, and small curtained windows to each side of the bed. Dee set Blackjack down. He hopped up onto the bed and started sniffing around. Apparently, he'd also seen the news specials on hotel room beds. I think every hotel room should come with a black light for sheet inspection.

Against the wall to our left, I noticed a large, heavy dresser, and next to that, a small fireplace. I saw a wardrobe against the right wall, and behind that stood a worktable and three chairs. To my utter delight, I saw a blue Ethernet cable wrapped around a wrought-iron lamp on top. They had Internet, which would make our lives much simpler – and safer.

We entered and closed the door. The room had dull, hardwood floors, which I liked; the rest of the room, not so much. There were area carpets on each side of the bed, and a large Persian one in the open area between the door and the metal footboard of the bed.

Nothing in the room matched. The carpets by the bed were floral prints, which clashed nicely with the red and black checkerboard pattern on the bedspread. The pillows were fluorescent green, orange and blue.

I couldn't see any pattern or style to the décor whatsoever, and thank god there were no paint-by-number landscapes on the wall. I had to assume the decorator was blind, or that they'd hired a high-priced professional to screw things up correctly.

Dee looked around and nodded. "This is nice."

Could have fooled me.

She looked behind us, and on a chair by the door were towels and washcloths. I also noticed two heavy white bathrobes hanging on the back of the door. Dee grabbed a robe and walked to the wardrobe. She opened the right hand door and stood behind it, her back to me. She draped the bathrobe over her shoulders and began to twist and squirm.

Every few seconds an article of clothing would fly out from inside the robe and land on the bed. It was amazing, how did she do that? In a matter of seconds, her blouse, slacks, and socks lay in a single pile on the bed. Her undershirt landed on the bed, and I turned away for reasons of modesty.

I turned to my left and continued my examination of the furnishings. I had failed to notice the large mirror over the dresser before, but I couldn't fail to notice that Dee's squirming reflection was visible there now, in spectacularly living color.

She removed her bra and turned toward the bed to toss it to the pile of her other clothing. The robe was open, and her body briefly visible as her first item of underwear landed precariously on the edge of the bed.

She was beautiful. Her creamy-white   skin almost

glowed, and I noticed the only tan lines were on her arms and neck. Her breasts were not large, but were amazingly well formed, and prominently visible as she bent forward to remove her panties.

At this point, I blinked my way back from Fantasyland and turned around to face the door. I started to feel a little guilty about my voyeuristic mirror experience. It felt more like an art lover than a Peeping Tom. I felt no lust, only appreciation.

Maybe just a little lust, but only a little.

The panties must have hit the pile, since I heard the wardrobe door close. I turned to find Dee, the robe tightly around her, walking to the foot of the bed. She picked up a small bag with an enormous shoulder strap, which she hung dramatically over her left shoulder.

She walked to the door, grasped the handle, then looked up at me coolly. "I'm going to take a bath. Stay here, and out of trouble, until I decide to come back." She looked at Blackjack who had curled up on her discarded apparel. "Both of you."

I don't claim to be smart, buy my instinct for self-preservation seemed to be making a comeback. I nodded my intention to comply.

Without another word, she took a step out, but stopped abruptly and looked back. "And the bed is mine."

She strode out and closed the door behind her. I heard her footfalls move toward the bathroom, then that door also closed.

I looked at Blackjack, whose head rested on one of Dee's socks. He looked at me from the corner of his eyes, then closed them and pretended to be asleep. He was going to enjoy our time here, and the bed. Too bad about me.

Some buddy.

I set the bags I was still carrying down by the desk. I'd

had a couple hours of sleep and would be fine for a while. I had other things to do.

First I examined the room, there wasn't much there. I opened the wardrobe and found a few wooden hangers on the right side. On the back of the door hung an iron and ironing board, which was a nice, but useless touch. The drawers on the left side were all empty, as were the desk drawers, not even any stationary. Across the room, I checked the drawers of the dresser. They were empty except the bottom one, which had a small book entitled The History of Farting in the back right corner. Was this supposed to replace the Bible?

Oriented and reasonably sure the room was safe, I grabbed Number One's bag and set it on the desk. I unzipped it and started removing the items I thought we might need. I soon had the phones, keys, credit card and money, driver's licenses and even some receipts spread out on the desk in front of me.

I now had time to examine them in detail. I started with the licenses. Both appeared to be genuine, no sign they had been altered. Both men, Gamal Rifaat and Youssef Haddari (Number One and Number Two), appeared to be from Liverpool. The late Mr. Rifaat had been in command. The Sig Sauer P250 he had been carrying was a very nice weapon, much better than the still functional military surplus Makarov carried by Youssef. Furthermore, Gamal had all the receipts. Can terrorists in Britain deduct mayhem from their taxes? Or, maybe they're on an expense account.

Gamal carried the best weaponry and paid all the bills, which meant he was in command. So, I started with his phone. I had taken the batteries out of both phones. I couldn't take a chance on them being traced or hacked. I now put the battery in Gamal's phone and waited for it to boot. Once it was active, I searched through the menus and put it into airplane mode, which supposedly turned off the radio. I wasn't an expert but didn't want to bet my life on anything, so I gave myself a two-minute time limit.

I first went through the address book. It was empty. I looked at the call history and found just one entry there, a call made only a few hours before I rearranged the contents of his cranium. I checked the minute usage, which was at almost two hundred for the month. If the phone had been used frequently, and there was no history, then Gamal had been deleting it on a regular basis. I guess he didn't have time to delete this one.

I pulled the battery from Gamal's phone and inserted it into Youssef's. I'll make it simple and just call him Joe.

This phone was the same, pay-as-you-go model. Joe didn't have an address book either, but fortunately he didn't bother to delete his call history. Unfortunately, all his calls were to Gamal, confirming that Gamal was in command. I pulled the battery from Joe's phone and looked at the receipts.

I wanted to find out where they'd been. There were several, but they were all from the Pembroke area, including his hotel receipt. They occupied rooms 213 and 215, and the receipt showed four guests. There were at least two others in the hotel, we had been lucky.

The keys didn't tell me much, an apartment or house key and a couple to desks, cabinets or padlocks. Unless I could visit his house and office, I would never know. Gamal had a respectable wad of cash, and I was about to count their money when Dee entered.

Wow, that was fast.

She wore only a white T-shirt and shorts. The first thing I noticed was that the warm water must have brought out the Freckles. She now had as many on her legs as on her face. All right, that was the second thing. First, I observed that Dee was not wearing a bra, and that she appeared to have a much greater lung capacity than I'd previously estimated from her reflected glory.

I dropped my gaze to her midsection. She had a slender waist, which I'd already established in my mind. Her abs appeared to be flat and firm. I looked down her body and noticed her legs again; even with the red spots, they were very attractive. When all else fails, look them in the eye; which I finally managed to do. I looked up at her sparkling green eyes, and found them glaring at me. I grabbed my duffle and walked toward the door.

"My turn."

She wrinkled her nose, but she may have been joking this time.

"About bloody time, Blackjack was beginning to complain."

Blackjack's eyes opened at the mention of his name, and he glanced over. He looked fine, so I grabbed the other robe and left the room. A good shower could be as refreshing as a nap.

* * *

Dressed only in running shorts under the robe, I returned to the room. I had washed out my clothes in the sink and had them draped over my left arm. They were still wet, but I could iron them dry in the room. As far as dressing, maybe I could try the robe thing that Dee did. I decided against that, I could hurt myself— pull a muscle or twist a knee.

Dee was at the desk, staring at her computer. The Ethernet cable trailed from her computer to the wall, so apparently we had Internet. Excellent! She glanced up, and

I smiled. I wanted to get on her machine and find out if Ham had anything for me from Langley. Before I could ask, she returned to the meticulous examination of something on her screen.

I walked over to the wardrobe to retrieve the iron and board. As I walked by, she lowered the lid on her laptop to make sure I couldn't see what she was reading.

Great, still keeping secrets.

I set my clothes on a shelf in the wardrobe, then set up the board and plugged in the iron. While it was heating up, I looked around the room for the TV. Intel is important, so I needed to check the news, just in case I was on it. I was also interested in if, and how, the death and capture of two terrorists at the port of Pembroke would be reported.

I moved to the center of the room and looked around. I couldn't see a TV, just an old clock radio that looked like it had been built from vacuum tubes and paper clips. The hands on the clock dial read six-thirty, but that was probably because they were broken and hanging limply down.

I finally vocalized my dismay, "There's no TV?"

Dee spoke without looking up, "People don't come here to watch the tube."

I tried to look over her shoulder at the computer. "No, apparently they come here for the online shopping."

Her only reaction was to lower the display, so I went back to the ironing board. I pulled my soggy undershirt from the wardrobe and spread it out on the board.

Minutes later, my white T-shirt was dry and looking sharp.

I held it up and tried to figure out how I could put it on without taking off the robe. I came to the sudden realization that Dee must be double jointed. I squirmed and twisted, just like she did, but all I managed to do was push the robe off my shoulders.

Shit!

I held the shirt out in front of me, and grabbed it by the bottom. Before I could pull it over my head, I heard Dee stand and walk toward me. She whispered, "My god!"

I spun around to see what had startled her, but she just stood there, staring at me. After a moment, she moved closer and examined my chest. She reached gently out, touched my arm, and spun me slowly back around. She removed my robe and set it on the bed. I then felt her touching my back, tracing one of the scars.

Her voice subdued, she commented almost to herself, "There are so many."

"Souvenirs! After the fifth one, I wished I started collecting shot glasses instead of just getting shot."

That usually got at least a polite chuckle, but Dee just gently touched the long straight scar on my right shoulder blade.

"How did you get this?"

"Machete. I was in a friendly West African nation that wasn't as friendly as we were led to believe. The local Army commander I was there to train had his own agenda."

I looked over my shoulder as Dee took a small step back.

"All those little ones?"

"A Taliban mortar attack while we were sleeping. The first shell hit in the tent next to mine. I was lucky."

She stared a moment longer, then spun me around again, staring at me like I was an alien creature with scales instead of skin. Finally, she stepped back to examine my lower body, which was just as scarred as the upper.

"So many."

"Some of my buddies don't have arms or legs to get scarred. Every day, I thank God I've been blessed."

She nodded, whispering, "More than Gareth, way more."

I was about to make a smart-ass comment about officers and desks, but that wouldn't be right—for Dee or for Gareth. She looked at my abs and chest.

"You're in such amazing shape, don't the scars—the injuries— you know, make it difficult?"

I was starting to feel like one of those frogs on the dissection table.

"Probably." I stepped back and started examining her. "Is it my turn?"

She turned red and rushed to sit at the desk and started examining the items I'd left there. She pointed at the phones. "Anything interesting here?"

I shook my head and picked up Gamal's phone.

"That phone," I pointed to Joe's, "has only been used to call this one. The call history on this phone has just the one number in it, an incoming call."

"What number, let me see. Maybe I'll recognize where the call was made from."

I shrugged, picked up the battery, and put it back into the phone. We waited patiently for the screen to light up and the phone to become active. I pulled up the phone history and showed it to Dee. She grabbed a pen from her purse and began to jot down the number.

Once she had the number recorded, she handed the phone back to me. I started to take off the back so I could remove the battery, when it started to buzz. I looked at the display, there was an incoming call from that same number as before.

Dee and I looked at the phone, then at each other. Things were looking up, now we could just ask who it belonged to.

Chapter 22

Through the Bluetooth headset he was wearing, Maliki heard the cell phone ring, meaning that Gamal may finally answer.

Maliki paced the dimly lit room, staring down at his phone's tiny display as it blinked in time with the annoying buzz in his ear. Still, there was no answering click on the receiving end of this call.

He looked back at the table where the last of his unwitting host's Cohiba Behike cigars was burning. He wished the General were there now, watching the five-hundred-dollar cigar disappear into savory smoke. Maliki smiled and wondered, had the cigar simply become the world's most expensive incense?

Besides, Maliki gave his host the box of cigars as a gift; a re-gift, actually. Raul Castro had personally given him three boxes a few years ago, one of which ended up in his hands now.

Maliki reached toward the phone to hang up, but was startled to have it answered before going to voicemail.

Instead of hearing Gamal's gruff voice, someone else responded.

"Kandahar Marriott, home of the Taliban special. Survive three nights and the fourth is free. How may we help you?"

It took a moment for Maliki to analyze this new information and understand what was happening. The voice was American, but he had certainly called Gamal's phone. This must be Deacon, but how was this possible? Maliki hesitated a moment longer, then asked with forced congeniality, "I would like to speak with one of your guests, a Mr. Gamal, is he available?"

Maliki walked to the table and slid a photograph from a stack of papers. One showed Sergeant Deacon speaking with a dirty, greasy man next to a wrecker as Major Jones' car was being retrieved. The other was of Detective Jones, also at the accident scene, standing with a group of her colleagues. She must be a strong woman to function that well under such stress. She was certainly a beautiful one. He listened again, aware that Travis had been speaking.

"Hello?" The voice said, "who shall I say is calling?"

"I am a friend of Mr. Gamal's."

"Then I'm terribly sorry, sir, there was a horrible Cricket accident and Mr. Gamal seems to have lost his head. Where would you like it sent if we find it?"

Maliki frowned. Gamal very well could be dead, which was unfortunate. And Deacon was still alive, which was unacceptable. Maliki needed more information, and decided to continue the American's little game.

"Just hold onto it for me, Mr. Deacon, I'll send someone to pick it up."

"I would much prefer giving it to you personally, along with a complimentary visit to our world-famous waterboard spa."

"That is so very tempting, but I must sadly decline. Now if you will excuse me, I have other calls to make."

Maliki was about to disconnect, but Deacon said something to Maliki that demanded his attention.

"I know what you're doing, Gamal told us everything."

Gamal didn't know everything. No one did but himself. And Maliki was sure that Gamal would have died before revealing the few details that he actually knew, but it was always best to be cautious.

"Gamal couldn't tell you much. In fact, he was there on vacation with friends. They were planning on taking the ferry to Ireland in the morning."

"The ones at the MotorLodge? They will need to take a cab to the ferry, then. And they shouldn't wait for Youssef, either."

Maliki frowned, how did this man know so much? Gamal and Youssef were well-trained and extremely cautious. Maybe he was simply guessing. However, he did know their vehicle had disappeared. If Gamal were indeed dead, maybe this Deacon character had their van. That would be incredibly good luck.

"Is Youssef dead as well?"

"No, but I don't think he's feeling well, a bad break if you ask me. He had the same kind of accident as Gamal, but he'll live. I made sure the MI5 agents they were watching got him prompt medical attention. Prompt-ish, anyway."

Maliki controlled his growing anger. The American did know too much. Maliki remained silent; he would need to be cautious with this Marine. He would let him talk in hopes of discovering more of what he knew.

Deacon continued, "You must have something really big planned if you're willing to kill MI5 agents to cover it up, I can't wait to find out what it is."

"I will be happy to show you! Tell me where you are, and I'll send my chauffeur to pick you up." Maliki remembered the surveillance pictures from the hotel and accident scene. "And if that lovely policewoman is with you, by all means bring her along. The more the merrier, isn't that what you Americans like to say?"

Maliki waited for an answer, but none came. The woman must be with him. Maliki had become a master at Psychological Warfare, and knew just how to press his new advantage.

"Please pass along my condolences to Sergeant Jones, I was deeply saddened to learn about her brother. It seems that accidents happen quite frequently these days. I understand Major Jones was a friend of yours as well. I regret that I didn't have more time to share with him the full extent of my hospitality, as I was able to do with your Lieutenant Ibarra back in Pakistan."

Again Sergeant Deacon remained silent, but Maliki didn't believe he had provoked the man so much that he would do something rash. Finally, the American spoke, "Yes, there does seem to be a lot of accidents happening these days. You should probably be careful."

"I am always careful, Sergeant Deacon, but you already know that."

This conversation had been extremely valuable, and the sooner Maliki contacted the right people the sooner this problem could be eliminated. In fact, that Detective Jones may be of value in creating a diversion. Yes, he could see a number of interesting possibilities.

"I'm sorry Mister Deacon; I have matters that require my immediate attention. Are you sure that you won't accept my invitation for a visit?"

"I'm sorry, no. I have a couple of things to do myself. And you will be careful, right? I wouldn't want you to have an accident before we've had a chance to meet."

"I promise, if we do meet, I will be in perfect health. Goodbye Sergeant."

Maliki hung up and immediately turned off the phone. He opened the back, removed the battery and the SIM card, then set it on top of the cigar. He took a new card from a small case he had in his pocket and inserted it into the phone. Once the battery and back had been replaced, Maliki made another call.

"Assad, take your brother and go to the MotorLodge in Pembroke. Pick up the men staying in room 213 and then activate the tracking device in Gamal's van. Find the people who took it and bring them to me. You should assume they are armed, but I want them alive. I have plans for them."

Maliki felt he could now move on. The LoJack device installed in the van would lead Assad and his team to Sergeant Deacon and his lovely companion. The two would be no match for his men, since their arrival would be a surprise. But then again, the Marine had proven very resourcefully and maddeningly capable.

Maliki would call Assad later and stress that they were to be taken alive; and unharmed—if possible.

Maliki first had other calls to make; he should begin damage control procedures immediately. The information provided by the stupid American would actually make things simpler for him. Maliki was an unsurpassed master of manipulation, both of people and of information.

Very soon, everyone in the entire world would know that.

He retrieved a much more expensive cell phone from the case on his belt. He scrolled down the recent call list and redialed a number. He wanted to make sure that Gamal's body was properly cared for, and that Youssef received medical attention.

Maliki looked at his watch as the phone rang through the headset, Maliki smiled. He held up the photos of Travis and the woman.

"You only have a few hours left, Sergeant Deacon. With such a beautiful woman at your disposal, I hope you will make good use of your time."

This was almost too easy. He stared at the photo of the red-haired female, such a waste.

Chapter 23

I heard Maliki hang up, and the line went dead. My body went through the process of removing the phone's battery on its own while my mind processed the new information it had just received. So far, my mind was not pleased with the results, and my body still fumbled with the tiny grey square of electricity.

Abdul al Maliki was in Wales. What the hell was going on?

That could not be a coincidence, no way, but what could be the connection? Also, the man seemed to be a much different person than what I would have expected. In Pakistan, I pictured him as a brutal, wild-eyed, fanatic with an uncanny instinct for survival. What I'd found here was a brutal, sophisticated sociopath with an uncanny instinct for survival. The latter was more dangerous.

Dee touched my arm. "What's wrong?" she asked.

I didn't answer. I still needed to think, process this data while it was fresh. I went back over the call in my mind. I also got the impression that he had significant resources at his disposal, and seemed completely at home in his current surroundings. I needed to reevaluate the way I was doing this. I was off my turf and he, apparently, was not.

"Travis?"

"Please, just a minute."

Worse, I still had no idea what his plan might be. I'd seen the complex ambushes he could devise, complete with rearguard elements to allow the safe egress for his forces. He knew how to conduct a small unit military operation. He was obviously capable of doing the same thing here.

In Pakistan, he knew how to negate our superiority in the air. By executing his attacks during poor weather conditions, he was able to compromise the attack aircraft, and even the Predator drones that were so lethally effective under other conditions.

In fact, he captured my lieutenant after an attack last year. They'd sent in a drone, but it crashed due to icing. Maliki set up a secondary ambush at the drone's crash site, capturing the demolition team and apparently destroying the drone.

I needed help, and wasn't sure where to get it.

Dee continued to watch me carefully. As I returned from my mental wanderings, she spoke, "Was that the man who killed Gareth?"

I nodded. "His name's Abdul al Maliki. He's the one responsible, though I don't know if he did it himself."

"He told you his name?"

"I already knew his name, at least his Jihad name. Not even the CIA knows his real name."

"How do you know this?"

"He's based in Pakistan. He killed my Platoon Commander less than a year ago. Even Gareth was after him back in 2008. He always managed to stay one step ahead of us."

"How do we find him?"

I shook my head; I still hadn't adjusted to the fact that he was here. I didn't know anything about where he might be. A phone tap may help locate him, but that would require going to the police. That was not an option any more. If there were future conversations, and they could record them and study background sounds, maybe they could discover some hint as to his whereabouts. I wouldn't hold my breath on that one, either.

Having a platoon as backup would make me feel better. Maliki always covered his ass. I had been lucky with Gamal, they were worried more about MI5 than about us. That had changed, we wouldn't surprise them again. Maliki would adapt, and he probably had everything he needed to do it effectively.

On the other side of the equation, when I found Maliki there would be no reading of his rights—well, maybe his last rites. If I couldn't get him until he was trying to escape from whatever carnage he had planned, that would be unfortunate yet acceptable. I just wanted the bastard.

I looked over at Dee, who sat impatiently with Blackjack in her lap, and asked, "Do you have Becket's number?"

The question surprised her, but she nodded.

"I think we should call him. This guy is better prepared than I realized, or could have imagined. I'm not sure we can find him on our own, and our chances go up if MI5 helps. Besides, we really need to convince them that he's here, and that he's dangerous."

Dee smiled and replied slowly, thoughtfully, "I'm very happy to hear you say that, I agree. This has all been so . . ."

She looked around the room, trying to find the right word.

"Unbelievable. Secret shipments, dead terrorists, stealing cars; I'm not trained for this. MI5 is."

She pulled out her cell phone and began to reinsert the battery. I stopped her.

"They are still after us."

She put the phone and battery back in her bag.

"Then we shouldn't call from here." She thought it over, "We should find a place, a crossroad, some distance away and with lots of traffic."

Dee stood and grabbed her bag.

"I know just the place."

Chapter 24

Dee felt more than a little guilty as she looked across the truck park. Travis had wanted to call Becket while they were driving down the M4 highway, making it impossible for Maliki to track their signal. She refused, and wouldn't tell the Travis why.

She felt certain that this was a call she should make in private. So at that moment Travis walked Blackjack on a large patch of grass, near the buildings across the park. She didn't call until they were well out of earshot.

She heard the phone ring for the third time and was about to disconnect when the ringing stopped and an irritating, high-pitched voice responded, "Becket here."

"Colonel Becket, this is Detective Sergeant Deirdre Jones, do you have a moment?"

There was a brief pause, then he replied calmly, "Of course, but I have another call on hold. Let me get rid of them, I'll be back directly."

"I'm not going to give you time to trace this call. We can speak now or I can disconnect."

"Very well, Ms. Jones. But I do wish to mention how much I enjoyed our last . . ."

"I really don't give a damn, do you want to talk or not?"

Clearly frustrated he replied.

"What is it you wish to talk about?"

"You need to know what's going on. We've uncovered a conspiracy, and are on the trail of a terrorist operating right here in Wales."

"Have you? And how did you arrive at this disturbing conclusion?"

Dee had no desire to recount the entire process, but was ready to lay out the significant facts and events they had uncovered.

"Neither Sergeant Deacon nor myself were convinced that by brother's death was an accident. In fact, Gareth made sure I would investigate if anything happened to him."

Becket interrupted, confused, "How did he do that?"

"Gareth left a message on my cell phone telling me to find Sergeant Deacon and investigate if there were a problem. It was almost as if he suspected he was in danger."

"I'm not sure I agree, but please continue."

"There was a problem, obviously. Travis and I have been trying to figure out why Gareth wanted us to follow him."

"By all means, let's talk about your terrifying terrorist plot. Why did you go to Tenby?"

She already suspected that Becket would know about their visit to Harbor Services and responded confidently, "Gareth had called me from there before he was killed."

"Before he died, you meant to say. And how did you find out about Naseem?"

She wasn't really surprised he knew about that, too. His agents in Pembroke would have certainly questioned Rys, and everyone else involved.

"That was Sergeant Deacon." That part was accurate, but she had no intention of giving him any more information than was necessary.

"He uncovered information in the office there that led us to Pembroke. He found out about Naseem and the cargo."

"Your cousin Dylan didn't help you with that?"

She had to be careful. Becket was obviously skilled and intelligent, plus he had the resources of MI5 at his disposal. She had to assume he knew much more than she'd anticipated. She spoke slowly.

"I felt bad about nicking Dylan's car, even more so because I've had to spend so much time inside it. He's not a very tidy person."

"My condolences," he responded sarcastically. "You're saying you didn't visit him because he also works at Harbor Services?"

Dee pretended to be surprised. She was beginning to feel the rhythm of the game they were playing.

"Is that where he works? I never knew, I thought he was a musician. I bet that's why Gareth went there, to say hello to his cousin. He said he was going to visit family while he was in country."

"I doubt Dylan was on your brother's itinerary for social reasons."

Apparently, Dylan hadn't told them anything, and he must have used their story about his car being lifted, or Becket would have sounded happier.

"When you speak with Dylan, if you haven't already, apologize for me if you don't mind."

"I wouldn't mind at all! Are there any other messages

you wish me to relay?"

"That's very nice of you. Please let him know that when Gareth's funeral arrangements have been finalized, I'll . . ."

Becket interrupted, clearly impatient, "You can tell him that yourself."

Dee smiled and looked at her watch. She needed to disconnect in the next minute, and there were things she needed to tell the pompous prat first.

"Fine, but you need to listen. We know the killer's name, Abdul al Maliki. We know you had men watching the dock. By now, you know they were being watched by a group of terrorists.

We found two on the hill behind their stakeout building, and suspect there were others staying at the MotorLodge nearby."

Becket was silent, then spoke slowly, "Where did you get that name?"

Becket sounded worried. Dee hesitated, but continued, "He called us on one of the phones we took off the terrorists. Travis talked to him and figured out who he was. He's here, in Wales, and we need to find him."

Becket now sounded angry, very angry, "I am trying to find him. And he's not in Wales, he's in London. Where I should be! Where I would be if I weren't chasing you two."

He paused to let this sink in, "And what do you know about those supposed terrorists Travis attacked in Pembroke?"

"They were there to attack your people. Travis managed to subdue one, but he was forced to kill another when they resisted. We also discovered that they were smuggling some kind of cargo into Wales through Pembroke."

"They were there to back up my team, not to kill

them."

Dee could hear a trace of gloating satisfaction in his voice.

"And you saw what was in the cargo you mention?"

Dee hesitated, what was he implying?

"No, we didn't see it."

"We did. We inspected it ourselves only hours ago. While most of it was clearly overpriced junk, that's not quite enough of a reason to kill someone."

"Those men had a sniper rifle, and were spying on your men from across the road. If they weren't about to kill your, wait . . . you knew about them?"

Becket hesitated a second, "I was informed, yes."

What? That couldn't be!

"I've worked with law enforcement people from all over Britain. Those were not policemen."

"No, they're with Pakistani Intelligence, here on assignment. You have no idea what you're meddling in, what you're mucking up with your insane investigation."

"Impossible."

"Ms. Jones, there is something horrific about to go down in the UK. We know about Maliki, and that yes, he is, in fact, involved. But that's all I'm going to say about it. We are in a joint operation with the government in Karachi, an operation you and your accomplice appear to be disrupting. In fact, a high-level official from Pakistan's ISI is here assisting us in the hunt. You are putting lives, important lives, in danger, Detective."

She tried to think. No, this couldn't be. How could it? Of course not, he had to be mistaken.

"My brother was murdered. I'm certain of it. We're just trying to find the persons responsible."

Becket spoke slowly, clearly, carefully choosing each word, "In hindsight, your brother's death does not appear to have simply been an accident; though I'm not ready to officially state it was murder. I will also concede that there may well be a connection between his tragic death and the violence we are hoping to avert. However, one thing is certain: your actions are only making a difficult situation more tenuous."

Dee was feeling lightheaded, was he telling her the truth? No, she had been there every step of the way. They had been tracking down the killers.

Becket interrupted, "And how much do you know about your traveling companion, Marine Sergeant Travis Deacon?"

She thought a moment then responded, "He was my brother's friend, I'm certain of that. In fact, my brother wanted," she hesitated, what had been her brother's intentions? "Anyway, he wants to find my brother's killer as much as I do, and he's more clever than I originally thought."

"No doubt! And what you're actually saying is that you really know nothing about him. Not a thing."

She looked across the car park. Travis had bent down to retrieve Blackjack's contribution to the world's recycling efforts. She continued to stare and had to admit that she didn't know anything about him.

"Would it surprise you to know that the FBI suspects him of murdering a policeman back in the United States, in Texas?"

He paused, and Dee's head started reeling. This couldn't be! She needed time to think, but Becket wasn't giving it to her.

"The dead officer's name was Hildebrandt. As a teenager, Travis Deacon almost beat Officer Hildebrandt to death. He was given the choice of going to jail, or joining the Marines. The Marine Corps didn't rehabilitate him as much as make him a more effective killer. Two years later Officer Hildebrandt was beaten to death."

Dee didn't want to hear any more. This did not correspond to the man she'd come to know! Or did it? What about the terrorists, or were they really Pakistani agents? Hadn't he beaten one of them to death just yards away from where she waited? He showed no remorse at all for the suffering and death.

But no, still no, that couldn't have been him. She began to think about it like a policeman. "Why wasn't he arrested and charged?" she asked.

"He had an alibi, one of his squad mates, and their Navy Department seems to be covering up for him. Even so, the police have no other suspects, just one crazed Marine finishing the job he'd started years before."

Dee was speechless. Was he telling her the truth? Had she been traveling with a cold-blooded killer?

"Detective Jones - Dee, think about it. These problems all arrived when he did. While he has a fantastic story, none of it has been proven. He has shown a total disregard for the law and for his superiors that have been trying desperately to contact him."

Again he paused for effect, and it was working.

"He's killed people without due process, without even knowing who they were! You're an officer, sworn to uphold the law, how does that make you feel? You have a decade of experience; use your instincts, does this feel right to you?"

She hadn't thought of it that way. She hadn't thought of it at all, really. However, now that she did stop to think, she couldn't help but wonder if Travis hadn't gone too far. She had driven around with a dead man in her boot, and never thought to question how or why he had been killed.

That was not like her, not like a detective at all. Becket

seemed to sense her uncertainty and pressed relentlessly on.

"Dee, no one blames you! You thought your brother had been killed—you may be right, and we may be wrong. Anyone would have wanted to investigate under those circumstances, but this is no longer simply an investigation into your brother's death. Others have also been murdered, and you need to extricate yourself from what may soon become a major crime."

His voice became softer, almost conspiratorial. He whispered as if Travis might be listening by her side.

"Detective Jones, have you considered the possibility that Sergeant Deacon is just using you? Turn yourself in; help us find out what's really going on. We have all the MI5 resources to back us. If you really want justice, work with us."

Dee's world was reeling. Had she really been that foolish? Travis was certainly a lethal weapon, hardened by years of battle, but evil? Would she have feelings of . . . could she have been so wrong? She stammered, not knowing exactly how to respond.

"I, I don't know. If what you're saying is true . . . Oh, my God. It can't be true."

She didn't want to consider the implications, and Becket didn't give her time to try.

"Dee, go to the nearest police station and call me. I'll have someone bring you in. Help me, help me find out the truth. We all agree there is an imminent threat, but do you really think a single American soldier is better equipped to prevent it than the entire British government? It's your choice. Make the right one."

She heard the connection go dead. She felt paralyzed, she couldn't move a single muscle.

She had no idea how long she stood there before Travis gently took the phone from her ear. She hadn't even see him cross the parking lot to her.

She barely noticed him bend down, look her in the eye, and attempt to get her attention.

"Dee, Dee! What's wrong? What happened?"

Dee couldn't answer; she couldn't even look him in the eye. She numbly turned and walked back to the car. She was finally jarred from her trance by the ghastly sounds and smells of an animal hauler approaching slowly through the car park.

Travis took her arm and moved her to the side, while he continued to stare carefully at the large truck and trailer. As the revolting riot of pig flesh and feces pulled away, Travis gave chase and slid her phone into a corner of the last pen.

Travis walked back and explained, "They're probably tracing it by now, let them chase the truck for a while."

But Dee had already turned away, struggling with the alarming information she had been given.

Could she really have been that wrong? What should she do about it? She unlocked the car and collapsed into the driver's seat.

Chapter 25

This was getting critical, and I didn't have a clue what to do. Dee just sat on the bed, back against the headboard, legs drawn up to her chest. A pillow balanced on top of her knees, with her head resting miserably on top of it. She didn't so much as stare at the wall as gaze through it.

She was so distracted that she'd ignored Blackjack when he curled into a ball next to her, and she'd been like that since she talked to that Colonel Becket. After ending the call, she simply got into the car and waited. She didn't say a word on the way back to the motel nor had she spoken since then. She hadn't made an intelligible sound since coming back to the room.

She hadn't even taken off her dirty shoes, which left brown dirt stains on the bedspread. There had to be a serious problem.

I'd passed the last twenty minutes examining Gareth's album in detail. Almost all of the people photographed were from Kabul, with a few from the provinces. All of them were the slice of life shots that Gareth loved so much, but they weren't cutting it for me. Maybe I had examined them too much. Maybe they were getting too familiar.

There was only one photo that stood out for me: it was of a boy riding a bicycle, trying to avoid a large truck on the narrow streets of Kabul. The boy was slightly out of focus, but that could easily be explained by the fact that he was moving. That's probably what Gareth wanted, the blur of motion, the living city of Kabul.

But it was still different from all the other photos in the album. And why did he put it here for me to examine?

I didn't need more questions. I needed answers to the ones I already had. Starting with what was going on in Dee's mind. What was she thinking about, or trying so hard to keep from thinking about?

I looked over at the bed. As if she could sense my interest, she raised her head from her knees and looked at me. She unfolded her legs and slid to sit on the edge of the bed, facing me but not looking at me. She reached back and began to scratch Blackjack behind the ears. The spoiled canine gave a satisfied moan and rolled onto his back, inviting her to rub his belly. She scratched vigorously for a second then spoke, still not looking at me.

"Colonel Becket thinks I should leave you and turn myself in. He said you're dangerous."

"I am dangerous, very much so, but not to you. And I think you should get away from me too, but I don't think putting yourself in his custody is a good idea, either. Dee, it's not safe, and it's getting less safe by the minute. Maybe you should get away. Work the case your own way, but from a safe distance."

Dee shook her head and finally glanced my way as she continued, "Becket also said you are just using me, but that doesn't seem to be the case."

"I have come to rely on you, you're amazingly smart

and talented. And you're unbelievably strong, you've held up incredibly well under the stress of Gareth's . . . the stress of everything that's gone on."

She hesitated, looking down. I could see a tear form in the corner of her eye, and she blinked it away. Then she looked up, her emerald eyes staring into my eyes. They were remarkably beautiful, even with the anguish and uncertainty reflected there.

I wanted to sit next to her, put my arm around her and comfort her, but that would have made things worse. I wanted her to be safe, which meant I wanted her away from me, but didn't know if I could let her go.

I tried to sound confident, "He's right. You should leave."

She stared at me a moment longer, then slowly shook her head as she spoke, "I don't know if I can trust you anymore."

"Then it is very important that you go. Our lives will depend on being able to trust one another. If you can't do that, then staying isn't safe for either of us."

A look of anguish darkened her face, and she rubbed her eyes with the back of her hand as she whispered, "But I want to trust you."

I was tempted to tell her that I wanted desperately for her to trust me as well, but I wasn't certain how that would come out, or be received. I was shocked, however, by her next question. "Becket said the men you attacked in Pembroke were Pakistani intelligence agents."

They weren't, but I knew I could never prove that. She asked slowly, "Who is Officer Hildebrandt?"

I tensed; I could feel my cheeks become hot. That name was like a flaming brand, a hatred burning deep into my heart. I hadn't thought of him in years, but I would never be able to exorcise the loathing in my soul at the simple mention of that name. I had to speak slowly, guarding every word. "He was a policeman, from when I was a teenager. He was new to Everton, the town where I grew up. He was the reason I had to join the Marine Corps."

She just stared, obviously knowing there was much more to the story. I hesitated. This was painful, but I finally continued, "I beat him up, pretty bad. If others hadn't stopped me, I would have killed him. The local officials and judges decided to let me join the Corps instead of going to jail. I was underage, but somehow they made it happen."

"Becket said you went back and killed him, is that true?"

I slowly shook my head. "No, I didn't kill him."

She looked at me hard. I could tell she wanted to believe me, but couldn't quite bring herself to do it. Trust was one thing, but I didn't want her wondering if I were a cop killer hiding in the military.

"I didn't kill him, but I would have. I arrived about a week too late."

I hesitated. This was difficult. This was a story I hadn't told anyone, not even my cousins back in Texas. I wasn't sure I could tell it at all. I looked at Dee's face, begging me to help her understand, to give her the truth about my life, so she could decide how to proceed with hers.

That complicated things, because I really wanted her safely away from me. She had been an invaluable partner in this, but I now realized my feelings might make things dangerous. I couldn't be sure that my priorities were sound; I didn't want my feelings for Dee to jeopardize my mission to find Gareth's killers, nor did I want my feeling to jeopardize our lives.

But either way, I had to tell her the truth. I needed her to trust me, to understand. Finally, she asked, "Then who did kill him?"

"I'm pretty sure it was a Vietnamese street gang, for the same reason I was going to do it."

"Which was?"

"Hildebrandt was a predator, a pedophile, a clever pervert. I caught him with my little sister Katie, and would have killed him if my uncle and the cops hadn't stopped me."

I had to pause. I hadn't thought about this in a very long time, and hadn't talked about it for an even longer time. The image of a skinny, golden-haired little girl flooded back into my mind. It must have flooded my throat also, since I suddenly felt decades of grief well up there. The emotion forced me to pause, and I was surprised at how strong the feelings still were—or maybe they were amplified by the situation and company. I wiped my eyes and forced myself to go on.

"That's why they let me join the Marines; they screwed up and didn't check his background. He'd been fired from two other police departments for 'hardship reasons.' He brought that hardship with him, and the local leaders wanted everyone to disappear. I went to the Marines. He just went away before the truth came out." I had to stop and take a deep breath, controlling my mind and my emotions. "After my first tour in the Marines, I started tracking him down. I discovered he'd gone from Everton to a place called Georgetown. From Georgetown, he went to the Houston area. He got a job with the Fairview PD."

I watched Dee as I talked, and couldn't tell if she believed me or not. At least she was listening, and some of the hardness and anguish had faded from her expression. I finished my explanation.

"He apparently raped the wrong girl there, from the Little Saigon area of Houston. One of the gangs mutilated and then killed him. It wasn't me, you can believe that. However, you also need to know I would have killed him. Katie, my sister, was never the same. What's worse, he got to stay on the streets, ruining the lives of other kids. I didn't kill Hildebrandt, but only because I got there too late. That's the only reason it wasn't me."

Dee looked at the floor, eyes blinking as she digested the truth about me. After a few seconds, she looked up at me and said, "I don't know what to say, how to react."

"You don't need to react right now. Becket told you to get away from me, I still think that's a good idea. So much has happened, so much is still happening. Make sure you know what you want to do before we get any deeper into this."

And, I want you safe. I thought, but did not utter aloud.

Dee stood and walked to the table, examining the open album. She slowly turned the pages. She stopped. Without looking up and in a small tired voice she said, "That's a big truck. The streets there are almost as narrow as in the old section of Tenby." She took a deep breath, exhaled slowly, and looked at me. "OK, I'll go. You can drop us at my aunt's house. It's close. Maybe it is the best thing." She looked at me, in obvious anguish. "But I don't want to leave."

I stepped closer, more urgently than I'd intended.

"And I don't want you to leave! These last days have been brutal, but you being with me—keeping me out of trouble—has made, has made it all bearable."

I took one more hesitant step closer, and she didn't back up. I began to wonder if she wanted me to . . .

What did she say? Which truck? Was she talking about the picture with the boy? That was it, a revelation, it was the truck I needed to look at, not the cyclist.

"What about the truck?"

Her face remained frozen for a second or two. The expectant expression on her face began to fade, to transform, spanning an emotional spectrum from surprise, to disappointment, to irritation if not anger. I had blown my chance, but I was back on task. Personal feelings had been instantly, unfortunately, stowed away.

I pointed at the picture of the kid on the bike in front of the truck. I noticed again that the child was out of focus, but not the truck.

"This truck?"

She regarded me coolly for an instant, then looked down at the album. "I assumed it was a picture of the truck."

Of course it was!

"You're right, great work Dee."

I had been so into the theme of the pictures, the people, that I missed the obvious. Dee's fresh perspective saw it immediately. It was the truck, the civilian truck carrying crates with U.S. Air Force markings on them.

I slid the chair back and dropped onto the hard, wooden seat. I grabbed the computer, pulled up the e-mail page of the website I'd been using for communications, and typed in a series of e-mail addresses. I only used two anonymous forwarding sites this time. It was a bit of a risk, but I needed an answer fast. The last address was Ham's personal e-mail. I had to use his personal address, the CIA filter would never let it through. I described the crates and markings, and gave him as much of the black stenciled numbers as I could read. The child's head blocked the last few digits from the picture. I could send him a copy of the photo in a separate e-mail.

I thought for a moment, and then asked for anything he could get me on Maliki. We needed all the help we could

225

get.

I hit send, and a message appeared on the screen telling me the e-mail was sent. I turned to the back of the album. Gareth had left a DVD in the pocket inside the back cover of the album. I was certain that it contained digital copies of the album's photos. I slipped the disk out of its cover and inserted it into Dee's computer.

It took a few minutes, there were dozens of photos, and they were large files. I would have to send them one at a time to stay under the attachment size limitations. It took almost a minute longer, but the directory of pictures now had a small, thumbnail picture beside the file names. I began to scan them carefully.

The picture I wanted was easy to find, the truck was clearly visible in the tiny file image. I again went through the process of making sure the e-mail would be untraceable, attached the photo, and sent it off to Ham.

It took a long time for the picture to upload through the motel's Internet e-mail system, and while I waited, I looked through the directory of pictures that was still in a separate window on the screen. Most of them had descriptive names, like 'Young Girl outside Bagram.' One, however, was simply named WHO. At first glance, I assumed it was of officials from the World Health Organization. They came to Kabul regularly on humanitarian missions. But when I looked at the thumbnail picture beside the name, I realized it was the three men in the café, whose picture I'd been examining the morning Gareth was killed.

I looked closer, examining the details displayed in the file's directory. The first thing I noticed was the date time stamp, telling me when the picture was taken or at least uploaded. It had been created only minutes before the picture of the truck. I looked at the other pictures, and none of them had been taken at that time. Were the two pictures related? If so, how?

I decided to examine that picture again, and on an impulse sent it in another e-mail to Ham. In the subject line, I simply put 'Please ID.' In the body of the e-mail I typed 'URGENT.' I didn't see how the two were related, but it seemed too much of a coincidence to ignore.

As I waited impatiently for the e-mail and picture to upload, Blackjack hopped down from the bed and scampered to the door. He lowered his nose to the open space underneath it and sniffed, then he began to growl.

I sprang from the chair and sprinted to the door, picking up the dog and rushing back to Dee. I dumped Blackjack into her arms and hustled her to the corner of the room, behind the wardrobe, where she would be out of sight from the door. I pulled the SIG from behind my back, and the little Makarov pistol from my pocket. I took it off safety and forced it into her hand.

"Take it, just in case! Point and shoot, it's ready to fire. You have eleven rounds."

I jumped over the bed to the opposite side of the room and knelt, only partially concealed behind the mattress. I took aim at the door, and reached to my back pocket for an extra magazine. Before I had the magazine completely out of my pocket, the room's door exploded in a spray of splintered wood.

A large, powerfully built man staggered inside, pushing a portion of the door in front of him. I saw an automatic pistol in his right hand, and everything slowed down to combat speed. My heart raced, but my mind had shifted gears into overdrive. I felt calm now, and everything seemed to move at half speed. I raised my pistol and did a double tap, two rounds to the exposed portion of his chest. I didn't go for a head shot because I could see he didn't have body armor.

I saw a submachine gun barrel protrude beyond the side of the initial intruder as he fell. I dove to the side as bullets ripped through the wall behind the bed. A lamp shattered and fell to the floor. I rolled into a kneeling firing position, waiting for the large man to fall and expose the man or men behind him. I saw three others rushing in, firing in a pattern around the room and trying to spread out inside. These were trained men, and probably experienced as well. I fired three times and a second man flew backward, his face now deformed by the 40-caliber bullet that struck him below the right eye.

The remaining two were on opposite sides of the room, sweeping their fire toward the middle, their automatic weapons discharging over five hundred rounds a minute between them. This made covering the entire room with searing hot metal an easy task. I got off another two rounds and rolled to the bed. I think I hit the one on the right, but he kept on firing.

The one on my left stopped. I heard a click, then his magazine clattered to the ground. It would only take a second for him to slam home a second magazine, so I looked under the bed. At this point, the man to my right was rushing forward, still firing, but I would have to deal with him later. Lying on my back, I extended my right hand and fired five rounds toward the shadows of the reloading attacker's feet.

I heard him scream, and I also heard the magazine from my other attacker's weapon clatter to the ground. I had only a second before he would be ready to fire again. I rolled to my side and was up on one knee, but instead of trying to load another magazine, the attacker charged recklessly forward, pulling a combat knife from his belt as he flew through the air.

I tried to swing my pistol around, but he hit me with a thud and we both rolled backward. With his left hand, he grabbed my right, forcing my pistol up. He twisted my weapon down against my thumb, which forced it from my hand.

My pistol clattered uselessly away, and my assailant still had a combat knife in his right hand. He attempted to drive the point of it upward, using his momentum to force the blade deep into my side or stomach.

I could see the fire in his eyes, and he screamed triumphantly. He thought he had me. With great difficulty, because of the pressure of his attack, I down blocked his knife hand, which forced the knife wide of my body. I prepared myself to absorb the impact of his bulk as he landed on top of me. He was heavy, but I controlled the air leaving my lungs.

He growled fiercely and tried to slip the knife again into my left side, which was probably his only move considering the proximity of our bodies. I grabbed his wrist, and at the same time raised a knee and drove it into his groin. He was fast, and managed to twist his body. The blow only partially connected.

His defensive maneuver did allow me to twist his knife hand. He howled with pain as his wrist rotated viciously. He didn't drop the knife as I'd expected though.

He next tried to head butt me. Instead, using his forward momentum, I threw my leg up viciously, and propelled him over my head. He flew several feet and crashed into a chair. To my dismay, he rolled nimbly to his side and was on his feet almost as soon as I was. He still had his knife at the ready.

I was breathing heavily but he was panting, near exhaustion. I stole a glance at the other attacker, who was swearing fiercely in Arabic and struggling to get to his knees on the other side of the bed. He placed his pistol on the bed and used both hands to pull himself up. He was only seconds away from getting into a firing position. I grabbed the bedspread and yanked it out from under him. He fell backward to the floor, and his pistol flew up, landing in the middle of the bed.

I looked around, then ran for the automatic handgun dropped by the first man inside. After only a step, I heard a scream and turned. The man with the knife was almost on top of me again. I used the bedspread as a shield and tossed it over his head. While he struggled to pull the bedding away, I stepped to his right and drove a sidekick into his knee.

He cried out in pain and staggered to one knee. I located my pistol, and was about to dive for it when I heard the click of someone chambering a round. The other one had retrieved his weapon and was about to fire.

I barely had time to grab the shoulder of the man next to me. I pulled him up as I pulled myself down behind him, and the staccato bark of the other guy's weapon echoed through the room. I felt the spray of shattered wood behind me, and the violent shuddering of rounds striking the back of the man between us.

I heard a pitiful moan from my human shield, and he began to slump. I tried to drag him to my right, shielding myself with his now dead body while I lunged to reach for my own weapon. I realized I would be several feet short, and from the corner of my eye could see the other one climb painfully to the top of the bed.

I quickly frisked the dead man in front of me, hoping he had a backup weapon within my reach. I found nothing. The living one on the bed now screamed at me in Arabic, consigning my soul to hell. I was sure several parts of my body were exposed, and at this distance anything visible would be an easy shot for him.

My only chance was to dive for my weapon, hoping his shots weren't fatal until I could finish him. I rolled for my pistol and heard a slow series of explosions, but these sounded different than the parabellum rounds the terrorist had been firing.

It was Dee. She fired again. The little Makarov barked two, three, then four more times. There was no return fire from our attacker, so I glanced at him as I grabbed my pistol and rolled into a firing stance.

Dee emerged from behind the wardrobe, in shock, standing completely rigid near the wall. She held her pistol uncertainly, extended to arm's length in her right hand, while Blackjack squirmed and barked viciously in her left. I hadn't even noticed the barking with all of the shouting and gunfire around us.

I could assess the situation now. I instantly saw that Dee's face was contorted in horror as she stared down at the man she'd shot, sprawled out on the bed. He was obviously dead. She had killed him. The shock of what she'd done was slowly beginning to work its way into her mind.

I jumped to my feet, and winced. I felt my right side. My fingers touched a small patch of warm, sticky blood. It was a little painful, but I couldn't feel any real damage to bone or muscle. I would ignore it for now.

I checked my Sig, and retrieved the fallen spare magazine. I then moved quickly to each of the downed attackers, collecting weapons and cell phones. They all had weapons, which went in my bag. Only two had cell phones, which I stuffed in my pocket. All were dead except the large one who had entered first. I considered a fatal blow to the larynx, but Dee was watching me. Instead, I removed his belt and used it to secure his arms behind his back. I

231

then stuffed a large wad of cloth, torn from his shirt, into his mouth.

I rushed to Dee's side and gently took the pistol from her hands. I held the left side of the weapon up, so she could clearly see the safety lever.

"This is how you put it on safe." I flipped the lever at the back of the slide up. "This is how you set it to fire." I slipped the lever down.

I put the pistol back on safe, then dug through my bag. I pulled out a spare Makarov magazine and inserted it. I then handed the pistol back to her. She hesitated, looked around the room then took the gun and put it into her pocket. She started to put an almost frantic Blackjack down, but I stopped her.

"Not yet. Dee, I need you to do exactly what I say. In two minutes put Blackjack down. Grab the computer and album, and find me downstairs."

I looked around, worried. How had they found us? What resources did these guys really have? It could be Becket, but how could MI5 have found us so quickly? I looked back at Dee.

"Your cell phone is still off, right?"

She nodded.

"I don't think these guys are Pakistani security agents, and it wouldn't make any difference if they were. What do you think about Becket now?" I asked. She looked around the room, and touched the pistol in her pocket.

I continued my instructions, "I don't know how they found us, but until we know we'll have to keep moving." I looked her in the eye and smiled. "Two minutes then come downstairs. Are you with me?"

She looked down. My clothes were covered in blood, a good portion of it my own. She surveyed the carnage once more and nodded. I smiled confidently back. "We will be fine."

I slung my bag over my shoulder, and sprinted out the door. I stopped at the top of the stairs, peering carefully over the railing. I assumed they would have a guard posted below, to keep anyone from coming up behind them or escaping down the stairs. There was a young man holding an MP5 assault rifle at the base of the stairs, covering the ground floor. He looked up the stairs and saw me. The look of shock on his face was soon replaced by a blank expression as two 40-caliber rounds passed through his chest near his heart.

I bounded down the stairs and examined the ground floor. The woman was still seated in front of the TV, a thin bladed combat knife protruding from her chest. I could see an old man lying in the doorway of the kitchen; it looked like he had been killed from behind with a garrote.

I looked out the front door, but didn't see anything out of place. I went to the back and saw a full-sized white sedan, with a nervous looking Mideasterner fidgeting behind the wheel. I pulled out the cell phone of the man who had died on the bed, and who I hoped was the team leader. I went through his call list, redialing each number.

On the third try, I saw the driver reach excitedly around the cab. He retrieved a phone and put it to his ear. In Arabic, with a low, rough voice that I hoped sounded injured, I commanded, "Come inside, now."

I hung up as the driver jumped from his car. He ran toward me, struggling to chamber a round in his assault rifle. As he neared the door, I fired two rounds through the window. He collapsed in a heap and skidded to a halt at the step.

I turned to find Dee standing behind me, holding the MP5 from the fallen man at the stairs. Without a change of expression, she opened the door and sprinted past the fallen driver, not even glancing at his body. Blackjack followed, as did I after taking the dead driver's weapons.

The driver had left the vehicle running, and Dee hopped behind the wheel. As soon as my butt hit the seat, she sped away in a cloud of dust and gravel.

Chapter 26

I felt my head throbbing. The pain was intense and the wound deep. I put my right hand to my face and felt it, the warm wet moisture falling in rhythmic, relentless drops.

I was crying, like a baby, like nothing I'd experienced since Katie's funeral. And the thing that got this started was stupid, ridiculous--absurd actually. This outburst had been triggered by our visit to Crymych.

Crymych, a town with no vowels.

My baby sister got me a tape for my fourteenth birthday, my favorite group: America's greatest hits. She'd saved her pennies and finally managed to buy that dusty old secondhand recording at the store in Carrizo Springs, what we thought was a city but was barely a town back then. The first song on the tape was 'A Horse With No Name,' which popped maddeningly into my mind when I decided Crymych was the 'Town With No Vowels.'

However, the young and innocent Kathryn May Deacon decided I had to have that tape because of another song, further down the list, 'Sister Golden Hair.' It became her song, because that's what Katie May was to me, my beautiful little sister with the golden hair.

She loved that song, they told me that was the song she listened to as she killed herself, two years after Hildebrandt; her favorite song, a bottle of prescription sleeping pills, then oblivion—and hopefully peace.

He killed her soul, and the mind and body finally followed. That outcome became inevitable when a judge forced me to choose, leave her and join the Marines, or go to jail. Either way I'd be gone, either way she'd be alone.

If I'd been there, I know I could have helped her, more than the shrink did. Damn right I would have killed the son of a bitch Hildebrandt. Sometimes I feel cheated that I wasn't there to choke the life out of the officer myself, to watch the light leave his eyes the way I saw it leave Katie's slowly, each time I visited.

And sometimes I felt like I kept doing this job because I had to punish someone, to watch evil men die before they could rob some other innocent of their lives—or worse. I had watched men die, and hoped to do so again very soon.

I realized that I was no longer crying. The hot dampness on my face was sweat now. Anger, I could handle anger. Anger had been my friend on several occasions. But the wound was still there, deep, to the heart.

I jumped as Dee opened the door and plopped inside, a satisfied look on her face. She barely glanced at me as she smiled eagerly at her computer. I noticed her hair again. It wasn't the same color as Katie's, but it was thick, beautiful hair that framed her face and highlighted her features with light. Dee had an impish, 'aren't you the clever one,' grin that Katie, the 'before' Katie, so often wore when she teased me.

Emotions again began to whirl and battle inside of me, but these emotions were different. These were emotions I would never feel toward my sister.

Dee looked up, cocked her head curiously and asked, "Did you hear me? I get the settings, so we can . . . my God, what happened? Are you all right?"

She studied my face with alarm, lingering on my red, puffy eyes. I shrugged, and changed the subject.

"Gas pain. Are we online?"

She gave me another skeptical look, then took her laptop and scampered into the back. She sat on the sedan's wide bench seat. I crawled over the large console and sat next to her as she entered a password into her computer.

After our little midday mayhem at the Tenby B&B, we had driven north. We called the police immediately after leaving the premises. Dee identified herself, filled in the constable as he took the report, then warned them that MI5 would try to cover it up. They were skeptical, but I hoped the dozen or so bodies would get their attention.

After the call, we stopped at a large sporting goods store just outside of town and bought several necessities. First was a first-aid kit, a good one, that had a variety of antibiotics, antiseptics, analgesics, and even a few items that didn't start with 'A.' Then came a couple of large, nasty knives, a set of binoculars, shoe polish that would have to do for camouflaged face paint, and a bag full of other goodies. From there, we drove to Crymych, about half an hour north of Tenby. I told her we should find a library. I needed to check my e-mail and a couple of websites. I was certain that most libraries in Wales, like back in the States, would have wireless Internet available. She drove to one, and I was right; now we were logging on.

Dee looked over, examining my face in the flickering blue light of the library home page. "Have you decided how they found us yet?" she asked as the library homepage finished loading. She continued to type away. I hadn't, in fact, figured anything out. I was too busy putting myself through a purgatory of guilt and regret. Instead of telling her that, however, I changed the subject again. "Have you decided whether you can trust me yet? I'm not sure I should tell you if you're going back to Becket."

She smiled. "Yes, I trust you. No, I don't know how they found us either. And maybe we're still not safe."

"The solution to that is to find them first. Go to the secure mail site I book marked.'"

I actually believed her, that she trusted me. Dee seemed different now, a little harder, with a more resolute cast to her face. The battle at the B&B had opened her eyes, but the world didn't seem any brighter.

She clicked the mouse a few times, and a login screen for the clean e-mail service appeared. She handed me the laptop. I typed in my username and password, and all of my e-mails appeared on the screen. There were two, both from Hamilton Dupree.

From the file size, I could see that the oldest was much shorter, and it didn't have any attachments, so I opened it first. It dealt with the photo of the truck, and was only two paragraphs long. It could have been condensed to two sentences, actually just one.

First, Ham suggested that the truck held radio equipment. They could surmise that from their size and approximate weight, determined by the compression of the springs on the rear of the truck. The partial part numbers were a big help, but not enough for a definitive identification. If he had to guess, his first one would be some type of ground control unit.

His second guess was a battalion-sized karaoke machine, but he ruled that out since torture was banned. I liked Ham.

I slumped back in my seat. This information was

extremely valuable; at least, it appeared to be. Valuable was good, but useful would be better. It would only become useful if we could figure out where it fit into the big picture puzzle we were trying to piece together. Then, it would progress from useful to helpful when we'd found enough of the missing pieces to figure out what the picture on this puzzle really was.

Time was not on our side; in fact, it was an axe blade hanging over our necks. Both Dee and I were absolutely sure that we had only days, or even just hours to solve the puzzle that got Gareth killed.

I looked over at Dee, who had picked up the computer, browsing the information and attachments in the second e-mail. I craned my neck to see the screen; it was an inter-agency CIA field assessment of Maliki. She read it closely and jumped when I put my hand over the screen. "That's confidential. I could have you arrested for reading it."

Without breaking her concentration, or apparently losing her place in the document, she slapped my hand away and mumbled as she read.

"So, slap the cuffs on me. Sometimes I kind of like that."

It took a second, but she realized her slip, and now she tried to change the subject. She pointed to a paragraph under the heading of "Suspected activities:"

"It says here that the SAS suspects Maliki of at least two attempted attacks on Prince Harry while he was fighting in Afghanistan, but there were probably more."

I started to say that 'fighting' didn't always describe what the Prince was doing there, but so what. Yes, he was probably surrounded by an unknown number of the finest soldiers the SAS had, but by God was he there; no running, no deferments, no excuses. You had to admire the British royalty for that, putting your life on the line was still considered a privilege as much as an obligation.

I only half-listened as Dee continued her commentary, but something set off a signal flare in my mind. What was it? What had she said that seemed so significant? I stopped her and asked, "What did you just say?"

She stopped and thought, then said, "The luxury box that Gareth got for us, to the Six Nations between England and Wales in Cardiff. I think he was trying to set us up."

She said that a little shyly, but I didn't pay any attention. That wasn't it, but I did think it was an odd comment.

"Why did you think of that?"

"Because of what I read, about Harry. The Prince is going to be in Cardiff tomorrow for the finals. Since it's England-Wales, I imagine a lot of the Royals will be there"

Prince Harry would be in Wales. Abdul al Maliki would be in Wales. There was no way this could all be a coincidence. I could see an obvious connection, but it was almost too fantastic to consider.

I looked at Dee, "I'm beginning to see a pattern here."

She looked up, puzzled. Then her eyes got wide, and her jaw dropped as I nodded my head. That was it, I knew it. She realized it almost as quickly as I did.

Maliki was going to kill Prince Harry, and as many of the Royal Family as he could. As I thought about it, I shook my head; that was insane! There was no way he could pull that off.

Dee echoed my sentiments, "No fucking way! That would be impossible."

However, as we looked each other in the eye, we both realized that it was true. Maliki was going to go for the biggest prize ever. And, from what we'd learned about him in the last few days, he seemed to be able to do anything.

He accomplished something that MI5 had totally failed at: finding us.

No, as I thought about it, I realized how crazy that idea sounded. Dee slumped back in the seat, deep in thought, and spoke without looking over to me.

"How could he do that? No, I can't believe it to be possible."

Not probable, but I'd learned that anything is possible. We needed to figure this out, thank goodness there was no rush—anytime in the next five minutes would be fine. I voiced the idea that was going through my mind, "He could try anything. In fact, I'm sure it's something no one's tried, or even thought of before."

But how did that information help? I attempted to organize all the facts we'd uncovered, to look at them again and in different ways.

"We should start by going over everything that's happened, consider anything and everything, no matter how bizarre it may seem, but let's do so with Harry in mind as the potential target."

I started with the accident. Gareth had been tortured, but not with the same intensity Maliki normally employed. It would be discovered at some point, but not for a few days; next week, after Harry's visit.

I heard Dee laugh and looked over, curious. If there were something amusing about the situation, I needed to hear it. She saw me staring at her and giggled again.

"Zombies."

I shook my head, really confused now. Or maybe the stress of the whole ordeal had taken more of a toll on her than I'd anticipated. She saw the concern on my face and frowned as she scolded me.

"I'm not daft! It's just something that Kareem, the missing Beeb from the dock, had said."

"Naseem," I corrected.

"Whatever. He said the big crate had dead people in it. Maybe that's Maliki's secret weapon. He'll turn a boat load of zombies loose in the stadium and let them eat their way to the Royals."

She must be really tired, she was laughing out loud.

"Or vampires! It could be the coffin of a giant vampire, genetically engineered to only drink royal blood."

She laughed hard again and leaned back in her seat. She rubbed her eyes and forehead with her hands, and moaned, "Dear God, God I need some rest. Sorry."

I sat there in stunned silence.

That was it! The whole thing made sense now, and for the first time I thought we had a very real chance of finding him.

I reached across her body to the computer bag. I needed to look at something, immediately. As my face passed in front of her, she looked up at the front of the car, startled. She put her arms around me and kissed me hard.

I don't want to say it was a passionate kiss, but her tongue was so far down my throat, I wouldn't need a prostate exam this year. Her hand was caressing the back of my head, and her lips were rubbing the skin off mine.

I thought about pulling away, but discarded that idea immediately. I was enjoying the experience way too much to end it right then. I responded, and returned the kiss with equal passion, when I heard a knock at the window behind me. I wanted to see who it was, but I really didn't want to stop kissing Dee.

There was another tap on the window, louder and more insistent. I turned angrily to get rid of whoever was intruding on our moment, and found myself looking into the face of an amused policeman. He used his billy club to motion me to lower the window, which I did.

His smile became a smirk as he looked us over.

"And what are you two doing?"

Before I could speak, Dee almost shouted, as if she were a little drunk.

"Just havin' a bit of fun officer, no crime in that is there?"

"Depends, miss, on just how much fun, and whether you're having it in public."

Dee giggled, with just a hint of vixen in her voice. The officer pointed at the computer. "What are you two watching?"

Dee slowly lowered the lid and smiled seductively as she responded, "Us, last night, just havin' a bit more fun for the camera. You can watch if you like!" She giggled again, "For five quid a minute!"

It looked like he was considering the offer, but then leaned in and looked us over carefully. He appeared to be disappointed that things hadn't progressed to the insert tab 'A' into slot 'B' phase, and stood.

"I suggest you find a better place for your re-enactment."

Dee spoke up immediately. I realized she didn't want me to talk and let him know I was American.

"Thank you officer, 'ave a good night!"

We both turned our heads to watch the Constable walk slowly down the street. When he finally rounded the corner, I smiled at Dee and asked, "Now where were we?"

She sat up straight and lifted the computer screen.

"Solving this case. And don't get any ideas, that was all for show." She handed me the computer case. "What the hell were you rambling about?"

After a moment of disappointment, I reached into a pocket of the computer bag, and retrieved a stack of papers. I leafed through them and stopped at the picture from the dock. It was of Rys' crew unloading the suspect cargo. I held it up to the light, examined it closely, and handed it to Dee.

The next page was the manifest of the cargo. I examined the weights and dimensions of each crate she'd written down by hand, then slumped back into the seat, amazed and afraid. I turned to Dee. My face must have reflected my concern, and she asked, "What?"

"You were half right. It was a coffin, but not for a vampire. It's for a Predator."

It fit, all of it! Once you recognized what the whole picture was, each of the puzzle pieces fit neatly and quickly into place. I held up the picture and pointed to the largest crate.

"That's a coffin, what they call the crates used to ship unmanned aircraft, called Predator Drones. Every year the CIA and Air Force lose a dozen or so, mostly due to weather. My Lieutenant was searching for one they thought had landed intact in a heavy snow pack when he was captured. Maliki killed and tortured him, the Predator was never found, until now."

I pointed at the other crates.

"These three here are probably the ground control radar. In flight, Predators are controlled by pilots in the U.S. using satellite communications. But for takeoff and landing, they use radio control units. As long as you have a pilot within line-of-sight of the drone, you can fly them anywhere."

She nodded, eyes wide, understanding immediately what I had said and what it meant.

"Like Cardiff."

"These drones carry Hellfire missiles that can be fired and directed with that radio if necessary."

Dee whipped out one of the cell phones we'd take

244

from our latest batch of assassins and dialed a number she had memorized by now. I heard ringing, and then a nasal voice say "Becket here." Dee started explaining what we knew, but I tuned her out. I knew what I needed to find.

Predators needed an airstrip, and it would have to be launched from a location close enough to arrive on station before the authorities could intercept it. There would only be a few places that a Predator could take off from, and hopefully they could find out which one quickly. I did a Google search on airstrips in Wales; there were only a few in the Cardiff area. I started with the closest field outside of Cardiff itself. I clicked on the link, and the field's information appeared on the screen. It was outside a town called Newport, and a picture of a nice little field finally appeared. It was in a rural area, trees on both sides, with a few general aviation planes and one corporate jet. They were all parked near a large brick building that looked like an old tower.

I was about to dial the number, when Dee began to raise her voice. Apparently, the conversation with Becket wasn't going well. I took the laptop and got out. I rested the computer on the nearby book drop, and hoped that Officer Perv didn't come back.

I dialed the number, someone answered on the first ring.

"Airfield."

The old man who answered was probably Welsh, and definitely pissed off, which was close to what I had expected. I worked out a clever cover story for the call, and jumped right in.

"Has anything strange been going on there recently?"

"Fuck yeah!"

That sounded encouraging, maybe I'd luck out on my first call.

Then he continued. "I've got an army of twats from Special Branch here, shutting everything down. Nothing landing or taking off until after the weekend. It's going to cost me a healthy chunk. I had people scheduled to land here for the Five Nations."

This wasn't what I wanted to hear, but I still found it interesting. I needed to find out more.

"Nothing at all can land or take off? Is it just you, or are other fields involved?"

"It's a no-fly zone, except for police and some military equipment scheduled to arrive. And everybody in South Wales is shut in. They better compensate us, by God, I'm losin' a fortune.

And they're making me stay at the field. I was going to the match, the bastards."

"Complete bastards, I agree. Thanks for your help."

No help there. I was happy to hear that Special Branch was in charge, and not MI5. Whatever the hell Special Branch was.

I called other fields, moving away from Cardiff. I called a place in Tenby and got the exact same story. I had no idea where to turn next. It's theoretically possible to take off from a road, if it was big enough, but assembling a huge aircraft by the side of the freeway didn't seem like a workable plan.

Dee stormed out of the car and marched to my side, shaking her head.

"Becket thinks we're the terrorists. Called our information fantasy, said that we were insane. He refuses to even look into it, claims he's got too much real security to see to and won't let us pull men away from it. He did promise to dedicate all of his resources to finding us after the festivities in Cardiff are finished."

"That will be too late." I pointed at the screen. "We

need to find the airstrip Maliki is using, but almost everything in Wales is locked down. And it has to be close enough to fly all the way to Cardiff under radio control, at least close enough so they can pass off control to another pilot in Cardiff."

How was he going to pull this off? I was sure there would be some kind of air cover protecting the Prince, if not in the air, then at least on call. The Air Force could land a Harrier jump jet in a parking lot across the street from the stadium, and have it in the air within minutes. Maliki, on the other hand, apparently couldn't take off, and couldn't fly in without police or military clearance.

Were we wrong? Was there another explanation? I turned to ask Dee her thoughts, but she was almost at the other end of the library. I shouted, "Where you going?"

She looked back over her shoulder. "This is a library. I'm going to look for a book."

I shrugged, why not? I wasn't getting anywhere. I continued searching. I searched for everything in Wales on 'airfields,' 'airstrips,' 'take off,' 'landing,' and every other aviation topic I could think of.

My search using the key word strip returned some interesting websites, more along the lines of 'let's kill some time, baby' than 'let's kill Prince Harry.' I did find a beautiful Russian student that would be willing to marry me and make me happy for the rest of my life. The 'rest of my life' part may be a problem. I didn't think she could get here that fast.

Dee walked up carrying a single, worn volume. It had a horrible orange cover, with the picture of an old, propeller-driven aircraft flying in formation on the front. The title was "History of the RAF, from World War II to Korea." She held it up and shrugged. "It's all they had."

I took it and leafed through it. It was a thick book and

looked comprehensive, maybe we'd get lucky. I went to the index and followed my previous search pattern, only mildly disappointed that 'Ilsa' wasn't listed as a subheading under strip. What was listed there was the category 'racing.' How did that relate to aircraft, were there separate air racing fields?

I turned to the page and started reading under the bold section heading "Converted To Racing Strips." On the opposite page were two pictures of what was obviously the same airfield. The top picture showed a small bomber, maybe a Mosquito, taking off. The other showed a shiny green car, brightly painted number and decals on the side and wheels smoking as it accelerated down that same runway, now a drag and racing strip.

A runway converted to a drag strip. It was certainly possible, and definitely our last straw. I went back to the computer and did a quick online search, and located three racing strips in Wales that were close enough to be candidates.

We started calling. Someone answered at the first one, and I could barely hear over the roar of engines and squealing tires. By the time it was quiet enough for him to speak, I'd hung up and called the last one on the list. Dee had called the second one, listened for a while, then hung up. I just listened and waited as the phone for candidate number three kept ringing. Finally, I heard a click, then a mechanical voice said: "Mail Box Full" and the line went dead. Dee shook her head when I looked over.

"I got an answering machine at the second place; they're closed until next weekend, but the message ended with 'Go Wales.' I bet they're at the match. They may still be a candidate, but I don't know. What about you?"

I shook my head. I'd had even less luck. "The first track is active. They're racing right now, so I doubt Maliki would be there. No one answered at the last one, and the voicemail box was full."

We looked at each other for a moment, both having the same thought at exactly the same time. Someone wasn't checking their voicemail. Why? Were they on vacation, reposing, or at home, decomposing?

Dee looked at the screen, and wrote down the address of the third track. I clicked on a little icon that said 'Map' and an interactive map with directions appeared. Dee looked at the screen and nodded. "Less than an hour away."

Making a decision was a lot simpler when you only had one good option. I shut down the laptop and we both got in the sedan. As she started up, I noticed the book on the console. I grabbed the book and got out, but Dee called after me, "You can't be serious!"

I ran toward the library door, dropped the book through the night deposit box, and hurried back to the vehicle. Dee looked over at me, half irritated and half amused, then said, "Are you hoping to join the friends of the library committee?"

I smiled, then winked. "No, I was just dragging things out a little, hoping another officer would come by."

She stared at me a moment, lifted her nose imperiously, and said, "Dream on!"

She put the car in gear, and we were off to the races.

Chapter 27

Abdul al Maliki examined the room carefully, like a stage manager might examine the set of a Broadway play on opening night. But this play would have a very brief run indeed.

His Lordship, General Philip Morgan-Thomas had landed, late as usual. Maliki wouldn't be able to prolong this meeting with his old and dear friend as much as he would have preferred. It was a question of priorities; he had an entire nation to violate and abuse, and so he couldn't spend too much time on a single citizen.

He lit the obscenely expensive Cohiba cigar, another from his host's personal collection, and rested it on the top of a Chinese Chippendale desk right next to a stainless steel butcher's saw purchased especially for that day's festivities. Maliki made sure the fine cigar burned deeply into both the wood and the rich leather inlay. This priceless antique had been in the General's family for centuries, supposedly a gift from the then Prince of Wales himself. Each time Lord Philip and he got drunk there in the study, the desk got older. In a year or two it would have certainly predated Stonehenge.

With the cigar burning ruthlessly into its polished surface, the desk was no longer priceless. In fact, it continued losing value quickly as the cigar went on burning an ugly black line across the top. The rich aroma of the cigar was now mixed with the acrid smell of burning mahogany and leather.

Maliki had also retrieved a bottle of wine, a Chateau Mouton-Rothschild that was the prize of Philip's collection. This exceedingly rare selection was being served in paper cups from a local fast-food restaurant, and condensation formed a vulgar wet circle on the wood where the overly chilled bottle was left open on the desk.

Maliki would have been satisfied with that, but Nadja now possessed a festering hatred for the General, who apparently enjoyed some truly aberrant sexual tastes. She suggested one last, painful insult to the nobleman. Maliki had no antipathy for inherited wealth; his family was equally favored in Pakistan. However, Maliki had enlarged and enhanced the power and wealth of his ancestors. Sir Philip was simply a drone.

Maliki refused Nadja's initial request, but she could be very persuasive. As a result, the General's two prized foxhounds sat motionless in the corner. Maliki had them stuffed and mounted sitting in chairs at a table with playing cards in their paws. The brown one actually had a Cohiba in his mouth as well. The dogs playing poker had been his contribution to the presentation, there was no doubt that his dear friend would be beside himself with anger.

Right on cue, his co-star entered stage left, accompanied by Karam and Talat. Sir Philip, to Maliki's delight, was in full costume. The General stood tall and thin, with a full head of wavy brown hair streaked with grey. He looked striking in his perfectly tailored uniform, cap tucked under his arm with medals polished and in perfect formation across his left breast.

Lord Philip wrinkled his nose as he entered, then looked impatiently around the room. Maliki helped the General by picking up the cigar and putting it in his mouth. Maliki then sat in the desk chair and propped his feet up on the desk top, next to the still smoldering scar.

Lord Philip stared blankly for a moment, then literally spat out his words in surprise and disdain, "What in the bloody hell do you think you are doing?"

Maliki blew a long cloud of bluish smoke into the air.

"I'm just enjoying a fine cigar and a cup of wine with an old friend."

Maliki looked at the wine bottle and its honor guard of horrid little cups. Sir Philip's face went blank as he gawked at the display, his mind did not process disrespect or derision. His face became the pathetic visage of the cast fool as he looked back at Maliki.

"I don't understand."

Maliki stood and set the cigar back down on the desk. He then walked to the General and amicably put his arm around the taller man.

"Philip, you never did. In fact, you are such a fool that I doubt you could ever truly grasp what has transpired around you."

Sir Philip glared at Maliki, then pulled away. "I don't have to listen to this. You've gone mad! I want you to leave my estate immediately."

"I plan on leaving, but not quite yet; and certainly not because you wish me to go. Besides, there are things I need to do, and things we need to do together. Here, have a cigar. It will help you relax as we chat."

Maliki walked to the corner and retrieved the cigar

from the stuffed dog's mouth. Sir Philip could only stare in disbelief as the man, someone he'd assumed was a friend, picked up a lighter from the poker table and lit the cigar.

Maliki offered the cigar to the General, but his friend simply glowered back and refused to take it.

"No matter, you won't have had a chance to finish it anyway,"

Maliki shrugged.

He carefully inserted the cigar back into the dog's mouth and patted its head. At this, Lord Philip came back to himself. He spun around and walked briskly toward the door.

"I'm calling the police."

Maliki waved a hand, and the two guards took the General by the arms and dragged him to where Maliki stood.

"Let me go this instant! I won't listen to another word," Philip said as he struggled to gain his freedom.

Maliki picked up a large, carved statue of a pheasant taking flight and slammed the base of it into his captive's stomach. The General doubled over with a groan and a whimper. Maliki lifted Lord Philip's head and glared into his troubled dark-brown eyes.

"Failure to listen will be punished, painfully. Do you understand?"

Lord Philip, to his credit, glared at Maliki and turned his head away. "Fuck off."

Maliki looked up at Talat, who slammed a massive fist into the old man's kidney. The General staggered, moaning pitifully. Maliki nodded and Talat pummeled him again, and this time the old man slumped, and then nodded his head. "I'm listening." Maliki smiled and spread his hands.

"Wonderful, because there are some things I've been wanting to tell you for a terribly long while."

Lord Philip struggled to raise his head, and he looked over weakly at Maliki.

"Why? Why are you doing this?"

"Precisely what I wanted us to talk about!"

Maliki walked to a section of the wall opposite the door that was covered with pictures, certificates and awards. On the far left were photos of a young Philip at school and in uniform. Maliki took down a picture of three young men in uniform, standing arm in arm in front of a small jet aircraft. He held it out to the General, smiling.

"Our first day of flight school, remember? They called us the 'Three Musketeers.' We'd been together since first year at King's College. A person with your titles should have gone to Oxford or Cambridge, but you weren't smart enough were you? My family was one of the most powerful in Pakistan, but as I was to learn—Pakis are Pakis, no matter how rich they are."

Lord Philip just glared back.

"At King's College we decided to save the world, so our next stop was Cranwell." Maliki stared at the photo. "After the Air College we all went to flight school, but here things began to change. It was subtle, but there. I learned, in many different but delicate ways that I would never be RAF. I was from 'over there.'"

Maliki took a menacing step toward the General, and spoke in a soft but threatening voice, "I believed we were comrades. I was a fool."

Maliki smiled jovially, then sailed the picture across the room. It shattered when it smashed into the wooden base of the wet bar. Maliki turned and took a step toward the center of the picture wall. There he retrieved another photo in a large, ornate frame.

"This is where I learned my place, learned what I really meant to you. More importantly, I discovered what every person from my race and faith meant to our colonial masters."

Maliki held up the picture to the General, who with difficulty raised his head to examine it. After a moment, he raised his eyes to his tormentor, confused.

"You don't even remember, do you? Your father was in Parliament, and an influential member of the House of Lords. Right before graduation you rushed over to us, almost dizzy with excitement. You stood straight, head high and proud, and declared: 'We are going to have an audience with the Queen! Right after the ceremony.'"

Sir Philip could only glance up out of the corner of his eye, a first hint of understanding breaking through his pain-clouded mind.

He looked at the picture again. Several beaming young officers stood at attention as a robust looking Queen Elizabeth addressed them. Sir Philip Thomas-Morgan and the second Musketeer were clearly visible; the dark-skinned Maliki clearly was not.

The General shook his head weakly. "All this because you didn't meet the Queen?"

"You still don't understand!" Maliki became angry. Decades of resentment proved difficult to restrain. "It's because my best friends decided I wasn't worthy to meet their Queen. I was smarter, stronger, and a better officer and pilot than either of you, but you actually laughed at the idea of a Paki officer being invited. I thought I had been your friend. Instead, I was merely your mascot."

Maliki paused, allowing himself to calm down. "I'm also doing this for bin Laden. I met him as a child, when he fought the Russians. He stayed with us a while after he was forced to flee Tora Bora in Afghanistan. He will be missed. He will be avenged."

Maliki walked over to the desk. The two thugs dragged

Sir Philip along behind, and slammed him roughly down in the wooden desk chair. Maliki pointed at the large computer screen behind where the cigar was still burning an angry channel into the desk's surface. Maliki pointed to a large, white, cigar-shaped object that almost filled the screen.

"You recognize this of course."

The General regained a portion of his strength, and glared at Maliki before he turned his eyes toward the screen.

"A Predator."

Maliki bent over the desk, and using a small computer mouse, he changed the picture to reveal a wide-angle view. He gestured to the screen and commented politely, "You'll recognize where it's located, as well."

Sir Philip glanced at the screen, then frowned and leaned closer. He shook his head and looked over at his tormentor, confused. "That looks like my hanger, here on the estate, but that's impossible."

"Difficult, but not impossible. And with your help, I will use this drone to kill Prince Harry and certainly others in the Royal Family."

Maliki watched with growing anticipation, as fear etched itself in his captive's features, and hopefully his soul as well. Maliki continued, "You have filed an official, military flight plan for your old de Havilland. You will take off from the estate here, and arrive in Cardiff tomorrow. Only it won't be your little red airplane making the flight. It will be this drone."

The General squinted at the screen, examining the drone carefully. Maliki bent and pointed at two long, cylindrical objects hanging under the wings of the aircraft.

"Yes, my old friend, those are Hellfire missiles. We recovered everything intact almost a year ago. We recovered another over three years ago. I was going to use the first to kill Prince Harry in Afghanistan, but the preparation time proved too great. Once we had perfected the process, bringing them here became a simple problem of logistics."

Lord Philip shook his head, fighting the realization that this was actually happening. "No," he muttered. Maliki put his hand on the mouse and moved the cursor, clicking to open a window that filled the screen. The image of the lethal drone aircraft was replaced by the real-time video of General Philip Morgan-Thomas seated in his chair with much of the room visible behind him. Maliki nodded to his security men, and they moved quickly to the chair. They secured the General's arms with Velcro straps. The captive looked blankly from one arm to the other, then looked up bewildered at Maliki.

Karam pulled out a rope and tied Philip firmly to the chair, as Talat pulled ski masks from his pocket. The General craned his neck to see the men behind him, then began to squirm, twist and shake violently, trying desperately to escape. Karam pulled a pistol from his waistband and smashed it into the base of the General's skull, dazing him. He slumped forward slightly, head lolling.

Maliki took the butcher's saw from the desk and bent down, face close to that of the semi-conscious man in the chair.

"Philip, let's not make this unpleasant."

They all laughed, except the General, who stared blankly at the saw. Maliki twisted his head to look at the screen and nodded. "We're recording. Let's finish this." He held the saw in front of Philip's face. "I read about this recently in an American thriller novel. A Libyan terrorist executed an old enemy with a saw instead of a knife. I thought I would try it myself."

The three pulled the ski masks over their faces and took up positions behind the chair, Maliki directly behind his friend, who was now thrashing violently. Maliki glanced at Karam, who struck their captive again at the base of the skull, causing him to go rigid and slump forward.

Maliki raised the saw over his head and began to shout.

"The British crusaders and their American masters continue to wage an unholy war on Allah and his people!"

Maliki grabbed the General by the head and pulled it back so his face was clearly visible on the screen in front of him.

"This man is a crusader, a General, in the British Air Forces. He has killed innocent women and children in the name of the ungodly! He will suffer here, now, and then again in the fires of hell for all eternity. This is his punishment."

The other two moved to hold the still-stunned General, trying to keep him from struggling too vigorously as Maliki pressed the point of saw blade against the right side of Lord Philip's neck. The masked terrorist forced the saw forward, ripping into his captive's soft flesh, angling the blade forward to sever the veins and arteries of the neck as quickly as possible. He especially wanted to sever the windpipe.

The General was screaming and begging, as he struggled futilely against his bonds and captors. Maliki hated this. The noise was always so pathetic and disgusting. He continued pulling and pushing the fine steel blade through flesh, and was impressed with how much easier the saw worked than the blade of a knife.

Yes, much better.

He struck an artery, and blood sprayed in all directions. It instantly began to pool on the fine Persian carpet. He decided against laying down plastic. He wanted the authorities to find the raw scene, in all its horrible splendor. There was a shudder, and the blood flow from the now gaping neck weakened then stopped.

The coward had died almost immediately! Did the pathetic weakling have a heart attack? This was a disappointment, Maliki had wanted his friend to suffer as long as possible. However, Maliki kept up even strokes with the saw for the audience that would see this tomorrow night. The blade struck bone, but Maliki forced it back and forth with brutal efficiency. He would never use a knife again.

Moments later, Maliki lifted the head by the hair and shouted.

"Allahu Akbar. Death to the crusaders!"

He held the head aloft for a moment longer, then looked over to Talat.

"Cut! That should be enough. Edit the first part. And have it ready by tonight. I will be in the hanger."

The General's lifeless body lay slumped forward against its restraints. Maliki dropped the head unceremoniously in the dead Lord Philip Morgan-Thomas' own lap, and strode out.

Chapter 28

I moved quietly through a narrow, six-foot wide strip of brush and trees. Dee and Blackjack were supposed to be waiting for me at a small country road ahead. To my left, I examined a pasture and to my right, I saw the still intact concrete of a World War II airfield. Both the pasture and the airstrip were protected by well-maintained, triple-strand, barbed-wire fences.

The sheep, grazing earlier in the pasture as I moved in to recon the facilities, were gone. They had slowed my ingress as some had their heads extended through the fence, trying to reach the longer grass outside their normal grazing area. Several stopped munching to watch me pass. I couldn't take a chance on startling them and had moved at a slower, non-threatening pace.

Thank goodness they were gone, nesting, or whatever it is that sheep do at night. This allowed me to pick up my pace as I distanced myself from the racetrack, recouping the minutes I lost maintaining the silence of the lambs.

I jogged on in a steady, terrain-grinding rhythm, which

allowed me to look around and appreciate the current landscape, much nicer than where I was a week ago. The contrast between here and Afghanistan was staggering. Green was much nicer than brown, and there were so many interesting shades of green in Wales.

Brown basically came in two shades, dull and duller. Maybe there were three shades, since parts of rural Afghanistan tipped the scale all the way to brutally dull.

I reached the end of the fence and stopped, inside a thin screen of trees. Just beyond lay the road where Dee would be waiting. Where Dee was supposed to be waiting, I didn't see the car.

I scanned the area, right and then left. I finally saw the car, about fifty meters short of where we agreed to meet. For some reason, she stopped too early. Besides being some distance off to my left, the car was off on the shoulder and headed the wrong way. The front right tire had passed well onto the grass, and the car was still running. It was dark, but I could see Blackjack in the driver's side window barking madly at the trees to my left.

Something was wrong.

I moved as rapidly as possible toward the car, staying in the cover of the trees. I looked at the vehicle; I could hear the barking now. Blackjack jumped back and forth between the front and back seats, still frantic about something happening in the trees ahead of me.

I began to run, and could now hear strange sounds ahead of me. First came a slight whimper, followed by the sound of someone crashing through the bushes. I then heard the disturbing sound of a moan, and I recognized Dee's voice.

I was almost there.

I heard more crashing, after which came the unmistakable sound of pants being hurriedly unzipped.

There was another urgent moan, followed only seconds later by another moan, but one of pleasure. I could see a path, where someone had forced their way through the bushes. I pulled out my SIG and hurried to follow the sounds.

I was there, but now there was the sound of—what the hell? I broke through to a tiny open area between three larger trees and found Dee squatting in the shadows, pants down and a look of absolute pleasure on her face.

She saw me and scowled, "Go on, what are you gawking at?"

I turned to face the road, removing the black watch cap from my face and head. "I thought you were in trouble."

"I bloody well was in trouble, I had to piss something awful."

There has been an ongoing debate about women in combat, and I'd served with women who were fantastic Marines. But, until they could issue a combat rated bladder, I still saw potential for problems.

Also, I was not happy about my possible exposure by having to run to her rescue, and I could hear that Blackjack wasn't happy either. With a little more irritation in my voice than I intended, I called to her over my shoulder, "If there's nothing else, I'm going to the car."

"There is something, dear. Since you're here, and my pants are already down, would you mind kissing my rosy red ass? Don't get pissy with me, you toss pot. I really had to pee!"

I knew when a skirmish was unwinnable and hurried toward the safety of the car. Blackjack stopped barking, both paws on the window, as I approached. He jumped to the passenger seat as I reached the far door.

Once I sat down, he jumped in my lap and started

licking the top of my head. What was it with this dog and my bald head?

I managed to pull the beast away, and reach under my seat for the disposable cell phone I'd stashed there. I turned it on and watched for it to acquire a signal, and then waited silently for it to connect to the network. It finally went active, but there were no voicemail, no text messages, and therefore, no answers. I turned it off and stowed it back under my seat as Dee plopped inside. She closed her door then turned to look at me as if nothing had happened.

"What did you find?"

"This is it. The runway is still in decent shape and there are a couple of old hangers the track owners use as shops or for storage. I checked the first hanger, inside I saw a fully assembled drone waiting at the hanger door. There were two men keeping guard near the second one, but I have to assume the second drone is in the hanger I couldn't get to."

She thought a moment, then asked, "Is it armed?

"The first drone had two missiles, one under each wing. The other one could have as many as four."

Dee turned and looked out her window a moment, then turned and nodded resolutely at me. There was a new resolve in her eyes, a stronger determination than I'd seen before.

"I'd still hoped we were wrong, simply paranoid. This is the real thing, isn't it?"

"Life or death."

Her gaze seemed to intensify; she sat a little straighter in her seat. "But you're not here for the missiles, are you?"

I had to be careful how I answered. Dee and I had different priorities for this mission. "The drones are not my only objective."

"Are they your primary objective?"

I should have told her what she wanted to hear, but I couldn't lie to her, not then. And after the library, all we'd been through together, maybe never.

"No."

"Travis, promise me, the drones can't take off."

I didn't think I could promise that. "The man who took your brother's life may be only a few hundred meters away."

"And the man who's about to make that sacrifice meaningless is sitting right here."

I didn't need the distraction right then. I looked at my watch and reached for the door handle. "Time to go. Besides I didn't think you liked the English, or royalty."

"I don't like British Rail, either, but I can't imagine life without it. I don't know whether this Maliki character knows it or not, but the Monarchy in many ways is Britain. You can understand that, can't you?"

Actually, I couldn't. My entire adult life revolved around loyalty to my teammates. I had never even registered to vote, and only cared about who was running things when they screwed with my ability to do the job.

Dee sensed that she was not getting through to me. "Gareth would go after the drones, even if it killed him."

She paused only for a second, and then went on, "I guess it did kill him. It's what I'm going to do, go after the drones. If you don't promise me, I'll go after them myself."

Shit!

I really didn't have a choice. We were running this mission together, mates. I felt my face flush, not that kind of mates. Not yet. But maybe? I guess that meant I was going after the drones.

"Travis?"

I felt her hand rest on mine. It felt warm, nice. I realized that I had been staring out the window, up at the stars. I also realized that my priorities had suddenly changed.

"I'm thinking, give me a minute."

I could still do this. I turned and put my other hand on top of hers. She looked at our hands, surprised.

"Drones first, but you have to do exactly what I say. Agreed?" She frowned slightly, thinking it over, but finally nodded.

And, she hadn't pulled her hand away.

"I move into position outside the hangers, and at exactly," I looked at my watch, "two-fifteen you drive down the road until you can see the main building through the trees. It's the tall one, remember?"

She nodded twice. She'd remember.

"Fire at the house with the MP5, on auto. Empty the whole magazine, aim for the upper level. Keep firing until they start to fire back. OK so far?"

She nodded again, but I was sure she would object to my next instructions.

"When you start taking fire, drive like hell toward Penilton. Use your cell phone and call the police, say you live in the area, and tell them you heard shooting from the track. A lot of it! Tell them someone's chasing you and they're armed."

"Not bloody likely! You think I'm going to tuck tail and just leave you there?"

"I need you to do this. Not only will some of the men leave to chase you, but I'm going to use your diversion to sneak into the hangers, grab some wire cutters, and slice the cables to the aileron, the wing flaps. If things don't go well, for us, Maliki won't know there's a problem until they try to take off. Then it will be too late."

The biggest benefit to my plan would be not having to worry about Dee. I reached into the back and dug through the bag behind my seat. Blackjack energetically started licking my head again, but I pushed him away.

I pulled out a set of two-way radios, wiped the dog slobber off my head with a sleeve, and set the channels. I then turned the volume down to the lowest setting and handed one of them to Dee.

"No voice, clicks only, just key the transmit button." I press the red button on the side, and there was a corresponding click from the speaker of her walkie-talkie. "I will click once when I'm in position, you acknowledge with a single click. Likewise, you click once when you're about to drive to the building and open fire, and I acknowledge with a click. If you have a problem, click three times and I'll get to you. Give it a try." She pressed the transmit button, and heard the click from my radio. I responded with a click. Everything worked fine, and she nodded. Dee grinned wickedly, then clicked three times and asked, "What took you so long?"

Excellent, her mind was right, and she had her emotions under control. I never really doubted that she was cool and professional enough to carry out her assignment. My part would be a little tougher, but this way she has a good chance to make it—better than mine.

I grabbed the door handle, stopped, then turned to face her. I smiled confidently.

"This will work, and you'll do great; I know it. Meet you back here in two hours."

Dee started to reach for me, then stopped, embarrassed. I smiled, and she smiled back. She grabbed my shirt, pulled me close and planted a quick kiss on my lips. Blackjack probably wanted to give me a wet one, too, but that would have to wait. She blinked, looking just a little embarrassed, and almost as surprised as I was.

Dee reached and touched my arm, then whispered,

"Thank you."

"If we're both alive at Gareth's funeral, you can thank me then. There's too much that can go wrong before that."

She just smiled shyly and nodded.

What the hell did that mean? Did she nod because she would thank me then, or because she knew things could go wrong? The more time I spent with Dee, the more confused I became.

I decided to take the initiative. "Dee, there's something I want you to know, in case things don't . . . just in case."

She blinked, and stared. She looked both apprehensive and expectant.

"They're called Panda cars because in the mid-sixties, they were black and white, or blue and white, and looked like a panda on wheels."

Her face went blank, and her jaw dropped. That would pay her back for pretending the kiss was nothing. I smiled. "I just thought you should know."

I hopped out of the car, and trotted silently back into the trees.

* * *

I neared my target, a group of buildings on the opposite side of the runway from the tower and road. This brought me closer to the second hanger. I wanted to get a look at it before I launched my assault, to determine the easiest way to disable that second drone. It would also leave me closer to the row of trees marking the northeast side of the property where I would begin my attack.

From there I could move through the trees and brush, and would be able to approach the house, where I assumed Maliki would be.

I arrived at the second hanger twenty minutes ahead of

schedule. The guards were gone so I approached from the rear, and discovered that we had a problem. A large section of the rear wall was gone. Inside was a rusted old pickup truck and a stand of weeds. This hanger had been abandoned, and unless there were two drones in the other hanger, and I'd just missed it, the second drone was somewhere else. And, I had no idea where that could be.

If the second drone were gone, what else—who else—could be missing as well?

I moved to hanger one. I could see the guards inside through the rear window. They were not asleep, but they weren't particularly alert, either. I moved back into the trees where I could observe both the house and the hanger.

I checked my watch, still ten minutes ahead of schedule and half an hour before Dee brought the party to life. I keyed the transmit button. Dee should have heard the single click. Almost immediately I heard the answering click, meaning Dee was all right. Everything was set.

As I lay down in the brush to gain better concealment, I heard faint, low voices in the distance, from well beyond the hanger. I slipped quickly to my left, trying to determine who, where and why. I saw two well-armed men exiting the old control tower building and getting into a small dark sedan.

The car cranked over, started, and without turning on the lights, they cruised carefully out of the gate and down the short drive to the road. I lost sight of them before they reached the road, and had no idea what they were doing. Should I warn Dee? I didn't know if they had a scanner, but I would've in their situation.

I had to risk it; I keyed the transmit button. "Dee, two men in a dark sedan are on the road. Click once if you understand."

The click came back immediately.

Excellent.

I slipped back to my observation point, lay back down and thought about the mission, mentally examining every detail for something, anything, I'd missed. That train of thought became quickly derailed when I thought about Dee, and the kiss outside the library.

I also realized this was no time for daydreams.

Chapter 29

"How the hell did things get like this?" Dee said to no one, or maybe to everyone.

Blackjack's head popped up from the passenger's seat, and he looked at her eagerly. Dee smiled; at least somebody would stand by her to the end. Which may not be that far away.

She picked up the machine gun and examined it again, careful to leave the safety on. She hated it. She had no desire to even touch the thing, this MP5, much less to fire it. What happened to the good old days when MPs were simply shameless politicians and deserted country roads were for shagging. She wanted another bath, with truly therapeutic bath oils and properly scented candles next time.

Dee thought about it, and decided being alive for breakfast may be enough for today.

She considered her options for Blackjack again, and regretted not finding a place to leave him. She felt terrible about exposing him to danger, but there were only two options now, let Blackjack out or keep him in the car. If she let him out, would she be able to find him again? She wasn't even sure when she'd be alive to come back. Plus, there were wild animals, and even larger dogs, that would pose a threat.

There in the car, she'd be able to watch out for him, but only as well as she'd be able to watch out for herself. Her little four-legged baby would do anything to protect her, but these bastards would have guns. Not a fair contest, and not an easy decision.

She pressed a button on her watch, which illuminated the numbers on the face. She held it for over a minute, watching the numbers tick past, seconds and then minutes. There was still a bit of time before she had to get moving, but she felt herself growing nervous. She decided to keep her mind busy by beginning her preparations. She had to do something; the waiting had begun to get to her.

"In the back."

Dee nudged Blackjack and he hopped eagerly into the back seat. She pressed a button on her door and rolled down the passenger's window, then did the same for her window. She looked around the car and wondered if that would be good enough. The building would be on her right, so she would be firing out of her window, but Travis had told her to roll down all of the windows. He said there would be a lot of noise and smoke. She started to roll down the back windows, then looked at Blackjack. She didn't think he would jump out, and so she rolled them all the way down. She second guessed herself, and wondered how he would react when the shooting began. Would he panic?

She rolled them up. How much smoke could there be? But, what if she needed to fire at the building a little longer, out the rear window? She rolled down just the rear window on the driver's side. Blackjack promptly hopped over and looked out, so she rolled it back up.

"Shit!"

Finally, she snatched the gun from her lap and tossed it over onto the passenger's seat. Dee grabbed the steering wheel, shook it, then screamed.

"What the bloody hell are you doing, Jones? You think you're Rambo, and this is a movie?"

She took a breath, slowly, then forced herself to take a second, even slower this time. If this were a movie, it would be Doctor Who.

She realized that her breathing was still coming fast and shallow, and so she forced herself to take slow, even breaths. She calmed down and felt better. In a little while, she would slip the car into gear, drive the three hundred meters ahead to where she would turn right, then in another quarter mile she would reach the track. As she drove serenely past, she would simply point that bloody gun out the window, pull the trigger, fire a shit load of bullets at nothing in particular, then drive like hell to town.

Piece of cake.

Simple.

No problem!

Bullshit, big FUCKING problem! But I can do it.

She nodded. She could do this. Things would be fine.

Everything would work out splendidly, then she could go home.

She had almost convinced herself that there would be no problems, when a car turned onto the roadway ahead of her. All she could see were the headlights, which approached her at what seemed to be a normal speed.

"Just someone coming home from a night out," she assured herself, but realized her hands squeezed the wheel so hard that it pinched the palms of her hand.

She thought about ducking down, but she'd waited too

long. Suddenly, the approaching car turned on its bright lights and slowed. Dee continued to sit, trying to look normal, but couldn't help but glance over as the other car crept passed.

In the other car, probably the dark sedan Travis had warned her about, were two middle-eastern men. The driver held a walkie-talkie radio to his mouth. Dee looked straight ahead, but from the corner of her eye she saw their heads turn to watch her as they drove past.

Now what?

The answer to that question became obvious when, several seconds later, she saw the brake lights from the other car burn a bright, angry red in her rearview mirror.

"Blackjack, come!" she shouted. The dog bounded obediently next to her.

The car in her mirror started a u-turn. She reached quickly across, opened the passenger's door, and gave Blackjack a push.

"Out, get out."

Blackjack gave a confused look back, then obeyed. Dee stomped the gas pedal and let the acceleration of her car close the door. She left him there. She had to. She had no idea what was about to happen, but she knew she didn't want him leaping about the car if things went bad. She really didn't want him in there if the bastards started—if things got really bad. And she couldn't think about what might happen if they caught her.

She pressed the accelerator harder, but it was already at the floor. She was starting from a dead stop while they were already at speed. The distance between the cars closed, and she looked over at the gun; no, not yet. She'd been trained in tactical driving, maybe she could stay ahead of them.

She looked in the mirror. They were almost on her. She reached over and pulled the gun onto her lap. Maybe she could pull ahead on the turn. She looked into the mirror, and her heart sank. Her pursuers were now almost on her. She wouldn't make it.

She grabbed the handgrip of her machine gun, then swerved and almost lost control as a thundering noise detonated from her right. It sounded like the roar of a racing engine, but why would it start now?

The answer came with three flashes from her pursuers and the shudder as bullets impacted the rear of her car. These bastards were shooting at her! The engine noise would mask that from the neighbors, so they wouldn't alert the police. Well, she had a gun, too.

She gripped the weapon and started to point it at them out the window.

Safety, she had to take it off safe. She flipped the lever with her thumb and held it out the window.

Take that you bastards!

She squeezed the trigger, and hell erupted next to her. The gun barked and bucked in her hand. The noise deafened her and made her right ear ring painfully. The flash nearly blinded her and little bits of something stung her face. She almost dropped the gun.

She just wanted to toss the damn thing and run, but Travis needed her. She held it up as best she could and squeezed again. She had to concentrate to keep it pointed back, and didn't notice that her car had slowed down considerably. The impact of the other car slamming into the rear of hers was a complete shock, and the violence of the collision jarred the gun from her hand.

She lunged after the falling gun, and between reaching out and the force of the other car pushing her sideways, she almost lost control. Her car crossed the lane to her right and skidded onto the dirt shoulder. She braked and fought the wheel, and managed to right her car. She yanked left to get back on the road, but the other car was there, blocking her. She slammed into the others, and both cars came to a skidding halt.

Dee hopped out and started to run back for her gun, but she slipped on the wet grass. She looked over her shoulder as she struggled back to her feet. The driver's door was pinned closed, but the passenger was already out and sprinting back toward her. She regained her footing and starting to run, when over the roar of the nearby engine, she heard the crack of a gunshot, and dirt erupted a meter or two in front of her.

There were two more shots, each bullet slamming into the ground closer than the previous. She thought about trying to run into the woods, but a small man appeared in front of her holding an MP5 of his own. Dee stopped and raised her hands in the air. At that moment, the out of breath driver, holding a large metal flashlight in one hand and a walkie-talkie in the other, arrived at his partner's side. He played the light over Dee, then looked at his friend. They began speaking in a language she didn't recognize, definitely not Arabic, and the small man nodded, agreeing with his partner about something.

The man with the light spoke briefly into his radio, then stuffed it into his pocket. He pulled a pistol from the holster hanging under his armpit, it appeared to have a silencer on it. He pointed it at Dee and approached her carefully.

As he reached her, the roaring engine sputtered once and died. As the silence returned, they heard a noise on the road behind them. The man with the light jabbed the pistol roughly into her side, and the other spun back. They could make out the sound now, barking, and close.

Blackjack had followed her!

"Go back!" Dee shouted.

The flashlight slammed violently into her stomach, and she doubled over. The man growled, "Shut up!"

He pointed the flashlight up the road and in the distance, a bounding black shape entered the limit of their vision. The man with the MP5 began to raise it, but the other spoke sharply and he lowered his weapon. The man with the light pushed Dee to the other, then took two steps toward her dog.

He raised the pistol, flashlight held next to it. They could see Blackjack clearly now.

"No!" Dee rushed toward the man, but felt a crushing blow as the MP5 slammed into her back and sent her sprawling. She heard a loud pop, then the heartbreaking sound of a squeal and a yelp from up the road.

The men laughed, and the man with the pistol fired again; but no sound followed. Dee struggled to her feet, fighting to get at the bastard who'd killed Blackjack. Before she regained her balance, the MP5 smashed into the side of her head, and she fell into blackness.

Chapter 30

I moved back into my concealed position in the trees behind the hanger. Someone had started a racecar in the yard outside, and I decided to find out what was happening. I'd crawled to the side of the building and looked in, but everything looked normal. I used the opportunity to take a couple of pictures of the drone with my phone, careful to leave it on for only a minute at a time.

The engine shut down, and I looked around to make sure I hadn't attracted any unwanted attention. I then checked my radio; it was on, properly set and about five minutes from receiving Dee's signal. I started to feel the adrenaline rush; my motor was revving, and I was ready and waiting to pop the clutch.

I'd just finished doing a quick survey of the World War II airfield, once racetrack, now terrorist hangout and resort. I had to give Maliki credit. This was a brilliant idea. After the war, some enterprising Welshmen acquired the property and supplemented their sheep herding business by using the runway for weekend races. This place provided everything the weekend speed freak could want. It had a machine shop, storage buildings, fuel tanks, and a couple of large hangers for getting the hopeful cars or motorcycles ready to race.

In some ways, it was even better for the weekend Muslim terrorist. The ample hanger was now home to a missile-equipped drone, and the roaming sheep provided the kind of romantic and recreational activities they usually only got at home.

The only other buildings that looked occupied were the control tower, and a house where the operators of the full-time farm and part-time track had lived, and probably died. The terrorists appeared to be quartered in the house.

Regarding the tower building, I checked that out as well. From nearby trees, I could see the exterior. Harsh security lighting revealed faded paintings of racing cars and the logos of several brands of beer covering the sides of the old control tower. There was also a freshly repainted track logo, a bright-red dragster with the front end of a World War II era, prop driven fighter aircraft – I'd say a Hurricane by the pointy nose.

I couldn't get close enough to be certain about who or what was inside, there were guards at the door and at least two people upstairs. It looked like the racetrack owners had converted it into a VIP gallery for race spectators. I was pretty sure the radio equipment would have been deployed there.

In addition, an adjoining concession stand had been built next to the west side of the tower facing the caravan park. When people in the UK heard 'caravan park' they didn't think camels, they thought Winnebago. Caravans in the UK meant trailers or recreational vehicles. I knew this because I'd managed to peek inside of the three caravans still in the caravan park. I would be sure to mention this to the police when they arrived, the next of kin would need to be notified.

The tower itself was a square, two-story building with very large windows facing the runway, turned track, now runway again. Those windows originally allowed British controllers to watch the takeoffs and landings of Wellington, or assorted bombers. For the last decade, however, it had been used as a takeoff and landing place for out-of-control Brits to get bombed and watch the races.

Terrorist now occupied the structure, and watched what was again a runway and its surrounding terrain, so they could bomb the Brits. The vicious cycle got more vicious each time around.

The actual runway, or drag strip, had been maintained well enough for a Predator to take off safely. And since it was no longer considered a runway, if anyone had decided to search for a place where drones might be launched, this would not have been on the list.

I looked across the small open space again, then down at my watch. This was a perfect spot; Maliki had things planned out to the smallest detail. I, on the other hand, was playing things by ear. I just hoped things worked out, which they were not since Dee was now late. I had a small earphone with my radio, and I knew the walkie-talkie still worked, because I'd tested it using the squelch adjustment.

The radio was now the problem. She should have signaled me five minutes before, and time was running out. I needed to start working on a contingency plan, fast.

First the Predator. I couldn't count on secretly disabling the drone any longer, so I silently circled the hanger looking for options. I could still see a guard inside, sitting in a folding chair next to the aircraft. I had to assume the other one was still there as well.

On the northwest corner, outside the hanger, I could

see an old gas pump, just a few feet from an electrical fuse panel. I hadn't paid any attention to it before, but now I could see there were weeds growing behind the pump, but not in front. The front area was packed gravel and appeared to receive regular traffic.

I also noticed there were several electrical conduits leading from the bottom of the fuse box and entering the hanger through the wall. In addition, another conduit from the box curved and went underground toward the pump, feeding power to the gas pump itself.

Besides fueling their own equipment, it would have made sense for the owners to have a gas pump on site. It would also have made sense for them to keep it locked. I crouched low and moved quietly across the open area between my concealed position and the pump, to find out if it was locked.

I reached the faded red pump without attracting the gaze or gunfire of any of the local killers, and then hid in the shadows behind the pump. The smell of gasoline was strong here, a good sign. A quick examination revealed that there was indeed a lock, but that it had been broken and was lying in the weeds below the lever. I still had to make sure the pump was operational. I quietly removed the hose from the side of the pump and lifted the lever, activating the pump. I heard the click that meant there was power, and silently squeezed the handle. The pump whirred, and a weak stream of gasoline poured onto the ground in front of me. I now had a flammable liquid, but how could I get it to the drone?

I turned and examined the side of the building. There was a large hole in the wall where a bundle of electrical conduits passed through to provide power to the building's interior. I scanned the area and found empty bottles and buckets strewn about. I filled three glass bottles and two of the five-gallon buckets with gas, then turned off the pump. Below the fuse box, I found several strands of discarded electrical wire and tied the lever in the handle of the gas nozzle open. If the pump was turned on, the gasoline would automatically flow out of the nozzle and onto the ground.

But I didn't want it to pour onto the ground. I had a plan. With some effort, I forced the gas nozzle through the wall where the electrical conduits entered the building. The gas would now flow directly into the hanger. I estimated that within a minute of the pump being turned on, gasoline would reach the drone. More importantly, it would have reached other items being stored in the hanger. I'd seen a car and a couple of motorcycles, a stack of what looked like paint cans, another oil drum, and two cutting torches with their accompanying oxygen and gas tanks.

That made a nice combination of things that burned, and things that went boom. If that weren't enough to set off the whole building, the fire would soon reach this pump and its storage tank. The resulting inferno would not only finish the job, but make enough of a conflagration to attract the local police and fire departments.

I moved one of the five-gallon buckets next to the gas pump, and another next to the wall where the nozzle poked inside. I set the gas hose into the bucket, and looked around for a cloth of some kind to use as a wick. There were actually a couple of oily rags sitting on top of the pump. I filled several bottles, then tore one of the rags into strips, and stuffed the strips into the top of the bottles.

I took my Molotov cocktails and moved back into the woods. I then set the bottles down in a bush opposite the pump, knelt and waited. This part of my new and improvised plan was now ready. All I had to do was run by, turn on the pump, and light and throw bottles of gas at the nozzle. The perfect ending to my perfect plan would then involve grabbing wienies and marshmallows to roast while I waited for the cops.

I looked at my watch. Rigging the hanger to burn and blow had only taken a few minutes, but Dee was now ten minutes late. I needed to move, but I really needed to know what was going on with Dee. I keyed my mike once, she should at least hear the click and respond with a click of her own.

After a few seconds, through my earpiece I heard two clicks in reply. I knew what that meant; Dee was not the one holding the radio.

Shit! Did I blow the drone, or try for Maliki first? If I blew the drone now, I could use the chaos to try to get to Maliki. He may even have come out of hiding to try to save the drone.

That was the smart thing to do. That was what I should have done. But, what about Dee? I didn't know what had happened to her, but I had to assume there was a problem. I may need the diversion later to save her. I knew what she would want, but I wasn't ready to play my best diversionary card without knowing what was at stake.

I needed more intel.

I moved toward the house, staying just inside the trees. Except for the road leading in, the entire property was bordered by a relatively dense barrier of trees and brush. This wasn't surprising. The nearest neighbor was probably a quarter-mile away, but the sound of high-performance engines and squealing tires would still be annoying.

The tree line curved left, and the house was set back away from the rest of the property. This gave the owners, and any visiting terrorist or assassins, a little privacy. Apparently, they didn't care about privacy anymore, since the open area around the house suddenly became bathed in light.

I could make out the house through the trees, and it appeared that every light, inside and out, had blazed to life. The yard around the house was now visible, though not quite perfectly, and I could see a head moving back and forth in one of the upstairs windows. With no shadows to conceal my approach, and now that there were armed guards pouring into the yard, my chances of getting into the house undetected were not good. Not zero, but not good.

That was when I heard a car, or cars, drive up on the other side of the building. I couldn't see who it was, but I quickly ruled out the pizza guy.

Again, I had to consider my options. I could go back and blow the drone, but I didn't know what would happen to Dee—or Maliki—if I did that. I could try to get into the house and hope that Maliki was inside. Once inside I could try to get to him, or I could just go look for Dee.

I slipped deeper into the trees, and stayed in the cover as I maneuvered around the house. The back door was much closer to the woods, and there was a hedge around the tiny backyard. I could see a face in the second-floor window there also, but if I had to go in, this would be the place to try.

Next, I moved around to the south side of the residence turned barracks, now turned fortress, where the garage and drive were located. I immediately noticed that the sedan I saw leaving earlier was back, parked next to an older pickup and large white passenger van with the racetrack's dragster, fighter plane logo on the doors.

I also noticed a new vehicle parked on the lawn. This one instantly became my biggest problem; it was the car that Dee had been driving. I had to assume she'd been captured and currently being held inside. This really complicated things, because there was no way in hell I was going to leave her there.

I continued examining my options, and noticed that the garage had a high ceiling. The house was two stories, but it had what looked like a bathroom window on this side of the building. Unfortunately, the only door on this side was the large garage door, and there was no way of getting that open without alerting everyone inside. I looked closer, and realized it would be possible to move next to the house unseen from where I was, and then crawl along the base of the building and probe for an open window or door.

I had a plan.

As I moved into a long shadow caused by the security lighting pointing at a corner of the garage, I heard a faint panting coming from my right. I slipped a half step deeper into the concealment of the bushes and raised my weapon.

In addition to the panting, I could make out the soft padding of running, limping feet. Around the corner of the trees, running down the middle of the drive was Blackjack; he was struggling. He was running on three legs, holding his left rear leg tucked into his body. I could see he'd been injured.

Blackjack labored on, in obvious pain and close to exhaustion. He kept moving resolutely toward the car.

"Blackjack!" I called out in a soft voice. He didn't hear. His whole universe now revolved around finding Dee and protecting her. "Blackjack, come!"

He limped to a stop, looking around.

"Here boy, come Blackjack."

Blackjack let out a pitiful whimper and lowering his head and ears. He managed to drag himself to me in the bushes. He collapsed there with a moan, panting raggedly. He lay with his left side facing up, and I saw a bullet wound in the thigh of his injured leg. Thank god the bullet didn't hit bone, but the nasty chunk of missing flesh had to be agonizing. I marveled, absolutely amazed that he'd made it this far. I felt ecstatic that he had survived, but also concerned. Things just kept getting more complicated.

Blackjack's eyes were open but unfocused, and his breathing was rapid and shallow. If he'd been a person, I would suspect he'd gone into shock. I couldn't spare much time, but I couldn't just abandon this little hero. I assumed our car still had a first-aid kit in back, as well as bottled water. It would only take a few seconds to treat his wound and give him some water. He would probably stay put if I could cover him up in the back seat of the car.

I gently scooped him up. He whimpered weakly but remained quiet after that. Staying in the shadows, I crouched down and ran to the car. I reached the passenger's side, luckily it faced away from the building, and knelt down. The doors were unlocked, and again I was glad the interior lights had all been removed. I laid Blackjack gently down on the rear passenger-side floorboard. I reached across the car and grabbed the first-aid kit. It had an antibiotic cream that I applied liberally to the wound. I was glad to see it also contained a topical painkiller. Finally, I gently placed a square, self-adhesive gauze pad to the wound.

I looked around, but found nothing I could use as a dish for water. I dumped the first aid supplies on the seat and laid the plastic box open in front of my wounded teammate. I grabbed a water bottle from the opposite floorboard and fill the improvised water dish to the top. Blackjack looked pitifully over at it, but simply slumped and dropped his head back down onto the carpet. I left the water there and covered him with Gareth's rugby jersey,

I then close the door and left. I'd done all I could. He was tough; he would hang in there for us.

I had also used that time to analyze my situation in

more detail. I had only one viable option. I could see men moving cautiously into the trees at several places around the house and control tower. They knew I was in the area, but didn't know exactly where.

I moved silently back into the woods and began to retrace my path to the hanger. I would make my way back to the drone, set off my gas bomb, and hope the diversion allowed me to get inside the house and rescue Dee. That should also take care of the drone, but I realized that the aircraft was not my top priority right now. I couldn't leave Dee. Blackjack wouldn't give up. I wouldn't either.

I slung my rifle. Without a good silencer, if I was forced to open fire, I'd also give away my position. I slid the heavy hunting knife out of its sheath and moved silently forward.

I'd made it around to the trees at the rear of the house when I heard movement ahead. Not footsteps, but the equally telling scrape of branches on cloth. I waited a moment longer, but there were no further sounds. Someone had taken up a position in the woods. They were waiting, stationary, pivoting in place to look around. I would have to move in a wide arc, avoiding where I thought the sentry would be. If he didn't make any more noise, he could be very difficult to find.

However, as I approached the task became easier. He was a Paki; maybe Indian. In our combat unit, we all use unscented soap and deodorant in the field, for a reason. The person concealed to my right had enjoyed a nice curry dish earlier on, an odor which carried well on even a light breeze. Fortunately for him, I would rather he stayed alive to announce that everything was quiet, than to go missing and have others start looking for him.

I slipped past and moved on.

In the woods to the north of the house, I detected

another curry scented ambush. This time the gunman was smarter. He'd picked a spot where the bushes were thinner, and had positioned himself just inside the far border of the trees. By watching the light from the house filtering through to him, he would be able to detect any flickering movement ahead.

I still had options. First, I could attempt to crawl through unseen, keeping myself hidden behind the low-lying vegetation. Second, I could neutralize the observer. The only way to be sure was to eliminate the threat.

I moved to the edge of the trees, even with the sentry, and stole to within a few meters of him. I tossed a tiny stone into the brush a few feet to his front, an old trick that still worked. He leaned forward, probably expecting to see a small animal of some kind. I doubt he actually saw anything, the blade of my knife passing behind his eyes and into his brain would have obscured his vision.

Silently, I eased him to the ground and moved on. I reached the corner of the tree line, where it moved to the north and toward the hanger, and followed it on. I moved faster now, with only a few meters to go before reaching the Molotov cocktails. I no longer cared if they saw me, I was about to create a huge, blazing diversion, so a little gunfire wouldn't be a problem. Besides, killing a few more guards would put me in a better mood.

I reached down and picked up the largest of the bottles and pulled out my cigarette lighter. The reassuring smell of gasoline told me the rag in the bottle's neck was saturated and ready to burn.

I crouched low and hurried toward the pump. I only had to flip up the lever and light the wick. Suddenly, two bright halogen beams seared into my eyes from a vehicle parked nearby. In one motion, I dropped the bottle in my left hand and dove over it to escape the lights. At the same time, I reached for my pistol. I would have to try to light the gas pump and fuel bomb with sparks from the rounds I would fire into it. Or maybe I could ignite it by firing into the electrical box.

Back in darkness, I had my weapon out, taking aim. But ahead of me I heard a scream of pain. It was a woman's scream. Dee's scream.

"I have a knife to her kidneys Sergeant Deacon."

I froze, squinting. My eyes dilated enough for me to make out the shapes ahead. A large man had his arm around Dee's throat. He squeezed and Dee struggled to get away from him, whimpering.

Two other men appeared, both holding AK47s pointed directly at me. I dropped my weapon. One of them strode forward, raising his rifle butt first. I stood defiantly as the metal butt plate of the rifle slammed viciously into my forehead.

Chapter 31

Abdul al Maliki strode into the library feeling very good about things; about his mission and particularly about himself. His success was assured, and even his minor distractions were about to disappear. He would see to that personally via teleconference.

He sat down in front of the computer screen and entered a code. Password accepted, the computer beneath the desk before him hummed back to life. He was anxious to speak with the pair waiting for him in the racetrack hanger, but first he wanted to make sure every detail was just right.

He straightened his smoking jacket, then considered leaving it open to reveal his muscular chest. The jacket had been a gift from Maliki to Philip, whose body now slumped in a chair but a few feet to his right.

The jacket was made from terribly expensive black silk, a custom-tailored copy of one made for the Prince of Wales in eighteen eighty-six—or so Maliki had been assured. It had cost him over three thousand pounds, and

Philip had been beside himself with appreciation.

No, not appreciation—joy. General Philip Morgan-Thomas never actually appreciated anything that Maliki had done for him. Maliki had considered having one made for himself, but realized a little patience would save him three thousand pounds.

Patience was about to pay off again. He clicked the icon for his video conferencing software, pulled out a Gitanes Brunes cigarette, and waited for the software to load. He picked up a heavy, gold-plated lighter from the table and lit up. The General had a smoking room, but only for cigars. It seems that cigarette smoke irritated his eyes. Maliki inhaled deeply on the French cigarette and blew a stream of heavy grey smoke into General Morgan-Thomas' vacant, still open eyes. Maliki chuckled. The smoke didn't seem to bother him any longer.

On the left part of the screen, the image of Ahmed appeared; behind him to the right lay the form of Sergeant Travis Deacon, strapped to a table. The far right hand portion of the screen held the lovely visage of Deidre Jones. Maliki had always found the combination of auburn red hair and deep green eyes to be terribly exotic.

"Sir."

Maliki's attention reluctantly returned to Ahmed.

"We have inspected the drone, and everything appears as it was. I have conducted the additional test flight as you instructed, all is working properly."

"Check it again. Sergeant Deacon is an exceptional soldier. We cannot assume he hasn't found a less obvious way of sabotaging the aircraft."

There was a muffled voice from the speakers; Travis was attempting vigorously to speak through the gag in his mouth. Maliki watched the screen as Ahmed picked up a large wrench from the table in front of him and slammed it violently into Travis' stomach. Travis struggled against his restraints, since they prevented him from doubling over in pain.

As Travis recovered, he tried to speak again. Finally, Maliki waved a hand and Ahmed removed a wad of cloth from Travis' mouth.

All eyes turned to Travis as he opened and closed his mouth and moved his jaw from side to side, trying to regain full use of his mouth.

"Marine!" Travis moistened his lips with the tip of his tongue. "I'm not a soldier. I'm a Marine."

"Of course, Marine. I appreciate someone who takes pride in who they are and what they do. I feel the same way about my endeavors."

Travis raised his head off the table and managed to look at the camera, not the television as Ahmed just did. The American knew exactly what was happening; Maliki realized that he shouldn't have underestimated this man.

"Absolutely!" Travis looked over at the TV screen. "There you are, wearing an expensive dinner jacket, smoking an expensive cigarette in a fancy library somewhere. You should be proud. You look like you're having a smashing good time."

"It's not the Marriott, but it will suffice. And actually, I have not been having a good time of late, thanks in some part to you. I'm impressed, but still irritated, by the fact that you found my drone."

"You mean your backup drone."

Maliki smiled. Yes, he definitely underestimated the Marine.

"Why would you assume that?"

"You have two drones, one unloaded a few nights ago, another several weeks before that. I would assume the primary aircraft would be with you. Since we are doing this via video call, with a half-second latency in the signal, I can assume that the connection is via Internet and not local. You and the other drone are somewhere else."

Maliki watched the screen with interest as Travis laid his head back down. The terrorist was fairly certain that Travis had some sort of plan that he hoped to execute. Maliki very much wanted to know what that plan might be.

"That is correct. In fact, I may be back in Afghanistan at this very moment."

"You're in the UK, and we know where. In fact, we've passed the details of your entire plan to MI5."

Maliki, of course, knew this to be a lie. "I don't think so. In fact, when you told MI5 about the racetrack, they didn't believe you."

This silenced Deacon, he and the woman exchanged concerned glances. Undoubtedly, they would now try to determine how Maliki knew this, but of course they would fail. It was, however, important that he discover what Deacon knew, specifically how they had found the track, and if they did, in fact, know of the estate.

"Please don't misinterpret my remarks. I am very impressed with your resourcefulness and analytical prowess. I never would have anticipated anyone finding the track in such a short time, with so little to go on."

"It was Detective Jones that figured out the location."

"Does the Detective speak for herself?"

"At times, but she also tries to honor your traditions. The police here are very serious about respecting racial and cultural diversity. She's aware that Muslim women are to speak only when they are spoken to, or given permission by a man," Travis continued, sarcastic, "Or maybe it's the gag."

Maliki waved impatiently toward the camera.

"But sir, she will scream," Ahmed hesitated.

"Then you will gag her again."

Ahmed removed the gag, and Dee didn't waste a second.

"You camel fucking piece of shit! When we get loose, we will track you down and ram a . . ."

The gag was again stuffed forcefully into her mouth.

Maliki was actually amused by the outburst, amused and subtly aroused. He examined Dee again, deliberately, then smiled.

"I did not find that to be very respectful. However, Miss Jones, you will find occasion very soon to scream again. I will pick the time and will personally provide you with a more tangible reason to do so."

Maliki looked at Travis. "I believe it would be best for Sergeant Deacon and myself to continue this discussion between ourselves. Are you amenable to that Sergeant?"

"Oh, absolutely, if by amenable you mean ready to shove a hand grenade up your camel fucking ass and pull the pin."

Maliki laughed and raised the cigarette to his lips. He looked up blissfully and inhaled deeply. He held the smoke in his lungs, savoring it, then slowly emptied his lungs in a stream of grey-blue smoke. Finally, he stared at Travis' image on his screen.

"I think that I'll bring you back here when I'm finished. Take the opportunity to get to know you better, inside and out so to speak. I'm sure my host won't object."

Maliki leaned forward and rotated the camera until the General's body appeared in the center of the screen.

"In fact, I'm sure he won't say a word in protest." He turned the camera back to its original position and continued, "But before that time, I would like to know how you found my 'backup drone.' It certainly couldn't hurt to share that bit of information with me."

"I would love to share that information with you! It was your new neighbors. As soon as your men moved into the area, the locals discovered that their property values had gone way down."

Maliki chuckled mirthlessly. "Possibly, but the value of the entire country is about to be significantly lessened. Ahmed."

The terrorist leader nodded to Ahmed, who walked to a small table where he picked up a cordless power drill. He pulled the trigger. The angry whine came through clearly, even over the computer's tiny speakers.

"I think we will save that for when Sergeant Deacon and I are together in person. The vice grips should be sufficient for now."

Ahmed set the drill down and picked up a pair of five-inch vice-grip pliers. They were locked in the closed position, but Ahmed pressed a lever on the inside of the thin, curved handle and the chrome tool sprang open with a metallic clang. Ahmed grasped the vice grips and squeezed the handle. The serrated jaws click together with a bite of metallic certainty.

"Let me formally introduce you to Ahmed, one of my lieutenants. Not only is Ahmed a superb pilot, but he is a true craftsman with hand tools as well. Ahmed, why don't we ask Sergeant Deacon again?"

Ahmed strode to Travis' side and pulled out a large combat knife. He slipped it under the front of Travis' shirt and slowly sliced through it, from hem to collar. Ahmed then carefully laid the shirt open revealing Travis' chest and stomach.

Ahmed stepped back and looked at the television in front of him, waiting for instructions. A wicked smile snaked its way onto Maliki's lips, which was enough to send Ahmed into motion.

Ahmed turned slowly to the Marine's side and examined the flesh just above his right hip. Maliki noticed there were no 'love handles,' but Maliki hadn't expected there to be any. He regretted he was not there to give Sergeant Deacon the personal attention this American so richly merited, but that would come later.

Ahmed pinched a one-inch chunk of flesh from Travis' side and pulled it away from his hip. He then closed the jaws of the vice grips until they tightly pinch the flesh. Ahmed paused and looked at Maliki.

"Sergeant Deacon, I would really like to know how you discovered we were here?"

Ahmed squeezed the pliers tighter. Travis grimaced in pain, but still lifted his head to examine what was going on. He lowered his head back down, then turned it to stare at the camera.

"If I tell you, will you let us go?"

"Of course, you have my word."

"Fine, we found out from monitoring local police reports."

Maliki considered this, what could his men have done to attract the attention of the local police?

"Please, go on."

"Sure. Apparently, your minions decided to enjoy their success a little early. There has been a sudden epidemic of sheep being sexually assaulted in this area. I've been told that premature celebration is a very common problem among terrorists—if they can get it up for celebrating at all."

Maliki should have expected this, but it still made him angry. He nodded to Ahmed, who brutally squeezed the handles shut, clamping the Marine's flesh in a relentless metal grip. Blood and tissue splattered the table. Maliki was disappointed that Travis did not cry out, but not too disappointed. There would be time for screams and pleading later.

Travis lay silent, grimacing, in obvious pain. He sucked in a long, rasping breath and struggled to control his body. In an amazingly short time he was under control, seemingly relaxed once more.

"I assure you, there will be nothing premature about your death. And since you seem so concerned about the quality of my celebration, I will modify my plans slightly. The body of Detective Jones was to have been discovered tomorrow morning in London, heavy with traces of plastic explosives. This was to lend more credence to the theory that an attack there was imminent."

Maliki's gaze now lingered over Dee's body as she sat bound to a chair.

"But I've decided to allow her the honor of celebrating with me. She will live, and be able to give you a first-hand confirmation that our celebration did not end prematurely. In fact, Miss Jones and I will enjoy a lengthy, and intensely physical relationship."

Maliki nodded, and Ahmed approached Travis again. He raised the vice grips so they were clearly visible to his victim, then lowered them once more toward the American's side.

Travis refused to cry out, as before. Good. Maliki was certain he would provide many hours of entertainment. The woman, however, turned her head and began to weep. He decided they made a nice couple, and wondered what they would be willing to do keep the other from his expert attention.

Chapter 32

Dee watched Maliki's face as Ahmed held the vice grips close to the camera. Ahmed turned the chunk of flesh back and forth, allowing his leader to examine every bit of the jagged pink surface, every drop of blood that still oozed and ran down the shiny metal head in thin red lines.

Dee never watched much television, but she couldn't help thinking that this was just like a movie. Things like this didn't happen in real life. She tried to turn her head, but a hand grabbed the hair on top of her head and twisted until she was again looking at the video-conference equipment.

The look of triumph and pleasure on Maliki's face was nauseating. This man was insane. As a police detective, she'd previously dealt with two violent criminals; both men, both acting out their abusive delusions on helpless women. The first one had actually tortured and mutilated his victims, four of them, before he was apprehended.

Dee remembered sitting across the table, looking into the criminal's face, actually able to feel this man's hatred of women. From the moment she'd sat across the interrogation table from him, she could sense the barely contained rage, a brutality seeking only the freedom to act. That man didn't care that he'd been caught, and the idea of a future meant nothing to him. His name was Abgaal, and he was from Somalia, and he brought his perversion with him.

The brutality Maliki was demonstrating, this unrestrained love of pain, was something different entirely. Abgaal hated women; Maliki simply enjoyed the suffering of others. In fact, Dee almost sensed that Maliki felt a grudging respect for Travis. This respect for a worthy adversary would make Travis' suffering all the more enjoyable for Maliki, and certainly less enjoyable for Travis.

"Once more!" Maliki's voice scratched out of the TV speaker.

Ahmed walked slowly over to the table. Travis watched him approach. Dee couldn't see the torture master's face, but she could picture a cruel and sadistic smile in anticipation that this would be the time that would bring Travis' screams and supplications.

Instead, Travis just stared at Ahmed's face. The only reaction came as Ahmed stopped at the table, and Travis calmly closed his eyes. Dee could see his eyes roll up slightly, and his face go slack, as if he were praying or getting ready to doze off.

Ahmed pinched the raw wound on Travis' side, but he didn't react. Dee watched, fascinated, as Ahmed pinched the flesh next to the growing, bloody wound above Travis' hip. The massive Arab pinched a large portion of flesh between his fingers, and the vice grips moved in tightly to engulf it.

Dee closed her eyes and started to look away. Fingers painfully ran through her scalp as the hand yanked her hair and forced her to face the table. A brutal twist and she opened her eyes. Ahmed had been waiting patiently, not wanting to proceed until his audience was in place, attentively watching his performance.

Ahmed's hand squeezed the handle. Travis shuddered slightly, but his expression remained the same. Blood sprayed and the body jerked as the torturer twisted the pliers and yanked another mass of flesh from his side. The only reaction from Travis was a short gasp and squint. Dee couldn't imagine where Travis' mind had escaped to in order to block out this brutality, but she was certain that it wasn't working all too well.

"That will be sufficient." Maliki said calmly.

Dee gasped. She didn't realize it until then, but she had been holding her breath. For how long she didn't know, but she found herself panting now to keep from passing out. She felt warm tears streaming down her face.

"Sergeant Deacon," Maliki waited, then spoke louder, "Sergeant Deacon!"

Travis didn't move. Maliki frowned, then his eyes shifted slightly, and he nodded.

Dee felt her head rip back, as if those brutal fingers were about to once again tear the skin from her head. It was so sudden, so unexpected—she screamed. Now Travis reacted. His head flung forward, eyes open in fear for Dee. She looked back, remorse and fear in her eyes. If only she could be that strong.

"That's better." Maliki was now smiling amicably at Travis from the screen. "I cannot tell you how eagerly I'm anticipating our time together. My time with your friend Major Jones was rushed, and my options were limited."

Maliki smiled viciously at Dee, "But let me assure you, I made the most of our brief time together."

Dee glared at the screen. Maliki extended his hand forward, palm up, and motioned for her to stand. She sat straighter in her chair.

Almost instantly Dee felt a lash of pain that consumed her shoulders in fire. The impact almost threw her to the floor. She had to fight to hold back tears of pain the sudden assault threatened to bring. She tried to sit up straight once more, but her throbbing back and shoulders would not respond.

Dee looked back. Ahmed dangled a three-foot long orange rubber hose in front of her eyes. A vicious smile contorted his face; not hateful, simply brutal. This would be about power and control, him over her. As Ahmed's eyes ran over Dee's body, she understood that he'd had other victims like her. Other women had felt his lash, and no doubt his touch. Lust was there, deep in his soul, ready to emerge once the sadist inside had been satiated.

Dee faced forward and stared at the screen, trying to decide if she should comply or continue to resist. Maliki looked into her eyes, then nodded again.

Again, the hose scorched her back with a rubber tongue of fire and pain. This time she collapsed, falling to her knees in front of her chair. Tears cascaded down her cheeks. This was a pain and brutality she had never known, had never even imagined.

Hands grabbed her and threw her back into the chair. She exploded forward as her back touched the chair.

"Miss Jones," Maliki said softly. The smug satisfaction in his voice was obvious, but Dee felt too much pain to react.

"Do I need to make my point again?"

Dee looked quickly up at the screen. Maliki smiled arrogantly back.

"Have no doubt, you will do what I want. Everything I want. Whenever I want it. You will live as long as you please me, and be punished severely any time you don't.

302

Now stand so that I may see you better."

Dee refused, and braced herself. After seconds of anticipation, the blow came, more violent and vicious than before. She fell face first onto the floor, sobbing in pain and humiliation. The realization in her mind was worse than the flames burning through her back. He was right. She could not resist much longer.

Hands pulled her to her feet, and two men held her arms securely between them. She rocked unsteadily on her feet, and looked for Travis. She saw the thin trickle of blood and fluid dripping off the table, plunging into a small, pinkish pool on the floor. He struggled to keep his head raised, staring coldly at the screen. His face seemed relaxed. Had he given up? No, it was a look of certainty; every molecule of his body now focused on one thing.

Maliki followed her gaze.

"Sergeant Deacon already knows his fate." Maliki turned calmly back to Dee. "And as someone who has probably broken horses in the past, he may understand yours even better than you do."

Maliki looked at Travis again, then back at Dee. He smiled and shook his head. "I am truly blessed of Allah. I cannot decide which of you I'm hoping to spend time with most, an extraordinarily pleasing problem to have."

Maliki leaned forward, his face filling the screen.

"I felt cheated in Pakistan when my time with your Lieutenant was cut short. Was that you Sergeant? The one who almost captured me? I was not happy that my talk with your superior was ended prematurely."

Travis just stared.

Maliki shrugged and turned to smile at Dee.

"And I felt especially cheated with your brother. Not only was time a problem, but I had to make sure they wouldn't immediately discover the truth of what had happened to him."

Maliki nodded to Ahmed. "Bring her to me. The two of us will celebrate our great triumph properly. Bring Sergeant Deacon to the estate of our gracious host General Morgan-Thomas. We will all meet there later, and can continue this lovely conversation in a more secure and relaxed atmosphere."

Ahmed stared at Dee for a moment, then walked to a small instrument table next to Travis. He held out a hand to one of the guards, who placed a small bottle in it. Ahmed held it in front of Travis' face; it was a salt shaker. Ahmed slowly moved the salt over Travis' fresh wounds, carefully and deliberately shaking a trickle of salt into the open flesh. Travis tensed but didn't make a sound.

Ahmed waved a hand toward the men holding Dee, and they dragged her toward the door. She looked over her shoulder at Travis, who was staring at her intently. He raised his head from the table and said, "Just hang in there!"

Dee tried to smile back. At that moment, she realized that if she got the chance, she would hang herself before letting Maliki have his way with her. Death had never looked so inviting.

She continued watching Travis. His head slowly lowered back down and his eyes closed. He again escaped to the refuge of his mind. This gave her some small measure of strength. If he wouldn't give up, she wouldn't either.

She watched as Ahmed slowly unscrewed the top of the shaker and held the open bottle over Travis' mangled side. They would make her watch until Ahmed was finished.

Chapter 33

Ahmed walked away, and I strained against the ropes and twisted my body on the table, trying to watch as they dragged Dee out the open hanger door. I craned my neck and twisted until my muscles cried out in pain, but this wasn't as painful as the missing flesh from my side. The salt would actually help, after the initial agony. It would also help it heal faster, but I had more important issues than that.

I held that position and watched, fighting back the urge to pull and struggle against my restraints. I watched them exit the hanger into the shadow, then turn right toward the cars. I knew they were going to divide into two groups, one to London and one to Maliki, but I couldn't be certain which would be taking Dee.

I had to do something. And if I planned to escape, it would require more mind than muscle. I relaxed my body and lay flat.

There was no way to be certain that Dee would be taken to Maliki, since the original plan was to take her to

London. What if I guessed wrong and went to the wrong place? That mistake would mean her certain death. Then I remembered the look in Maliki's eyes. He wanted Dee there, with him. I had no doubt where she'd be taken. I only had to find out where 'there' was.

I realized that subconsciously I'd actually been struggling against my chains, apparently the idea of her in the hands of a sadistic piece of shit was more potent than morphine for making my pain disappear. I thought again about Dee as Maliki's prisoner, it would be a living hell. A quick death would be better for her than the slow, cruel one he would inflict.

I couldn't let that happen.

I wouldn't let that happen!

All I needed was a weakness to exploit, anything or anyone, but I needed it now. I raised my head and scanned the hanger for a means of escape. I counted seven others there in the hanger. Four of them were technicians preparing the drone. Two of them were guards left to take me to the estate, wherever that was. Lucky number seven seemed to be in charge.

He was old and round; a short, slimy-looking guy who yelled and gestured madly at the technicians. He was an Arab, with slicked-back hair and a bushy, Imam-looking beard, wearing a red, long-sleeved shirt. He reminded me of a dwarf.

Wasn't one of Snow White's dwarves named Slimy?

Since my guards straightened up every time he looked over, I assumed he was in command. His bulky frame and pudgy face gave no hint of physical strength, so he was probably just in charge of preparing the drone for its mission.

There would be a pilot in the tower, to launch the drone and get it to a hand off point near the target. I had to assume there would be guards there as well, but that wasn't an immediate problem. The tower wouldn't figure into my plans until I'd escaped.

I examined my restraints as closely as possible. There were thick Velcro straps holding my wrists and feet to the table, which would have to be released when they moved me. That would be my first chance to get free, but probably not my best chance. Still, if I saw an opening, any opening, I would take it. It would only take a few rounds in the engine to disable the drone, then I could rescue Dee.

An overpowering rumble filled the hanger. I twisted around, trying to find the source. The roar came from a large motorcycle, in a dark corner near the front of the hanger. The sound was deafening. One of the technicians sat proudly on top, grinning as he revved the engine.

The sound continued, and I saw more movement to my right. The large Kawasaki racing bike masked the sound of the drone's propeller as it started to spin up. I arched my back and watched the drone as it moved toward the door, and the motorcycle rolled out ahead of it.

The motorcycle made a clever diversion. No one would notice the growl of the drone over the rumbling of the motorcycle, and a racing bike wouldn't cause any alarm around these parts at all.

The drone rolled smoothly out of the hanger door and turned left toward the runway, followed by the technicians. I clearly heard the bike continue to thunder angrily outside, but the Predator seemed to have just disappeared. A minute passed, maybe longer, before the technicians began to jump up and down, waving their hands in the air and pounding each other on the back. I had to assume the weapon had taken off, and the countdown had begun.

They celebrated; all I could do was wait.

The motorcycle shut down soon after. I heard more

shouting outside the hanger, and tilted my head back in time to see the technicians running past the open hanger door toward the cars. Slimy wobbled his way toward me and waved two guards to the foot of the table.

Two guards grabbed my ankles as they prepared to loosen the Velcro straps. Out of nowhere, I felt a coarse rope loop under my chin and pull my head back over the edge of the table as the straps on my ankles fell slack. Slimy lay below me, the rope looped around my neck, ready to crush my throat if I caused any problems.

This little shit might be a butterball, but he knew what he was doing.

The guards undid my wrists, thrust my arms together over my stomach, and slapped on a pair of handcuffs. These guys were competent, bordering on professional. Escape would be harder than I'd anticipated.

The guards slid me off the table and stood me up, facing the door. The larger guard stood to my right side, my strong side, and the little one took the left. They got this part right, also. I pretended to swoon, then dropped to my knees. I wanted them close, this way they'd be forced to help me walk.

Slimy took the handcuff key from the little guard, then ordered them in Arabic to take me to the car. They yanked me to my feet and dragged me out of the hanger. I glanced toward the runway, but the drone had indeed taken off.

Maliki's endgame had begun, and his opponents hadn't even taken the field yet.

They hustled me out of the hanger. We headed toward the cars, and only the one we'd been driving remained. This was a break.

I looked left and saw a dark sedan reach the exit gate and speed toward the road; the others were gone. As we neared the car, I pretended to stumble again.

The guards had to hold me up while the Slimy pressed the remote and unlocked the car. I got ready as he opened the rear passenger's door.

"Blackjack!" I yelled.

From his hiding place on the floorboard, Blackjack's snarling head launched itself at the shocked little Arab, who actually whimpered and lurched backward into the larger guard holding my right arm. Slimy regained his footing and tried to run, but stumbled as Blackjack sank angry jaws into his left calf.

I jerked my right arm free from the falling guard and clenched my left arm tight, pinning the smaller guard's arm fast against my side. I swung my hip out and knocked the guard to my left off balance. I then lifted him off the ground by his arm and slammed his head on the top of the still open door. His head rebounded violently, and he crumpled to the ground, dazed but not unconscious.

I looked at Slimy. He lay sprawled out, screaming on the ground, while Blackjack chomped viciously at the back of his neck. The Arab was not an immediate threat, so I continued to survey the situation.

I stepped toward the large guard who had drawn an automatic pistol and was almost back on his feet. With the side of my right foot, I kicked into the back of his knee, and he fell with a grunt. I pivoted and drove the heel of my right foot into his exposed kidney. His face contorted with pain, as he screamed and crumpled to the ground. I kicked the pistol out of reach, and it spun away from him.

The smaller guard was almost back on his feet, so I kicked him in the side of the head. He slammed violently into the side of the car. He doubled over and almost collapsed. I grabbed the back of his shirt to keep him from falling. I pulled him toward me, and we backed away several feet from the car. Then, with all my force and weight, I rushed forward and I slammed his head into the side of the car. He collapsed, now unconscious and bleeding from a nasty gash over his right eye.

As he fell to the ground, I turned back to the others.

The larger guard struggled painfully to his hands and knees, but Slimy had managed to get Blackjack off his back and stand up. He danced to avoid the dog's snapping jaws, and he struggled to pull his gun from his pocket.

I located the small guard's fallen weapon and dove for it. I grabbed the gun and rolled onto my good side. Hands together, I aimed at the dancing Arab. Blackjack had his full attention, so he didn't notice me.

"Blackjack, come!" I shouted.

The dog kept nipping at his attacker's leg.

"Blackjack!" I yelled louder.

They both stopped and looked over.

"Come!"

Blackjack started to move, but then turned to get back at his prey.

"Come. Blackjack now!"

Blackjack reluctantly hobbled to my side.

"Drop the gun!" I yelled in Arabic.

Slimy lowered his gun and pointed away from me. He held perfectly still as he assessed the situation. I really didn't want to shoot him, not without questioning him first. I could probably learn enough from the other two goons, but he was in charge, and therefore, the one I really wanted to chat with.

He looked at his two fallen cronies, then turned his still clever eyes toward me. He slowly lowered the barrel of the gun to the side, then fired. Two rounds slam into the head of the big guard.

Shit! I hadn't wanted to shoot him. I was paying for my hesitation. He managed to put two rounds into the other guard before I got off a shot that struck him in the shoulder. He staggered back, right arm dangling limply at his side, but with his left hand, he took the gun from his right.

I fired a shot into his leg, and he crumpled to the ground. I ran toward him but arrived just as he put the pistol barrel under his chin and pulled the trigger. His head exploded, and along with it my best chance of finding Dee and Maliki.

Angry, I rushed to the dead Arab and stuffed his pistol into my belt. I fished through his pockets and pulled out all of his keys. I put the car keys in my mouth and found the handcuff key. I discarded the rest. As I started to open the handcuffs, I heard the distant, rapid-fire explosions of an AK47. I then felt the sting of flying gravel on my hands and chest.

I located the source of the gunfire. Two men stood on the observation ledge of the tower. The gunfire must have attracted their attention. I dropped the handcuff key into my pocket and ran toward the car. I looked at the unconscious man, but knew I didn't have time to toss him into the car.

"Come!" I yelled as I ran around the car, which partially blocked us from the riflemen. I opened the driver's door, and helped the limping dog across to the passenger's seat. I then jumped behind the wheel. I inserted the keys, when the car shook and a spray of glass struck the side of my face. I turned my head away from the gunfire as another round smashed through the windshield, closer, stinging my head and face with diamond sharp shards.

I started the car and fumbled with handcuffed wrists to put it in gear. My muscle memory was working against me in this God damn backward vehicle. I really had to concentrate on what I was doing.

The car now in drive, I jerked the wheel to my left and stomped on the gas. Two more rounds crashed through the windshield, one barely grazing my right shoulder. I bent to my left and pushed Blackjack safely onto the passenger's side floorboard as we bounced across the grass toward the exit. "Stay!"

I fishtailed onto the gravel exit road and sped down into the cover of the trees as another bullet exploded through the rear passenger-side window. I skidded onto the road and turned right toward the town. I had to concentrate on my driving to avoid ending up in a ditch. I kept an eye on my rearview mirror, but didn't expect to be followed. They couldn't leave the tower until someone else, probably in Cardiff, took control of the drone.

I tried to brush glass off my shoulders and chest as Blackjack tried to hop up onto the passenger's seat. I checked the rearview mirror again. No cars were following so I pulled to the side of the road. I carefully brushed the glass from the seat, then lifted him up. He sat, back straight, but I could see the pain reflected in his eyes and ears. Even hurt, the tongue lolled out of the side of his mouth. I could clearly see the huge, canine grin on his triumphant, panting face.

As I pulled back onto the road and carefully drove on, he looked at me and barked twice. I knew what he wanted to say, and I felt exactly the same.

Through clenched teeth, I congratulated him, "Yeah big guy. We kicked some major terrorist ass back there."

He stared at me a moment longer, then struggled to lie down. His wounded leg tucked tightly against his body. He rested his head on the seat and closed his eyes.

I stopped in the middle of the road and dug through my pocket. I located the handcuff keys, then managed to remove the cuffs. My hands free again, I rubbed my wrists, then tossed the cuffs and keys into the back seat. I reached over and scratched Blackjack behind the ears as I hit the gas pedal. He moaned in appreciation, or maybe in pain. Either way, we'd done good. We were back in the game, and still had a chance to win this war after all.

I turned my attention to the road, and had to swerve back into my own lane. We only had a chance if I could learn to drive.

Chapter 34

We'd escaped. Blackjack and I were in awful shape, and the car was in an even worse condition. As soon as I'd become proficient enough to drive the speed limit, the left rear tire exploded, and the car practically swerved off the road.

I'd managed to keep going, but the sound of flapping rubber had soon given way to the grinding whine of metal rim on pavement. Things apparently weren't bad enough, since steam then began to coil up from under the hood, condensing on the windshield and forcing its way into the car.

Keeping things together demanded my full attention, but I still couldn't stop myself from worrying about Dee. Plus, my mind kept trying to figure out where Maliki might be. On top of that, I couldn't reach my cell phone, which had become lodged under the passenger's seat.

I really needed to catch a break.

A new grinding sound started under the hood, startling Blackjack. The car then began to shudder. Resigned to the inevitable I looked for trees or tall bushes where I could conceal the car.

I couldn't be certain we weren't being chased, and I didn't have time or ammo for another firefight. They would have certainly overtaken us by now, what with the speed we were going. We were probably safe, but probably didn't cut it. There was no room for error, so there was no room for risk.

Up the road, off to the left, I saw what looked like a shallow gully with tall weeds, brush, and a few trees growing up. I then saw a pair of headlights drive around a bend in the road a few hundred meters ahead. I suppressed a growing sense of anticipation. If I worked this right, I could solve my two biggest problems at the same time. As usual, though, there was still a lot that could go wrong.

I sped up just a little. I wanted to speed up a lot, but the car was past the point of any real acceleration. As my car, the bushes and the approaching vehicle converged, I swerved wildly. I moved my car into the right lane heading straight for the lights. I then jerked the wheel madly back and forth, and pulled left, aiming directly for the bushes.

I hit the brakes and slowed to what I hoped was the optimal speed, grabbed Blackjack, and leaned down to my left and covered the dog. The car bumped and bucked as it left the road, then jerked and jolted us as we entered the thicket.

With a jarring crash, we hit something, a boulder or tree trunk. My back slammed against the dash, and Blackjack whimpered. Fortunately, we were not going fast enough for either of us to be injured.

I sat up and looked around; the bushes only covered part of the back windows. The trunk had popped open, and we were not deep enough into the vegetation to completely hide the car. I needed to move quickly. I turned off the lights; the car engine had died on its own. With my right shoulder, I forced the door open through the damage and brush. I checked to make sure the guard's 9mm was still in my waistband and got out.

I looked around the backseat, salvaging as much as I could from the first-aid kit. I grabbed my phone, which must have slid from under the seat, then lifted Blackjack gently out. I hurried up the slight incline and back toward the road.

To my relief, the approaching car stopped, turned around, and returned to the accident scene to render aid, or at least to gawk. To my great relief, it was a sporty looking Jag; we would be able to make excellent time in that. The diminutive driver was out of the car, head barely visible over the top of his vehicle, searching anxiously for survivors.

He saw us moving toward him, and waved as he asked, "Over here, are you all right?"

As I approached the car, he reached back inside and removed his keys from the ignition. Standing back, he carefully closed the door, pointed the remote directly at the driver's door, and pressed the button. I was too far away to hear the click of the door's locks, but mister fastidious lowered the remote, then bent to look through the window, making sure the doors had actually locked.

Finally, after making sure no one was going to spring from the roadside weeds and steal his car, he walked toward us—after looking both ways, of course. Since I was almost there by that time, he didn't have far to go.

He was short, slender if not thin, with a rebellious crop of wavy brown hair. His eyes were dark, probably brown as well, as was his complexion. As I hobbled up, his eyes got huge.

"My God, man, lie down. You're injured, let me

317

examine you."

I walked past him. He followed me, still talking. "I'm a doctor, well a psychiatrist, but still a doctor. I have a first-aid kit in my boot."

He wasn't wearing boots. Right, his trunk. I walked straight to the passenger-side door and jiggled the handle. "No time, we need to go."

He examined me with disdain. "You're filthy! I'll just call an ambulance, if you don't mind."

He didn't know it yet, but Mr. Clean did not want to get between me and rescuing Dee. But, I'd try being nice.

"I'm sorry. I'll be happy to pay for your car to be thoroughly cleaned, but we need to get moving."

He considered this a moment, but finally pulled a cell phone from his pocket and started to dial. He stopped, and looked up with interest as a round from my Sig passed a foot or so from his left ear.

Interest, terror, either way he stopped dialing. Now that I had his complete and undivided attention, and had taken the first steps toward clarifying our relationship, I explained further.

"A friend of mine has been taken hostage, and I'm going after her. Either you drive, or I will."

At this point, I looked into the woods where the rear end of my car was still visible. His gaze followed mine. He spun back toward me, eyes wide.

"The dog stays."

"The dog goes! Your spot is the one we're negotiating."

His look of horror slowly faded, and he pressed a button on the remote. The doors unlocked and he reluctantly moved toward the driver's side.

I yelled at him in my command voice, and he jerked to a stop. "Not yet. Open the boot."

I had set Blackjack gently down on the seat and stood back up, and still the trunk was closed. I glared and walked menacingly toward him. At that point, I heard the trunk miraculously pop open.

I walked up, grabbed his arm, and we marched over to my wrecked car. I positioned him next to the trunk, pulled out an AK47 assault rifle, and stuck it in his chest. Instinctively, he raised his arm to hold it, then he stared at it in shock. Quickly, I set the other three rifles on top of the first. His face turned white. His mouth opened wide, and his eyes opened even wider. Finally, he was able to stutter and squeak a response, "Good God, man, where did you get these?"

"Off dead terrorists. Do you think we should just leave them here for some kids to find? Take them back to your car."

He hesitated a moment, then struggled back toward his car. I grabbed the pistols and other equipment.

* * *

I was amazed at how comfortable the ride was, but a lot of cars feel smooth on a good road, at about thirty miles per hour. Percy, his full name was James Percival Gordon, looked much older now than he had at first. It was the hair, the old youth in a bottle trick. Dr. Gordon had a country home that he wouldn't be visiting today. He liked Americans, voted Conservative, and wanted to crap his pants every time he saw my gun.

He was also a conservative driver, to the point that he was becoming a potential gunshot victim—my hand moved closer to my pistol every plodding, agonizingly slow mile. I found a way around that by actually pulling the pistol and putting the muzzle against the beautiful, polished hardwood dash of his Jag. After a brief discussion of whether bullet holes were covered under his warranty, he sped up.

Now making acceptable progress, I pulled out my cell phone, turned it on and called Brian. He answered on the first ring.

"Brian, it's Travis."

Brian's voice boomed from the speaker. "Where the hell have. . ."

"Listen! I don't have much time."

Brian fell silent. He knew the drill. I gave him the details.

"It's Maliki, Abdul al Maliki from . . ."

"I know who he is," Brian interrupted. "Go on.

"He's taken Dee. I got away, but I need you to help me find her."

There was only a brief pause on Brian's end and then he asked, "How?"

"They left in two cars. I don't know which one she's in. One was a four-door Audi, dark almost black. The other was a large white van. It's got the track logo, a speeding red dragster with the front end of a prop fighter plane. That will be easiest to spot, if we get them, we at least have a place to start."

"That won't be easy, mate."

"I know."

I looked over; Percy was staring at my side. The large square of missing flesh from my side was oozing blood and fluids onto his leather seat.

I snapped at Percy, "I told you I'd pay to have your car cleaned!"

Percy looked up with a start and stared ahead.

"Brian, call Constable Sheri Wells, she's Dee's friend. Tell her Dee's in desperate trouble. Find out if she's willing to break a few laws to help."

Brian asked the next logical question, "Why not go directly to the police?"

"It will be too late! Maliki will strike before they do anything."

Another brief pause before he asked, "Strike where?"

"He's smuggled Predators in through Pembroke. Two of them have Hellfire missiles. Gareth found out, that's why Maliki had him killed. Maliki's going to kill Prince Harry, and as many others as he can."

I felt the car swerve violently. Percy stared at me with a look of horror, but managed to get himself, and the car, under control.

"Harry is already scheduled to attend the match in Cardiff tomorrow," I continued to explain to both of them. "For some reason, MI5 is convinced there's an attack planned for London, and that somehow I'm involved. MI5 is trying to keep us from talking to anyone. It doesn't do any good to talk to the police. Dee tried and failed. They've been told we're helping the terrorists."

Brian paused, then spoke slowly and carefully. "Sorry, Travis, this sounds fucking insane."

"Of course it's insane, but so is putting bombs in the subway, or putting explosive vests on kids and the mentally disabled, then sending them to the market. Does any of what those bastards do ever seem 'sane' to you? The question you need to consider is if it's possible."

Brian thought it over. I continued, "Brian, someone killed Gareth. What else would they be willing to do?"

From the corner of my eye, I say Percy nodding his head vigorously.

"Look Brian, all I want to do is keep Dee from reaching Maliki. Please, help me find the van. Call Wells, see if she'll help."

"Help him!" Percy called toward my phone.

"Who was that?"

"My chauffeur, I hijacked his car. He's a psychiatrist and is going to be the star witness when I plead insanity."

Brian seemed to have a new concern. "Travis, what about protecting the Royals?"

"They have security. They can take care of themselves. Dee only has me."

"I can't let them get Harry, or anyone else. I swore an oath, so did Dee."

I wasn't going to debate this with Brian, or anyone else. This called for a creative application of the truth.

"Brian, Dee is the key. I think they're taking her to Maliki, if we find her in time we can stop their attack. They're probably nearing Swansea on their way to, or past, Cardiff."

It could have been true. I hoped it was true.

Brian's voice changed, a professional soldier now. "Fine, I'll call Wells, then do what I can. I'll call you back."

"No, I'll call you in half an hour. I'm turning off my phone, so they can't track me."

Brian replied calmly, "Right, half hour. Out."

"One more thing! Call Dee's cousin Dylan, tell him what's going on, maybe he can get to Cardiff and help us look." I gave Brian the number and finally disconnected.

I started to take out my phone's battery, but stopped. I paged through the saved pictures, stopping on the ones of the Predator in the hanger. I typed in the address of Ham's personal e-mail address in Washington and sent them off. I knew I was taking a big risk not sending them anonymously, but the option of being clever or discreet disappeared when Dee did. Percy eyed me with interest, watching as I sent a message for each picture.

"I should take out the battery. They may still be able to track the phone, but I need my CIA analyst friend to help," I explained.

Percy nodded, then looked down at my still-seeping side.

"How did that happen?"

"It was an unfortunate, cosmic confluence. Nature dictated that a very large set of vice grips—like big pliers—and a sadistic Arab terrorist with a passion for pain, come together at my once virgin side."

Percy looked back at the road; he was concentrating, but not on his driving. He drifted right into the oncoming lane. He returned to the present and swerved back in his own lane before glancing over at me.

"What you were telling your friend, is that true?"

"Yes."

"Even the part about pretending there was an attack planned for London tomorrow?"

"My friend Dee's body may be found there early in the morning to make it seem real and imminent."

"I heard on BBC that the Queen has decided at the last minute to go to Cardiff for the match."

We stared at each other for the briefest moment, then Percy looked back at the road. I turned the phone over and took out the battery. I felt the car accelerate.

JP Gordon had entered the game.

We flew over a small rise in the road. The car left the ground and slammed back down in a shower of sparks. Blackjack whimpered, but Percy just leaned forward in his seat.

I patted Percy on the shoulder and urged him on, "God save the Queen!" I looked over at him and smiled, "With a little help from Percy."

Chapter 35

"I've always fancied myself a bit of a daredevil."

Percy didn't look at me as he spoke; apparently being a hazard to everyone on the highway required his full attention. Our speed once crept up to over ninety, but he had been forced to slam on his brakes behind the little green Toyota in front of us.

Percy pounded on his horn and flashed his lights, and finally managed to force his way past a truck in the slow lane to our left, then accelerate past the panicked teenaged girl in the green Yaris. I gently reminded the good doctor, again, about our predicament.

"Percy, if we get stopped, we'll be arrested."

He leaned forward, a now fiercely serious look on his face.

"They'll never take us alive!"

"I've created a monster," I mumbled.

He smiled and looked over, "Not really, but I am laying the foundation for a temporary insanity defense, in case we are detained. Hey, your idea."

"You're not going to start drooling are you?"

He looked over again and nodded, barely skimming by a large black sedan that had just changed lanes ahead of us.

"Not a bad idea, if it comes to that."

My phone rang. I assumed it was Brian. I'd called him earlier, and left the phone active. I didn't want to leave it on, but the need to communicate made it necessary. He and Wells were searching the motorway north of Swansea, and he had a couple of his SAS buddies going west from Cardiff. Dylan was also on the road ahead of us. I felt that tiny jolt of adrenaline that comes when the shit and the fan begin their collision course.

I answered the phone, "Travis."

It was Dylan, "We've got 'em!"

"Who's we?" I wondered.

"You and me! Do you want me to tell you or not?"

Yes, I did. The tiny jolt injected enough adrenaline to power the country of Afghanistan for a year. However, as he went on, I got more confused. It sounded like he sneezed, but I think he was saying the name of a city. He then finished by making no sense at all.

". . . and catch them by the time they reach the country road to Cairo."

"Where?"

He answered, but with the same nonsense. I turned to Percy and asked, "Is there a place called Cairo near Swansea?"

Percy thought a moment, then shook his head.

"My friend says they're on a country road to Cairo."

My chauffeur frowned, in deep concentration, then had one of those Eureka moments. He nodded, accelerated, and gave me a smile. "We're close, minutes away, and it's pronounced . . ."

He went on to say the same damned jiberish as Dylan.

326

I was getting just a little tired of these Welsh names. Percy saw my frustration and tried to help.

"It's a city. It's spelled C-w-m-r-h-y-d . . ."

"Just drive, please!" I interrupted.

Percy glanced at me out of the corner of his eye, laughing. I truly had created a monster. I put the phone to my ear and told Dylan, "My driver knows where it is, five minutes. Can you slow him down?"

I heard honking, then enjoyed Dylan's truly amazing command of obscene language. After a second of hesitation he went on, just a hint of concern in his voice, "I'll come up with something." Then he yelled a string of obscenities about sheep shaggers and diaper domes. Seconds later I heard "Shit!" and the sound of squealing tires.

I listened closely, but there were no other sounds for almost a minute. Finally, Dylan filled me in. "I ran 'em off the main road, at the A48, first exit past the 4067. They're on the off-ramp."

I passed that information on to Percy, he nodded and said, "We're passing the 4067 right now, one minute."

I relayed back to Dylan, "A minute. You armed?"

"You know better than that."

"Apparently no one told the guys behind you. They have assault rifles. Keep slowing them down, but just drive away if they start shooting."

"Hurry, I think I can keep 'em behind me on the off-ramp, but . . ."

I heard a crash, and a grunt from Dylan, "The bastards rammed us!"

The bad guys were getting impatient.

I felt a jerk as Percy swerved left onto the off-ramp. I set Blackjack on the floor and picked up the MP5. I then told Dylan,

"We're on the ramp, right behind you." At that

moment, Percy jabbed me in the arm. He then pointed behind us. In the distance, I could see the flashing lights of a police car. I watched for the van in front of us, while keeping track of the police behind. I saw the taillights ahead as Dylan shouted into his phone, "I see your lights."

Good. I looked back, then told Percy, "I don't know if the cops know which car is ours. Turn off the lights, maybe they'll just drive past us."

The lights went off as I heard the sound of squealing tires in the phone, and suddenly, ahead of the van, a pair of headlights illuminated the side of the road. Dylan had been spun sideways and skidded to a stop, blocking the entire off-ramp with his car.

I looked right, and through the driver's window. I saw the police car speed past us on the freeway. They'd missed the ramp, but improved their life expectancy by letting us deal with the terrorists. We were about thirty meters from the van, and I could see two men exiting the passenger's side. I didn't know if the driver was also getting out. Any doubts about being careful were eliminated when I saw the second man raise the heavy frame of an AK47 assault rifle to his shoulder, aiming it at Dylan.

"Stop!" I shouted to Percy.

We started skidding, and I reached across and hit the Jag's horn. The sound startled the shooter, who spun to look. This gave me time, and I jumped out of the car before it came to a complete stop. I rested the front stock of the MP on the now open door and shouted in Arabic, "Drop your weapons."

He answered by firing a five-round burst, missing badly. I yelled to Percy, "Get down!" The second man opened fire, and two holes appeared with a shudder into the windshield.

I fired once into the second man, lower abdomen, for

two reasons. It would probably be below any body armor he was wearing, and it wouldn't kill him. Not immediately at least. No one would die until I knew what happened to Dee. Then, we'd have to see.

The man stumbled backward into the first man who had turned to look at Dylan, trying to decide which of us posed the greatest threat. He staggered a few steps, and looked down at his fallen comrade.

I slipped into the vegetation to my left and began to move forward. Ahead of me, I saw a shadow in the headlights of Dylan's car also moving into the bushes and trees. Good, he'd be safer there.

I looked back at the van. I still only saw two men. One down, and the other one now fired at Percy's car. I raised the MP and aimed. I wanted to go for his right shoulder, that would make it almost impossible for him to fire accurately. I hesitated. I'd never fired this weapon before. If it were even just a little off, I could kill him or worse, send a round past him and into the freeway traffic beyond. He fired another burst toward Percy, and I fired in return, aiming low so the dirt would stop any errant rounds. I'd taken the safe route, aiming for his legs. This had put him down, but he would still be able to fire. As I'd feared, I saw him struggling to get into a firing position, and moved to my left a few meters. I had a feel for the weapon now. I aimed, and took the shot I'd wanted at first. The round passed through his right shoulder and out his back. He fell backward lying on the ground in front of the van.

I heard a voice from my left, "Travis!"

"Here!" I answered, and a second later someone emerged from between two large bushes. It wasn't Dylan.

Instead, Merrick stood there. He held his hands out to his side so I could see he wasn't armed, and carried an eager look on his face. "What's going on?" he asked.

"Same old shit. What are you doing here?"

"Dylan came to me, we talked about Gareth." He looked over at the van. "We just going to let them mount up and drive away?"

I held out the MP5, "You still want to kill me?"

He shrugged, "No, but I may kick your ass when this is over."

I shrugged, and tossed him the gun, then a fresh magazine. I pulled out my Sig and turned to the van just in time to see the rear door of the van swing open. I pointed to the front of the vehicle and whispered to Merrick, "Take left, but I need them alive. I have to find Dee."

He slipped carefully toward the van as I heard a siren. Through the trees but on the other side of the freeway, I saw a police car, maybe the same one, speeding back the other way. He'd probably found a cross over and had turned around. If there were another cross over behind us, they could get here in minutes.

I looked for Merrick, but he was almost over at the first downed man. He looked up as the lights in the van came on, temporarily blinding him. The driver jumped out of the still running vehicle and ran toward the bushes across the road, firing wildly over his shoulder as he tried to escape. Merrick raised the MP and shot the fleeing driver in the lower back. He flew forward, arms and legs spread wide, his body forming an 'X' in the air. He remained that way as he fell forward and landed on the ground.

I hurried to the side of the van. I could see the unmistakable triangle sights of an AK47, silhouetted in the headlights of the cars on the motorway behind. The police car was still heading away from us, so we had a few minutes.

I saw a dark face peer around the van, then look back at the Jag. The gunman at the rear of the van turned and ran toward the car, rifle aiming directly at where Percy would have been sitting. The Sig bucked once in my hand, and the running terrorist spun counterclockwise from the impact to his right shoulder. The assault rifle flung forward, skidding to a halt under the Jaguar's front bumper. He collapsed to the ground, but was still too close to his weapon.

I ran to the van's rear, covering the downed man with my pistol as I moved. I hesitated briefly at the threshold, then spun to cover the van's interior with my Sig.

I had hoped to find Dee tied and gagged in the rear, but the van was empty. I looked back toward the Jag. The terrorist there had retrieved the fallen assault rifle.

I yelled to him in Arabic, "Throw it here, now!"

He looked at the pistol aimed directly at his head and complied. He then lay on his side, wounded shoulder elevated, and began to recite the Koran as he rocked back and forth in pain.

I shouted to Merrick, "Clear."

He replied, "Clear."

The battle scene had been secured, but the now audible siren meant that our future was not. Covering the terrorist with my Sig, I ran to the man I'd just shot. I grabbed the discarded assault rifle and slung it over my shoulder, then stomped on his injured shoulder with my left foot. The wounded Arab cried out in pain. I spun him onto his face, dug my knee in his back, then holstered my pistol. I quickly frisked him, removing a small automatic pistol that I then stuffed into my belt.

I yanked him to his feet and threw him onto the front of the Jag, then went around to the side of the car. I put my head in the driver's side window, and found that Percy had thrown himself down across the passenger side. I was about to make a comment about it being safe now, but I realized the hero shrink was protecting Blackjack with his body.

I reached in and touched Percy's leg. "It's over," I said to him.

Percy looked up at me, then peeked over the dash and surveyed the scene. He looked at me again, and seemed just a little peeved. "Is it always so noisy?"

"Pretty much. Percy, thanks for everything, but I need another favor. Get Blackjack to a vet, as soon as possible. In fact, call an ambulance for him right now. And when the police come, tell them everything. I don't care what you have to do, make them believe you. The Royal family is in danger. They can't ignore this."

Percy nodded. I grabbed the semi-conscious terrorist by the belt and dragged him with me to the van. Merrick had two of the others on their stomachs by the open rear door. I looked at him. "The driver?"

"These guys aren't very sturdy," Merrick said shaking his head apologetically.

"These guys are going to help us find Dee." I threw my man into the back of the truck.

We each took one of Merrick's prisoners and tossed them inside. Merrick looked back down the road and announced, "The police are almost here."

"You drive. I'll ride in the back."

He hurried into the front seat and took off. We reached an intersection, and he turned left into a small, residential area. Merrick looked over as he drove calmly down the narrow street.

"Where's the dog?"

"He's in the car, but he's been shot. Percy, the guy with the Jag, will make sure he gets to a vet."

Merrick nodded. "Too bad he's not with us. We could let that little beast, what's his name? Blackjack? We could let him loose on these fuckers until they tell us where Dee is."

I didn't think that would make them talk, but something else began to form in my mind. I remembered the truck hauling pigs at the truck stop, and the outline of a plan appeared. I grinned at Merrick and asked, "Are there any pig farms in the area?"

Chapter 36

Merrick shook his head and scowled, appalled. Blood coated my arms, almost to my shoulders. Little meaty chunks of flesh and guts clung stubbornly to my body, and the heavy apron I was wearing.

Aside from being appalled, Merrick's angry face reflected a great deal of frustration. On the drive to this farm where we'd come to chat with our Islamic guests, we had argued about Dee, and about what our priorities were. When Merrick found out about Maliki and his plans for the drones, he, like everyone else, wanted to dedicate all of our efforts to stopping him.

My priority was Dee; I could never completely wipe the image of her in Maliki's control from my mind. Merrick took a step closer as I finished honing a large skinning knife and set the sharpening stone down on a nearby bucket.

"You really enjoy that?"

"Hey, it beats going to the opera, right guys?"

I gestured at the fence to my left, where the two superficially wounded terrorists stood bound and watching the action. The other we patched up and left secured in the car. At first, our guests refused to look, but soon they were staring, unable to look away. They didn't know our plan, but I'm pretty sure they knew it would involve them.

I had already done a lateral incision on a large sow, and after cutting the throat, I could begin to move the beast's insides to the outside. In less than a minute, I stepped back to inspect a pile of pig heart, liver and other assorted delicacy-making goodies. Sniffing and grimacing, Merrick asked, "How did you get so damned good at something so damned disgusting?"

"On our ranch in Texas we have a lot of feral hogs, wild pigs running loose. They're dangerous, like three-hundred-pound rats, but they breed like rabbits. We cull them and donate the meat to local food banks."

I gestured to the far end of the nearby pen, where a very old man with thin grey hair and overalls operated a tractor, digging out a trench in the muck.

"It's better than what Keri's doing."

Merrick nodded in vigorous agreement and we both stopped to watch the tractor's front blade scoop out another reeking mass of mud and pig shit.

I continued, "And it's definitely better than what these two are about to enjoy."

They still pretended not to speak English, but at that comment they exchanged panicked glances.

I looked at my watch, then up at Merrick.

"When will Brian and the others get here?"

Merrick looked back at the road, about twenty meters behind us.

"Any minute."

We needed to hurry. I turned as I heard the tractor approach, front bucket tilted up like a cradle, waiting for an arriving child. Keri stopped with the bucket pointed away from us, put the transmission in neutral, and set the brake. He got down and inspected my work, then nodded approvingly.

A word about Keri, the oldest and skinniest man I'd ever seen. He appeared to weigh about twenty pounds, if he was carrying ten pounds of change in his pocket.

He owned the pig farm that we'd found only a few miles from our combat site. I'd knocked on his door and asked if I could buy three pigs, that I needed to question some Arab terrorists. Without a word or change of expression, he grabbed his filthy old cap and led us to the pens.

He offered us the pigs for free, but only if he could help. Turns out that Keri Collins was a veteran, from his attitude toward our captives, and his age, I assumed he'd fought with King Richard in the Crusades.

Merrick, however, did not share our enthusiasm. In fact, he tried to stop us several times. Now he walked to stand in front of the tractor, like he intended to use his body to stop us. He looked at the pigs, the terrorists, and then to me.

"Please tell me again, what are we doing and why the hell are we doing it?"

"It was your idea," I replied innocently.

"It bloody well was not my idea!" He exploded in frustration.

"You wanted to go Blackjack on them, so that's what we're doing," I shrugged.

I'd previously related the story of U.S. Army General John "Blackjack" Pershing, who fought Islamic madmen in the Philippines a century ago. There were reports that he used an innovative, if culturally insensitive, approach to pacification. Some claim he ordered his soldiers to dip their bullets in pig's blood, and that the bodies of any fallen insurgents were buried with pig entrails on top of them. Pigs are unclean to Muslims, and the goal was to discourage their continued rebellion.

True or not, I felt I could improve on the process. I had to improve on the process; Dee needed me. I was her only hope. I walked to where the swine's remains hung and nodded to Keri. He released the chain holding it up, and we lowered the stinking carcass into the front bucket of the tractor. Our terrorist companions shifted and stood on their toes, trying unsuccessfully to see what was happening.

I then walked over to terrorist number one, and asked him in English, "Where is the girl? Where is Maliki?"

He glared back defiantly, so I asked again in Arabic, "Where are Maliki and the girl?"

He spat in my face, which only made the ensuing events easier. I pointed to the tractor and went on, still in Arabic. "We are going to put you into the body of that pig, sew you up inside, and bury you under the ground where those foul animals are kept." He glanced at the pens, then back at me as I continued.

"I believe your soul will remain there, trapped, unable to escape through the filth. What do you think?"

He looked at me, in shock, then turned to stare at the pens. I gestured to Merrick, who reluctantly helped me march our defiant prisoner to the tractor. We stopped in front of the pig carcass, and here his defiance began to fade. Keri brought me a large cloth sack, which we lowered over the frantic terrorist's head.

Merrick grabbed my sleeve.

"Don't do this!"

"I will find out where Dee is," I answered.

Merrick looked pained, almost as hollowed out inside as the hog in the bucket of the tractor. He looked away, then turned back and met my eyes. "You don't want to live

338

with this for the rest of your life, mate. Believe me, I know—I live it every day."

I nodded to Keri, and we moved our prisoner closer to the tractor.

The second man now began to shout and struggle against his restraints. I nodded to Merrick, and he hurried over to get him under control. It didn't take much, since both of them stared, eyes wide, and watched as Keri and I picked up the hooded terrorist, now crying and pleading, and lower him toward the front of the tractor and the waiting carcass.

He became a kicking, screaming, crying baby, and promised to tell us everything. We stopped, stepped back, and stood him up and removed the hood. Keri seemed disappointed.

I turned him so he faced away from his accomplice at the fence, and questioned him extensively about Dee, Maliki, and their plan. Satisfied that he'd told me everything he knew, which wasn't much, I walked over to our second prisoner. I spoke casually in Arabic to the stricken man, "The soul cannot escape through the prison of unclean flesh. Eternity is a long time to spend in darkness and filth. One second would be too long for the strongest man. Too long for your companion."

I pointed toward the tractor, and was about to explain his fate if he failed to cooperate, when he began to babble uncontrollably.

"They are in Cardiff, but I don't know where. Believe me, on the heads of my children, I don't know where they are!" He whimpered and cried, "Please. This is all I know. Do not put me in there!"

"The woman?" I asked.

"Ahmed took her to Maliki, in Cardiff. They will fly away after the attack. That is all I know!"

He started to squirm, trying desperately to free himself. I took his arm and moved the struggling man toward the tractor, but he went limp, like a protesting two-year-old, and I lowered him to the ground.

Merrick stood over him. "Think he was telling the truth?"

I nodded. "He was too scared to lie. Besides, they both said the same thing. I doubt that either of them knows where the drones' controllers will be located, only that Maliki's in Cardiff. It's not much, but it's a place to start."

We carried him back to the fence, and laid him down on a patch of grass. Keri marched the first one over and shoved him down next to his unconscious companion.

Merrick looked at them a moment, then turned to me and studied my face. "You weren't going to do it, were you?"

I stared back, not sure how to answer him. We had both faced the same crisis. How far do you go to save someone you care about from torture and death? I thanked God I didn't have to find out the answer to his question myself.

"Over there!" Keri shouted, and pointed to headlights now turning onto his drive.

We watched several cars approach. I recognized Brian's car and walked toward them. The cars pulled into the parking area by the house, and Brian, Sheri, and another half a dozen men got out. As they hurried over, Brian looked around at our interrogation room and pulled out his cell phone.

"I'm dialing 9-9-9. This is bloody harsh."

"I've already called an ambulance. And it's not as bad as it looks, found out that Maliki's in a hotel in Cardiff. There's a second radio control unit, but I have no idea where it could be."

Brian still wasn't happy, and poor Sheri looked like she wanted to faint. We talked about finding Maliki and the other radio, and disagreed about that, too. We knew the radio control units for the drones would need to be high up to keep a line of sight. Brian and the others believed they would be in the hills outside of Cardiff. This would be the normal location for us to set up, and Brian knew of several places around the city that provided perfect cover and control.

I, on the other hand, thought Maliki would want to be close, with both controllers, to witness his success first hand. My plan was to search downtown Cardiff. That matched with what our guests had told us. Brian thought I only cared about finding Dee, and maybe he was right. I shook my head. No, I had to trust my instincts. They'd be downtown in a hotel.

Brian didn't look happy, but he knew we had to split up. Keri, who had walked over to us, talking on his iPhone. He hung up and frowned.

"They're almost here. At least let me bury one of the blighters. The ditch ready."

We shook our heads. Keri frowned, "You got about five minutes." I looked at Sheri, then at Merrick. "I need a ride to Cardiff,"

Merrick shook his head. "I'm with the big guy on this one. He'd never get out of Cardiff, so he'd never go there."

I looked back to Sheri. She looked over to Brian and said. "We should at least check it out."

Brian shrugged, then looked at me. "We'll be up in the hills."

Brian tossed Sheri his keys. As we hurried to his car, I checked my watch. It was a little after six in the morning, and we had no idea what Maliki's schedule would be.

I asked Wells, "How long to Cardiff?"

She shook her head, "Normal day, a little over an hour. I'd say at least two with what's going on."

As we got into the car, I heard Brian call to the others, "Gather in, we're running a recon in the hills above Cardiff."

I felt certain they were wasting their time, but didn't try to stop them. In fact, I wanted them out of my way. I wanted Maliki alone, with no interference, and certainly no witnesses. I would find him; I had no doubt about that.

Chapter 37

Maliki snatched up a vase from the end table, spun, and hurled it across the living area of his penthouse suite. He looked around for something else to destroy, not even watching as the almost priceless antique shattered against the polished oak writing desk in the opposite corner.

He yelled into his phone, "Find them!"

Maliki closed his phone, then paced around the white leather couch, stopping at the large picture window facing the nearby Millennium Stadium. He took a deep breath, released it, then took another. He slowly let out his breath. He couldn't let himself get upset. He didn't know the details, but he certainly knew what had gone wrong, Sergeant Travis Deacon.

First came word that the troublesome American had escaped from the racing track, and now the mujahedeen he had dispatched to London had disappeared as well. Maliki now suspected that the Marine had finally convinced the people at MI5 of the true target of his plan.

This would explain why Colonel Martin Becket,

wunderkind of the anti-terrorist agencies in Britain, would soon be at his door. The Colonel had called and informed Maliki to stay in his room, that he would soon visit the hotel. He could be there at any minute. Maliki's problems had increased quickly; Becket's surprise visit, his diversion in London was now thwarted, and a rogue Marine was rampaging loose through the country. It seemed as if all of his preparations faced an uncertain climax.

All soldiers know this axiom of battle, that no plan survives the first shot intact. However, Maliki excelled as a tactician. The core of his plan would survive. He would be successful, and the heart of every man, woman and child in this arrogant, degenerate nation would be blackened forever.

But first he needed information.

Right on cue, he heard a knock at his door. He strode over and peered through the tiny peep hole into the angry face of Colonel Martin Becket. Maliki hesitated a moment, deciding on how best to play the situation, then opened the door and stepped back as Becket stormed into the suite.

Maliki spoke before Becket could open his mouth.

"Congratulations! The London attack has been thwarted."

He walked over and gave the Colonel an enthusiastic pat on the back. "I had every confidence in your abilities."

Becket stared blankly for a moment, then shook his head. "Please, Asif, whatever are you talking about?"

Maliki had not considered this, but he now wondered if Asif Rabbani, the name he used as an officer in Pakistani Intelligence, would also die today. Would the fire of his Jihad burn so fiercely that his old identity would be totally consumed? An interesting question, but he had to complete his mission first. "We just intercepted radio traffic, stating that one of Maliki's teams headed to London had been

344

intercepted on the M4 highway and was eliminated. The plan has been called off; brilliant work, my friend."

The Colonel scowled, deep in thought, then mumbled to himself, "Is that true?" He looked at Maliki. "That bloody American, Deacon, instigated a shootout west of here, on the M4 as it turns out. Several Middle Eastern types are either dead or missing."

After a moment's pause, Becket looked uncertainly at Maliki.

"Could we both have been wrong? He had clearly gone off the reservation regarding orders and authorization, but could he have been after the same group, in a different way?"

Maliki walked toward the bar and smirked, "Either way, it will soon be over."

He poured them both a drink of bottled water. He knew that Becket would not drink alcohol on duty. He handed the glass to Becket and asked, "If it is indeed over, I assume that everything else will continue as planned."

Becket shook his head. "When Special Branch heard about the attack, right here in Wales, they canceled everything, for everyone. Except Harry! The Prince is a bloody nightmare, as we discovered in Afghanistan. He will not hide, or even be cautious. It was a miracle that he made it back from that hell hole over there alive."

"I know I was surprised," Maliki smirked.

"Harry will still be there to award the cup, though he'll be arriving at the stadium at nine instead of ten."

Maliki looked at his watch, alarmed. "That is less than an hour away."

Becket nodded, and Maliki asked, "The Queen?"

"Special Branch will secretly move her party to the airport at Bristol when Harry leaves for the stadium. I'm not sure what happens from there."

Maliki processed the new information. "They will be in the open for several minutes, and the traffic will be a mess," he spoke to himself as much as to Becket.

"A bloody nightmare! They would be gone already, but Special Branch and the police have to secure the route up North Road to the A48 and then shut down access all the way to Bristol. It's not a very good route, but no one will know about it ahead of time, so it should be safe."

Maliki pulled out his cell phone, a new plan already taking shape in his mind. He had to be sure, though, and addressed Colonel Becket, "Beckie, you're sure they won't fly out of Cardiff?"

"You know I hate that name, and yes, Cardiff is definitely out. They can't clear the airspace over Cardiff, too many aircraft already in the air. In fact, Philip should be landing here shortly. They will have everything in place at Bristol International by the time her motorcade arrives."

Maliki smiled broadly, "An excellent plan, a plan I can work with."

The now jubilant terrorist put his arm around his friend and walked him toward a closed door to their left. He opened the door to reveal five armed men. Two other men restrained a struggling woman on the bed.

Maliki gestured to the large man now aiming a pistol at Becket's chest.

"This is Ahmed, my assistant." Maliki pointed to the bed. "And you already know Detective Jones."

Becket froze, staring at the battered detective, arms tied to the heavy wooden headboard. She also froze when she saw the Colonel. Becket spun toward Maliki, realization turning to shock and fear.

"You!"

Maliki bowed his head.

"Me." He looked up smiling. "It has always been me.

Everything you are and have is because of me."

Maliki held out his hand toward Ahmed, who handed his superior a large carving knife.

"Dear Beckie, I can't tell you how disappointed I am about our change in schedule. I had hoped we would enjoy your leisurely death, much as Philip and I enjoyed his."

Becket just stared, confused and shocked, clearly not comprehending all that his friend related. He shook his head, ever so slightly, and whispered, "Why? How?"

"I no longer have time to explain why; you can ask Philip when you get to hell. The how? You made that quite easy. For all these years, it was my information that made you a success. I provided you with the names, dates and locations that helped you enjoy unequaled achievement in your war against militant Islam, along with all the accompanying rewards. What you didn't know, was those were the names of my competitors, of my enemies. You became a legend, all the while making me rich and clearing my path to leadership, allowing me to take control of the largest force in all of Pakistan."

Becket dove toward Maliki, "You bastard!"

Ahmed swung his pistol and struck Becket in the face. He staggered as two men rushed to restrain him.

Maliki sneered at Becket, then looked at his watch. He turned to Ahmed and said, "We have less than an hour, get to the roof and make sure everything is prepared. We now have separate targets for each drone." Maliki put his hand on Ahmed's shoulder and smiled. "I will finally kill young Harry, and how do you feel about turning a Queen into cat food?" Ahmed returned the smile and hurried out. Maliki took a step toward the struggling Colonel, who had stopped fighting and was staring blankly at his captor. Maliki bowed slightly.

"We are out of time, my friend, so let me give you

347

this."

Without warning, Maliki drove the knife into Becket's chest, right through the heart. The momentary expression of shock on the Colonel's face became no expression at all as he slumped face down to the carpet; dead in a rapidly forming pool of blood.

Maliki allowed himself a brief moment of satisfaction; staring down at the lifeless body of his lifelong friend. With a determined stride, he moved to the bed where Dee stared in stunned silence at Becket's body.

He sat on the bed next to her. She met his eyes defiantly.

"Miss Jones, we are truly blessed of Allah. Not only is my jihad still possible, it has actually become easier. I never anticipated a clear shot at the Queen herself. This will indeed be a day the world will never forget."

Maliki ran his hands over Dee's body as she struggled to get away from him. He looked up at the large man to her left, who slapped her viciously across the face. Stunned, she stopped moving and struggled to simply remain conscious.

"And then will come a night which you, also, will never be able to forget."

Dee shook her head. Her eyes began to clear, and she focused hatefully on Maliki. He gently stroked her cheek.

"What is the expression, we will party like there is no tomorrow? Depending on the party, for you there may be no tomorrow."

Maliki stood and hurried toward the roof, and his destiny.

Chapter 38

Nothing could have prepared me for the mayhem of game day in Cardiff. Madness surrounded me everywhere I went. I had to wonder if a terrorist attack might not actually improve things. Or, if anyone would notice a change.

I wanted to find Dee and Maliki, but what I found, no matter which direction I looked, were crowds of enthusiastic, drunken Rugby fans. Thousands of brightly clad maniacs surged and buzzed around me, reveling in the excitement of the approaching sports Nirvana. I'd been to New Orleans during Mardi Gras; this felt the same.

The closer I got to the stadium, the heavier the crowds. I realized a foot search would be impossible. Motor traffic was worse. I had to leave Sheri about a mile outside the city center and run to the stadium. I'd called her a few minutes ago; she'd only moved a block closer.

Sheri had called all the hotels in the area. She used the story of looking for a Pakistani man who'd left his phone in a bar. No luck so far.

I started to worry that I'd screwed up. I realized that it

would be impossible for Maliki to get out of the downtown area by car. I had no doubt that he wanted to see the destruction close up, but not at the risk of being captured or killed.

Time was almost gone, and I needed help. I surveyed the area, there had to be a cop around somewhere. I hurried down a wide walkway to my left, and ran into a couple wearing white jerseys with a large blue 'O2' on the front. This was the English team jersey. They also wore large hats that looked like lions.

They both took deep breaths and screamed, "Go England."

I replied with, "How 'bout them Dallas Cowboys!" and pushed past the confused pair.

I saw the top of what looked like a policeman's cap, and walked over. Since I was probably on the most-wanted list by now, I had to question my sanity and my decision-making ability in general. But, the only thing that really mattered was finding Dee.

I shoved my way past a group of teenagers in red Welsh jerseys, and found the cop trying to keep people from using a trash can for a toilet. I moved next to him, pretended to be drunk, and shouted, "I lost my hotel."

He looked me over coolly, another drunk fan. A Yank to boot. "What's the name?"

"If I knew that, I could just stop and ask directions! It's a tall one, by the Stadium."

He looked toward the sky. He could be begging for patience, or just waiting for the right one to be revealed to him. Still gazing skyward, he recited a list, checking off each one on his fingers. "We've got the Barcelo, Hilton, Big Sleep, the Lodge." He paused, receiving his next inspirational download, then resumed. "There's the Sleepers, Marriott, Park Plaza, the Flat . . ."

"Wait!"

I stopped him as a little bell went off in my head. Maliki said something, but what, when? Was I just imagining things? No, I just needed to remember. I relaxed my mind and let it flow back.

I remembered. *It's not the Marriott, but it's OK.* Or something like that. He said that while I was his guest in the hanger. I though he was referring to the Marriott where Gareth and I stayed, but maybe he meant something else.

"Marriott!" I stopped the policeman. "How do I get to the Marriott?"

He looked around briefly, then pointed south. "The quickest way's to get on Wharton Street, right there, and go left. Turn right on Trinity, it will run into the Hayes past St. David's Hall. Stay on Hayes to Mill and go right. It's a little ways down Mill Lane."

I thanked him and quickly walked toward Wharton. I pulled out my phone and called Sheri.

"Are you almost here?"

"Hell no!" Sheri did not sound happy. "I'm moving in the wrong fucking direction. There's something going on, an army of constables descended on the area and is forcing everyone out."

That was probably significant, but I had no idea what it meant. I needed some information, and hoped Wells could get it for me.

"Sheri, I need you to call the Marriott. Ask if there are any Middle Eastern groups staying there."

She interrupted, "I already called. They don't have anyone from Pakistan."

"I know that, but I still think they're there. Just call and ask questions. There has to be something or someone."

"Fine." She hung up, frustrated, but I knew she would do her best.

I hustled down The Hayes, almost to Mill Lane, when Sheri called back, excited.

"I talked to the assistant manager; she was a bit bitchy, by the way. The only thing out of the ordinary was the Egyptian TV people there to broadcast the game back to Sandland. Turns out they rented the Penthouse and most of the floor below it. Also turns out they set up some satellite and radio equipment on the roof 'cause they couldn't get a good signal from street level."

I turned right onto Mill Lane and saw the large, red-brick Marriott up ahead on the left.

"That has to be it, great work!"

"Not so great, there's no way I can get to you. They're locking things down pretty tight around here."

"I can handle it. Call Brian then Merrick, and let them know."

The hotel was on my left. I hurried past a little outdoor dining area and saw the entrance. To my right, I saw several bags stacked next to a wall. Nearby a tall, black man in a suit was yelling into his cell phone. His head was down and his hands covered his ears, concentrating. I walked to the bags, grabbed a large briefcase, and hurried inside.

I strode up to a man wearing an ornate red uniform, standing next to a luggage cart, and grabbed his arm. I hoped he was the head bellman.

"I'm Reggie, from Crown Electronics. Some guy named Ahmed called. The inverse transducer on their uplink modulator is fried. He said something about roof, or penthouse." I held up the briefcase. "I need to get up there to fix it, now!"

The Bell Captain, his brass nametag said 'Burton,' looked skeptical. He glanced across the lobby at the large, dark-wood check-in desk, as if he were about to walk over there and ask them what to do. I grabbed his arm.

"Burton, he promised me an extra two hundred pounds if I got up here in twenty minutes. Take me up there in time and we split it."

Burton thought about it for a second, then asked cautiously, "Who called?"

"Some guy named Ahmed, said he was with Egyptian broadcasting or something. Hurry Burton, I'll get up there eventually. You can either get paid for doing it now, or bitched at for keeping them waiting. You know how those types are."

That proved to be the clincher. Burton pulled an electronic key card from his pocket and led me to a freight elevator off to the side of the lobby. He inserted the card, and the elevator door opened immediately. We entered. He pushed the "P" button. The door closed, and we started up.

After the first ding, I set the briefcase down. I pressed the button for the third floor and pulled the Sig pistol from behind my back. I held it up for Burton to see and explained.

"Burton, I'm really from the CIA, and those guys in the Penthouse are really from al Qaeda." I considered that an exaggeration, not a lie.

The elevator dinged again as we passed the second floor.

Burton looked scared, but he held it together pretty well.

"So I have a dilemma. I have to stop them from launching missiles and killing Prince Harry, but I can't do that if I let you go and you warn them. Do you have any suggestions?"

There was a third ding, and the doors slowly opened. Burton stood straight, smoothed the front of his uniform, and turned to face me.

"I could walk down stairs and call the police, and hotel

security, and let them decide how best to proceed. However, what if they are innocent, and I don't warn them? What if you injure them?"

"Injuring them is where I'm going to start, and they are not innocent," I said as I patted him on the shoulder. "But I'm in a bit of a hurry here. Harry's life depends on us."

Burton looked down, then gave me a little smile as he said thoughtfully, "They don't tip at all."

"Then they can't be innocent. Let's go with your first idea, call the cops. But warn them, anyone going up there needs to be wearing body armor and have a shit load of fire power. Security may want to wait for the police." I raised my shirt to expose the blood-soaked bandage on my side. "These guys are vicious. They almost got me once already."

Burton looked shocked. He nodded and turned to exit the elevator. I stopped him.

"Oh, I'd also suggest you quietly evacuate the hotel, starting with the upper floors. They have bombs."

Burton's eyes got big, but he didn't flinch. He nodded, stepped out of the elevator, and turned to face me. I handed him the briefcase as the door closed.

There was a tiny jolt as the elevator resumed its ascent. I checked the magazine in my pistol. It was full. I touched my left pocket and felt the two spare magazines there. I heard two more dings, but the next ding signaled a text message to my phone.

I grabbed my phone and retrieved the message, reading with difficulty in the weak fluorescent lighting of the elevator car. It was from Ham, but before I read the whole message the door opened, and I found myself in an ornate lobby. The brass placard in front of me said 'Penthouse,' and the sign over a metal door to my left said 'Roof.'

The decision of where to go first was made for me,

since the door to the Penthouse began to open. I rushed to the door, slamming it into the large man who stepped into the lobby. I knocked an automatic pistol out of his hand and slammed the butt of my gun into the bridge of his nose. He went limp as I pushed past him and rushed through the doorway. He slumped to the ground, dazed and barely conscious.

I rushed in and dove to my right, rolling behind a chair and coming up into a firing position. Another man had been sitting in a chair watching TV, and had to reach for his weapon. He was quick, now firing at me with his assault rifle. As the fusillade moved from the door toward where I now stood I fired twice, both rounds hitting him in the chest. He and his chair tumbled backward.

I ran back to the door. The man I had left there was still dazed, but had managed to pull out his cell phone and was screaming into it in Arabic. I kicked the cell phone out of his hands, and slammed my pistol into the side of his head. He collapsed.

I looked back to the second man, lying partially concealed behind the chair. He wasn't moving, so I dragged the now unconscious man back inside. I closed the door and slid on the security chain. He was still out cold, but I couldn't just leave him. I turned him sideways and rolled him up in the Persian carpet in the entry area. I then dragged him and the rug into the coat closet, stuffed him inside, and shut the door.

With a glance, I surveyed the room. The man I'd shot hadn't moved. I continued looking around and noticed two doors. I ran toward the closest one but stopped when I heard muffled screaming from the opposite side of the suite. I couldn't be sure it was Dee, but it was definitely a woman.

I rushed to the other door and listened outside.

Whoever it was, she was gagged. I tried the door. It was locked. I didn't have time to search for the key. If there were another guard inside with her, she could be in danger.

I took several steps back and rushed to the door. I lowered my shoulder and the thin, interior door disintegrated into a shower of splinters. I again dove to the side and came up in a kneeling position, pistol ready, but the woman thrashing on the bed was alone.

I made another survey of the room. Keeping my gun on the bathroom door, I hurried to Dee and removed her gag. There were tears streaming down her face.

She coughed and choked from the influx of air. She held up her hands to me and said, "There's no one in there, or the closet. The others are outside?"

"Taken care of."

I set the gun on the bed and looked around. I hurried over to a writing desk in the corner. I snatched a bone-handled letter opener from the drawer, and used it to hack through the cords binding her hands and feet, and she threw herself into my arms, sobbing. "You're alive! Thank God." She looked up, "I knew you'd find me."

She rested her head against my chest, crying softly. I enjoyed her in my arms for a moment, then for a moment longer, but I knew we had to get moving. I lifted her unsteadily to her feet.

"Let's get out of here."

She almost collapsed in my arms, then managed to steady herself and stand. She stood there, taking mental inventory and making sure her body was working again. She then bent down and picked up my pistol.

She gave me a stone-cold glare.

"Maliki's on the roof, and I'm going to him."

Chapter 39

Dee yanked open the stairway door; she wanted to charge up to the roof and kill Maliki. I slammed it closed before she could take a step. I was on board with the kill Maliki part, but running after him in a rage posed a significant health hazard.

She wheeled to face me with a look of rage and frustration, stopping her may not have been the best move on my part; she was charged and determined. I'd just given her an assault rifle and about thirty seconds of training, instructions that skipped safe and went straight to lethal.

"Not yet!"

I took the butt of my rifle and smashed a mirror by the door. I carefully picked up a long, triangle-shaped section and moved to the side of the doorway, then lay down by the side of the doorframe and looked up at Dee.

"Open it slowly, about a foot."

She understood, nodded, and slowly opened the door. I slid the mirror shard through the open door, and angled it to give me a view of the entire stairwell. I examined the top for evidence of a person or weapon, and then the walls for shadows or any flicker of light. The stairs and landing appeared vacant. Several seconds passed before I finally felt secure enough to move. I stood and put my hand on her arm. "I go first. You wait here and make sure no one gets out."

She meant to say, "Good plan," but she was upset; "Go to hell" came out instead. She turned and tried to push past me into the stairwell. I grabbed her shoulder hard, maybe harder than I intended since she winced.

"Stay behind me. Don't fire unless I tell you to! I will be moving around, and you'll have more of a chance of hitting me than them if we're not together on this. Understand?"

She nodded, but I could still see a burning fury in her eyes. I didn't know if she would be able to control herself once we found him.

"Dee, I know you are ready to do whatever it takes, but being motivated does not stop bullets. You've seen the scars."

Uncontrolled emotions were dangerous; it was the time for a cold, hard killing machine. I moved closer, bending down to look her in the eyes. I waited until she controlled herself enough to hear me.

"If you want Maliki stopped, if you want him punished, we have to do this right."

The fire in her eyes flared, as if hatred alone could burn through anything in her path. I held her gaze, cold and hard, and the broiling flame of her gaze became a searing ember of determination. I smiled and nodded, but she simply turned to the door.

I took up position next to the door, and moved her to the wall by my side. I reached down, turned the knob, and threw open the door to the roof.

Nothing happened, so I glanced quickly up the stairs and pulled back out of the doorway. Still nothing, so I spun into the doorway, weapon ready. I bounded up the stairs and called back to Dee, "Let's go, weapon pointed straight up until contact."

I took the stairs three at a time, knowing she couldn't keep up. I stopped on the landing and looked up the stairs. All clear, so I moved to the next landing.

At the top of the next flight, I noticed another narrow landing and the door to the roof. There wouldn't be room for both of us up there. Dee stood behind me now, breathing heavily, but not out of breath. That would change in a minute.

I held out my hand, "There isn't room for both of us up there. You stay here, while I check it out. When I go out on the roof, run up the stairs behind me."

She glanced up the stairs and nodded. I bounded up the stairs and stood next the door, back against the wall. I'd give a year's pay for a good satellite view of the roof—and a couple of grenades.

I looked down at Dee and mouthed, "Ready?"

She nodded. I knelt as low as possible, braced myself, then opened the door just a crack. I expected a volley of bullets to throw the door viciously against my bracing shoulder, but nothing happened.

I pulled the mirror shard from my pocket and used it to view what I could of the roof. I could only see to the left, and a little to the front. I saw a large air conditioning unit to the left, and there was a low wall about ten feet in front of the door.

I adjusted the mirror to look up. The sky was blue, broken only by white wisps of clouds floating high above and the dark metal of an assault rifle pointing down at the door.

I never thought this would be easy.

I stopped and drew a battlefield map in my head using all the information I had, or could reasonably imply. Orienting myself, I pulled up a mental schema of the building itself. The door to the penthouse would be facing east, so this door would be facing south. If Maliki wanted to see his victory first hand, he would be on the north side of the building to our rear.

If his men were defending Maliki's position, they would probably be behind us as well – except Mister 'Death from Above' on the thin metal roof above. I let the pieces come together and nodded. This may work.

I put my finger to my lips for silence, then motioned her up the stairs. As she arrived, I bent low and whispered, "Follow me out, do exactly as I say!"

She nodded. I looked up, estimating where I'd seen the muzzle. I aimed my MP5, and pulled the trigger. A long volley of 115-grain, 9mm ammunition pounded through the roof. There was a shout, then the sound of a body landing outside the door.

I stomped on a shell casing, flattening it. I threw the door wide open, and kicked the casing under it, flat side first, wedging the door open. "Let's go!"

I ran out and spun right, scanning for fire or movement. It was clear, so I had Dee move behind me. I looked around and saw the large, commercial air conditioners only a few meters in front of us.

I looked back at her and yelled, "Wait for my commands!"

I sprinted across the three meters to the large air conditioner and took cover. Automatic-rifle fire tore into the machine's metal, only inches behind me. I estimated there were three of them, at least one with an AK47. I wasn't sure the air conditioner would provide adequate cover from the assault rifle. I reached around the edge of my cover and fired. I fired again and waved for Dee to join me. As she sprinted across the open space screaming, she drew fire from our attackers. This allowed me to slip around the corner and fire carefully at them. They were standing behind a brick wall, twenty meters away. I fired, and chunks of brick erupted around them. One fell back, at least one round hit flesh.

Dee was next to me now, eyes wide open and near panic. She wasn't trained for this. I pushed her behind me, and was about to look around the corner when a flurry of rifle fire pounded against our cover. A 7.62 round from the AK managed to find its way through our cover and punched a hole in the metal panel just above my head.

I ducked instinctively, and Dee jumped back. When the firing stopped, I leaned around and fired a ten-round burst, then I pulled back as the air conditioner protecting us shuddered from the impact of their concentrated fire.

Dee cowered just a little, frightened but not panicked. She was doing better than I hoped, but that didn't mean either of us would live through this.

"I don't know if I can do this!" she said as she looked over at me with fear in her eyes.

"You're doing great, just do as I say."

"There are so many of them, what do we do?"

I looked up. "This is where I normally call for air support."

More rifle fire hit the air conditioner, now coming from our left as well. Someone was trying to flank us. I looked left, then spun and staggered as a round penetrated the air conditioner and struck my hip. Dee screamed, but I regained my balance quickly. It was a glancing wound, and wouldn't be a problem until the adrenaline pumping through my body wore off.

I aimed my rifle around the corner and emptied the magazine toward where the attacker had been. I pulled back just in time, as bullets chewed huge chunks of metal from the corner of the air conditioner. The men with Maliki were good, and probably experienced. Dee was not. They could just wait where they were. I could not. I had a chance on my own, none with her.

I ejected the spent magazine, and inserted another. I had three magazines remaining. I looked to our left, trying to anticipate where the next rounds would come from. Instead, I heard my name being called.

"Sergeant Deacon! Can you hear me?" Maliki wanted to talk.

I answered, "Yes, are you ready to surrender?"

He laughed. It seemed like a very confident and relaxed laugh to me.

"I think not. And I hope you don't think it rude if I don't extend you the same offer. I'm ready to see you both dead."

I didn't answer, trying to estimate his position from the sound of his voice. He spoke again, but he had moved. "No witticisms? No glib comments? I'm a little disappointed."

I shouted back, "You'll never get away with this!"

He laughed, "Of course I will. Right now, both the Queen and Prince Harry are leaving their hotel. They will soon be fighting their way through traffic in heavily armored limousines, but we both know what a Hellfire missile will do to even the most heavily armored vehicles. Both drones are on station now. We have commandeered an Air Ambulance, which will be here in minutes. Ahmed and I will fire as it arrives, and be gone before anyone knows what happened."

He paused to let us consider the situation. "I like my

chances, Sergeant Deacon. Much better than yours,"

Honestly, so did I. A Life Flight chopper, that's how he was going to get away. The sky would probably be full of them. He had this planned out with military precision. He may actually pull this off.

At that moment, someone behind Maliki began to swear in Arabic. I heard Maliki ask, "What do you mean?"

My phone vibrated with an incoming text message as the other man, probably Ahmed, shouted to Maliki in reply, "I don't know! It just went blank!"

I grabbed Dee's arm and moved her behind me.

"We've got to get out of here!"

"What's going on?" she asked.

"Air support, stay behind me."

I emptied the magazine of my MP5 as we hurried toward the door from the roof. We were almost there before they opened fire, effectively this time. I staggered as a round hit my right leg, but at the same time I felt Dee collapse, dragging me backward.

At that moment, I heard Maliki shout, "You bastard!"

He sounded alarmingly close.

I leaned toward the cover of the doorframe and fell, pulling Dee along with me. As I hit the ground, I pulled Dee close, and we rolled for cover. The door was still open, and we rolled through in a heap. I stopped, pulled out the cartridge, and slammed it shut.

I pulled Dee to her feet. "Keep moving!" I yelled.

I supported Dee with my arm, and we limped, stumbled, and swore our way down the stairs. We were just past the second landing when I thought I heard the door open behind us. I grabbed my rifle, slapped in a fresh magazine, and helped Dee lean on the rail.

"Keep going." She had lost her weapon, so I gave her my pistol. "Get out, the police should . . ."

At that instant, the whole building shook. Smoke and debris rained down on us from above and we both tumbled down the stairs.

Chapter 40

I found myself in a claustrophobic universe of grey fog and silence, struggling to regain consciousness. It was a place I'd inhabited several times before, usually followed by time in the hospital. The grey fog of dust and debris was the result of an explosion on the roof, and it eventually settled. The concussion to my ears would pass quickly. Or it could last for days, depending on the damage.

I struggled to a sitting position, but couldn't see anything more than six inches from my face. I was still alive, I could tell by the pain in every cell of my body. Being alive and in pain was always better than the alternative.

My mind cleared, and I remembered Dee. In a panic, I looked and felt around for her in expanding circles around my body. After a few seconds I became concerned, we were together when the roof exploded.

There, I felt a leg! I slid my hand further up the calf and discovered it was only a leg, it ended just above the knee. I felt down to the feet. It was wearing a heavy boot, and I almost gasped in relief. Dee was wearing running shoes.

I sat straight and looked around. I thought I heard a sound, but with the high, piercing ringing in my ears, I couldn't be certain. I listened carefully and heard it again to my left and down the stairs.

I took inventory of my body. I moved my hands and feet, one limb at a time. I followed this quickly with a visual inspection and found everything there and everything functional, more or less.

I struggled to my feet, leaning heavily on the twisted railing beside me. I picked my way carefully through the wreckage, down toward the next landing. The faint sound was unmistakable, a whisper, a woman's voice; Dee's voice.

I staggered faster down the steps, and there she was, sitting with her back to the wall, shouting. I could see her chest heave, and her throat was constricted from the effort, but my damaged ears could barely hear her whisper.

We saw each other at the same time; I stumbled forward as she tried to stand. I was beside her in two long strides, but she had slumped back to the ground, pain contorting her face. Her hand reached down to grab her left leg, and I could see it was broken. She reached up to me, wanting me to help her up, but I shook my head. I needed to make sure there weren't other injuries that required immediate attention.

I gave her a quick inspection. Except for a severely broken leg, two bullet wounds, dozens of cuts and an untold number of bruises from falling debris, she was fine. Oh, and she probably had a concussion as well by the look in her eyes. I helped her to her feet and placed her left arm over my shoulder. Together we hobbled down the last flight of stairs to the penthouse lobby. The damage there was slight, but dust settled everywhere. An overturned vase was the only real clue to the carnage above.

We hobbled over to a side chair next to the elevator, and I eased her down. She closed her eyes, but it was more from pain than relief. She tried to straighten out her leg and screamed out in pain. I heard her scream, sort of. This was encouraging from an auditory perspective, but it made me anxious to get her to a doctor.

I walked to the elevator and pressed the button. Nothing happened. I pressed several times, but the light did not come on. I heard Dee's voice and looked over. She was shouting at me, so I moved close to hear.

"The elevator won't work if there's a fire. Besides, the motors or gears may have been damaged. We'll have to take the stairs."

"You're too banged up, and that leg looks bad." I watched to see if she heard me. Her hearing may have been as impaired as mine. She nodded, so I went on, "I'll get an ambulance crew to carry you down."

She looked down at her leg and nodded again. I pulled out my cell phone, but it was broken. I turned to enter the penthouse to see if the hotel phones were working, but Dee grabbed my sleeve and pulled me toward her. She shouted at me, and I was happy to find that my hearing was coming back. She glanced up at the ceiling and asked, "What happened?"

"Air cover," I smiled. "I told you about Ham, my friend back at CIA headquarters?"

She nodded.

"After I got away from Maliki's men at the racetrack, I sent pictures of the drone. Not only to prove it had been captured and restored, but I was hoping they would be able to track it from the tail numbers. Ham found out that the racetrack drone belonged to the CIA. Ham then had the brilliant idea of actually trying to take control of the drone. It took a while to dig up the communications settings and details, they had been deleted from the system since the drone was presumed to be lost. Then they had to load the information, and then locate the drone with a satellite capable of the necessary communications. After that . . ."

Dee interrupted, "Is there a bottom line?"

I smiled. "They took control of that drone, but couldn't get the information on the one Maliki had. The solution was to take control of the first drone, and fire a missile to destroy the communications equipment for the second one."

I smiled and pointed to the roof. "It worked."

Dee looked at the open door to the penthouse, hoping to look through to the outside world, then asked, "The Queen? Harry?"

I smiled and nodded. "I'm pretty sure they're all fine. We stopped them Dee; we did it."

The corners of her mouth turned up in a contented little smile. She closed her eyes and let herself lean back into the chair. She began to relax, peaceful, almost happy as her head rolled back to rest against the chair.

I realized that seeing her happy made me happy, but unfortunately, it didn't make me healthy. I could no longer ignore the fact that my whole body hurt. Every muscle was beginning to tense and ache. My hearing was still a problem since the ringing had been replaced by a course rasping sound that I didn't recognize.

The rasping sound got louder, and I put my hands over my ears, which made it almost disappear; which was also wrong. That meant the sound came from an external source.

I turned around and discovered that the external source came equipped with a long, wicked looking knife, which it thrust mercilessly at my back. Someone was trying to stab me.

I spun and thrust up my left arm, blocking the knife but suffering a slash to the forearm. I rolled stiffly to the side, muscles resisting every move, and I managed to roll to my feet.

What I saw was frightening. In front of me stood a man, what had once been a man, his body practically burned to a crisp. The breathing came in grating croaks, as my attacker forced air in and out of its lungs. No doubt the flames from the Hellfire attack seared his lungs as well as his skin. I stared into his lidless, almost demonical eyes, but the face was so distorted I didn't have a clue who it could be.

I felt for a weapon in my belt. I was unarmed. I looked for something to use as a weapon, since I wasn't sure which of us had the more debilitating injuries. If I could get a chair, a lamp, anything, I could end this in seconds. Instead of turning toward me, though, he raised the knife high as he moved toward Dee.

I lunged forward, and my muscles and wounds cried out in painful protest. It felt like I was moving in slow motion as I hit him from the side, and we both tumbled to the ground. I grabbed the wrist that was holding the knife with my right, and with my left, I reached up and grabbed his throat.

He roared, more like a wounded lion than a human being, and hit me in the side of the head. I couldn't believe his strength. His heart must be pumping pure adrenaline through his body, and the nervous system had clearly shut down from the overload of pain it had to endure.

He hit me again, harder. He twisted his body, throwing me to the side. We both struggled to our feet and stood, facing each other. His face contorted, teeth almost glowing an unnatural white against the charred black of his face. I realized this was supposed to be a smile, a gruesome, ghoulish smile.

His raspy voice was alarming, but his words were even more frightening, "Sergeant Deacon, I will end this. You couldn't defeat me in Pakistan, and you won't do it here."

Maliki! Somehow this monster had survived the missile. He would have been the first to recognize what had happened, and I'm certain he would have fled. This must have allowed him to escape the kill zone of the attack. The immediate kill zone, anyway, since I had no doubt that anyone so scorched and burned could never survive. The only question now was who would die with him.

Without warning, he lunged forward and thrust the knife toward my midsection. I swung my left arm to block it, but realized my hand was hanging limp. I glanced down and saw that Maliki's first attack had been much worse than I realized. The deep, wicked gash had severed muscles and tendons. I partially blocked his attack, but the knife still sliced into my right side.

Maliki's death's head smiled again at the sight of my wounds. He stood straight, then began swaggering as he ducked, feinted and swayed toward me, closing in for the kill.

It was almost comical. He looked like a marionette under the hand of a drunken puppeteer. His intentions were clear, but his muscles no longer responded quickly nor exactly to the commands his overloaded nerves were sending.

But, my condition was worse. Many of my muscles did not respond at all.

I circled left as he approached, savoring the success he believed would soon be his. I tried to move faster, but couldn't outrun or outmaneuver him. My only hope was to delay the final combat until the damage to his body could overcome the rage still controlling it.

But the raspy voice sounded strong, even confident, "I will be back. I will finish my mission if it kills me."

I shook my head, didn't the fool know he was dead? How could he think he could survive, much less escape? I circled, and noticed the glimmering reflection of the broken mirror on the floor. Moving faster than my body felt it should have to endure, I hurried toward the glass.

I knelt painfully, grasping a long, thick sliver of glass. I struggled to my feet and continued to circle, but discovered that Maliki was no longer looking at me. He walked slowly toward the wall. He stopped just feet in front of the half-empty frame of the mirror.

His left hand went up, tentatively tracing the outline of his face. Fingers brushed by the charred slits that had been his nose. He staggered back. I imagined his lidless eyes going wide in shock.

He roared in rage, then spun to face me. He raised his knife to attack, but I had moved first. I drove my glass weapon deep into his throat. The impact of my assault sliced my fingers, but also knocked him backward. He stumbled, falling to the ground.

A pitiful gurgle replaced the rasping horror of his voice. His right hand moved tentatively toward the glass dagger in his throat. He thrashed back and forth, and tried again to speak. Then the bastard rolled to his side, struggled to his knees, and tried to stand.

No! You will not get up.

Maliki tried to stand. I shook my head, when would this end? I staggered toward him, bending to pick up his knife as I moved. I swayed drunkenly as I stood, staggering, almost falling as I struggled to stand. I looked at the zombie of a man kneeling in front of me. Maliki was all I could see. He rose to his knees, head turning toward me. I had no idea what he was thinking, feeling – he had no face, so there could be no expression to read.

I stumbled forward, slowly raised the knife above my head. Maliki reached out to grab me with a charred, withered hand. He growled something that sounded like: "Hell's fire awaits you," but I didn't care.

I brought the knife down with all my strength, backed by the full weight of my tortured body. The blade struck the top of his skull, and slipped effortlessly through bone and into the tender tissue beneath. The blade jarred to a stop as the hilt reached bone.

Maliki went rigid, shuddered, then fell stiffly to the side. Vacant, lifeless eyes stared back—he was dead. I fell to one knee, feeling cold. My head spun wildly, and it was difficult for my eyes to focus. I recognized the symptoms of shock, resulting from severe blood loss. I looked over at Dee, who was struggling to dial her cell phone. How cruel would it be to die so soon after finding something truly worth living for? I tried to consider the irony of that, but passed out on the floor instead.

Chapter 41

From our left, rifles fired over Gareth's casket. Blackjack cocked his ears and turned to stare, but didn't make a sound. He was a real trooper now, proudly wearing the Purple Heart medal I'd hung on his collar. His rear leg no longer required a sling, but the long, nasty scar would endure; a reminder that dogs can be heroes too.

Dee, sitting at my side, had become much more than a trooper to me. She was now—well, we'd see how things worked out. The honor guard fired the second volley of a 21-gun salute, and out of the corner of my eye, I saw her wipe away a tear. The final volley thundered inevitably across the small, family cemetery. As the echo died in the beautiful Welsh countryside, the attendants lowered my comrade to his rest. The honor guards lowered their rifles and snapped to present arms, a tribute to a Brother in Arms.

Brian, in full uniform, was second in the seven-man formation. In front of him was the Prince, who had insisted on participating. Harry, as he wanted me to call him, seemed like a regular guy. We'd talked after the funeral, and discovered we had been to some of the same places in Afghanistan. We even swapped a few lies about what we'd done there. He really got excited when I invited him back to our CIA base to run some ops with us. At that point, two very large men from Special Branch became even more excited than Harry and hustled him away.

I'd never really thought about it, but being a Prince can actually suck at times. Having to answer to an entire nation severely limits your options. I bet it's even tougher to get leave time from being a prince than a grunt.

I turned to watch as the coffin reached bottom, and thought of Gareth. I would remember him fondly. I would miss him forever. The loss was partially tempered by the memory of Maliki dying before my eyes, as my hands squeezed the final breath from his lungs. May he burn in hell forever.

I heard a voice, and looked over as the chaplain offered a final eulogy. He finished, and Dee took my good hand as Gareth's SAS mates passed by to offer a final salute. Then came a procession of friends and well-wishers, who walked solemnly past. Many dropped flowers into the darkness below.

Finally, the family approached. Dee, limping badly in her new cast, brought up the rear. She wore a long black skirt and jacket. I wore a light black suit and sunglasses to hide the cuts and bruises. She insisted that I walk with her, for support. The truth was, she seldom let me leave her side at all. I didn't want to read too much into it, but did anyway. I was in love, and not even a plate full of cockles could ruin the way that made me feel.

We went back to our seats, and soon the ceremony was over. Almost immediately, a tall, thin man in a police uniform walked over. He bent and kissed Dee on the cheek then offered his hand to me, bowing slightly.

"Inspector Hill, Dee's immediate supervisor. It's a pleasure to meet you, though the circumstances are rather unfortunate. To further the unpleasantries, I must inform you that until inquires into the events of the last few days are completed, you are to remain in police custody."

What? This really sucks.

I thought being a hero would get me some consideration. Maybe I can get Harry to put in a good word. Can a prince make a royal decree?

Inspector Hill continued, "Detective Jones will fill you in on all the details and requirements of your detention." He bowed to me again, smiled at Dee, then walked toward a large group of police officers near the road.

I turned to Dee, offended and confused, "What's going on?"

She shrugged, a little indifferently, I thought.

"Standard procedure, we can't have our witnesses disappearing on us, now can we? The bad news is, until further notice you're under house arrest. The good news is, your confinement will be served in my house. I have some rather innovative interrogation techniques I hope to try out."

She bent painfully and kissed me on the lips. "Believe me, Sergeant Deacon, you will be begging for mercy when I'm through with you."

I looked into those beautiful, clear, emerald eyes; both pain and hope gazed back. I was ready to beg right then that she would never be through with me.

END

ABOUT THE AUTHOR

After serving in the Marines Corps as a commissioned officer, author Rick DeMille started a career in information systems and currently manages the technology department for a small energy company in the Dallas area.

His interest in writing was revived when he wrote a Y2K guide which was distributed through a local outdoor supply company and he began writing short stories, several of which were published online by websites such as BeWrite.com. Furthermore, his short stories won various contests, including those sponsored by 'Darklines,' 'Eros and Rust,' and Magellan Books from Australia who also included one of his short stories in the ADUMBRA anthology.